THE

NEW NOBILITY.

A STORY OF EUROPE AND AMERICA.

BY

JOHN W. FORNEY.

" You see yon birkie ca'd a lord,
  Wha struts, and stares, and a' that,
Tho' hundreds worship at his word,
  He's but a coof for a' that;
    For a' that, and a' that,
    His riband, star, and a' that;
The man of independent mind,
  He looks and laughs at a' that.
The rank is but the guinea stamp,
  The man's the gowd for a' that."
               BURNS.

NEW YORK:

D. APPLETON AND COMPANY,

1, 3, AND 5 BOND STREET.

1881.

NOTE.

THE whole idea and scope of this volume are my own—and some of its early chapters; but the body of the book, especially the middle and last passages, is the work of my gifted personal friend, Rev. William M. Baker, of Boston, Massachusetts, who kindly responded to my invitation to edit and finish the "New Nobility." He has written much for the secular press, and has had a large clientage; but I think that he has never shown more talent and heart than in the assistance he has given to me in these pages.

J. W. F.

CONTENTS.

4 CONTENTS.

THE NEW NOBILITY.

CHAPTER I.

THE WRATH OF THE GODS.

THE Middle Railway station at Brussels is very like all such establishments on the Continent. Clean, decorous, and well attended, it is as different from an American depot as a French railway carriage is from an American railroad car. There is a bureau where you buy your ticket, another where you wait for your luggage until you have seen it weighed, and then pay for it, and three rooms for the first, second, and third class passengers. You enter the one answering to first class, and wait till the train that is to carry you to Paris rolls into the large and well-lighted station. The doors of the several carriages stand wide open; you select and secure your seat, then look around to study human life, so interesting in this foreign multitude. Brussels is a lovely city at all times, with its parks, galleries, cathedral, fountains, boulevards, theatres, and factories; but on this beautiful August day it was specially attractive, and there was an unusual bustle at the railway. The silver wedding of King Leopold and Queen Maria had just been celebrated; and the last of three days of processions, music, banquets, and speeches, all the populace taking part, had closed the night before in a blaze of illumination. Thousands of foreigners had come to enjoy the spectacle; the two sovereigns were much beloved, and the King had made himself particularly agreeable to the factions still warring upon each other in the Legislature and the press.

The Middle station was thronged with tourists, and additional carriages had to be added for the departing visitors. The guard was sounding the farewell whistle, and closing the doors of the carriages, when two men bustled into the smoking compartment just as it was being locked for the journey. In a moment the last signal was given, and the long train moved toward Paris with the noiseless ease peculiar to the iron roads of the Continent. It was a lovely morning. A copious rain had cooled the air and freshened the autumnal roses which poured their fragrance into the open windows. There were now four men in the smoking section; two, seated in opposite corners when the others came in, were quietly enjoying their after-breakfast cigars. They were dressed for the journey in dark colors, and it would have been difficult to decide their nationality. They might be French, German, Prussian, American, even English. They bore the stamp of gentility, and they resembled each other closely enough to be father and son. There was no doubt about the other two, as they lighted their cigars and began an animated conversation. They were English in dress, manner, and movement, and, when they spoke, the dialect was unmistakable.

"I never saw a more beautiful woman," the younger exclaimed to his companion, "never a more perfect style and presence."

"And never have I seen you so carried away. She is indeed lovely. Did you mark her voice?"

"Yes; and that completed the charm. She was not French, not Italian, nor German; and, although she spoke without accent, I do not think she is English."

"You are too bold; you startled me; you tried to enter the compartment; and I was amused at the easy dignity with which the elder lady informed you that the *coupé* was reserved."

"Yes, that was admirably done. I am eager to find out more about them."

"Do you know, I half suspect they are Americans?"

"Impossible! What, that elegant creature the product of the vain and vulgar Yankee race!"

"Come, come, old man; there you are again! What have the Americans done that you should be so unjust to them?"

"I have no patience with them; and I never meet them that I do not feel repelled. My disgust is instinctive. You say I am unjust; I reply, that if I am, I can not help it."

"Well, I do not care to dispute the point; but I predict that you will live to repent your hasty judgment."

The younger Englishman, and the most impulsive, turned to the two other men in the smoking section, who were quiet listeners, and as if he expected, or rather exacted, their approval, suddenly exclaimed:

"You have heard this discussion. Am I not right about these Yankees?"

It was a blunder, made worse by the characteristic English *insouciance* of the question; and both the silent strangers started as if the question had been a blow. After a brief silence the elder—who had laid a firm grasp upon the shoulder of his companion as if to hold him down—threw his cigar out of the window, and said, in a low and severe voice:

"I am an American; and I will add that, if I thought you had known it, I should have resented your insolence at once."

"What, sir, my insolence!" said the Englishman, quickly rising in his seat; at which the younger American stood up as if to defend his father—for so indeed he was.

"Yes," said the elder, as he sternly motioned his son to silence and his seat. "Yes, your insolence. I have been forced to listen to your abuse of my country; and I should have treated you with the contempt you deserve, if you had not asked me to endorse your language. But now I almost thank you, and in return I will give you a little gratuitous advice. Be sure, as you grow older, to think twice before you attempt to air your prejudices in the presence of others. My country people are full of faults, and have much to learn from others ; but the last school I would advise them to study in is the society of the English, of which you seem to be a very fair specimen."

These words were spoken deliberately, in a cool, cultivated voice. The American was angry, but collected and dignified. He looked like a man of character, and as the clear, incisive sentences fell from his lips he gazed steadily into the Englishman's face, who, on his part, turned upon him a fiery and astonished stare ; but, before he had time to recover himself, the long train stopped at the busy railroad town of Mons, the most important station after leaving Brussels, where there are two trains for Paris, one hundred and twenty miles distant. The doors of all the carriages were unlocked and thrown wide open, as is customary, to allow the passengers to alight, and the four men found themselves descending to the level platform of the Flemish station in silence. While the two Englishmen were smarting under the strong language of the American, the latter, taking his son by the arm, quietly walked into the carriage in which the two ladies were seated who were the innocent causes of the explosion. The Englishmen saw their unpleasant dilemma at a glance ; and they had no time to recover from their new surprise, when they were hurried back to the smoker's retreat, as the train moved off on the route by Traumont, Compiègne, and Creil, to the gay capital of the French republic.

CHAPTER II.

MERELY A MECHANIC.

GEORGE HARRIS was born in one of the oldest of the American States, Pennsylvania, on the 30th of September, 1817, and was nearly sixty-one at the opening of our story.

Trained in the common schools under the great system instituted by Thaddeus Stevens and George Wolf, afterward perfected in the Philadelphia High School by men like Alexander Dallas Bache and John Sanderson, he was a blacksmith's apprentice before fifteen, and the owner of a little shop in old Spring Garden before he was nineteen. He was a good workman and a close student, and his intelligence and ingenuity soon attracted attention; he had no rich friends, but he was a careful reader of the busy world around him. His forge and anvil were his college; and the little he had gathered at school prepared him for the great future which accident opened to his young ambition.

One of the dreams of these early days was the beautiful vision to which in after-life he gave practical expression. It was the legend of the "Iron Worker." When Solomon's Temple was about to be opened, the blacksmith, finding himself omitted from the invited guests, boldly marched into the temple just from the forge, and taking the king's own seat, insisted that, since it was he who had made the tools with which the builders wrought, without him the splendid dome had never been constructed. King Solomon heard the appeal, and the blacksmith sat by his side at the royal feast.

When young Harris was pushing himself into business, full of health and vigor, he was unexpectedly called upon by an agent of the Russian Government, who had been referred to the ambitious and skillful mechanic, and invited to visit St. Petersburg, to undertake the equipment of a great Russian railroad; to construct machine-shops, to build locomotives and carriages, and to educate in skilled labor the youth of the Empire who might be the leaders of the next generation.

It was an unexpected call, and yet the High School boy found himself equal to the new responsibilities; he gathered around him men of capital by his brains, and his frankness won mechanics like himself. He called them in from other cities and States, and by his energy and intelligence pleased his royal employer, improved his own fortunes, and made a

name for high credit and integrity, which was freely awarded
to all his associates. His organization was in a few years
one of the most effective in Europe, the model for many
others.

Russian and American diplomacy have had a long and
congenial relationship; and nothing is more interesting than
that the two great antipodean systems should have come so
near together. The Continent, given up to absolutism on
one side of the globe, has gravitated to the republicanism of
the Continent at the other. Peter the Great, the anonymous
Muscovite shipbuilder, who traversed Europe, at the beginning of the eighteenth century, as a common laborer, was
only the antitype of Benjamin Franklin, the American print-
er, who traversed the other end of the same planet at the
close of the same century. Each had his mission and each
executed it.

When George Harris and his assistants left the United
States for St. Petersburg they had rare advantages. The
workers in iron in the first century of American independence, from Franklin, with the key that attracted and directed
the lightning, to Fulton, Fitch, Watt, Arkwright, Stephen-
son, Siemens, Edison, and others, have been the pioneers
of a destiny that is a religion in itself, the missionaries of a
new and powerful evangelism.

By a strange coincidence the State of Pennsylvania seems
to have supplied most of the American ministers to Russia,
and most of the builders of Russian railroads and Russian
ships. Since 1814, of the forty-nine ministers and secretaries
of legation appointed by the President of the United States,
twelve have been citizens of Pennsylvania. The presence of
such citizens at the proud court of the Russian Czar as William Wilkins, James Buchanan, George M. Dallas, Andrew
G. Curtin, George H. Boker, and Bayard Taylor undoubtedly prepared the way for the skilled mechanics, manufacturers, and shipwrights who were called from the same State
to the Russian capital by the successive emperors of that
great autocracy.

CHAPTER III.

FAMILY TRAITS.

ALL genuine women grow into manners; society is their true school; imitation is their final finish. They carefully copy the rare styles, sunned and ripened by the ages. The quickness of female intuition is an inspiration. How magical their skill in colors, in costume, furniture, flowers, and music! How refined and rapid their perception of the right tone of the voice, the best pose of the body, the sweetest expression; and when their natural gifts are turned to books, and the young mother teaches herself and trains her child at the same time not only the finest manners but the best morals, there is nothing more enchanting!

Such was Margaret Harris, the wife of George Harris, when she was seated with her daughter in the railway carriage at Brussels. Ten years younger than her husband, her daughter was born in St. Petersburg nineteen years before, having twice visited the United States with her parents and her brother, the last time during the Centennial Exhibition of 1876.

If there was a close resemblance between George Harris and his daughter Mary, and this although the father was as rugged in appearance as the daughter was beautiful, in her his strength had refined itself into loveliness, but it remained strength all the more. There was nothing between mother and daughter to show their relationship except the voice; and by that organ the family could be traced. Nature is in nothing more cunning than in the magic music of the human tongue. One may lose the trace of a face, the years that have surged between the outposts of youth and age have utterly changed the features, and you have stood wondering before the stranger till the old, unforgotten tones recalled the friend as if from the grave of the past.

So, when you heard Mary Harris, you also heard her mother and her brother. If Longfellow could have listened to her voice, he could have more truly written that " The intellect sits enthroned on the forehead and in the eye ; and the heart is written in the countenance. The soul reveals itself in the voice only."

Taller than her mother, and lighter, she had the startling beauty that comes with golden hair and dark eyes, and when she spoke you thrilled at the sweetness and depth of her voice. Its clear metallic ring was like a challenge, and there was an invisible echo (if I may be pardoned the paradox) like the sound that follows a melodious bell. Her tone at first seemed a defiance when she answered you ; but it was only the consciousness of perfect innocence, and the mastery of a pure woman over herself. Fond of her mother and her brother, she was very proud of her father. She cherished her mother, but she had a possession in her father ; at once a property, a partnership, and a worship. His views of men and things were hers, and he was equally her teacher, her protector, and her guardian. Educated, if not by him, at least under his eye, nothing aided him more than her literary excellence, her knowledge of languages, her grace in society, and her precious good sense; and the world at first regarded her more self-willed than sentimental.

But at last, much the strongest resemblance was that between Mrs. Margaret Harris and her son, in personal likeness, because in identity of character. That identity lay in the common sense ; common, at least, to these two.

"I am sorry for the dispute in the carriage with the Englishman, because it seems to have disturbed your father," said Mrs. Harris to her daughter, the morning after their return from Brussels, as they sat together in their Paris apartments at the Hôtel Bristol.

"Yes," was the reply ; "it was awkward, but I can quite understand my father's anger. It was impertinent on the part of the stranger. But then it was very like some of the English. There is nothing upon which he is so sensitive as an attack upon his country."

"But he is usually so prudent, and he specially dislikes

anything like a scene. I wonder what the exact cause of the altercation could have been?"

"And I have asked Henry, but my brother is as reserved as my father."

It would have been easy to satisfy her curiosity, but George Harris was not sorry to let the matter drop, although he could not help thinking about it a great deal.

As to the son, he was this much like his mother that, when he evaded explanation, every one felt with him that the matter was of importance, and that he had not as yet accomplished his purpose, whatever it was in regard to it.

CHAPTER IV.

APOLOGY.

THE splendors of the foreign embassies in Paris have not been lessened by the successes of the Republic. But the English Legation, the German Legation, the Italian and Russian Legations, the Chinese and Turkish Legations, are far more palatial than the humble offices of the American Minister. Paris, like London, is a diplomatic center, and the rival movements of Russia and England are as keenly conducted and as vigilantly watched as they are in St. Petersburg and London. It was a day reception at the Russian Minister's. The Grand Duke Alexis had come over to see the Exhibition; and the imperial droschka, with three fine steeds abreast, had been a new attraction to the cosmopolitan pleasure-seekers, as it sped out of the great horse-show on the broad boulevards on the opposite side of the Seine, and dashed up to the embassy. Crowds were pouring into the gates of the Minister's hotel, and he stood in his gilded saloon to welcome his guests. The handsome prince had just alighted from his Cossack chariot as George Harris, his wife, daughter, and son were ascending the flowery stairs

leading to the drawing-room of the Legation.   Nothing
could have been more graceful than the recognition of the
Americans by the Grand Duke.   That lovely day shone
down on no lovelier creature than Mary Harris ; nor in that
brilliant throng was there a more pleasing sight than the
family of the cultivated American.   All nations were represented in their beauty, wealth, and learning, and in their
highest rank.   The Prince of Wales was present with his
retinue on his fortnightly visit to Paris, and, together with
the royalties of other powers, had come to the Russian levee.
To these were joined all the ministers of the French republic
and the representatives of the other powers.   After due
homage to the Russian Minister by Mr. Harris and his family, and as he was conversing with other Russian friends,
and his wife and daughter were engaging their American
acquaintances, the rare charms of Mary Harris attracting
universal admiration, a well-known English diplomatist approached George Harris and addressed him with easy famili-
arity.   They had met in Washington during the Rebellion,
while Lord Lyons was the British Minister, at the house of Mr.
Seward, the American Secretary of State, who held Mr. Harris
high in esteem, and they had frequent subsequent interviews.

"I want to ask you a kindness.   Some days ago you had
a dispute with a young countryman of mine in a railway carriage on the way from Brussels, and this is the first time he
has seen you since.   He is here this morning, and asks to be
presented to you, that he may apologize for his part in the
affair " ; and the envoy waited for the reply.

"It was a hasty and awkward difference," said Mr. Harris ; "and I am almost sorry myself for my own impatience
with the young man."

"Then I feel that I am not mistaken in your good nature," the diplomatist responded, as he beckoned to the
young Englishman of the smoking compartment, who quickly
advanced, and the envoy spoke :

"I am glad to make you *better* acquainted with Lord
Conyngham, Mr. Harris."

And the two men shook hands, the handsome nobleman remarking :

"And I beg you, Mr. Harris, to accept my thanks and my apology at the same time. You treated me as I deserved, and taught me a lesson that will last a lifetime."

"Let me reciprocate your frankness at least. If my advice proves to be so useful, I am not sorry for the necessity that made me offer it."

And with some more words the young nobleman lifted his hat and stepped aside, but soon returned with a lady on his arm, who laughingly greeted the other Englishman.

"This is my sister, Lady Blanche, Mr. Harris, who must be my intercessor with your wife and daughter, to make my forgiveness complete."

It was so quickly and gracefully done that the lady was almost instantly introduced to the two American women who stood close to her ; and it took only a few minutes to include Henry Harris in the general reconciliation.

Even the British statesman, who had been in diplomacy nearly forty years—had served in Greece, Italy, America, Turkey, and France—never witnessed a more interesting scene as he watched these pleasant courtesies, and certainly never saw two more charming or more charmingly contrasted characters than these two lovely girls, Mary Harris and Blanche Conyngham ; and the elegant courtier, as he left the new friends laughing and chatting, quietly whispered to Lord Conyngham, "Has she come at last ?"

CHAPTER V.

THE TROCADÉRO.

BLANCHE CONYNGHAM was more than an English girl of fashion. The only daughter of a peer of the realm, and sister of the heir to a large estate, she was as unspoiled as if

she had been reared in a lower sphere. She was fortunate
in the rare gift of unconscious beauty, and when she met
Mary Harris and her mother she captivated them by the
honesty of her manner and the candor of her conversation.
To say that she was pleased with them was to repeat what
all others said who first met these superior women. The
three rode to the Exhibition in the same carriage, leaving
the three men to follow ; and they had a little feminine talk
as they rolled up to the main door of the Trocadéro ; but
they were meanwhile silently occupied in a mutual and womanly inventory of each other.

"You are not strangers in Europe, that is easily seen,"
said Lady Blanche.

"Oh, no," said Margaret Harris ; "I have been a long
time abroad, and my daughter was born in Russia."

"I have never seen your vast country, but I read about
it a great deal ; indeed, I think about it every day. Do
you return soon?"

"Next year, and for good. This is our last visit to Paris,
and I feel a little sad at leaving familiar scenes and dear
friends."

"But then we have a home awaiting us, and many who
long for our coming," said Mary Harris.

As Blanche looked at her, a new light filled her eyes, and
the rich voice of the American girl touched her heart. Mary
studied the bright English face opposite with a sweet
smile.

The crowd was hastening along the broad vestibule of
the fantastic temple, and strains of music poured through
the wide edifice, while the silvery waters dashed over the
broad steps under the towering fountains with their gigan-
tic figures, and from the sweeping balconies of the Trocadéro
you saw the animated perspective leading to the main temple
of the Exposition. As the ladies descended from the chariot,
they found Lord Conyngham, George Harris, and his son
already arrived to receive them. Naturally the young nobleman walked with Mary, Blanche and the others following

down the broad stair to the great highway over the bridge across the Seine.

"These World's Fairs are schools, not shows, to me, and they always give me rather saddening reflections. There is so much to see and to think of, that I tire at my own incapacity," were the first words of the young man to Mary.

"Yes, I can quite understand," she said ; "but I always take refuge in gratitude to God that all these wonderful things were made by his creatures, and so are a kind of worship of him."

"I never heard such a view of the Exposition ; but it is very true," was all the other could say.

"Is it not the right view?" she asked modestly ; "how much better these modern manifestations of the industry and skill, the science and genius of our men and women, than the preparations for conquest and war ! They seem to me to mark the contrast between the past and the present."

This was so different from what he had expected, and so different from what he had been accustomed to, that Lord Conyngham could only look and listen. At last he said :

"I do not think our English women reflect so deeply as you do, and indeed I have not heard those of your country speak like you ; but it is very agreeable."

Mary made no reply, but, looking back, she said to Blanche :

"Lady Blanche, you must rescue me from your brother. I frighten him by my sermon, and then he flatters me. Is that his way?"

"My brother is not easily frightened, and, like most Englishmen, not much given to compliments, but I think you have been surprising him. What is it, Alfred?"

"Only this : Miss Harris has been giving me a new cause of the good wrought by these World's Fairs."

"I am neither philosopher nor prophet ; but nothing," Mary added, "overcomes me as a woman more than these evidences of human improvement, as I see them in such places, and I can not help thinking that when our fellow-creatures show such great powers, they are new witnesses of the greatness of God. It can mean nothing else."

"Mary was curiously affected at Philadelphia two years ago," said her father, joining the group. "When she first saw the Corliss engine in the American Exhibition, she said it overcame her like the sermon of an eloquent preacher, and I confess it impressed me the same way."

"Now, father dear, we will change the subject, if you please. May I not ask you to show me the English pictures, Lord Conyngham? There is one Turner that you must explain. It is quite beyond me."

CHAPTER VI.

EARL DORRINGTON.

EARL DORRINGTON, the father of the young Lord Conyngham, had a weakness for Paris, and belonged to that large class of Englishmen who always seek the Continent in November. He was so much attached to Nice and the South of France that, with his long absences there and in the gay French capital, he was almost a stranger in his own ancient halls. He took little or no interest in public affairs, was rarely seen in the House of Lords, and beyond a sort of idolatry for his daughter Blanche, lived in and loved the world that had always treated him as one of its spoiled darlings. He was not yet sixty, and there were few handsomer men, and none more blameless or gentle. He was a sincere aristocrat, and inherited as a part of his family religion a firm conviction of the inferiority of the common people. Of his own purity and perfection he was so sure that he felt no pride in them. They were a sort of property as inseparable to himself as his hands or his head. He no more doubted that he was placed apart from those not well born than he did that his valet and his butler were

created only to wait upon him. His daughter was his
prime minister, and although all his generosity was vica-
rious, the world believed that the luxurious Earl was liberal or benevolent on his own motion. But Blanche was
his almoner. She had large sympathies and quick percep-
tions, and freely indulged them, and as she accompanied her
father in most of his travels, and wrote his name in all her
charities, generally without consulting him, he had an un-
deserved reputation for good deeds not his own ; nor did his
languid manner stand with the public as a contradiction to
his registered charities. He was too well bred for controversy. He accepted Blanche as the most perfect of her sex
—his wife having died when Blanche was born—and he
rarely questioned her actions. The Earl and his children, as
he called them, had the best quarters in the old Hôtel Meu-
rice, on the Rue Rivoli, now richly renovated, and as they
only met at dinner in their superb private parlor, that was
the occasion for the report of the day. They were not often
alone at that hour. Their English and foreign acquaintance
was large, and when they were not engaged with others they
had invited guests of their own. The luxury of the rich
English nobility is nowhere more lavish than while they are
in Paris. They enjoy life in a quiet and costly exclusive-
ness, and if one were to attempt to describe what is known of
their outlays, one might fear to be misunderstood. A few of
the wealthy commoners go beyond them, but, as the titled
British families are nearly all very rich, they live lives of
almost fabulous extravagance, and when they settle down
for a season in Paris their expenditure is boundless. The
English nobility as a rule have large estates and incomes,
and Earl Dorrington was one of the most fortunate.

He was first in the drawing-room, waiting, in full dress,
for his son and daughter, who had given the day to the Russian reception and the Exposition Universelle, and as he sat
looking over " The Times " we will take his photograph. He
was, as has been said, a man of sixty, with iron-gray hair and
short whiskers, a face without a moustache, and that quiet-

ude which comes of inherited independence and comfort.
Tall, like his son Alfred, the young lord, he had less of the
affronting self-assertion of the latter, and more of the winning air of his daughter. Men who do not work themselves,
and have others to work for them and attend to their slight-
est wish, fall insensibly into a contempt for others. Such
men are an intrusion, and worse, to sensitive minds, and the
more so because patricians such as these come at last to a
conviction that they own what they never deserved. But
the Earl had a gift of hiding this trait, and rather won upon
those who disliked it in others. There were no guests to-
day, and he waited pleasantly for the entrance of his son
and daughter, and greeted them warmly as they came in
from opposite doors. Certainly they were a handsome pair.
The young lord had his father's height, and as he stood
forth in his black costume and white cravat, his long, shapely
English limbs, and his fine head rising from his broad
shoulders, his striking face laughed in the consciousness of
perfect self-enjoyment. Blanche looked like him; but, in
her delicate blue dress, a deep-blush autumn rose in her hair,
her small, white, unjeweled hands, a bright solitaire in each
delicate, shell-like ear, and her sweet face all aglow, she was
rather a contrast than a comparison. Her father saluted her
with his best grace, and led her, like a knight of the olden
time, to her appropriate place at the head of the table, seat-
ing himself opposite his son.

"And what of the day, sweetheart?" was his first greet-
ing as he took his sherry and declined the soup. "You have
had heavenly weather for your ride. Pray tell me all the
good things you have seen?"

"First of all, papa dear, I have seen a charming American; and so has Alfred; and we are both in love, if you
please."

"What, at first sight? An American—and what is his
name?"

"It is a lady, your lordship, and although this is my first
look, my brother is more fortunate."

Needless to say that the Earl knew nothing of the adventure on the rail, and he replied, with very little curiosity in his tone :

" One meets all the world in Paris, yet it is not necessary to fall in love with it, even at second sight. The Americans are always demonstrative ; I prefer to read about them."

" Then, dear papa, these are exceptions. They are almost as composed as if they were great people, like the English ; and, you know, we are the greatest on the round globe. At least, that is your opinion."

Then Alfred spoke to the Earl :

" These strangers have interested me. They are a better strain than I have been accustomed to. They are quiet, accomplished, wealthy, and gentle, and the father has a sort of English pride of country ; the mother is very well poised, and the daughter is an angel."

" I never hear," the Earl said in reply, " of an American's pride of country without a smile. As I never dispute, especially with strangers, I listen to and wonder at the Americans. They have no past ; no great families ; no great leaders ; no literature, and no gifts of governing ; and no matter how well-bred or educated, they amount to nothing. They are the green fruit of the orchard. The world must be controlled by educated experience. All experiments are temporary. Mankind was born to be managed by the ripe minds. It was so in the Pagan eras ; it is so to-day ; it will be so to the end ; and America is only an accident, and accidents are sudden and suddenly perish. We may improve by the accident of its existence, but we shall survive and dominate."

Such was the school of Lady Blanche and Lord Conyngham. They talked for a long time over their elaborate dinner, and this was all that was said about the Americans ; but Mary Harris was not one soon to be forgotten by the young nobleman.

CHAPTER VII.

FIRST ACQUAINTANCE.

GEORGE HARRIS and his wife and children regarded Lord Conyngham and Lady Blanche with interest. The father was impressed by the manly deportment of the young lord, and Mary Harris was pleased with Lady Blanche. Mrs. Harris saw more than the rest, and Henry, her son, like most brothers, only regarded Conyngham as a very well-bred snob, without once thinking that his sister was the magnet.

George Harris quietly observed :

"The young lord is a type of his class—a very large, and, I fear, an increasing class, the chief ingredient of which is the conviction that other men are born to contribute to their wants and luxuries. These people can not understand mankind. Not to know is born in them. I do not complain ; it is their destiny. Nor do I expect them to like the United States. If I had been spoiled as they have been ; if my ancestors, instead of honest, hard-working people, had been raised to give command, to obey nothing but their own instincts, and to expect all below them to fawn and flatter, I should to-day be as much in love with myself and as fond of thinking others my inferiors as these simple moles, the amusing drones of the British nobility. You can not expect an eagle from the nest of a peacock. Like makes like."

"But, father," said Mary with beautiful animation, "do you not think that the daughter Blanche is the exception that proves the rule ? She seems a different sort."

"And so she does. I was quite pleased with her *naïveté*. She has courage too, and talks sometimes as if she knew more than she cared to tell. Did you observe how long she stood before that very bad painting of Mr. Lincoln in the poor collection called the American Art Gallery ? "

"You did not hear her questions about him," said Henry.

"I had to ask mother to help me out with the story. She was much affected by the narrative of his low beginning, trying career, and tragic end. We are strange creatures to these English," he continued, "but not more than they are to us. It is a fashion, I think an affectation, with them not to know anything about our country, and I have more than once been vexed, for I never *begin* to talk to them about home, by an Englishman asking whether I lived in North or South America."

"But, father dear, you often say that events are compelling the English to appreciate our country," was Mary's rejoinder.

"Yes, my darling, but compelled appreciation can not be sincere. It is like the respect that comes from fear, a sentiment that begins in envy and ends in hate. I am sorry to believe that the English rulers will always regard us in the one or the other light. Even now they are divided between envy and hate."

"But, father, not the English people."

"I said the rulers ; no, thank God ! not the English people ; and that increases the feeling of the rulers—a feeling daily strengthened by their dependence on us and our independence of them. Our Declaration of 1776 was but the first step toward our independence of them, which is yet to culminate and give place to such a dependence of England on us—no, such a unity of England with us as few dream of as yet."

"Do you not think, George, that the success of the Union army left a severe scar on the heart of the English aristocracy?" quietly asked Mrs. Harris.

"It is not pleasant to know this, but I meet it almost daily, and it is often difficult to keep down my anger among the English. I could not believe how deeply they desired our defeat ; and now that they are suffering more and more in their trade, and getting deeper and deeper in debt, and we are improving daily, and even competing with, instead of buying from them, their resentment is only natural. What

2

folly in them to fight the inevitable ! Not even English
pluck is sufficient for that, and they must know that we and
they are but at the beginning of vast changes, and all in one
direction."

And this was the other side of the medal.

CHAPTER VIII.

THE PARISIAN PALACE OF PEACE.

No just ideal of the Paris Exposition would have been
possible had it not been preceded by the Centennial at Philadelphia, two years before ; and as nine or tèn millions of
people witnessed the latter, they need only be assured that
its French successor, though unspeakably grand and complete, lacked many of the unforgotten peculiarities of the
American memorial. In one respect they were much alike.
They had the same transcendent mission. Before the American International all the great Expositions had been royal
saturnalias, originated and organized by the Russian Czar,
the British Queen, the French Emperor, the Austrian Monarch, the Belgian King, or the German Kaiser, and the
resulting rewards were almost exclusively scattered among
court favorites. The assertion was common that art was the
offspring of aristocracy, that genius only ripened under a
regal sun, and that a modern republic was another name for
severe utility. The Philadelphia Centennial dispelled the
offensive dogma by the grandeur of its scheme, by its superb
perspectives, architectural and rural, by the almost articulate
perfection of its marvelous system, by the magical variety
of its machines, by the solved problems of its inventions, and
by the almost inspired succession of its other developments
in art, science, agriculture, and mechanics. The connoisseurs
of Europe who came to criticise remained to applaud ; the
foreign artists who feared that their models might be stolen

remained to copy those of the Americans; and the people
of two worlds mingled in admiration before the novelty and
majesty of the spectacle. No court favorites absorbed the
awards of this republican jury. Impartial judgment and
refined discrimination settled the prizes on the meritorious,
without reference to rank or condition; and they may now
be found in every European capital, the recognized badges
of republican good taste and justice. The French Republic
followed in turn, and this was its triumphant season. The
prophets who predicted failure were silent before its mag-
nificence. Never before had French genius a grander opportunity; never had art reveled in a more complete temple.
The air was full of freedom. There was a carnival of classic
liberty. There were order without arms, culture without
coercion, temperance without austerity, and subordination
to laws made by the people themselves for themselves. The
festivals that crowned this unequaled pageant were all festivals of peace, and Paris proved to her foes that the best
way to govern the French people was to govern them least.
The trade of soldiers and the crime of war, that guilty saturnalia of France, the Third Empire, the fierce logic of the
Commune, and the grim German conquerors, had perished or
passed away, a succession of horrors, the ghastly harvest of
force, the grim holocaust of an incredible treason. The
American Centennial was the apotheosis of freedom in the
New World, a better and brighter deification of human
rights because sanctified by the blood of the martyrs, and
the French Exposition was the joyous feast of the deliverance from despotism of one of the oldest nations in the Old
World. Both had been satiated with internal conflict; both
were tired of the horror of brother warring upon brother;
and both sought and found safety in these magnificent expressions of industry, reconciliation, and fraternity.

And it was in this spirit that all the nations came to
Paris in that year of our Lord. No one failed to catch the
contagion of the example. No orator was needed to empha-
size a lesson that spoke for itself always and everywhere.

For the first time the European monarchs saw that the
European masses would fight no more save for themselves.
A new gospel of progress had been declared. The French
Republic meant victory because it meant peace. As you
walked these long corridors, crossed these golden pave-
ments, and looked down these glittering perspectives, the
monarch you met was the multitude ! And he felt that he
was master. He came from all the human climes : the
swarth Nubian, the silent Chinese, the passionless Turk,
the stolid Swiss, the ruddy English, the ebon Moor, the light
Caucasian, the grave German, the gay American, the black
African, the olive Italian, and the frowning Spaniard. What
a fable to say that mankind prefers to be ruled by mediocrity !
What a lie to insist that hereditary government is essential
to civilization ! The world is getting wiser, and the profoundest lesson it is acquiring is that the kings of men must
be kings of mind, and that inherited titles are no more com-
petent to control humanity than inherited disease. The citizen of a republic is judged by his character and his record,
and "in a republic a title is no more than a counterfeit bank-
note."

The greatest wonder of the Exposition was that it happened when it did. The wounds cut deep into the face of
the fair city, in '71 and '72, were still unhealed. The marks
left by war were visible almost at the very doors of this festival of peace. German soldiers, who marched beneath the
Arc de Triomphe and down the Champs Elysées in full
panoply of battle, with their music of victory echoing and
re-echoing from the walls of the closed and barred houses,
sipped their *petits verres* in the cafés of the Exhibition, and
talked like brothers with men hardly more than yesterday
their deadly foes. To stand in the courtyard of the Grand
Hôtel de Rivoli and look over upon the ruins of the Tuileries
was almost to smell the cans of the *petroleuses*. The rising
walls of the new Hôtel de Ville recalled the yells of the fren-
zied Commune, and as you saw everywhere how Paris now
rejoiced you could not but remember how she wept ; you

thought of the immense sum France had surrendered to Germany, and then of the vast expense of the great world's show, and you had to honor this people for their indomitable courage, energy, and perseverance, and to marvel at their seemingly inexhaustible wealth. They had failed in a war which they had undertaken with hearts as light as upon a *fête* day, and confidence so strong that it would have been treason to think of disaster. They had cried *À Berlin!* until they believed no power, divine or human, could save the cohorts of King William from defeat. They were crushed by the terrible result, and Paris lay bleeding nigh unto death. But they dried their tears, they opened their workshops, they rebuilt, they redecorated, and they called the world to come and visit them.

CHAPTER IX.

THE AMERICANS.

No American family was better known in Europe than that of George Harris, and this for two reasons. First, because they seemed to be almost omnipresent. You saw them in Rome, especially if you went where new streets were being opened—where excavations were bringing to light an earlier and nobler era than that of the Cæsars ; most of all, would you be sure to see them in the new schools and churches wherein is being nursed the infancy, at least, of a grander epoch than that of the Popes. If you seated yourself in the magnificent Scala of Milan, you were sure to see at a distance, if not the father or the mother, certainly Henry Harris and his sister. The family came upon you as you lingered under the lindens at Berlin ; among the treasuries of ceramic art in Dresden ; along the picture galleries of Vienna, or as you drove in your droschka down the streets of St. Petersburg. Perhaps nowhere did the father and son find as much to interest them as in the English Parliament. The Chamber of Deputies, in France, was more exciting, but they were too well acquainted with the French not to know that the history of France is but the explosive utterances of a national character, from which, and through the future also, the sparkle, the foam, and the intoxication are as inseparable in the man as in the champagne springing from the same soil.

"The English are slow of movement," George Harris remarked to his son one day, as they sat in the Strangers' Gallery during a debate in the House of Commons, "but they never recede. Of course you and I know the sure result to which England is tending, but I admire the ponderous slowness with which it advances. See the scorn and apathy with which so many of them are listening to John Bright. Look at him: his whole manner is that of a man who is slowly straining as if to lift a vast weight. He knows that destiny works in and with him, but that it works with imperceptible omnipotence."

"And I was thinking," his son replied, "of the colonies of England. Apart from its general influence over other nations, it drags after it half the world in its vast dependencies. Like a locomotive drawing an enormous train, and upon an up-grade too, it must move slowly."

"Yes; and the work given England to do has developed," the father added, "both English pluck and English brawn. But were ever people so unlike as the French and the English! No wonder that for so many centuries they regarded themselves as natural enemies, cat and dog, bound to fly at each other on sight. Each does its own work in its own way."

Neither father nor son uttered it, yet both added it to himself, "And America is the power which impels both."

But there was a second reason why George Harris and his family were so well known over Europe. Wherever you met them you could not fail to be struck with their appearance. In Italy or Germany; in Sweden, Russia, or France; by porter and by prince, by *concierge* at the door of their hotel or by the nobleman who received them at dinner, by wayside peasant and by king, queen, or czar, father and mother, son and daughter, were regarded as belonging, in some way, to the nobility. The parents had sprung from the common people. At one time they had been very poor, had to struggle hard and to live scantily, yet with success had come something more than merely the aspect of wealth.

"Look at Disraeli over there," Henry Harris had said to his father at a dinner given by the Mayor of London; "why is it that you would know that he is a public man if you were to meet him by Lake Nyanza? It is the same of Bright, of Gladstone. You can see that they have been long accustomed to face opposing or applauding multitudes. Their countenances are noble, yet worn like cliffs washed by the seas."

"Every man wears his character in his face," the elder Harris replied. "At last, my son, we always know people for what they are! Lord Conyngham, for instance—I read him from the moment he first spoke to me."

"But a young man grows, changes," Henry Harris hastened to say.

"Yes; and I saw *that* in him, too; possibility of change, docility of development, if I may so style it. Strange to say, it was this which checked my anger, even in the first moment of exasperation at him. But we will not speak of that again. Besides, hush! we can not catch what that gentleman down the table is trying to say."

"Why can't the man say what he has to say?" Henry Harris murmured to himself. "Why will an Englishman persist in mumbling, hesitating, repeating, whenever he rises to make a speech? Because great men write illegibly under press of business, lesser men do so too; they will, in that at least, be like the Rufus Choates and Horace Greeleys. Prime ministers hum and haw in Parliament, and, therefore, Tom, Dick, and Harry must do so too. But I will listen if I can."

The family of George Harris seemed to live in public,

and it was a very broad public, since it embraced all Europe, with occasional visits to Egypt and Syria. Had they been in America, they could have contented themselves upon the banks of the Hudson or the Delaware. There they would have been happy even in a home comparatively secluded, and surrounded by friends few and choice. Being in Europe, it was different. Wherever their home might be for the time, as pleasure or business demanded, they were always "abroad," so far as feeling went.

"That is one of the peculiarities of the Americans as of the English," Lord Conyngham remarked one day to Henry Harris. "Arabs and Turks, Spaniards and Russians, people wonder at us wherever we go. 'Why can't they be quiet?' they say to each other of us. . 'Is their own land so dreadful that it is impossible to live there?' I don't understand it myself. We have a St. Vitus's dance; we can't settle down to save our lives."

"I suppose," Henry Harris made answer, "that it is part of our force. Our mission is to revolutionize the world, you know. We are missionaries, you observe, my lord. So long as there remains a Chinese locked up in his ancient costume, a Turk in his harem, a Zulu in his jungle, we must go after him."

"They certainly will not come to us," Lord Conyngham replied.

George Harris and his household seemed to be, as has been said, almost everywhere, and yet wherever they went they carried their home with them. Mr. Harris had married his wife because he had loved her, and as they strove together to establish themselves in the world their mutual affection had deepened as part of their mutual development. As their children grew up they had been taken into the close companionship, and therefore into the steady growth of the parents. Before leaving America the father and mother had been separated from the rich more by their independence of spirit than by their poverty. From the great mass of the laboring poor they were held apart still more by their habits

of thrift, of self-denial, of deliberate purpose to lift themselves to higher levels. Thus, and from the outset, the
household had been nurtured into the nearest intimacy with
each other, as aloof from those around them. When they
came to Europe this feeling was naturally intensified. The
pressure of business, stern and steady, their ignorance of
the ways of the people about them, as much, sometimes, as
of their language, the deepening of the intention to advance
in things to which all lesser success was but a stepping-stone
—all this had tended still more to isolate the household from
the world about them, and to throw them upon themselves.
Had they remained in America, they could not have been so
thoroughly at home when together as was now the case.

"At last our happiness lies in that," Mary Harris said to
her brother, as they walked together one day through the
wonders of the Exposition at Paris; "whatever we see during the day—pictures, statues, machinery, distinguished people, marvels, absurdities—whatever we see or hear during the
day, is really enjoyed only after we have come together at
night, and while we are talking it all over together before
we part for the night. Besides—"

"Well, besides what?" her brother asked, for his sister
had ceased to speak, and seemed indifferent to the brilliant
scene around her—to be thinking instead, her eyes cast down.
Neither of them observed that Lady Blanche and her brother
were examining a superb set of Limoges faience near them.

"Besides what?" Henry Harris repeated.

"I ought not to say it;" the fair girl lifted her laughing
eyes to her companion's; "but do you know, I never see anybody I think quite as much of as I do of those at home."

"Of course you love them most; I do."

"Yes, but it is not that; you mustn't make fun of me,
Henry, but I can not help thinking that my father and mother are superior to everybody I meet. If the French Government had said to father, 'Here are the millions; we do not
understand such things, and you do; build an Exposition
Building for us;' don't you suppose he could have done it

at least as well or better than it has been done?   When I
saw Marshal MacMahon for the first time I said to myself,
'If my father had commanded in your place, *he* would not
have been whipped by Von Moltke, I can assure you.'   It
may be absurd, but last night at the opera I thought, while
the people were applauding the prima donna so vigorously,
'Ah! if you only heard my mother!'"

"Why, she can not sing!" and her brother laughed aloud.

"No, but she could if she would.   Look at what my father has made himself.   Suppose he had gone into music instead; and so of my mother: there is nothing on earth that
they could not do if they tried."

"I suppose you think father would have made an excellent czar?" her brother asked, humoring her affection.

"Certainly; I have never seen the Emperor that I have
not said to myself, 'I only wish I had the opportunity to tell
your Majesty so,'" the sister gravely replied.

"Nonsense!" her brother exclaimed, and they strolled
on.   But the sister did not tell him that she had almost as
exalted an opinion of him as of their father.   There was not
a picture she passed, a statue she saw, but she entertained a
secret belief that Henry could have done it a little better if
he had given his attention in that direction.   The brother
would not have expressed it, but, really, he had the same
feeling toward his father and mother and sister.   Had their
lineage been the best in Europe, the members of the household could not have had greater pride of race.   Their line
extended back, it is true, not for a thousand, but merely for
some sixty years or so; instead of a hundred ancestors, val-
iant knights, belted earls, noble dames, there was only one
father to boast of and one mother; yet, and because an entire
genealogy was condensed in these, they were that much the
more prized and loved by their children.

"I suppose," Lady Blanche said to her brother, when the
others had passed out of hearing, "that it is their belief in
themselves which gives them the bearing of princes."

"And the odd thing about it," Lord Conyngham replied,

"is that they never do or say anything that looks like boasting. They assume their nobility as matter of course. They are curious people, the Americans. I am every day more eager to understand them. I have had men who toadied to me until I could have kicked them into the kennel," he added to his sister Blanche; "but, in the case of young Harris, if there is to be any toadying, by Jove! it is *I* who must do it. He is a modest fellow, and yet you feel toward him as if he were a royal duke."

CHAPTER X.

GEORGE HARRIS BREAKS HIS SILENCE.

AMONG many curious places in Paris, old and new, there is none more cosmopolitan than "The Bodega," occupying the corner of the Rue Rivoli and the Rue Castiglione, part of the costly hotel-palace, "The Continental." Its furnishing is a mass of gilding, carving, mirrors, upholstery, magnificent *repoussé* altar-pieces, and bold arabesques, oil paintings, mosaics, and furniture of inconceivable shapes and prices. The Bodega is to this huge pile what a chapel is to a cathedral; what a wine vault is to a great castle. It is the resort of the daily cosmopolitan multitude, who come there to smoke, to lunch, and to enjoy the distillations of their various countries, while they converse and trade. The various wines and liquors are exposed in pipes, and the customers served by draughts drawn from the spigots by the active servants of the place. English, French, Germans, Italians, Americans, Dutch, Mexicans, Turks, Africans, India princes, all ranks and nations, gathered here during the Exposition, from morn till night, and even English ladies did not hesitate to meet here for their ale, sherry, port, and gin. One saw them frequently, and frequently alone, and, although you never saw them insulted, you never met at the Bodega an American woman. Upstairs are spacious parlors where almost every day men of all nations meet to gossip, large rooms looking out upon the Place Concorde and the gardens of the Tuileries, and sometimes you meet odd characters and have curious views. In this spot some friends had met together by themselves. Yet the ample doors were wide open, and the scene was free to all, and quite public. The impromptu speech, given presently, had numerous impromptu auditors.

There was a large party—men of all nationalities. Two handsome rooms were thrown open, but the company mostly gathered in the one with George Harris, where there were plenty of chairs and easy lounges and American rockers. The Frenchmen and other foreigners could all understand English. Everything was very cheerful. For ˋa while light subjects only were started, but presently they came upon a more serious topic, and one from "home." It was a marked sample out of those cases now and then occurring in the United States, where a newspaper editor had exposed the private life and wickedness of a candidate for public office, and even mentioned his relatives with opprobrium. The enraged candidate had deliberately sought the editor and shot him dead.

By insensible degrees, as this affair was discussed, it rapidly assumed a gravity which spread like a cloud over the assembled groups, and became a sort of rallying-point, or center of defense, for the Great Republic and its society, institutions, and prospects. There was a small minority on one side ; on the other was the majority—among them several Americans—with plenty of out-and-out denunciations, and rueful prophesies of evil to the land where such things seemed characteristic and ingrained.

As the voices raised and multiplied, and matters became almost threatening, a gentleman who was standing in the door sang out :

"Here comes the Old Gray. Now let's hear what he has to say about it."

The person so designated as he entered the room was

received, it was plain, with affectionate welcome by all the Americans. Many rose and advanced; every countenance lit up. Imagine a man of slow movement, six feet tall, stoutly built, with blue eyes, red and tanned complexion, white or almost white beard, mustache, and hair very profuse, quite untrimmed, and the latter falling over an enormous shirt-collar, snowy clean, flaring wide open at the throat, free of necktie, and with proportionately vast cuffs, turned over at the wrists. The shirt-collar and wristbands, with their unusual blanch of copiousness, having first been observed, you saw that the name by which his friend announced him was fully warranted. He was dressed in an entire suit of light English gray, loose sack-coat, trousers, vest, with overgaiters on his ankles, all of the same material. Nor must the hat be forgotten, a soft nutria, mole-colored, broad-brimmed, and of specially generous crown—a characteristic hat, the kind which travelers will remember seeing in New York and some of the old Southern cities.

Answering the friendly greetings of the crowd by a few words, but plenty of expressive nods, smiles, and hand-claspings, he accepted a seat near George Harris, while a brimming glass of red wine was filled, and put by his side.

"You are just in time," said Mr. Harris, " to settle this quarrel of ours ; " proceeding to state the points of the argument—the case that the American newspapers had been printing and commenting on, while the foreign press found in it a typical bit of democracy, an omen of disruption.

The Old Gray leisurely proceeded to drink before he gratified their inquiries. There was quite a silence through the rooms. What he said came out slowly at first ; then, as objections, questions, and cross-questions accumulated, he went on with more decision and animation.

"I am in the midst of friends," he said, looking around ; "not only fellow-Americans, but fellow-Europeans. If you really want my notions and theories, you must allow me to give them in my own way."

We will not undertake to render literally what followed.

The minority rested in peace, content to leave their case in the old man's hands. The majority comprised some very skillful and able speakers. All were entirely courteous, yet heavy blows were struck upon both sides. We will content ourselves with giving the gist of the new-comer's utterance.

It was an advocacy of freedom—some would have called parts of it a rhapsody. It was no rhapsody, however, for the American possessed all the cautiousness and even wariness of Monsieur Thiers himself, but more heat and emotion, and had learned, though less in books and systems, far more of men and actual life. He boldly defended the spirit of license in the press, in legislative assemblies, in criticism. "Excesses are unavoidable—they prove the rule," he said. "Weeds even show that the soil is rich. Nature itself is freedom.

"I speak strongly," said he, "because I find many good people who think the only remedy for too free action is in severer penalties and tighter restrictions. Do not misunderstand me either. Of course, the rules of the civil, criminal, and common law, the same in all countries, must be absolutely adhered to and enforced. Then I believe in immense margins for America, and for all modern peoples; they are necessary to growth and development. I want a tough, gristly, athletic race, in my country, North and South. I want a proud, full-voiced, even turbulent democracy; and if we can't have that without some excesses and evils—as how can we?—I will do the best I can with the evils. Believe me, we are to revise and reconstruct some of the hitherto accepted points of public opinion for the use of the New World. Not the great laws of right and wrong, for they are eternal; but under them, and fully owning them, we are to take our own way—as, indeed, we substantially have done now for a century. Of that way, the States, as they now stand, are the fruit.

"The principle of freedom, I do not object to your calling it license, carries in its train not merely its own great good, but many great evils, like the principles of Nature itself. Few understand America—few even of her own children. As I said, she proceeds on her development in her own way, perhaps unwittingly to herself, on immense scales, like those of geology ; her aims are vast ameliorations in the future ; she is unable to stop her mighty strides to heal every temporary fault and defection.

"Compacted as we are to be—for, as far as now appears to me, our Union is indissoluble—our varieties and paradoxes are immense. Our republic is not only a new dispensation, a new.departure in itself ; it needs a new dispensation of free speech, free criticism, tough cuticles, unprecedented toleration. What, more than these, can supply that tremendous concrete and perpetual attrition our diverse elements so need ?

" We are certainly blocking out and dovetailing together in the United States the great democratic edifice of the coming world, not for or out of ourselves merely, but out of all races—British, German, Scandinavian, Spanish, French, Italian—and as the legitimate result of past time. Not for the States alone, I say ; the United States of America is merely a model in small for the United States of the World ; the whole world, and all lands, and all good men and women are inextricably involved in our success.

"Yes, few understand America. I have sometimes thought I have not met a single person who fully appreciates her. The most hardy, most patriotic, most sublime, most *balancing* spirit of time and humanity yet—more heroic than the old Greek or Roman—is to-day brooding in our average American-born people, in the agricultural regions, and the good strata of workmen in cities. It is a latent, generally slumbering power, but sometimes it awakes. It will always certainly awake when fit occasions come. It awoke in '61, and took shape. It put down the Secession revolt. The politicians with their rings and frauds ostensibly manage our politics, I confess, but the people back of everything really hold the last tremendous verdict, and will give it and relentlessly execute it whenever they choose. To me it is enough. Any day, any moment, the power I speak of—and it is unerring, deathless, willful—may burst into action, quick and resistless as lightning. Then the evil birds of our politics will scatter to their dark holes, like the swarms of bats they are. My friends, few know the real America. It does not know itself. It is not on the surface.

"Not more surely is the material universe, with all its contradictions, one grand scheme of development, often through rough and forbidding processes, than the American Union is. It is never going to be great in .conquests, as Rome ; nor in the classic arts, as Greece ; nor rival the special points of the Middle Ages ; nor compete, at least, I hope not, with the current European capitals in their *bon ton,* or operas, or the special refinement of the few, or what they call *culture* and *society.* Though 'ladies and gentlemen' are included in its scope, it is quite indifferent to them, and could get along perfectly well without them. Not so other nations ; in those select classes flows the heart's blood of other nations. But we are a People, averaged, dilated, religious, sane, practical, owning their own homes—fifty millions, as the next census will show—sublime masses, such as the world never saw before. Faults enough there are, and miseries enough, and frauds enough, and the poor and unemployed, no doubt. Yet where else is Man so brought to the front ? Where are the ideals of all enthusiasts, and all the past, already so realized ? "

As the old man ended there was silence for a short time. His earnestness had made a deep impression, not only on the foreigners, but on the Americans themselves There was not only such vehement faith, but such original touches, novel presentations, such weird effects withal, it almost seemed as if the "spirits of the mighty dead " were hovering in the room.

Jefferson, Rousseau, Hegel, Buckle—ay, old Socrates, and a greater than Socrates—would have found, if so, that their hopes, ardors for humanity, their overarching dreams, were here alive and active to-day, adhered to without diminution, without remitting a particle—nay, with increased confidence, perfect trust in God's purposes, and demands larger than ever, tempered well with—but undauntedly meeting and in defiance of—all the exceptions, sarcasms, evil prophecies, of the most inveterate pessimist.

CHAPTER XI.

AN AMERICAN EVANGEL.

THE American Chapel, Rue de Berri, Paris, with its simple front and plain interior, in the midst of numerous costly and venerable Catholic monuments, resembles a Quaker woman in the midst of a crowd of jeweled queens, and its ministrations are almost as exclusive as the Roman service is universal. It is, like all the purely English churches on the Continent, attended by the traveling and resident English and American Protestants, and avoided by the Catholics of the different races. The prevailing Continental religion is Romish. An Italian, French, or Spanish convert to Protestantism is, or was, almost as exceptional as a recusant Hebrew or a Christianized Turk. You are told by the priests that there are no changes from Catholicity except to infidelity, and that outside of Switzerland, Germany, Holland, Sweden, and Norway, Continental Europe is completely subservient, skepticism excepted, to the Pope. In France, however, the real leaders of aggressive thought and purpose are certainly not in this category, and they thoroughly represent the French masses. There the republican chiefs accept the mission of war upon priestly domination in politics and education as second to if not a part of their party philosophy, and the people support them. If the leaders do not logically drift into the Protestant faith, it is doubtless because there are too many Protestant creeds and doctrines; hence, too many divisions. The French republicans hold that the modern Catholic Church is the conscientious foe of all human liberty; that no doubter is ever permitted in that microcosm, and that such a doubter never raises his voice until, like Luther in the past or Hyacinthe or Döllinger in the present, until a Lacordaire, Lamennais, or Montalembert appears to cry out against abuses which periodically overthrow dynasties and thrones. These men insist that the Roman hierarchy is a political machine and nothing more; that it can live only in the atmosphere of slavery, aristocracy, and privilege; that its armies are the cohorts of ignorance, bigotry, and suppression of speech and the press; and that there can be no genuine liberty in the world until the Catholic Church is radically changed or utterly destroyed. Protestantism is too divergent and discordant for such strong minds. None of the republican leaders of France are demonstrative in church matters, while the Orleans and Bourbon princes are nothing if not Romanist, and the late Napoleon and his Spanish Eugénie derived from their Catholic connections incalculable advantages. It is only of late that the Gospel, and in a form more primitive even than Protestantism, seems to be revolutionizing France, and at its deepest foundations, because among the very humblest of the people.

The Protestant chapel in Paris was a common ground for American and English worshipers. The British Dissenters and the American Unitarians, Presbyterians, Baptists, Lutherans, and Methodists, were specially attracted every Sunday during the Exhibition, and the Harrises were very regular in their attendance. It was announced that a young clergyman of Philadelphia, a friend of theirs on his visit to Paris, would preach on the coming Sabbath. Lord Conyngham and Blanche were only too glad to promise their presence. George Harris had a great desire to induce the Earl to hear the young divine; but, knowing his nature, and his indifference to all things that savored of religious dissent, and his inherited respect for the Church of England, not to speak of his growing belief that American ideas and inventions were, to use his own words, "undermining the institutions of Old

England," he concluded to speak to Blanche, who instantly responded :

"I will secure his attendance, Mr. Harris, never fear, and think I can pledge him for the sermon ;" and the dear girl made her demonstration to the Earl with all the cunning impulse of her sex.

"I want you to ride with us to chapel on Sunday, dear papa," she said the next morning at breakfast, in the tone she always used when she wanted to be most acceptable to her fastidious father.

"Certainly, Blanche ; I have never attended our service, I regret to say, since my arrival in Paris."

"It is not our service," she said ; "it is the American chapel, and you are to hear a very interesting young American clergyman, and I have mortgaged you for an hour, if you please, sir."

"Blanche, when are you to finish this American craze? I confess I am getting dreadfully bored, and now I am to be dragged to the altar to be scolded by a Puritan in the pulpit. No horror is more terrible to me than to be forced to listen to one of those dogmatic doctors of divinity who glory in hammering their auditors into their conclusions. No, Blanche ; I must be excused. I am satiated with Yankees."

"No, you are not, you darling, handsome papa ; not satiated, but fascinated."

"What do you mean, Lady Blanche ? How fascinated? I am incapable of such an emotion."

Not even Blanche could have induced the Earl to go if she had not been able to say in conclusion, of the preacher : "His wife is a lineal descendant of the famous Lord Collingwood, who succeeded Nelson at the battle of Trafalgar, and whose mausoleum at St. Paul's you admired so much."

So Blanche carried her point as usual, and at the time fixed the two families attended church. There were too many prominent people present to make even this distinguished party more attractive than others ; but a lovely

woman is always a sensation, and charming Mary Harris was
too well known not to be a special magnet.   Character is
that element in a woman that disarms envy, and Mary, admired by men, was worshiped by women because, while she
knew a great deal, she assumed to know nothing.   Lady
Blanche, herself an English beauty, and as beautiful for her
good sense as for her honest heart, was of a haughtier bearing, as was natural to her rank and personal charms.   The
Earl and George Harris and Mrs. Harris sat together, leaving the four young people in the second pew from the
chancel.   The young preacher was indeed the American
Lacordaire.   That Frenchman, who died before he was sixty,
and who was one of the great triumvirate of which Lamennais and Montalembert were a part, tried to harmon-
ize the largest love of human liberty with fervent attachment to the Catholic Church, and he employed journalism,
with his two associates, as an early agency in his mission.
The American also had served as an editor of a great newspaper, and to that school was undoubtedly indebted for his
large-hearted liberality and copious command of language.
Lacordaire was singularly graceful in form and style, and
seized upon the current topics of the times when he attracted his immense audiences at Notre Dame, and the same
was true of the American.

The minister emerged from the vestry while the organ
was sending forth a strain that seemed like the song of a
choir of angels floating in from a distance.   He ascended
the sacred desk with an air of grace and dignity which at
once attracted attention, and even the old Earl yielded to his
conviction that the American presented a fine presence, for
he leaned over to his daughter just to ask : "Are you sure
that he was born in the United States ?"

"Quite sure," she replied.   "The Harrises tell me that
this is his first visit to Europe."

The Earl made no reply, but he fixed a searching gaze
upon the minister, which was scarcely removed during the
service.

As the music died away the speaker arose, and, taking up a neat gold-edged hymnal, he announced those beautiful lines by James Montgomery :

> " Our God is present in this place,
>   Veiled in celestial majesty ;
>   So full of glory, truth, and grace,
>   That faith alone such light can see."

The singing was congregational, and at its conclusion a Scriptural lesson was read, and a very fervent and comprehensive prayer was offered. Then another hymn was sung, and a collection taken for the benefit of the British Bible Society, which had incurred a great expense in consequence of the free distribution of the Divine Word at the Exposition. The appeal for a liberal contribution was not in vain. The collection plates were well loaded with napoleons, which the Earl did not fail to regard as a very proper recognition of a " British " society.

After announcing the text, which he did in a peculiarly reverential tone, the clergyman alluded to the promised thousand years called the millennium. Millennial glory was the burden of prophetic song. It was the grand object of prediction from one end of the sacred book to the other. He then brought to view some of the most important instructions of the Bible touching the great subject, and after a learned but brief exposition of the doctrine, he led his hearers into the contemplation of the present as contrasted with the past, with the view of showing what mighty changes must be wrought in the condition of human society in the centuries which yet lie embosomed in the future.

He said : " On the banks of the Rhine stands a noble and colossal triumph of Gothic architecture, the foundation of which was laid over six hundred years ago. Tens of thousands of ardent pilgrims have entered Cologne for the sole purpose of beholding the perfection of its marvelous details. And where the Tiber quietly rolls under the shadow of St. Peter's there is an imperial collection of rich paintings, rare marbles, and elaborate frescoes, which are serving the world as models, for we have no such ideals in these times. We gaze in admiration at these contributions from the human brain and heart and hand; but they issued out of a long, slow growth, from a point far back and low down in the past. Go back into that past, and I predict that you will discover little to praise. You will find a very rude virtue among the few—nothing more. As one of my gifted countrymen once said : ' Were you to sleep where men slept then, and eat what men ate then, and do what men had to do then, you would break out into the most piteous moaning and whining and complaining that ever afflicted human ears.'

   .   .   .   .

"In that long, dark night of the world there were a few men who, according to Dr. Oliver Wendell Holmes, carried in their brains the *ovarium*, the eggs of the next century's civilization. They have been given to every age, and they have not lived and died in vain. Their names start to life as we think of the marvelous changes which have taken place in the aspect and condition of human affairs. And as we are so far in advance of what has been, so the future shall exceed everything that is on these lines of thought, genius, industry, and happiness.

"Since I have been in Europe the cry of 'hard times' has fallen upon my ears without cessation. It is very painful to see the condition of the struggling masses in these old countries—the men who do the real work that a few may live in princely luxury. I pity those who lie at the bottom of society, *sans* comfort, *sans* money, *sans* friends, *sans* hope, *sans* everything. Oh, let us sincerely commiserate all who must suffer so dreadful an experience ! But I pray you to remember what your ancestors were in those centuries long gone. England was once a wilderness, and the Greek and Roman merchants used to give shocking accounts of the ferocity of the nomadic tribes that lived there. Where the great cities of London, Birmingham, York, and Carlisle stand to-day, your ancestors dwelt in the rudest huts, with the ground for a floor, a hole in the center for a fire, and another in the roof to let the smoke out, and the skin of a wild beast served as a door. It was many generations before the people lived better.

"England is like another land. But it has a very large quota of poor people. So have we in America. But cross the Atlantic and you shall see a wonderful country, not only in extent and in population, but one that is truly the best poor man's country on the earth. You shall see the real civilization of this age: vast flourishing States, crowded with toilers who are better paid than ever their class was before; noble institutions for free education; great charities in every city and town; broad avenues and streets, paved, swept, and lighted; good drainage everywhere; substantial houses for rich and poor, in which the chambers are carpeted and decorated; cheerful fires and light; libraries and music; paintings, and engravings, and etchings; churches, and asylums, and newspapers, and so on *ad infinitum*. Truly, we can not be thankful enough that we live in the nineteenth century. Our civilization is brightening. Its sun is gilding the mountain-tops of the future; a still better day is dawning on the world."

The effect of this fresh and peculiar style was seen on even the English, as the American proceeded to speak of the dawn of intelligence and the advance in letters, art, and science and government. The discourse closed with a panegyric on religion, in which the clergyman said:

"Even of much of the skepticism of the times, it must be said that it is a struggle to find out what the truth is. Like old Aurelius, men are stretching out their hands for something which the abstractions of the schools can not give. Like one of the Latin sages, they want a God who can speak to them and lead them. And they shall yet be satisfied in Him who could look through human eyes, and shed human tears, and hear with human ears, and love with a human heart. Reason does not rise up against the divine and human one because he is not real, but because he is an unparalleled and startling fact. St. Paul was right : 'Without controversy, great is the mystery of godliness. God was manifested in the flesh.'

"And as the world moves on to its brightest and best day, God has written on its horizon, in letters of light, 'Progress!' Humanity is looking toward fairer skies, and God, who beholds all the dwellers upon earth, bids them 'go forward,' as he did his ancient people. There may be Red Seas and broad wildernesses and open enemies yet to be met and mastered, but they will all disappear as the spirit of the living God leads the way."

Here the service ended with an earnest prayer, a song of praise, and the apostolic benediction.

CHAPTER XII.

A RETURN TO NATURE.

THERE is a certain magnetism in men as in minerals, especially when it is aroused by any exciting cause—devotion to country, for instance. It draws men together into an army which strikes and slays as if it were with a single sword. It so chanced on this occasion. Henry Harris had some time before this been brought into a degree of companionship with Lord Conyngham. The nobleman had apologized so heartily for the rudeness which had characterized his first meeting with them that the family had made a point to show him how entirely they had forgiven the matter. But Henry Harris was specially attracted to Lord Conyngham. They were both young and full of an energy which had not been sapped and squandered in vicious indulgences. Moreover, there had been a certain outspoken boldness in the conduct of the exasperated patrician which showed that, however wrong and violent, he was not a mere fop, smiling and nerveless.

Lord Conyngham had long been familiar with the reputation of George Harris. He knew that, like Peter the Great,
he was one of the creators of commerce and wealth, and he
admired him as one always admires force. Moreover, the
young lord had stirring within him the ideas of a new era,
and one of these was that he who organizes men into bands
of skilled workmen is nobler than even a Frederick the Great
with his thoroughly drilled grenadiers; that the master mechanic who hurls his iron across an empire in railways is
nobler by far than a Napoleon who sweeps it with grapeshot.
The mortification of the young man at discovering who it
was he had so thoughtlessly offended was intense, the more
so as he came to know the family better, and he cordially
reciprocated every evidence of their good-will.

One day when there happened to be, as was often the
case, a sharp discussion at the Bodega ·concerning America,
many things said by Americans present had savored of
boasting. Lord Conyngham chanced to be standing near
Henry Harris. Neither took part in the discussion, but the
American had observed with pleasure the interest with which
his friend had listened. There was a rising color in the
young nobleman's cheek, a kindling light in his eyes, which
caused Henry Harris to say to him:

"Of course I believe in America, but you must not think
that we believe in brag."

"By no means," the other hastened to say.

"Thank you; but if there be a thing," Henry Harris
added, "which I particularly detest, it is anything that looks
like self-conceit. We had an American statesman of brilliant
qualities and splendid services whom neither my father nor
myself could endure. If you look at his portrait, or his bust,
you will understand why. He is the very symbol of arrogance. I saw a marble head of him in the Exposition last
week, and I almost shook my fist at it when no one saw me.
'For you,' I said, 'to have your head thrown back in haughty
defiance is sheer affectation. Other men might do it, but
although pure yourself, *you* know our political defects too

3

well.' There are faults in our American civilization, my lord," Henry Harris added gravely, "terrible evils, which may wreck us some day. Our country is colossal in this also. Besides, for me to be conceited because I happen to be born in the Great Republic is as if a fish were elated because it was born in the Atlantic. But I must leave you."

"I will walk with you;" and as they gained the pavement Lord Conyngham added, "Where do you happen to be going?"

"My sister and mother begged me," the other replied, "to meet them by a certain old statue in a little forest near Versailles. They have taken a sudden fancy to have a kind of picnic. Here is my carriage."

As young Harris said it, he saw a species of desire yet hesitation in the eyes of the other which caused him to add frankly, "If you have nothing better to do, my lord, I would be delighted to have you ride with me."

"Thank you," his companion replied, "but I also am engaged to ride with my sister Blanche. Versailles, did you say?"

The other caught at his meaning. "Join us there," he begged. "It is a glorious day; my mother and sister will be delighted to see Lady Blanche and yourself."

And thus it came to pass some hours later that these five persons were seated together upon the rustic benches in one of the most secluded nooks near Versailles. Lord Conyngham and his sister had come on horseback, but at the urgent invitation of the American ladies Lady Blanche had dismounted, "if only for a moment," they said, and with her brother had sat down among them.

"There must be something of Eden itself in the air to-day," Mary Harris said, after they had talked for a time upon a variety of topics. "I could not endure to stay in the house. Paris itself was too close and confining. I am like my brother—I want to be in the open air whenever the sun shines."

Evidently all present were of the same opinion. It may

have been the verdure of the grass beneath them, the trees clustering about them as if Nature would clasp them to her bosom with the embraces of her leafy boughs, the soothing seclusion which came to them like the sound of tempest upon the roof in the distant roar of city noises, but the same mood was, for the moment, upon all. They were wearied with the wonders of the Exposition, and the repose was, for the time, more delightful than sleep.

And thus it was the most natural thing that Henry Harris should find himself talking at last of his wildwood experiences. Two years before he had returned to America upon business for his father among the iron mines of the West, for it was one of the peculiarities of the railway king to go, so far as possible, to the fountain-head for his iron, as he did for his science and his principles. His matters had taken less time than he had supposed, and young Harris had accepted an invitation from a hunting-party, and had gone a thousand miles or so farther west. He could not sit still as it came back to him now. Getting upon his feet as he talked, he stood beside one of the towering trees, his hat cast upon the turf, his cheeks glowing.

"I had been upon the steppes of Tartary, but this was different," he said. "It was not only that the American plains were more fertile, and every way better stocked with game, and beautiful, but that I realized that it was the New and not the Old World I was in. Here was neither peasant nor czar. Ah, ladies, you can not imagine how delightful it was!" And he told them of the prairie, rolling east, west, north, and south, like another Pacific; of the peculiar transparency which made the remote mountains by day and the moon and stars by night seem so near; of the keen exhilaration, as if there were champagne in the very air and oxygen even in the brilliant moonlight.

"Of course," he went on, "it was fun alive spearing big fish in the cañons, shooting deer, charging down upon buffalo moving in battalions. And then we had a hand-to-hand fight with a cinnamon bear or two. It looked like murder to kill prairie-hens and antelope, but your conscience cheered you on instead when it came to a fair fight with a grizzly. You see, it was by no means so certain that *he* would be the one to be killed. It was a question even more doubtful when, soon after, I had an unavoidable 'difficulty,' as it is called, with a desperado from Pike County. You must pardon my enthusiasm," he added, hesitating, and with something of a flush, "but I found myself back in my boyhood out there, and it makes me a boy again merely to think about it. Boys like to eat, you know. Well, I never knew, even when I was a hungry boy, what sincere pleasure there is in eating as I found it to be then. When we rode of an evening into camp, tired, wet, with perhaps a bruise or two; excuse me, but, ah! how delicious the coffee did smell, and the trout, the wild honey, the juicy buffalo-steaks, the bits of antelope and venison. These Frenchmen, with all their sauces and cookery, know nothing about it. They do not have the appetite, you see—appetite which is at once boundless and exquisite!"

"Why, Henry!" his mother said, "we would think you were—"

"An epicure? No, madam," her son interrupted her with a joyous face; "I was Adam back again in Paradise! One never knows how delicious a drink of water is until you stop from a hot ride, to lie down upon your breast at a mountain spring, and drink, with your face in the water, and drink, and drink, and dr—" But his words were drowned in laughter; he seemed to be so much in earnest.

"And there is sleep," he began again.

"Sleep?" Lady Blanche asked, opening her beautiful eyes.

"Yes, Lady Blanche, sleep," the other persisted. "In this artificial life of ours we lie down and wake up as a matter of course. No one thinks anything of the quality of his sleep. It was different out there. We would halt at night, kindle our camp-fire in the bottom of a hole for fear of drawing the Indians upon us, cook and eat an enormous supper. Then every man would change his horse to a new patch of grass. We staked them out, you know. After that we would lie down, our feet toward the fire, our heads upon our saddles, in the deep, soft, aromatic, mesquit turf. Next you took a good look, as you lay, at the immeasurable sky overhead, thought of the almost immeasurable America about you, inhaled a full breath from the pure air, drew your felt hat over your eyes to keep out the sun-like splendors of the moon and stars, and then you slept, slept, *slept!* It was like—like eating pudding," he added, with a laugh. "There was an absolute pleasure, gratification in it, satisfaction; I mean such, I suppose, as babies have. Ah, when you woke in a flash, with the sun high up, it seemed to be all over in a moment, but it was grand!"

The young American had become a boy again as he spoke, and a very handsome one, the ladies thought. His enthusiasm had changed those around him into children also. It was a sensation wholly new to Lord Conyngham and his sister. Accustomed from birth to a ceremonious life, one of routine and social tyranny, nature asserted itself in them. They recognized the truth of what young Harris had said, as thirst does water.

"A leading English magazine lately spoke," Lord Conyngham said, after a good deal of further conversation, "of your West under the title of 'our great wheat-fields;' *ours*, you observe. The fact is, we are at last but one people."

It was sincerely assented to as the party broke up. So far as England and America were represented by those present, the unity of the Anglo-Saxon race was becoming apparently a substantial fact. Possibly this idea occurred to Henry Harris with special clearness as he took leave of Lady Blanche. The young nobleman had carefully refrained from glancing at Mary Harris when he laid down his propositions, and the American girl must have had some other reason for coloring so when her eyes fell in the general assent which followed.

CHAPTER XIII.

HASSAN PASHA.

As has been said, wherever in Europe the household of George Harris chanced to be, the place they enjoyed most was that which for the time they called their home. Whether it was in their rooms at the hotel, or under the striped tents which shielded them from a Syrian sun, it was there they found, whatever the landscape which lay around them, however interesting the city in which they sojourned, their chief happiness. However fatigued by the travel or the wonders of the day, an hour or two was sure to be spent by them together at night in summing up and comparing impressions as to the events of the hours going before. This was to the older, as to the younger people, really the most enjoyable time of all.

Upon one such evening in Paris, not long after the little episode at Versailles, the family had been passing in review all they had seen in the Exposition since their coming. Except the father, each had given his or her opinion as to what had been best worth seeing.

"And now, papa, what do *you* like best?" Mary Harris asked in the end.

"The people," her father replied. "The pictures, the various fabrics, the machinery are interesting, of course, but I am most interested in those from all parts of the world who have produced the objects we all admire. From the first I have found my attention riveted upon these. Many of the wonders in the Exposition are duplicates, but no two of these men and women are exactly alike. Whatever the nationality, people," Mr. Harris added, "interest me—there is no other word which expresses it—beyond their art, their science, their religion. Every day I find myself turning more and more from what a man says or does to the man himself."

"The future of the world—and it will be as much more

wonderful than to-day as to-day is beyond a century ago—the future," Henry Harris assented, "is with the people."

And this was another peculiarity of George Harris. To Earl Dorrington, the multitude through which he passed was little more than a swarm of insects. If pressed, he would have acknowledged that he belonged to the same species, and yet the habit of his life was to except Englishmen from men in general as the heaven-born superiors of the rest of the race, and himself as of a divinely appointed lineage, even more loftily superior to the masses of England than were these to such lesser *infusoria* as the Spanish or the Italians. The last Bourbon of the line, Henry V, as he styles himself, was not more intensely a legitimist. George Harris was, on the other hand, in ready sympathy with every man he met, and from whatever country. Entirely at his ease with earl as with czar, he was almost as courteous to his courier or his porter as to these. To him the grand old Tory nobleman was but one of many millions of men, in not one of whom there was not something to deplore, but much also to admire. The Earl was insular, in plain words, provincial. The American was metropolitan, a noble of the Order of the Universe. The fact must be added, if the Earl was proud, George Harris was, in a sense, as much more so as his order was grander and more enduring.

It was by reason of his interest in people that George Harris was never so happy as when in conversation with some one among the throngs in Paris who was a distinct type of his own land. Among these was an Oriental personage—Hassan Pasha by name—who was known all over Europe for his reckless splendor of living, the high stakes he played at the public gambling-tables and at private games of hazard, the great sums he had lost and won, his profligacy of morals, his elegance of manner, and the elevated positions he had held in the foreign and domestic service of his government. It was his wealth and family influence, rather than his personal qualities, which paved the way to the important dignities which he had enjoyed. There was something sphinx-like in the expression of his features. The eye scrutinized you with a gaze that seemed to penetrate your inmost thoughts, but it revealed nothing of the workings of the mind and heart of its master. It was clear and lustrous, as the Oriental eye always is, but it seemed to be trained to absorb, not reflect impressions. It was drilled and disciplined to such a degree that it never lost its self-control, so to speak. There was a studied reserve in his conversation and bearing, also, that puzzled and mystified, and yet fascinated. Piqued at the impenetrability of this strange nature, one was always seeking to find some crevice in the armor through which a lance might be thrust. He read others, but he would not allow them to read him ; not that he was a better judge of character, but because he had perfect mastery of himself. He had asked to be introduced to George Harris that he might make the acquaintance of his daughter.

"I have always admired," he said to Mr. Harris afterward, "your countrywomen. In the East we are accustomed to one style of beauty, but the Americans seem to blend together the choicest charms of the finest types of the Old World. I presume it is from the commingling of races. As Rome was formed out of various peoples, and a new and improved race was created, so the Americans in every sense of the word may be regarded as a new stock, strongly differing in many respects from their ancestors."

"Perhaps," said Mr. Harris, " the moral stagnation of the East leads to physical degeneracy."

" Not at all ; physically, the people of the East are among the finest specimens of humanity. From them sprang the great Aryan race that has overspread the world, the foremost in the march of civilization and in intellectual ability. The only difference between you and us is that Christianity promotes progress, free institutions, and activity in every department of life. Mussulmanism is perhaps too conservative, too much inclined to adhere to the past, and too distrustful of the future to plunge into the bold enterprises which keep Christian countries in a state of perpetual agitation. I admit your superiority in the arts of civilization, but I do not think the time will ever come when the West will subdue the East. The Orientals follow the practices and profess the religion which, bating certain modifications, the progenitors of Christianity professed four thousand years ago. Mussulmanism, instead of being a dead faith, is not only at this day professed by nearly two hundred millions of people, but it is spreading with wonderful rapidity over pagan Africa. By the aid of twenty million Moslems resident in China, it threatens to become the dominant religion in that vast empire, and it is undermining in India Buddhism, Brahminism, and all other of the opposing Eastern creeds. The Moslem Caliph may be compelled to abandon Constantinople to the Giaours and to retire with the faithful into Asia, the cradle of our faith and race, but that will not blight the prospects of Mussulmanism."

"Is woman," timidly asked Mary Harris, who was present, "for ever to remain in the East in her present abject condition?"

"We do not look upon her position in the same light you do," the Oriental replied with a bow and in smoother accents. "She is with us precisely as she was during all the Patriarchal period, such as is described in your holy book, which you call by the same name as we do ours—the Bible, Koran, or *Book*. We do not think she was created to invade man's sphere, but always to be his comforter, helpmate, and slave. When she leaves the domestic retirement which is the proper theatre of her existence, we think she loses her natural delicacy and unsexes herself."

"Well," replied Mr. Harris, "I see I can not convert you to our way of thinking. I must confess I admire to a certain degree the confidence you feel in your destiny and the faith you have in the future; but how is it that with all this Oriental intensity of feeling the Turks have always been so friendly to the United States? I hope it is because you sympathize with our people and their institutions."

"Don't deceive yourselves," answered the other. "We like the Americans simply because they let us alone and do not interfere with us as the English, Russians, and French are constantly doing. The truth is, we know very little about you, except that in a short time you have become a powerful nation, and that you are undermining the prosperity of our enemies. We wish you well, and that is more than I can say of other Christian nations. But let us dismiss this discussion, for we are trenching on subjects of conversation unsuited to neutral ground such as this."

CHAPTER XIV.

LOVE FIFTY YEARS AGO.

ONE evening the family of George Harris were assembled as usual in the parlor of their hotel. They had seen of late many a painting, historical and otherwise, but, unconscious as they were of it, they themselves composed a group which contained within itself profound significance. Beside her husband upon the sofa sat Mrs. Margaret Harris, a certain breadth in her brows, a soft yet steady command in her eyes, which breathed of motherhood and serene common sense. Place a crown upon her head, a scepter in her hand, and she would have satisfied your conception of an empress, and yet she was saying to her son and daughter:

"Yes, when your father married me I was as poor as himself. As you know, Henry, my father was a wheelwright. He was as honest and industrious as my mother was good and loving, but misfortunes came. My brothers died, my mother became an invalid, my father was disabled by the falling upon him of a wagon beneath which he was at work. I was not more than fourteen when the support of the household devolved upon me. It is strange," Mrs. Harris added, thoughtfully, "I was a frail, timid girl, yet the very pressure of things seemed suddenly to change my whole nature. I worked for a dressmaker, I walked miles at a time to carry my bundles to customers, I read and went to school as much as I could between times, and my health became strong. It was as if a new life had arisen within. me; I was happier than I could possibly have been other-wise. And then—"

"And then I met her going home one Saturday," her husband interrupted. "Her face was at once the brightest and the best I had ever seen. Such a thing as marriage had not entered my mind before. How could I afford a sweetheart and wife, with the attendance at concerts, the confection-ery, and dresses it involved? Yet as soon as I saw that open face, as sweet as it was sensible, as strong as it was pure, as—"

But the wife had laid her hand upon her husband's lips, blushing as she did so like a girl, and the son and daughter laughed aloud.

"Oh, well," the husband continued, holding his wife's hand in his own, "I was a hard-tasked mechanic, working all day, and reading as much as I could at night. Nobody as I was, your mother took compassion on me, and—"

"I only hope you will be as true and manly a man, Henry." It was Mrs. Harris's turn to interrupt now. "To me your father was the king of men, but I would not allow even him to help me support my parents. We loved for a long time before we could unite our fortunes. It was a year after, first my mother and then my father died, that we were married."

"It is not often we talk of such matters," Mr. Harris added, "but let me say, for once and all, that my marrying your mother was the wisest thing I ever did. From our first acquaintance we were companions in the truest sense of the word. I have never taken a step until after consultation with my wife. In every practical sense, she has been of inesti-mable help to me," and the husband lifted the hand of his wife to his lips, and kissed it. Sincerer homage empress never had, but the son and daughter glanced at each other with a smile. There was nothing they had known better, and from their childhood, than the influence upon their father, as upon them, of their mother.

. "Let me say only this," George Harris continued, "that your mother was of most service to me when I began to prosper. It is almost impossible for a man not to become a little intoxicated as money begins to pour in, but it was your mother who calmed me in prosperity as she had aroused and encouraged me in our days of adversity, for we had dark times also, I assure you."

The man who spoke was broad of chest and strong of limb. There was a certain square solidity about his countenance. His head and beard were white, his eyebrows bushy, his manner, like his voice and his gait, was steady and deliberate. For more than half a century he had dealt so closely and exclusively in iron that his entire nature had assimilated itself, in the best senses at least, to that metal. So much was there of system and of sternness in his whole aspect, that his imperial employers, as well as the thousands whom he employed, understood, and from the outset, that here was a person not to be trifled with. That he was not a tyrant, a Nero of the workshop, a Caligula of the tunnel and the railway bridge, was, and to a degree of which even he himself had no conception, owing to his wife, for although in a purely womanly sense, she was stronger than he. Not that he was not always iron, but that, in the uncooling ardor of his affection for her, he was as molten iron in her hands, and she gave direction and shape, and in a measure of which she herself was unconscious, to all that he was and did.

"I do not know how we came to talk of such things," George Harris continued after a while, "but there is one thing more I wish to add, and then we will speak of something else. The longer I live, Henry, Mary, I am satisfied that the grandest quality at last is that most uncommon of all things, which we call common sense. Let me say it but his once, my dear Margaret—your mother, children, is the

most sensible woman I ever knew—sensible ! You are laughing, Harry; well, perhaps I *have* said that before. But I say
it now because I want to tell you what is the secret of her
sense, of all sense. You know I am not a religious man. Almost all my life I have been so situated that it was impossible for me to go to church, even to know when Sunday came
for that matter, at times at least. Very well. But, from
the hour I first knew her, the soul and sweetness of your
mother's excellent sense has been her steady faith in God.
That is all."

At this moment visitors were announced, and soon after
the parlors were a scene of lively conversation, a little excellent music now and then, and a good deal of laughter and
enjoyment.

CHAPTER XV.

BROTHER AND SISTER.

AMONG the many American families in Paris during the
Exposition there was none whose rooms were more frequented than those of George Harris. There were some in
which there was a more lavish display of wealth, others in
which literature and art had a stronger sway, but in none did
people seem to enjoy themselves more. No one asked himself or herself why it was, but there was a certain alternative
from Parisian life therein which was turned to as a relief.
Neither in the head of the family nor in his matronly wife
was there a particle of affectation, and the children of such
parents had too much of their father and mother in their life-
long training, as well as in their blood, not to resemble them.
Once properly introduced, and you felt as much at home
with Henry Harris as if you had come upon him on a fishing
excursion. He was most like his mother, especially as there
was much of her gentle energy, too, in his eyes and bearing.
He had not struggled upward as his father had done ; had,

so to speak, none of the scars of the contest. The prosperity of the family began before he was born, and he had been carefully educated. In fact, his father would gladly have given him a university training. Like most men who had educated themselves, Mr. Harris had a sort of superstition in regard to an academic course, an idea that it imparted subtile and mysterious faculties as well as attainments. But the son was too much like the parents from whose original nature he had sprung to consent, and he decided to enter into the business of his father; decided with so much inherited decision that there was nothing for his father to do but to yield, and with a secret satisfaction, too, to his choice. Speaking Russian, German, and French; having had all the advantage of travel and association with the best society; kept by his intimacy with his mother and sister from wild courses, young Harris was, with his open brow and fine eyes and frank ways, the most popular of men.

Mary Harris was some three years younger than her brother. Strange to say, she was, as has been said, most like her father, except that his features, eyes, very character, had been so refined and transformed in her that people wondered at her loveliness even while they were struck with her likeness to her rugged parent. Dearly as she loved her mother, she seemed to cling even more closely to him; while her brother retained for his mother an almost childlike affection. He had been one of the rare instances of a boy in love with his mother, and he was only the more so now than when he had worn frills upon his bosom and trimming upon his little jacket. None the less was he the manliest of men; such a mother could have been so loved only by a youth of that sort. Although she hid it, her love for her son was the one direction in which Mrs. Harris's common sense was threatened with being overmastered. Toward him she was like a girl again, because he was to her so much of what his father had been when she first knew him.

"One can not help liking them," Lady Blanche said one morning of the Harris household to her father, the Earl

"There is an air of nature and freedom about them which one so rarely finds. I hate to live in the ball-room and the opera-house for ever. One becomes as weary of one's retinue of admirers as one does of her trains of silk and velvet."

"I have no objection to your associating with the people of whom you speak, up to a definite point," the old nobleman replied. "We are not in London. This is Paris, and we are in Paris during an exceptional period."

It was as if the Earl had said, "We are not in our castle just now. In our condescension we have come down to see the villagers dancing about a May-pole. It is merely the folly of an hour;" and he smiled as he sat at his breakfast-table, with conscious superiority.

"A definite point, my dear; you will not go beyond that," he added, adjusting his napkin.

"I think," his son said, maliciously, "that you would have opened your eyes a little if you had seen Blanche on horseback yesterday; she rode as if for a wager."

"I rode with him because he rides better and faster than my escort generally dares to do," Lady Blanche replied with spirit.

"With *him?* May I ask who *he* is?" The Earl demanded it with dignity.

"With Mr. Henry Harris," his daughter replied promptly, with unusual distinctness and perfect equipoise. "But I consented to go only when I learned that Alfred had agreed to accompany Miss Mary Harris. Who cares? It was a beautiful day. We had good horses. I never enjoyed myself more. We were speaking of Mr. Harris's family. Whenever I am with them I feel," she continued, with heightened color, "as if I had got out of doors. It is like being out with the hounds. I can not endure to be eternally in the drawing-room! I greatly prefer my freedom."

The words were spoken with such force, such fire, in fact, that both the Earl and his son looked at her with sudden surprise; she had at the moment a peculiarity of beauty they had not observed before.

"May I beg, Lady Clara Vere de Vere, to learn the species of game in this instance?" her brother asked, in ironical
accents. "Deer, is it; or is it but a fox? I am interested,
since I know so well that you will be in at the death. And,"
Lord Conyngham added, "when you are the Diana, the game
dies hard, terribly hard, you know that; we all do!"

There was evidently an allusion to something in the past
which Lady Blanche, at least, well understood; but her eyes
were full and clear, although her cheek paled as she replied
to her brother, her gaze unflinchingly upon him, a little sadness in it too.

"You know, Alfred, it was not *my* fault."

"What are you speaking of?" the old Earl demanded
the moment after. In such lofty and serene heights did he
habitually dwell, that the conversation even of his own children sounded as if below him. "It was of hunting, was it
not?" he added.

"Yes, sir; and I was telling Blanche to be careful next
time," Lord Conyngham said, with a cruel fun in his eyes.

"Very proper, Alfred. It is wrong, if it can be avoided,
to ride down a dog or even a farmer's wheat. I am afraid
we have trampled down many a turnip-field in our time."
The Earl was stately even in his regrets. The field was
highly favored to be so trodden.

"Poor Harris," the brother whispered to his sister, for it
is not only to their fags that Eton boys and Oxford men are
brutal. "Poor Harris! I would beg of you to have pity
upon him; but then, you know, it is merely a question of a
turnip!"

It is worse than a matter of fags and fagging. That may
have diminished of late, like bull-baiting, cock-fighting, and
the ferocities of the prize-ring, but the English love for hard
blows is in the bone and blood. To this hour old Rome sur-
vives in Britain. It was when the combat in the arena was
cruelest that to plebeian and patrician it was sweetest.
Strong natures can give and take severe blows, often with
only less enjoyment of the taking than of the giving. In all

England there was not a more polished as well as aristocratic household than that of Earl Dorrington, yet even the play therein was that not of kittens, but of young lions. No nobleman more of a gentleman, no lady more of a lady than Lord Conyngham and his sister, and never brother and sister loved each other more—they were lion-like in that also—but they did not spare each other.

"His heart is less to me than a turnip," this Boadicea, this genuine Englishwoman, now replied to her brother; "but you," she said, "you, my poor brother, *you*—" And she laughed as he colored almost painfully under her clear, steady eyes.

"My dear children," the Earl remarked, from his serene summits, "what are you speaking of?" And, rising from the table and standing at the window, he looked down upon the crowded and busy streets of Paris. No, it was not as if the lord of the castle had descended to the villagers; it was rather as if a benevolent naturalist were gazing upon the ways of the ants at his feet.

CHAPTER XVI.

ISHRA DHASS GUNGA.

HASSAN PASHA, the Oriental of whom mention has been already made, was a frequent visitor at the parlors of George Harris. Neither the father nor his son Henry were, however, the chief attraction. For these he had the admiration which even the most languid and luxurious nature has for men of energy, but he had no desire to be such a man himself. In his secret soul the most intelligent and vigorous of the infidels alive was to this Mohammedan but as a strong and spirited Arabian horse, to be used when need be, and which he would manage if he could with an iron bit, since there was such a thing as being dashed by one's horse to the ground. Both speed and spirit were enjoyed by Hassan Pasha, provided he could be master, and not called upon to exert himself particularly, but he had no more wish to be himself a Frank than he had to be a horse.

The attractions lay in Mrs. Harris and in her daughter. As a rule, women were no more to him than the playthings of an indolent hour, as sweet and as devoid of intellect as flowers ; they were merely a higher and more delightful kind of roses, in fact. But Mrs. Harris reminded him of certain sultanas whom he had known, women of ability who had ruled Turkey from behind the throne. As to Mary Harris, he had a species of curiosity which is characteristic of the Oriental. He had never known a slave, Circassian or Georgian, who was more lovely. She seemed to be as soft, as modest, as gentle, as obedient, as if she had never left her mother's side for an instant, and yet, " Her father deals in iron," he thought, " but in her the iron has been refined into steel. When I hinted the other day that women were made for the service of men, there was the glint of a Damascus blade in her eyes. ' Do you really think so ? ' she asked, but tone and glance reminded me of the way in which Saladin could cut in twain by a turn of his keen scimitar a veil of gauze which hung over him afloat in the air. How divinely she plays, too, and what a power of soul she can pour into her songs ! Ah me ! if—"

But what Hassan Pasha would have been capable of, had he possessed the power of which he every day regarded himself as unjustly deprived, who can say ! Certainly no gentleman could have conducted himself with greater propriety when visiting in their hotel.

He was conversing with Mary Harris there one evening when the name of Lady Blanche was mentioned. His face slowly darkened as he said : " She is an Englishwoman of the purest type, very noble, very beautiful. But do you remember, Miss Harris, hearing of Cadijah, the first wife of our prophet ? " he suddenly added.

"Yes, and of his younger wife, Ayesha," the lady replied.

" Well, they were the wives of the Prophet of God," the Oriental said, gravely, "and yet even then they were not proud, were merely simple women. Picture to yourself Sarah, the wife of Ibrahim—Abraham, you call him—was she a haughty dame? Your Bible does not say so. It tells of her kneading three measures of meal ; think of Lady Blanche doing that ! And then there was Rebekah at the well ; when Eleazar came with his camels, he made it the only test of the one who was to be the bride of Isaac, not that she should be even beautiful, but that she should offer to water his thirsty camels. And if you draw a picture of Rachel, she must have a jar upon her head. Of the wife of Moses it was the same, was it not ? "

"May I be allowed ? " The question was asked by a gentleman who had drawn near as they conversed, for the rooms were filled with visitors coming and going.

Hassan Pasha bowed somewhat coldly, but Mary Harris said, with her brightest smile, " With pleasure, Mr.—Signior—"

"My full name is Ishra Dhass Gunga," the gentleman corrected her, with a happy face.

"I know that well enough," the lady hastened to say, "only I do not know always what is the variation which I should use of *Mr.* We are here from all parts of the world. Sometimes I must say Herr, sometimes Monsieur, now it is Signior, then it is Don, or my lord, or your excellency. If it is an American, I am always safe in calling him Mr."

"Pardon me, do you think so ? " the new-comer demanded. "I never feel that I am as polite as I should be with an American unless I call him Captain, Major, Colonel. One must discriminate, though, and I try to estimate the man, and according as I like him I brevet him with anything military up to General, and there, alas ! I am compelled to stop. Please call me plain Ishra Dhass."

There was something irresistibly pleasing, to the lady at

least, in the speaker. He was a Hindoo who spoke English perfectly, because he had been educated for the service in a government college in Calcutta. Hassan Pasha, who had drawn himself up into his stateliest height, was a taller man, but the Hindoo was admirably formed, his dark face glowing like that of a frolicsome boy. His features were delicate, his eyes of a lively black, his hands small and in continual motion, but it was his genuine good-nature which struck you most. His teeth were not much larger than grains of rice, and whiter, in contrast with the dark bronze of his complexion, and he seemed to be always laughing. Not that he was at all silly, nor that his manners were part of his toilet. That he was entirely natural was too evident to be denied. He was dressed simply, in the Hindoo style, a white turban upon his head, and seemed to be entirely at home. From the opening of the Exposition he had been in Paris, and seemed to know and to be greatly liked by everybody. Wherever there was a group of ladies or gentlemen in corridor or parlor of the great hotels, you were tolerably sure, especially when you heard them laugh, to find Ishra Dhass as the center about which they were drawn. His humor was inexhaustible. It seemed to be part of his perfect health. Withal he was a gentleman. The modulated tones, the deferential manner, the entire independence of the man, made that very evident.

"Oh! I am a Brahmin," he would say, when flattered upon his knowledge of the world. "You know that we are gods in our own land. Very poor gods we are," he would add, with his merry eyes, "almost as poor as the Vishnus and Sivas my people pray to. They and we, all of us, are nothing but clay at last."

Being of as high caste as the highest, he was as free with even Earl Dorrington as George Harris could have been —much more so, for the American had a certain ruggedness of his own, while the Hindoo was supple, smiling, full of his genuine good-humor with whomsoever he was thrown.

"Will you pardon my intrusion?" he now said, with all

politeness; "but I could not help hearing what his Highness," and he bowed to Hassan Pasha, "was so eloquently observing in regard to your sex," and he bowed with unaffected deference to the lady. "You are right, sir. It is impossible to think of Ruth as holding herself haughtily the day she went home to her mother-in-law, Naomi, with her gleanings gathered into her veil. With six measures of barley upon her shoulders, how," he demanded, with his frank smile, "*could* she hold her head erect with pride? Ah, but she *was* erect; she was as straight as an arrow, because," he added, "from her childhood, she had been taught to bear burdens balanced upon her beautiful head. One day I was at the house of a nobleman in England, his guest, I am happy to say. He had a lovely daughter, about fourteen years old. I happened to be in her father's library when she came in for an atlas, and she had a trayful of sand on her head. You observe, she was too frail; had a tendency to stoop, and her governess made her do it to give her a stronger chest and a more graceful carriage. When she saw me she started, upset the sand, and down it came over her shoulders in an avalanche. She began to cry, but I told her it was what I used to see my dear mother do every day at home, only it was water she bore, not sand, and we had a good laugh over it. We became excellent good friends after that, I assure you. But, as I said, forgive me; I interrupt you."

"Not at all," Hassan Pasha said, in his politest manner. For the best of all reasons—at least, for the strongest reasons of which a Mohammedan is capable—he had the sincerest hatred for the Hindoo. Deeply as he despised and hated, even abhorred, the Russian, English, French, of Ishra Dhass he had an opinion stronger still. But he was outwardly polite to French, English, even to Russians, and he was so now. With as little compunction as though he had been a sheep instead, he could have killed this pleasant, smiling Brahmin, or, rather, could have had him killed by a slave, with an indolent wave of his hand; but this was not Asia; he was in Paris.

"I merely desired to add," Ishra Dhass continued, "that I have the honor heartily to agree with your Highness in one thing."

Hassan Pasha allowed himself almost to manifest his surprise as he looked at the speaker. Ishra Dhass, however, was perfectly aware of the sentiments of the Turk toward himself, and, instead of addressing himself to him further, was saying to the young lady : "It is a matter in which I fear I do not have your sympathy, Miss Harris. Not, at least, as yet. Europeans, Americans, you are—you are so sure you are right, right in everything! We Orientals," comprehending the Pasha with a wave of his supple hand, "are, you think, left hopelessly behind! Wait; please wait a few years. In some very important matters, matters you do not dream of, the sun is to rise upon you, as it always has done, and in everything of highest importance—is to rise upon you from the East. Never, since the world began, has it risen in the West; never! In the East it is to rise again, and ah, what a glorious day it will bring!"

It was said with such unfeigned enthusiasm, such certain assurance, as of an inspired prophet, who was also a joyous child, that both the Turk and the American lady looked at the Hindoo with astonishment. He seemed, for the moment, to be almost transfigured as with the certainty of what he said.

"What do you mean?" his companions asked, rather with their eyes than their lips.

"Asia has been mistaken, mistaken for centuries, sadly mistaken. But Europe and America have been mistaken too," he added, with a certain glad confidence, "frightfully mistaken. I will explain some other time; not now. It was your speaking of Eastern women which caused me to intrude. Your Highness is right. It is Sarah, Rachel, Ruth, who are the nearest to Eve. They are the models. There is another woman—the noblest, because the simplest and most purely woman of all. But," and he looked the Pasha steadily in the eyes, "I will tell you her name another time ; t now. See ; the company are taking their leave."

"What woman were you speaking of?" Mary Harris asked of him, soon after, in the doorway, as he left. "I am curious to know."

"My friend the Pasha dislikes the topic," the smiling Hindoo replied, "but you know already whom I mean. You yourself are named after her, and she lived in Syria eighteen centuries ago."

CHAPTER XVII.

WOMAN AS A SLAVE.

THE day following the conversation just recorded, Henry Harris was speaking of Hassan Pasha among a party of gentlemen, of whom Lord Conyngham was one. The Turk had made a peculiar impression upon almost every person present.

"It so chanced," the young nobleman remarked, "that I was once thrown with him a good deal. My father, my sister, and myself had been some years ago spending the winter in Rome. In the spring of the following year we unexpectedly joined a party of friends who embarked at Naples on an Eastern tour. The boat touched only at Messina, and thence steered directly for Constantinople. After leaving that port we were hurried, in quick succession, through scenes of wonderful interest and beauty. As in the case of all travelers in the East, our thoughts were more occupied with its past history than its present condition. The halo of the classic ages still envelops this region with a fascinating spell. The names of its heroes, statesmen, and philosophers are associated with its plains, seas, and historic sites, while Olympus, Parnassus, and Ida recall the mythologic fables to which the imagination of the ancient poets gave birth, and which, to this day, are themes of inspiration to poets and painters. The imperishable character of Greek civilization and letters is one of the most striking

facts in human history. There is not a classic student who
does not long to visit the scenes where lived and acted the
great men of the Homeric, Periclean, and Alexandrian eras,
and to muse over the remains of fallen splendor, and, on the
spot, to study the causes of the decline of states and the
ruin of empires. The most learned of our party, who at
the same time was one of the most pleasing of narrators,
supplied the place of a guide-book, for he knew all the
famed localities as if he had been born among them. We
sat around him spellbound as he pointed out Cythera, the
birthplace of Venus ; as we glided by Lesbos, he spoke of
Sappho and her woes ; and when the tumulus of Patroclus
loomed in sight on the Asiatic shore, he recapitulated the
legendary story of Troy. But the crowning glory of this
realm of poetry and romance was the sight of Constantinople as it emerged from the morning mist, with its forest
of gilded domes and minarets flashing in the beams of the
rising sun, Europe and Asia divided only by the narrow
channel of the Bosphorus, the Sea of Marmora spread out
before it like a mirror to reflect its beauty, the refulgent
atmosphere bringing out in clear outline the snow-clad summit of the Bithynian Olympus, and the picturesque land and
water scenery that spread around on every side.

"The day after our arrival my father sent his card to
our Turkish friend Hassan Pasha, whom we had met in London, at his *yali* or villa on the Bosphorus, to know when we
could call on him.

"'To-morrow,' he replied, 'if you will bring your son
and daughter with you.'

"We were not a little surprised at this general invitation,
and my father intimated to the servant that there must be
some mistake.

"'Not at all ; the Pasha is quite European in his ways,
and the khanem, his wife, follows his example as far as he
will allow her to do so.'

"We had finished a late breakfast when the carriage of the
Pasha was announced to be in waiting to conduct us to To-

phane. There a *besch chifte*, or five-pair-oar caïque, in a
short time carried us to the villa. It was an elegant building of Oriental architecture immediately on the edge of the
Bosphorus, with large gardens on either side glowing with
flowers of every hue. We landed on the garden side, and
had hardly set foot on shore before the Pasha advanced to
meet us. Our reception was more cordial than I thought he
was capable of. He seemed to make an effort to throw off
his usual reserve of manner in order to put us at ease and
please us.

"'Permit me,' he said, with a pleasant smile, 'to divide
you, and to introduce Lady Blanche to the khanem in the
harem. After they have chatted together they will join us
in the *selamlik*.'

"A eunuch, as black as Erebus and as ugly as such creatures always are, bowing obsequiously to the ground, led
the way to the harem in the second story, on the other side
of the house. My sister was conducted to a spacious saloon,
spread with Persian carpets, in the center of which a fountain bubbled over a tier of marble basins into a reservoir in
which goldfish were playing. When she was seated on the
divan, which overlooked the Bosphorus, with all its animated sight of sailing and steam craft passing by, and
caïques darting across the channel between the two conti-
nents, she was served with pipes and coffee, sherbet and
sweetmeats.

"'I am glad to see you in Turkey,' said the Pasha, meanwhile, to my father and myself. 'It is not the country it
once was, nor are Constantinople and its environs such as they
were in the time of Solyman the Magnificent and some of
his successors. Man, however, can not mar the beauty of
nature. Probably it flourishes more when most neglected
by him. There, on the opposite European shore, you see the
fortress which Mohammed II built on the eve of the conquest of Constantinople, and whence he set forth to besiege
and take that city from the Greeks, who had held it for fifteen hundred years. It is a monument of our former power

4

and superiority ; but, like the empire to which it gave birth,
it is falling to decay.'

"For some time we talked of themes of mutual interest,
when the Pasha whispered a few words to a servant. The
officers and servants in the vestibule retired into the interior
of the *yali*. Their disappearance was followed by the entrance of the wife of the Pasha with my sister. She wore a
transparent *yashmak*, which she lifted from her expressive
features as she took a seat beside her husband. She was
the daughter of one of the most distinguished and rich-
est princes of the empire. Her father had enjoyed all the
pleasures and aspirations of private and public life. There
was no luxury he could not indulge in and no ambition that
he did not gratify except that of supreme rule, and in the
general break-up and uncertainty of Oriental affairs he even
cherished the idea of one day becoming the successor of the
sultans of the house of Othman. He died, however, before
he might have played a conspicuous part in the fifth act of
the Oriental drama. He loved his eldest daughter as the
apple of his eye, and gave her entirely into the charge of an
English governess, who educated her to a familiar knowledge
of English, French, and the elements of modern learning,
and gave her such an insight into modern life that she lost
all sympathy with Oriental manners and customs. She was
denationalized in every sense of the word. To my sister she
had previously said :

"'I have been trained as a European, and I am to live as
an Oriental. I know my future. I am married to one whom
I never saw before marriage, who shuts me up in his harem
to consort with other wives of as low instincts as himself—
dull, vapid creatures, with minds as blank as a sheet of white
paper. It is a pity that I was not permitted to remain in
blissful ignorance of a better state. To my surprise, I am
taken to the balls of the foreign embassies. I look on, however, from a gallery. I do not participate. My position is
altogether false. I am neither Christian nor Mohammedan.
Pity that I ever knew a foreign tongue or met a foreigner.'

"It was at this moment that a female servant informed the khanem that her company was desired in the *selamlik.*

" ' Let us go,' she had said, ' and for a while, at least, act and speak like free creatures, and not like slaves. How I envy the condition of Christian women ! '

" With this, throwing a Cashmere shawl over her shoulders, preceded by her confidential slave, she had entered the saloon of the *selamlik.* Casting off her Oriental manners, she conversed with the Earl and myself on a great variety of subjects. She had read of the homage paid to women in Europe and America.

" ' It may not be a proof,' she said, ' of your superior civilization, but it certainly is of your superior humanity. Where man recognizes woman as his helpmate and not as his slave, he doubles his happiness and he gives his children new reasons for respecting their mother. God never designed woman to be a degraded creature. I receive and reciprocate the visits of Christian ladies, but I feel all the time that I am violating the customs of my own people, and that I am only rendering myself unhappy.'

" We tried to parry this sad train of thought with complimentary remarks, but we saw that a barbed arrow had entered her soul and could not be extracted. The finale to this story of domestic contrariety is that the Pasha, not long after our visit, went to Europe, and his wife was remanded into a state of Oriental seclusion, where she lived without any intercourse with the gay Frank world, with which she once had a partial acquaintance, and for which she had such strong sympathies. During our stay in Constantinople the Pasha was untiring in his hospitality ; but with him, as with all other Orientals, we could perceive an invisible barrier of separation that, while they manifest a decent respect, externally,'for each other, will for ever keep Mussulmans and Christians apart."

" Have you ever asked after her?" Henry Harris inquired as the other resumed his cigar.

" Yes," Lord Conyngham replied ; "and that is why I

have said as much as I have about our visit. I knew at the
time that it was contrary to Oriental etiquette to do so, but
he had himself gone so far that I thought I could venture.
And very sorry I was that I did so. He evaded the question, but Lady Blanche learned in some way that the poor
thing was said to have disappeared, eloped, committed suicide—it was not known which."

The young nobleman had spoken so much more than his
wont that the company were not surprised when he added:

"I beg that you will notice him, gentlemen. To me it
is as if he had stepped out of the 'Arabian Nights' Enter-
tainments.' Unless I mistake, Hassan Pasha will give the
world some startling sensation yet."

CHAPTER XVIII.

IRRESISTIBLE ATTRACTION.

IT is not in chemical compounds alone we find that strong
drawing of things toward each other which we call elective
affinity. If certain gases are attracted into one to form
water; if certain other gases cling together to compose air;
so it is the instinctive union of certain people which is the
making of genuine friendship. It was thus with the family
of Earl Dorrington and that of George Harris. Not that
the Earl could enter either closely or cordially into alliance
with any one outside of his household. He could combine
with the Tories to make a party, could be one of a cabinet
to form a ministry, but with these, even with son and daughter, he still was, as has been sung of Milton, "a star, and
dwelt apart." In the case of Lady Blanche and Lord Conyngham it was different. The blue blood was in their
veins, it is true, but the world was changing, and they were
changing with it—unconsciously so.

"Lady Blanche is the queen of her sex; the most beautiful, by far the most desirable woman in the world," Henry Harris said to himself every day, yet he always added, "but I will take good care that she shall never know I think so."

"Of all men I know, he is one of the few who deserves to be in the Peerage," Lady Blanche felt, rather than allowed herself distinctly to think, in regard to him. "And if he was, then—" But there she always arrested even her most secret feeling, not before the blood, proud as it was, had flushed her face. For it was a little singular that if Lord Conyngham had addressed his sister of late as "Lady Clara Vere de Vere," Mary Harris had taken occasion, by way of sisterly precaution, to read Tennyson's poem of that name to her brother Henry, from beginning to end, and over and over again.

"Lady Clara Vere de Vere—"

The lines began to ring in the ears of Henry Harris with absurd persistency ; he caught himself even muttering them aloud when by himself :

> "'Lady Clara Vere de Vere,
>   Of me you shall not win renown:
> You thought to break a country heart
>   For pastime, ere you went to town ;
> At me you smiled, but unbeguiled
>   I saw the snare, and I retired:
> The daughter of a hundred earls,
>   You are not one to be desired.'"

Only the young man would always add, also strictly to himself : "That last line is false. *This* Lady Clara is one to be most earnestly desired. Of course she cares nothing for a fellow like me, but, in case she should try to amuse herself with me, I will show her that all the iron is not in my father's veins, nor the pride in hers."

The truth is, the young American had been very carefully trained. In an incidental conversation with Earl Dorrington, George Harris had, without the remotest allusion to his own case, explained the matter to the Earl, who had been speaking with a stately scorn of the *parvenus,* the newly made rich men of England and France.

"Your view is in some sense the true one," George Harris had gravely replied. "A century or so ago, when men began to grow rich in New York and elsewhere in America, they were so taken up with making money, it was so unusual a thing to have a hundred thousand or so, that they were intoxicated thereby. Being addled by their money, men allowed, even encouraged, their wives and daughters to rush into extravagance, their sons to dash into reckless dissipation. But a generation or two of ever-increasing wealth has begun to cure all that, at least with us. Our men of a hundred thousand dollars, 'a plum,' as it used to be called, have given place to our millionaires. These have grown up accustomed to vast wealth. As one result the very rich man now educates his son to be a millionaire, as a farmer educates his boy to be a farmer, or as a machinist trains him to be a machinist, or as," the master mechanic added with a slight inclination of his head, "a nobleman brings up his son and heir to be an earl or a duke. As America grows older it grows wiser, steadier, stronger, I trust."

"Assuredly so," Earl Dorrington replied, and thought no more about it ; but that was undoubtedly the way in which George Harris had, with the hearty coöperation of his wife, brought up his children. Henry Harris had long known that he would possess considerably over a million. He had become accustomed to it ; the fact had become as much a part of the order of nature to him as his nobility had to Lord Conyngham. Although of an ardent, even impulsive, soul, the young American, combining in himself the characters of his father and his mother, was cool, determined, thoroughly sensible.

"I could die for her," he was coming to say to himself, as he saw more and more every day of Lady Blanche, "but I do not intend that she shall make a fool of me. Although," he always added in the same breath, "she has, of course, no such intention. I do not suppose she gives me a thought. Among her swarm of admirers I am hardly remembered."

Odd as it may seem in so truthful a person, he thought, really, nothing of the kind. He was pretty confident that Lady Blanche *did* care a good deal for him; was even sure of and greatly elated thereby. "But that is my self-conceit!" he always added.

Now if Henry Harris had said to his sister when she had been administering her preventive poetry to him, "My dear Mary, you say all that merely to hide your own feeling in regard to Lord Conyngham," if he had said that, it would have been very rude; but it would have been true, perfectly true, however she might have denied it, denied it indignantly and with glowing cheeks.

It was the same with the young nobleman. His sister had never been without some unfortunate suitor. Many of them had been unexceptionable, all of them had been very much in earnest, two or three had been desperate, in the case of at least one there had been a tragedy. And yet Lord Conyngham had rarely troubled himself concerning her matters. If she was as warm-hearted as she was beautiful, Earl Dorrington himself was not quite so proud—if such a superlative may be allowed—as was she. Why, then, should her brother indulge in such frequent warnings in regard to this young American millionaire? He had always been arrogant, always bitterly hostile, to Americans. At times he would flash out in contemptuous allusions to their exhibits at the Exposition, to this individual and that, man or woman, who were marked in their Americanisms. But why not let his sister alone in regard to Henry Harris?

"It is because you never cease to think of them yourself, of one of them at least," she said to him suddenly one day. "I am told," she added, "although it is a low thing to say, that it is the thief who is loudest in his cry of 'Stop thief!' Take care of yourself, my poor Alfred, and I will care for myself."

"Why do I hear so much said concerning the Ameri-

cans?" Earl Dorrington asked on this occasion from the
head of the table, for they were at dinner. "For my part,
of Americans I am grown weary. When I was younger it
was not so. Sydney Smith very well observed then, 'Who
ever reads an American book?' Now I am disgusted with
the unceasing allusions to American newspaper enterprise,
American literature, American machinery. When I was at
Harrow and since, 'the roast beef of old England' was next
to King and Constitution; now it is of American beef I continually hear. At least at our own board let us escape allusions so frequent to the people in question. I weary of it."

"I fear you will become exceedingly fatigued then, sir,"
Lord Conyngham said. "It appears to me that we are coming to hear of nothing but American locomotives, American
flour, honey, eggs, mutton, apples. The republic of France
is merely a French translation of the one over the Atlantic.
What with their revolvers, phonographs, telegraphs, yachts,
school systems, monitors, spiritualisms, and a thousand things
beside—"

But at this moment the Earl touched a bell near his
plate, and the portly butler made his appearance. He was
a larger man than his master, purple of face from much
port, white-headed, double-chinned, as grave of aspect as an
ambassador.

"Excuse me, Alfred," said the Earl, "but I must speak
of it while the subject is up. Wilkins!"

"Yes, my lord," said the butler.

"Allow nothing American to come upon my table. Neither here nor when we return to England. Do you hear?"

"If your lordship will allow me—"

"I will *not* allow you. Nothing American! That will
do."

"I wish to add," the Earl continued, as the butler withdrew, for dessert was on the table, at which no servant was
present unless company was being entertained, "that the
American republic, like the French, is but the accident of
an hour. It narrowly escaped destruction during their civil

war. The horrible corruption of General Tweed and his kind will speedily cause it to collapse. There are respectable persons among them. Mr. George Harris seems to be of the kind, but—I am weary of America. We will dismiss the subject. You were speaking a little while ago, Alfred, of Mr. Gladstone—"

And yet, singular as it may seem, the friendship between the two families appeared to increase every week. As if by a controlling destiny, the young people especially were thrown together, now in one place and then in another, almost every day. They seemed to find increasing pleasure in it too. For them the world was changing faster than they knew, and it did not revolve any slower for the fact that omnipotent love was lending its shoulder to the change.

CHAPTER XIX.

THE MARBLE LIE.

AT an early period after the opening of the Exposition, Mrs. Margaret Harris had said to her son and daughter: "As you know, I am not very fond of what is called art. My tastes are too simple. You laugh at me for preferring the congregational singing at the Protestant Church to the grandest music either of the opera or the cathedral. It is the same of painting and sculpture. There are really but two works of art in the Exposition which have fastened my attention."

"Which are they, mamma?" Mary asked, eagerly. "There is one which I love to look at more than any other. But your two; which are they? Are they English, Spanish, Belgian, Italian?"

"No," Mrs. Harris said, with a smile, "I will not tell you. You and Henry must pick them out for yourselves. I will give you only this clew: both are admirably done, but one represents a falsehood, the blackest falsehood of which I can conceive ; the other is truth itself, truth to nature, I mean."

"Please tell us ?" her son entreated. "It is the first time we have heard you express a special interest in such things. Which are they ?"

"No," Mrs. Harris said, shaking her head good-humoredly, "I will leave you to find out. I am almost anxious to see if your education has so changed the mother in you—yes, and I think I may say the father in you too—that you will not hit upon them for yourselves."

It was said in such a way as to awaken quite an interest in the mind of Mary in particular. Being a woman, she had more curiosity than her brother, but she said so much about it to him as they wandered, afterward, through the innumerable statues and paintings, that he also grew eager to make the discovery.

"It reminds me of when I was hunting antelope in Colorado," he said to her. "We men are made to pursue things, as much so as a deerhound is to chase a buck. Besides," he added, "when I *do* find them I intend to buy them, if it takes my last cent. I have not made my mother a present for a long time. It is the first occasion upon which she has expressed a desire for anything of the kind."

Every week or two Mrs. Harris would ask, of an evening, "Well, Henry, Mary, have you found them ?"

"Mamma takes a singular interest in her ideals of art," Mary remarked to her brother one day when they were in the Exposition. "Last night she told me that she would make, to the one who finds them, a gift. The one of us who hits upon what she calls the greatest falsehood she has ever known to be represented by an artist shall have something valuable. But you need not think she would accept it if you found and bought it, for she says she would not have it in her house."

"And what will she give us if we find the other, the representation of truth she spoke of ?" her brother demanded.

"I wonder what it is?" Mary Harris exclaimed, with enthusiasm. "She told me that she would make you or me, whichever of us finds that, the best present she ever gave. Of course, it is not for her gifts that we care, but it will gratify her so. Suppose we devote to-day to a deliberate search for her masterpieces?"

It was a dull and disagreeable day. Moreover, a long-anticipated *fête* was taking place in a distant part of the city. They had never seen so few persons in attendance, and Henry Harris, his sister leaning upon his arm, slowly and carefully examined with her a vast number of the works of art which adorned the Exposition. They had settled upon nothing when they withdrew to dine, but they renewed the search afterward. It was nearly time to leave the building before they could agree to abandon the attempt. The day had grown darker and darker; a silence had fallen upon the vast spaces usually thronged by a laughing multitude chattering in all languages. Both had grown weary of the interminable diversity of artistic effort in bronze and marble, upon ivory and canvas. Battle-pictures, heathen divinities, martyrs, Madonnas, landscapes, representations of luxury and of poverty, of comedy and of tragedy, of innocence and of vice, had been passed in review in vain.

"Let us give it up for to-day," the brother remarked to his sister, at last, after they had almost settled upon and then had abandoned this picture or work in marble and then that. "Come, Mary, they will be expecting us; let us go."

"In one moment. For," she added, slowly, "I have found it," in almost solemn tones.

Henry Harris glanced up at the work of Doré before which his sister was standing. It represented a female figure, draped with a hood and somber garments. Between its knees, as it sat, stood a winged and beautiful youth in the full flush of innocent enjoyment, eager-eyed, abounding in life. The hands of the austere female form lay calm and strong upon either side of the youth, and from the one sinewy hand to the other extended the thread, as of its life. In the right hand of the awful form were the shears, in the act of closing upon the tiny thread; and Mary Harris pointed silently upward to the contrasted faces of the two. That of the youth was open, joyous, utterly unconscious of danger, while, immediately over it, inside its half-concealing hood, the face of the woman appeared, old as eternity, with cavernous eyes, cold and rigid features, passionless, inflexible. Neither love nor hate was in that terrible aspect; only unreasoning, unfeeling, unalterable doom.

There was no need for either to tell the other that it was a symbol of Fate. The artist had done his work with too terrible a fidelity for any mistake concerning that.

"Yes," Mary Harris said, after they had gazed upon it in silence for some time, "I know that this is what my mother spoke of, and I do not wonder that she was so deeply struck by it. For it is a lie," she continued, with deep feeling. "Heathen genius ascended, in that, to the highest summit of its ignorance of God. That horrible fate is the sublimity of its despair of knowing anything beyond an inexorable law which, as philosopher and poet agreed, governs alike men and gods. And my mother is right," the girl added, with energy; "it is to-day a *lie;* the blackest of lies! There is no such thing as fate! Now we know better. We know that God is our Father, and we know that God is love;" and the voice of the speaker faltered, her eyes were full of happy tears, and the two turned and walked away in silence.

"Yes; you have found my falsehood," Mrs. Harris said to them that night, "and you need not fear that I will forget my reward. I knew that you would find it, my dear," and she drew Mary to her, and kissed her with unusual affection. "And now, Mary, Henry," she added, "which of you will find out my ideal of truth—purely human truth? Take your time for it."

CHAPTER XX.

THE BIRTH OF ADVENTURE.

IT so happened one day that Lord Conyngham and Lady Blanche came upon Henry Harris and his sister as they were standing before a large painting representing a battle. These last had been in vain search of the remaining work of art in which their mother was so deeply interested.

"I am almost sure that I know which it is, but," Mary Harris had said to her brother, "I found one of the two, and I am determined that you shall have the reward for finding the other."

"Shall I ?" her brother was just saying when he observed their friends near them, and, after due salutation, the young people fell into conversation concerning the mass of conflict and rolling smoke, charging horses and desperate men, before which they stood. The cheek of Lady Blanche took an additional color as she gazed, her form became more erect.

"I wonder you gentlemen are not somewhat ashamed of yourselves," she remarked. "How can you see in this and in so many other pictures the glorious struggles of heroes, and be contented to do nothing? That you should be a man, Alfred," she added, "and be satisfied to find your only laurels at billiard-tables and in parlors, at balls and concerts, astonishes me. At best your only field of victory is a tennis court or a garden party. If I were a man—" and she turned upon her brother with kindling eyes. Lord Conyngham took her indignant looks coolly enough, until, at last, he detected the milder eyes of the fair American fastened upon him, and then he colored somewhat and moved uneasily.

But if the wrath of Lady Blanche had little effect upon her brother, long accustomed to it, in glancing from his armor it smote and slew the other gentleman. It was not that she seemed so beautiful, that her pride was as that of an angry angel—it was not this merely, but that she gave words to a deep and long-concealed purpose of his own. He now felt sincerely ashamed that he had put off the execution so long. He said nothing, however.

"What can a man do?" Lord Conyngham hastened to say, addressing himself to his spirited sister, but really speaking to the other lady. "Shall I proceed to slap the cheeks of that gesticulating Frenchman in continuation of Waterloo? Yonder is a solemn Spaniard. His people once fought us at Trafalgar. We beat them then from behind our floating walls. Shall I burst over the stronger bulwarks of propriety and knock him down? We are the protectors of the Turks. There stands my mysterious friend Hassan Pasha to approve, and, if necessary, come to my assistance; shall I rush upon the Russian prince I see by the fountain, and pitch him in? Very good, I am willing," and he began with a solemn air to tuck up his sleeves.

"Nonsense, Alfred," his sister said without a smile, although the rest were laughing, "you know that 'peace hath its victories as well as war.'"

"Assuredly so, as my father observes; but what exact conquest shall I set about?" Lord Conyngham demanded. "I already do my best to add to the oratory in Parliament. You were eager to build model cottages upon our estate, and you know I almost became a bricklayer in carrying out your wishes in regard to that. Shall I rush over to Ireland and stir up the Home Rulers? Shall I build a hospital? establish a new Tory journal? organize an expedition to the North Pole, or an emigration to Australia? Here is Mr. Harris to help me; shall I turn American and invent a new mowing machine? devise a big balloon to bring over a prairieful of cattle at a time? Shall I—"

Lady Blanche glanced at her brother with some surprise; generally he was not so quick to answer her attacks. Like most of his rank, he had seemed to be merely a man of fashion, content to enjoy himself however and wherever he could. Now he appeared to be aroused. Mary Harris seemed to be uncommonly interested in the carnage going on upon the canvas before which they stood, but her color was heightened; evidently she was listening with deep interest.

"I will tell you what I will do," the young nobleman continued. "Until Dizzy contrives to plunge us into an imperial onset upon Russia, I will get my father to allow me to try the latest invention in rifles upon a few American Indians. What do you say, Mr. Harris? Could I get a shot at Sitting Bull if I went over? There is the Comanche brave, what do you call him—the Man-afraid-of-his-Squaws, isn't it? But, no, poor beggar! *he* suffers enough already at their hands. I wouldn't have the heart to shoot at *him*, unless, indeed, he wants to be put out of his misery. But, joking aside," and the young nobleman confronted his sister seriously as he proceeded, "will your ladyship be good enough to tell me precisely what you would have me to do? Whatever it is, I pledge you my word that I will at least try."

Mary Harris lifted her eyes with hardly concealed admiration at the one who spoke. Trained in all physical exercises, too, he was an athlete out of employ.

"I remember how it was in the Crimea," she ventured, for Lady Blanche did not know how to reply. "I have read all I could lay my hands on about the Redan and the Malakoff, and how the young Englishmen from the London clubhouses fought like tigers. So it was in our civil war, North and South; the men who could endure most, too, were those of the best blood among us—I mean of the best breeding and education. I am sure that my brother and—and you, my lord," she added, modestly, "would do your duty when the time came. Yes, I am sure of it." She laid her hand, as she spoke, upon her brother's arm, but there was that in her voice which made the nobleman thrill with satisfaction. It was as if her hand had been placed upon his arm instead.

"Thank you, Miss Mary," he said with more feeling than he usually showed. "Do you know," he added, "I am trying to induce your brother to go with me on a hunting excursion in Alaska, Nevada, Oregon, somewhere in your immense America. I am eager to go there. If I get tired of buffalo and elk, of wild-cat and panther, I will turn farmer. Your very husbandmen are heroes ; you have, I am told, ten thousand acres in wheat under one fence ! "

Henry Harris had remained silent as if in thought. He now remarked :

"I saw something in one of those harvest-fields when I was over there which was the oddest of sights. It was a ripe field of twenty thousand acres, my lord, a yellow sea of wheat. There were four fine horses attached to a machine, which not only reaped but bound what it reaped into sheaves as it went. I was watching it reap and toss the bound sheaves out as it rolled on. Suddenly the horses took fright, for they were not half broken, and dashed off through the center of the wheat, where it was thickest and ripest, the machine at their heels. As they tore along the machine reaped and whirled the sheaves, tightly bound, to the right and the left as usual, only ten times faster. It was one of the most amusing sights I ever saw."

The young American went on to speak of other experiences of his in his own country, and it was the Englishwoman now who listened with most interest ; there was so much of the breadth and vigor of the New World in the one who spoke, a noble something which every day charmed her more and more, by reason also of its freshness in distinction from her somewhat wearied experiences.

The next day the two men met at the Bodega, and engaged in a long and animated conversation.

"Think well of it, my lord," Henry Harris said, as they parted. "As you see, it is a hazardous enterprise, but it is also, as I believe, a thoroughly sensible one. It will carry us deep into England, Germany, Russia ; upon a serious errand, I assure you. If you determine to go into it with me, let me know as soon as you can. It is best to say nothing about it meanwhile. I have long intended to try it, and will, whether you go with me or not ; but I will be glad of your company."

And the American and Englishman shook hands with cordial good-will when they separated.

CHAPTER XXI.

ISIDORE ATCHISON, ARTIST.

ONE afternoon, about a week after the discovery of the "Fate" which was Mrs. Harris's supreme symbol of falsehood, Henry Harris and his sister had wandered into the section of the Exposition in which were displayed the contributions of American sculptors. The Old World greatly surpassed the New in this respect. As the Exposition harvested more than two thousand years of artistic effort, and from all the fields of the Eastern and ripest half of the planet, America could not have been expected to vie with the rest of the race in this respect, especially as its young energies have been necessarily given to things more essential to existence ; and yet, even in this respect, there were among its exhibits at least the buds and beginnings of the grandest results.

"It is a significant fact," Henry Harris said to his sister, "that art in America seems to be given over, and every day in an increasing degree, to woman. It is one of the many things I do not understand ; do not understand, because as yet nobody understands that which is only beginning to be born. One only knows that woman is the reserve force of the race."

"What do you mean ?" Mary Harris asked.

"This : men have had their opportunity for nearly six thousand years. By hard work in the field, the shop, the council-chamber, upon the decks of ships, and on the battle-ground—yes, and in the pulpit, the editor's office, and the halls of schools and universities—in these and other places men have accomplished the civilization of the world up to date."

"Men are, at last, only what their mothers, sisters, and wives make them," Mary said, defiantly.

"Very true, and to a greater measure than any of us imagine. But," her brother added, with energy, "woman is going to be the last, the most powerful, the *completing* force of history; not by becoming more like men, but by remaining distinctively woman. Hassan Pasha, Ishra Dhass, are right; woman is to become more Rachel-like, Ruth-like, Eve-like—oh, I do not know how to express it!—more purely and intensely feminine, unlike men—you know what I mean—*woman*-like, than she has been for ages. But, to a degree of which neither Turk, Hindoo, nor anybody else dreams of, she is, as such, to save the world. I can't tell how, but I am certain of it! It may be, by becoming a new and supreme power in literature, in art, as well as in morals —who can say? Look, for instance, at *this*."

They had halted before the head of an old man cut in marble, and he added : "I do not know why it is, but I can not get rid of this bust. It struck me when I first saw it; almost every day I find myself drawn back to it from the farthest parts of the Exposition. Look at it. You see it is the bowed head of an old scholar, apparently. See how thin the hair is, how hollow the temples, how refined the nostrils, how broad the brows. The eyes are sunken, and gazing downward; the shoulders are weighed down as if under—"

"A cross," his sister added.

"Precisely. Now," the young man continued, as he led her slowly from point to point, so as to obtain a complete view of the marble, "what do you think is the one idea expressed by the artist? Unless I am an idiot there is but one idea, only *one;* what is it?"

"A person would be blind as well as dull not to see that," his sister answered, with a suppressed triumph. "The artist has made patience, endurance, serene trust, absolutely visible. He has turned the abstract virtue into living stone."

"*He!*" her brother exclaimed. "*He!* Do you not know, Mary, that it is not a man—it is a woman—who created it? I am astonished at you! No, I am not; a woman can do justice to everything else in the universe except to a woman. Dean Swift made that discovery, bitter and bad as he was, years ago. It is a woman who carved it."

"Do you think so?" Mary asked, incredulously.

"I *know* it! Look here, Mary, I will make a bet with you, a one-sided bet; that is, if the artist is not a woman I will give you the finest watch I can find in Paris. More than that, I will have Worth make you the most beautiful dress he has ever turned out if this marble is not the one my mother picked out as her idea of truth. What do you say?"

Mary Harris glanced around, saw that no one was very near, and clapped her hands in triumph.

"O Henry," she said, "if you only knew it, you are an artist yourself! I would not be surprised if you are a genius. For some time I was almost certain that this is the work mamma meant. Last night I asked her, and she said yes. But I was determined not to give you a hint, to let you find it out for yourself. I am so glad! Because," she added, "it shows you have something nobler in you than mere genius. If I was sure that everybody knew you were my brother, or that nobody saw me, I would kiss you! Mamma will be so delighted! But," and she shook her head, "it never occurred to me that it was a woman's work. I don't believe it is."

"Let us ask some one." As Henry Harris said it, he observed that a lady was standing half concealed behind an equestrian bronze not far off. She was dressed in black, and had a veil over her face.

"Will you be so kind, as we have no catalogue—" Mary Harris ventured to ask of her in French. "Do you know who is the artist in this case?" and she pointed to the bust. The lady paused a moment, and then lifted her veil, revealing the face of a lovely girl.

"It is the work of a Miss Isidore Atchison," she said in English; but her eyes fell, her cheeks were suffused with color, and Mary Harris saw that her large hazel eyes were swimming with tears.

"I thank you," the inquirer added, and turned away eagerly, while her brother lifted his hat and bowed.

"Didn't you understand?" the sister asked her brother,

when they were out of hearing. "It is the artist herself. As sure as you live she heard what we said ; how could she help it ? I am so glad she did. And did you see how pale she was ? Poor thing, she must feel lost in this great ocean of people. I'm afraid you did not see how proud and pleased she was by what she had heard us say."

"I saw her," Henry Harris said, "saw her distinctly. I intend to buy the marble, and make it a present to my mother."

"Suppose we go right back and talk to her now," the sister said impulsively. "She had such a lovely face. Come, let us go."

"No," her brother replied, deliberately. "I would rather not attend to it to-day. I have reasons. Besides, I want to go and tell my mother about it first."

CHAPTER XXII.

FATHER AND CHILD.

On the same day as that upon which Henry Harris had found what his sister described as "Patience on a pedestal, smiling at Grief," there sat an old man in an attic room of a building on one of the obscurest streets of Paris. The apartment was small and poorly lighted by two dormer-windows in the roof. In one corner stood the iron bedstead occupied by the man at night ; in the other, and so placed that the light could fall upon it from above, was a strong wooden stand, upon which was a heap of something covered with a coarse, wet cloth. Small and poor as the room was, it was scrupulously neat, as was the clothing of the aged tenant, who was seated at a table, his back to the window which opened over his bed. He was carving flowers in wood, a bouquet of roses and lilies standing in a vase at his right hand. It seemed to be a work of difficulty, for he was toil-

ing with his left hand only, while the other lay paralyzed in
a pillow placed in his lap. The white hair was scattered in
thin locks over the noble head, the shoulders were bowed,
the temples were hollow; you would have recognized at a
glance the sublime serenity which had made so deep an impression upon Mrs. Harris and her children as reproduced in
the marble at the Exposition. Evidently the old man was
an artist. You saw it in the refinement of his face; in the
slow but sure movements of the skilled hand; especially in
the air, almost of distinction, which clothed his whole person
as if in an aureole. It seemed a matter of course that the
carving should be admirably done, yet even then you could
not but be surprised at the manner in which the hard oak
actually bloomed, beneath the sharp tool, into almost the
blush of the rose and the fragrance as well as delicacy of the
lily.

Suddenly the artist paused, sat with tool suspended, a
new light in his eye. He had heard, although no other
could have done so, the sound of a footstep upon a distant
stair, and knew whose it was. He was right. A few moments after, the young girl whom Mary Harris accosted at
the Exposition entered the room and stooped down and
kissed him as he sat.

"Oh, no, father," she said, "not so late as this." And
she took the tool from his hand, drew the table away out of
his reach, kissed him again to hush his remonstrances, and,
taking off her wrappings and hat, carried them into a smaller
room, a mere closet, in fact, curtained off from the other.
She then busied herself to prepare the evening meal. The
fare was simple, and it did not take long.

"How well you are doing them, father!" she exclaimed,
as she removed the carving and the flowers from the table,
covered it with a clean cloth, set upon it the modest furnishing for their supper, crowning the whole with a teapot,
which sent up its fragrant steam from over a spirit-lamp.

While they are at table their history may be told in few
words. Zerah Atchison had been an artist from his child-

hood, in an obscure town in Virginia. He had studied hard
in such books as he could secure, and had worked steadily.
While qualifying himself to be a great painter, as he hoped,
he had taken portraits, had condescended to lay aside brush
and easel and become a photographer even—anything in
order to perfect himself, meanwhile, by severe study. His
delight in beauty was not confined, however, to that of the
ideal world. While painting the portrait of the daughter of
a wealthy planter near Richmond, he had fallen in love with
and married her. Then came the civil war. As it began, a
daughter was born to them. But trouble came to them as
to all of their region. The artist was not a young man when
he married, and by no means a rich one. Always of a delicate and sensitive nature, his health had been impaired by
the wholly unaccustomed life he had led as a soldier in
the trenches and upon the battle-field. After that came
the ruin of his father-in-law, who lost everything in the result of the war, and who died soon after. But the severest
blow was the death of his wife, which followed speedily upon
that. Shattered as he was, Mr. Atchison would have given
up the struggle, and himself been swept away in the vast
wreck which burdened the ebbing tide of the Rebellion, if it
had not been for his daughter. What, in case of his death,
would become of her? The will of the man—the heart,
rather, of the father—reënforced his expiring energies. Toiling at whatever offered as well as he could, he contrived not
only to sustain, but to give his only child an excellent education. His strength revived as she grew. It was not only
that she became more lovely with each passing year, nor
even that, under his careful training, she developed an artistic power superior to his own—his affection had awakened in
her an unbounded devotion in return. To her he was as
a mother too; she gave him in return the love she would
otherwise have shared with brothers, sisters, friends, for
the circumstances of their case had isolated father and child
from almost any other association.

"And now I am so glad we came to Paris," she said, as

she sat at table with him. "When your little accident happened"—it was thus she characterized the paralysis which had smitten his right arm—"I saw that *something* must be done. After a while you consented, and here we are."

"You poor child," her father said, not sadly, only lovingly; "and now that we are here, what then? Even if I could go to the Exposition with you, what could I do? In this great Babylon we are lost among the crowd."

"More than Daniel was? More than Esther was?" she demanded.

"At best it is like an immense garden, this vast Paris," her father continued, "and you, Isidore, you are like—like—"

"The smallest of humming-birds; and yet," she added, with a laugh, "there is not a flower of the myriad but has its honey even for me."

It is no wonder that the eyes of her father lingered upon her. Slight as she seemed, she was elastic and strong. Like a Mother Carey's chicken, she had been born in the storm, of war at least; had been cradled amid the blowing of its sulphurous winds, the rolling of its red billows, and her character gave a certain daring to her very beauty.

"You are of the pure Greek type, my dear," her father now said to her, somewhat irrelevantly, "except that, as I have always maintained, the head of every Venus they produced is invariably too small. Yours is not."

"Dear father," she laughed, "you have told me that *so* often. Please don't."

"Yes," her father persisted, and as if it were a question of mere art, "but you are growing more beautiful every day. You ought to excel Aspasia, you are so many centuries older; riper, I mean. Besides, you have had such a severe strain upon you as even Antigone never knew, devoted daughter as she was."

"And I have had my father and my father's faith," she added, "but I broke down to-day;" and she told him at length of the visit of Henry Harris and his sister to her bust, and what was said by them. "I could not help hearing them," she explained. "It is such a poor little bit of marble, you know. If it were a huge equestrian statue like the one near it, if it were a dancing nymph, a convulsed gladiator, a Hercules in the agony of his poisoned robe, something of that kind, it would be different. But people pour by it in torrents like a river. Turks, Persians, Chinese, Spaniards, Americans, very few of them do more than throw an instant's glance at it. There is so very much to see, people have so little time. I told you weeks ago how that wise-looking, motherly lady stopped so long to look at it. Do you know, father, I am sure that the lady and gentleman who praised it so to-day are her daughter and son? It was not alone that they resembled her so much in their faces; their way of speaking and their calm manner are the same. Are they Americans?" she demanded of herself in the same breath. "N-n-no, they do not have the sharp, eager, hurried look of newly arrived Americans. They must be English, and I would not be surprised if they are English people of rank."

"You have not been annoyed again, Isidore? Hassan Pasha has not dared—" her father began a few minutes after, with a shade of anxiety.

"Do not fear for me, father; I can take care of myself," she said, with a change of face.

"And now she looks like Electra!" her father murmured, almost forgetting his question.

"I think at last," he continued, as if to himself and abstractedly, "that the soul of her beauty lies, yes, in her genius. It illumines her like a lamp within alabaster."

"O father," Isidore exclaimed, "a looking-glass should merely reflect; it ought not to talk also. You criticise me as if I were a plaster model." And then her face grew still brighter. "But you mistake," she said, and her voice faltered as she looked upon his patient face. "It is not my genius, as you call it; the only genius I possess, is to love."

CHAPTER XXIII.

COSMOPOLITAN COMPANY.

ONE evening Earl Dorrington had a large party to dinner. Lady Blanche had seen to it that, so far as was possible in Paris, their apartments should resemble those at home. With the Earl, her brother, and herself, the word English meant comfort as well as the highest civilization, and she had done her best to obliterate France from the memory, at least for the time, of every guest also. The table groaned with the old plate, and Wilkins, the portly butler, seemed to be, in his black suit and white cravat, more purple and portly than ever, as if he would bar out the least glimpse of anything other than "Hengland." Earl Dorrington, to do him justice, made an admirable host, and there was something pleasing in the manner in which his son and daughter lent themselves to the work of making their guests enjoy themselves. It was as if Pride clothed itself, for the hour, in the garb of Service, and Wilkins himself was cold and reserved, a haughty aristocrat in comparison to them.

After dinner the ladies grouped themselves for a moment around Mrs. Margaret Harris. It was not merely that she was a comely dame, that her dress and diamonds would compare with those of any of the ladies of rank present, but it was that she had, as has been before observed, a certain air of quiet command which arrested the attention of every one. It was but the impression which good sense always makes, but it is not often that common sense is a woman, and is immensely wealthy, and wears such jewels. Moreover, the lady spoke in a low tone, and seemed to be by no means desirous of monopolizing the conversation. She had enjoyed, however, and for years, an opportunity of seeing the world from more points of view than any other woman present, and her long and ample acquaintance with people of all prejudices and nationalities enabled her to come at the general average and essence and result of things beyond

5

even the two or three women of genius—authors and artists, French, English, American—who were present.

The conversation at the table just before had ranged over the leading topics of the time—the German Empire, the prospects of the Count of Chambord, Henry V, the hope of the Legitimists, Russian Nihilism, the struggle between Conservative and Radical in the French Republic, the opening of Africa, the prospects in America. With instinctive good-breeding every one dealt only in such assertions as could not by any possibility hurt the feelings of any other of the variety of persons present. As a rule, the ladies were more interested in the opera and the fashions, but the Exposition was like a colossal kaleidoscope in perpetual revolution, and it stimulated the minds even of these to higher thought than usual. Moreover, all felt that society was in a state of transition.

"It is true," Earl Dorrington had remarked from the head of the table, "that change is the order of the day. Nor do I deny that great discoveries are being made of a scientific nature. Assuredly so. But every wheel revolves upon an axis. Birth, blood, rank, divinely appointed authority, are the axis at last of all movement. Wealth, talent, ambition, success, inventive science even, and art, are useful in their way, and yet "—with a wave of the hand—"how transitory! Amid the orbits of the universe the Deity remains in absolute rest. So does that which bests represents the divine government upon the earth. Else," and the Earl paused as he was wont to do in Parliament until he had secured the deepest attention, "else would all things rush into hopeless chaos and confusion. Wine with you, M. de Fortou."

There had been so much conversation of the sort that the ladies had taken the topic with them into the drawing-rooms. Not that the Earl had spoken unchallenged. Men of many varieties were present, and much had been said for and against. The Earl did not object; if a less sublime illustration than his own may be used, all conversation upon politics was to him as the coruscations of the kind of fireworks known as Catharine-wheels; however the many-colored lights flashed from it to the right hand and to the left, however the myriad sparks might fly, all rotated at last and ended in the central spike which upheld it. As near as the Earl could make out, he and what he represented was that central support. Everything beside was but the flurry and the many-colored flash of the instant.

"I do not pretend," Mrs. Margaret Harris remarked to the ladies about her, "to understand our times. As a woman and an American, I have, of course, my own views, and yet to me the progress of events is like the process in a cask of wine. None of us know the many ingredients, the secret chemistries, going on over the world. What we all are sure of is that the fermentation of men and of nations, as of grapes, is according to a divine law. The process I do not comprehend; concerning the result, I have not the least anxiety."

"Kismet!"

The lady looked up. Hassan Pasha had entered the drawing-room and was standing beside her daughter near by. He had uttered the exclamation in a low tone, but Mrs. Harris smiled at him and shook her head. "Not at all," she said; "my daughter will tell you," she added, "what we all think of Doré's representation of Fate."

"I will be delighted to hear; to her even Fate must surrender," the Pasha replied with a bow, and he turned away the more willingly to listen to Mary Harris as at that moment the Hindoo, Ishra Dhass Gunga, came into the room with a number of gentlemen.

The wise Brahmin had, when he first arrived in England, brought letters from the Episcopal Bishop of Calcutta, as also from the Viceroy and lesser officials of British rule in India. The Queen had herself received him with favor; he had addressed many convocations of various kinds in England and France; and everywhere he had been received into the best society. If the truth must be told, the Brahmin was at the time the rage in many circles.

Even the Frenchmen present had to confess that the Hindoo seemed to enjoy life yet more than themselves. With his snowy turban, flowing robes, laughing black eyes, he seemed to be the incarnation of enjoyment as he was of health. With it all was a certain smooth and flowing manner, as of perfect breeding. And yet, supple and smiling as he was, people had come to know that he was as thoroughly informed in regard to Europe as in reference to India. He was vigorous too, and as alert as an acrobat.

"He is *enfant terrible,*" was the remark often made of him, so frank was he in many of his sayings. Even when people were most startled, he laughed and did not care. He was petted, was in splendid spirits, enjoyed to his finger-tips the excitements of the time, and yet, as all came to know, the current which lifted and bore him on was that of a purpose which had taken possession of the whole man, a purpose deep and strong.

"Our friend Hassan Pasha hates me," he had said to Henry Harris, as they came up from dinner, "as if I were a cobra, a deadly viper. Do you know why?"

"The Pasha is a devout Mohammedan, and he is aware," the other replied, "that you have become a Christian. And yet one would suppose he would be glad of anything which strikes at the worship of idols."

"It is deeper than that. I will explain to you some day. But I do not hate him," the Brahmin said. "Ah, no! if he were the deadliest of reptiles I would seek so much the more eagerly—you have heard of snake-charmers?—to charm him. I will be glad to tell you about it. Nothing is more interesting. Not now."

But that was said just before. Now the ladies and many of the gentlemen had grouped themselves in the Earl's drawing-room about the Hindoo. The fact that the Queen of England was in the act of becoming Empress of India added to the interest in him. Earl Dorrington had joined the group. Lord Conyngham had contrived by this time to draw Mary Harris from the Pasha, and, by a singular coincidence, her brother was engaged in conversation with Lady Blanche at the portfolio of engravings upon the other side of the room. George Harris was not present, having been suddenly called back to Russia upon business.

"Pardon me, my lord, but I can not enter now into the question of Christianity in my land," Ishra Dhass was heard to say to Earl Dorrington. "We accept it as the power which is to revolutionize India. But our hope is more daring, your lordship; we intend to revolutionize England also, and the world," and, notwithstanding the dignified aspect of the Tory Earl, the Hindoo went on:

"I am not speaking now of the throne, nor of the nobility, my lord; although monarch, noble, army, universities, press, all England, all Europe, and America too, must utterly change as the result. It is upon your idea of Christianity that the whole modern civilization rests. Roman, Greek, Protestant, and all the sects of Protestantism, it is that which sustains and shapes everything. Communism, Nihilism, Irish grievance, American corruption, Indian misrule, Austrian weakness, German arrogance, French uncertainty, Russian despotism—all is the result of your European misconception of Christianity. That is the reason you fail in regard to Turkey, to India. Ah, ladies and gentlemen, you are so terribly mistaken! The whole planet is a bulb which breaks into bloom here in Paris. 'How grand!' we say, 'how beautiful!' 'how glorious!' We are advancing to sublime perfection! And you are so highly cultivated, so learned, educated; you are, ladies, the wisest and most beautiful; you, gentlemen, are the most cultured and masterful the world has ever known, and yet—"

The voice of the Hindoo had become low and persuasive; he bowed deferentially to the brilliant circle about him. Then his eye kindled, his dark cheek took the crimson of the pomegranate. "Strong and beautiful as you are," he proceeded, "ah, heavens! how ignorant you are! Asia has taught you everything you know of God, everything. You have perverted it all. Asia," and the voice of the orator thrilled those present as with a force of prophecy, "Asia must destroy your crystallized Christianity, and teach it to you over again. Your fossilized Christianity—ah-h-h-h! it is become false, false, *false!* Eighteen centuries have polluted it!" The horror of his face, the gesture of his hand, were very striking.

"It is not," he added, as if in alarm, "of the Christ that I speak. To thee, O Son of God, *salaam, salaam!*" and the Hindoo bowed his head in reverence as before a visible presence. "I will not speak of it now. Is not this a dinner party? I forgot myself," he added. "At some other time gladly, not now. But your established Christianity, my lord, believe me, it must go." And the merry audacity returned to the Hindoo's face as he bowed to Earl Dorrington.

CHAPTER XXIV.

MATRONLY SUGGESTION.

MARGARET HARRIS was a good woman in the best sense of the word. She had grown with the growth of her own country, and strengthened with the strength of her experience in other countries. She had walked the thorny paths of poverty and the shining avenues of fortune with her husband, and she could sympathize with the poor and make allowance for the rich. It was her husband's greatest pleasure to call about him, when he was at his own home, and gave his brilliant receptions, the companions of his early life; and Margaret was never more graceful and sincere than when she was receiving their wives and daughters. Both seemed to understand the real uses of wealth, and also to fear and shun its abuses. She was as sensitive as her husband on this subject. In their eyes there was little difference between the insufferable arrogance of the aristocrat and the vulgar display of the parvenu; and if there was any mercy for either of these extremes, they withheld it from the first, because he ought to have known better. Margaret never concealed her contempt for the pretentious insolence of some of the so-called better classes who flaunted their inherited social superiority, and like her husband, George Harris, she frequently showed it. But nothing could describe her grief when she met beautiful American girls who seemed to recollect nothing but their accidental good fortune. Enriched by the sudden luck of their fathers, they made the tour of Europe only for enjoyment, and rarely for instruction. What a gentle providence she was to such girls, as she kindly assumed the right to admonish and advise them! The handsome matron, surrounded by these bright Americans, talked to them like a modern and a better Zenobia, and they regarded her with mingled love and reverence. Mary Harris, her daughter, sat with her mother, and seemed the living model of her frequent familiar colloquies. Margaret would say :

"We have such lovely girls in America that I want them to be as perfect in mind and manners as they are in person, and, oh! if they only knew how they make me suffer sometimes in society, I am sure they would be more guarded. I can read these foreigners when our girls forget themselves. It is so easy to acquire good style. I am told that behavior is born in most people. I deny it. I believe that we are all not only improved by contact and imitation, but that we are made better and purer. The best of us are the merest copyists. We are all influenced by our examples. We all study those who are set over us. How important, then, that we should have the best to follow and the purest to obey! I pity from my soul a rich girl, American or European, with no mother to guide and teach her. Mere wealth without brains is a curse, especially to a woman. I have seen it turn men into brutes and tyrants, into infidels and blasphemers. I could name many in England, France, and America that have used their money as savages have used their captives, only to gratify their own passions, to humiliate their inferiors, to laugh at benevolence, to scorn all public benefactions, and to die at last despised by their own contemporaries, and punished by a profligate, ignorant, and spendthrift posterity."

"But, dear Mrs. Harris," said one of the American girls, "you told us the other day that wealth was a great advantage, honorably acquired and properly used, and I remember how you pitied the lot of young women at home or abroad without money." It was Ellen Ellsworth who spoke. She was a reigning New England beauty, and one of the wealthiest of the American colony.

"I am glad, Ellen," said Mrs. Harris, "that you remember that interview, because you can yourself be a splendid example, if you will, of what I meant to teach; and I should be an impostor if I attempted to decry honorable wealth. My object was to induce our rich girls to add to their material gifts the graces of a Christian life and the culture of a high intelligence. No young woman, with or without money, who studies these counsels will ever lack for happiness, whether married or single. That, the result of a long experience, is my deliberate judgment."

"We have had quite a number of marriages between Americans and English, Mrs. Harris," said Ellen, as if to change the subject and ask a question.

"Yes," said Margaret Harris, and her cheeks glowed as she looked at her daughter Mary; "but how few have ended well! That remark of yours, Ellen, starts a problem. Is it not true that few English or French come over to us for wives? Is it not true that our girls come to Europe, and get foreign partners here? Do you ever reflect how rarely American men marry foreign women?"

As the stately Margaret spoke, it was interesting to study the group that listened to her. There were four, besides her daughter, and most of them the children of rich Americans, and it was manifest that her conversation impressed them. A dark Southern girl, Virginia Josselyn, who seemed to be a great favorite in the Harris family, said :

"I think that most of the American girls who visit Europe return to their homes the better for their experience, and more than ever proud of their country; and, dear Aunt Margaret, I can answer for myself that I see many things in America with different eyes after my foreign travels. I am taught both ways."

"My darling, I know it of you, as I know it of myself. When I accompanied my husband to St. Petersburg, more than a quarter of a century ago, I was very 'green' and ignorant. You see, we were both poor young people, George and I, and knew nothing of society and style. He had a busy, wearing life, and I had, for some time, little to do but to look, listen, and learn; I sometimes shudder as I recollect my loud voice and painful ignorance; and now that I see myself in others, it makes me nervous when I find my own imperfections repeated in them. I know how you have profited by your advantages, all of you, my children; and if I am sometimes a little too frank, you must charge it to my love for you and your parents."

And now the servant entered, and they followed their Zenobia to lunch.

CHAPTER XXV.

A DESCENT.

ONE afternoon Henry Harris entered an old and tumbledown house in a part of Paris the most in need of, and yet the farthest removed from, the improvements of M. Haussmann. The streets were narrow and dirty; the courts and doorways swarmed with ragged children who, thin and pallid as they were, quarreled and fought, or laughed and chattered among themselves, as much at home as if in palace yards or country fields instead. Young Harris was accompanied by Lord Conyngham, and two men, of the laboring classes apparently, followed them at a little distance. The four ascended flight after flight of rickety steps, having to feel their way at times along the greasy and dilapidated walls. Doors were open on the right hand and the left, and they could not help catching sight as they went of draggled women and frowzy-headed men, sleeping, gambling, eating, talking, cooking, or washing their clothes. Once or twice they had to step over a man lying drunk or asleep in the passage-way, and as they reached the highest landing they heard loud weeping in a miserable apartment. Glancing in as they passed, they saw the cold and pinched face of a little girl lying, with a woman sobbing over her, upon the excuse for a bed. For such a poor little body there seemed to be, to their rapid glance, a singular abundance of golden hair, and Henry Harris, who had taken off his hat, said as he replaced it and went on :

"I am glad of it."

"Glad of what ?" his companion asked.

"Glad it is dead."

As it was said, the friends entered a door which Henry Harris unlocked, and were followed by the laboring men. It was a wretched place, dimly lighted from the roof, the dirty walls scrawled over with obscene designs, and in opposite corners were beds ; a table, an old chest, and a chair or two completed the misery of the scene. On one side of the room a blackened door opened into an apartment yet smaller and darker.

"Go in there," Henry Harris said to the men who had followed them, "and we will make the change as soon as possible. Make haste."

"My lord," said one of the two, "you must hallow me to protest. Hif your father, the Hearl—"

"That will do, Judkins," Lord Conyngham interrupted him. "Hold your tongue. Go !" And the valet followed his companion, who was the servant of Henry Harris, into the dismal closet.

"My man Toffski is a moujik whom I picked up in Russia years ago," the American said. "We have had some queer adventures together, and he has a power of holding his face silent as well as his tongue beyond anything I ever knew of except in the figure-head of a ship. Now, as soon as we can."

In half an hour the gentlemen had exchanged clothing with their servants, who, transformed apparently into gentlemen, but with their hats down over their eyes, had received many final charges, and departed.

"As is the case of almost everybody," Henry Harris said, "we have been under the eyes of the police since we entered Paris. Since we are neither pickpockets nor burglars, we have not been so closely watched, however, but that our men will serve as our substitutes, as they go home, at least. *We* are, you know, nothing but common laborers, not worth the watching."

The transformation was wonderful, From head to foot, cap, blouse, heavy shoes, coarse stockings, and all, the friends seemed to be but units of the masses of *ouvriers* they were soon to mingle with, mere drops of a turbid current.

"Now, my lord," the American said, "we have already considered our plans long and, I hope, thoroughly. You go with me of your own request. It will be a severe trial. To begin with, your name is Tom Perkins. Well, Tom, how goes it?"

The young nobleman shrank almost as from an insult, and then laughed. "It is only a new way of sowing wild oats," he said. "We are off on a lark, that is all. Oh, I'm all right, Jack! It *is* Jack, isn't it? Jack Peters? The fact is, I have lived exclusively upon the mere surface of things all my life. Of course," he added, seriously, "I have always known that there were depths beneath me. God knows I have seen too much of the poverty and crime of London, seen it from my club windows, or from my cab, not to know that. As you have said, however, I really know almost as little of the lives of the millions under me as if they were living in Africa instead. I can read about them, have read about them, but that is not like seeing for myself.

Lady Blanche is always urging me to fit myself to take as active a part as possible in Parliament. Well, I am going into training. Oxford and good society have done what they can. I will try the depths a little. Call me Tom or anything. When a man makes a dive into deep waters he must strip, you know."

The American looked at his friend. with pleasure. The young nobleman had laid aside, with his ordinary clothing, his dandyism of manner, also his drawl and unconscious affectation. If his haughty bearing had disappeared for the moment, his manliness was the more evident.

"If you had joined me on a hunting excursion in Africa or America, you would have had to dress roughly and fare hardly," young Harris suggested.

"Certainly. And I can stand more than you imagine; can box as well as fence, can run as well as dance. We will get along," the false Tom Perkins said, with a jaunty air. "As to my slang, I have tried it in chaffing matches among the barges up and down the Thames, and it is all that can be desired."

"Well, I think we understand each other," Jack Peters remarked. "I wish we could stoop a little more as we walked, but we would be sure to forget to do so, and we had better be natural as to that. Remember that we are engineers out of work. I *am* one, you know. When we visit Russia I intend to run a locomotive, and you are my stoker, you observe. Oh, we are in for it !"

The eyes of both sparkled. They were young, in high spirits, a little tired of society, not without ambition, and with that superfluity of energy which is wasted, in other cases, in gambling hells and worse places. Moreover, they were thoroughly satisfied that the game was worth the pursuit. Most of all, each aimed in his secret soul at winning in the end the hearty admiration and astonished approval of the woman he loved best.

"Even yet I do not fully understand Communism, day laborer as I am," Jack Peters observed. "It is increasing,

under one name and another, in France, England, Russia.
What I hate worst is that it is beginning to threaten even
America. Whatever it is, Commune, Nihilism, Socialism,
International, *Descamisados*, Society of the Russian Red
Cock, or what not, I am determined to study it as thoroughly
as I have ever done a bit of machinery. I have often crawled
through boilers, hunting for the weak places, and I am very
curious to understand these societies, these rotten places of
our social system, which threaten to destroy civilization by
their explosion. But you will have to swear off from soap,
will have to drink execrable beer, to smoke some detestable
tobacco," he suddenly added, with a smile.

"I can stand it if you can," the other laughed ; "my
stomach is as strong as my arms. Late dinners have qualified
me for everything. Go ahead."

"This room is our abode whenever we are actually going
—behind the Falls, we would say of Niagara ; through the
sewers, they would style it here in Paris," Jack Peters added. "You have a key, so have I. There are arms hidden
under the loose plank in the other room. More useful still,
we have gold in our belts, which is the best ammunition on
earth. We will make our first essay to-night. Whenever
you think fit you can give it up. And now—" and the
American lifted his hat to the other respectfully, and added,
"Good-by, my lord."

"I bid you good-by, Mr. Harris," the nobleman said as
gravely, and lifting the coarse hat upon his own head by way
of farewell.

"Why, how are you, Jack Peters ? " the nobleman added
in the next breath, and with a total change of manner.

"Bless me, but it is Tom Perkins ! " exclaimed the other,
grasping the offered hand with rude cordiality, and they
laughed and left the room together.

Some hours after, Lady Blanche was riding in her carriage accompanied by Mary Harris. A *fête* was going on, the
streets were crowded ; their horses were halted for quite a
time by the press as they passed the ruins of the Tuileries.

"Do you see him? the wretch!" Lady Blanche said to her friend in the heat of the crush.

Mary Harris glanced in the direction indicated. Two coarsely dressed workmen, their caps over their eyes, were loitering near by, and one of them had the impudence to lift his hand to his hat as he caught the eye of the haughty Englishwoman.

"I dare say they are some of the miserable creatures that destroyed this very building," she said, indignantly, as they drove on at last. "My brother would have been tempted, had he been with me, to knock him down."

"Ah, Tom, you forgot yourself that time," the other workman said to his friend.

"That is a fact. Did you see how angry she looked? Anyway," the insolent Communist added, "they did not know us."

CHAPTER XXVI.

"THE HAMMER AN' DOWN WI' 'EM."

THERE are many institutions in London which illustrate the adage that "birds of a feather flock together." The magnificent club-houses have each its own peculiarity of members, army, navy, Tory, Whigs, reform, radical, literary, and the like. So, on a greatly reduced scale, of the innumerable hostelries. Some are used almost exclusively by men connected with the press, others by traveling salesmen, "bagmen," as they are called, some by coachmen, others by valets. At some only cabmen are to be found, in others only costermongers would feel at home. Just as there are hospitals for those diseased only of the eye or the ear, the nerves or the lungs, a refuge for those affected in some one way, and for such alone, so are there certain pothouses frequented exclusively by definite classes of the otherwise unfortunate.

In one of the worst streets of London there is, for instance, an ale-house having as its sign a naked and muscular arm grasping a hammer, with the legend beneath, "Down wi' 'em." This place, familiarly known as "The hammer an' down wi' 'em," is the resort especially of workmen out of work, generally tailors and cobblers. The room opening upon the street is but a narrow entrance, with the inevitable bar upon one side, plentifully supplied with liquors, and a barmaid rosy enough and portly enough to be cut up into half a dozen ordinary damsels. Passing through this, you enter into a large room, having a low ceiling of blackened beams, the floor sanded and set out with small deal tables and chairs, the walls garnished with pictures of martyrs, such as Robert Blum, Robespierre, Blanqui, Cobbett, Tom Paine, and—with an astonished look at finding himself in such company—George Washington. At one end is a raised platform, upon which any one can sing, play on any instrument, dance, or make a speech, subject, however, to the approval of the nightly audience, an approval which had a singular facility in turning into clamorous displeasure if need be.

One foggy evening this room was crowded with guests, every man having his beer or gin before him. Among the mugs and pipes were dingy and beer-stained copies of Reynolds's "Weekly Newspaper" and other radical sheets, which —bitter as their bitterest beer, strong as their strongest tobacco, intoxicating as their worst gin—circulate by the half-million copies among the lower classes of England. At a table, and playing checkers, sat two workmen, who had dropped in on several nights before, and who had become known to the barmaid as Jack Peters and Tom Perkins. They were near the platform, and one of them kept in his mouth a short clay pipe, a mug of ale at his elbow. They had listened to a good deal of noisy discussion on previous occasions, but the interest centered to-night upon a little bald-headed cobbler, who looked as if he had been effectually weaned from soap and the breast at the same date. He had no coat, his dirty sleeves were rolled up at the elbow ; his eyes, red, small, and watery, twinkled through brass spectacles.   The two new-comers had heard frequent and hearty encomiums upon a certain " Ol' St'istics," who had been unavoidably absent before, owing to a prolonged " drunk." This was the man.   His money, and with it his liquor, had given out at last, and he was now welcomed back with enthusiasm.   Hardly a man present but urged upon him a share of his ale or tobacco.   Occasionally there had been cries of "Ol' St'istics !   Ol' St'istics !" but the clamor became so unanimous at last, knuckles, mugs banged upon the tables, and heavy feet swelling the noise with stamping, that the cobbler arose at his table, and remarked with modest self-depreciation :

"Much obleeged ; same to you.   Arter my leetle attack of—of gout—"   But his piping voice was drowned in laughter, which gave place to cries of " Take the platform, St'istics !   take the platform, ol' feller !" and he was escorted thither with an affectation of airy politeness by a dilapidated tailor.

"I have just arose," the cobbler began, "from a prolonged illness," and he indulged in the delicate cough of an invalid ; " but I will do my best.   You see I sticks sich items as I can lay my hands on against the wall before me as I works by a bit o' wax, and I hammers at my last an' larns, sews an' larns, pegs an' larns.   It's a gift, an' I'll share it.   What'll you have to-night ?"

There were various demands of " Church !" " Army !" " Ships !" " Bishops !" " R'yal family !" but the calls for " Aristocracy !" finally prevailed.

"Very good ; listen," and, closing his eyes, the public favorite repeated in a rapid, sing-song manner what he had learned by rote.   "There is, in this here England o' theirs, not *ours*, five hundred an' twenty-five nobles.   That is, twenty-eight dukes, thirty-three marquises, one hundred and ninety-four earls, fifty-two viscounts, two hundred and eighteen barons.   These robbers own an average of twenty-nine

thousing one hundred an' forty-eight acres each, an' every
highwayman of 'em plunders us on an average of twenty-
nine thousing two hundred pounds a year each." There was
a relish, almost as of savory food, in the mere mention of so
much money on the part of speaker and hearer. The cobbler smacked his lips as he added, "Anything more you
want to know?" And the oracle opened his eyes and looked
around in triumph.

"Yes, give us a bishop or two," was the cry.

"Very well." The speaker closed his eyes and chanted
from memory: "The pay of the Archbishops of York an'
Canterbury, with the Bishops of London an' Durham, is
forty-four thousing four hundred an' forty-four pound. Bishop of Ely has seving thousing pound a year; so has the
Bishop of Winchester. Eight more bishops get five thousing
a year each; an' eight smaller ones get over four thousing
pounds. One hundred and twenty-eight canons in the ca-
thedrals get one thousing a year. Any more questions?"
And the speaker waited, with his eyes closed behind his owl-
ish glasses.

"Tell us about the bigwigs," was the cry.

"Very good," the oracle replied. "The Judges of Ap-
peals gets from five to six thousing pounds · each every
year," chewing the sums as if they were so much bacon or
tobacco. "The Master of the Rolls has six thousing; the
Lord Chancellor, eleving thousing pound every year; the
Lord Chief Justice gets eight thousing; the Members of the
Privy Council, five thousing each; the Vice-Chancellors the
same; also the puisne judges, whatever that is, an' every
circuit judge the same. Any more?"

"Yes, yes; the R'yal Family," was the cry.

"Very good. An' there is a lot of 'em hangin' on to 'em.
Stewards treasurers comptrollers," the speaker rattled on,
without pause of punctuation or taking breath, "chamber-
lains vice-chamberlains lords in waiting gentlemen-at-arms
yeomen masters of the horse masters of the hounds equerries
mistresses of the robes ladies of the bed-chamber maids of

honor clerks of the robes deans physicians ordinary and extraordinary sergeant surgeons dentists chemists an' every man an' woman of 'em is paid from one up to two thousing pound a year!" And there the breath of the speaker gave out. He rolled out the amounts with gusto, his hearers having evidently a delight in the naming even of so much money, as if in the glitter and rattle of that many shillings, crowns, and sovereigns poured out before them.

"But the princes? the princes?" vociferated the delighted crowd; and the cobbler, whose memory was really as accurate as it was wonderful, went on with rapid, monotonous chant: "Duchess of York has five thousing pound; Duke of Cambridge, twelve thousing; Duchess of Mecklenburg-Strelitz, three thousing; Duchess of Cambridge, six thousing; Prince Leopold, fifteen thousing; Duke of Connaught, twenty thousing; Princess Louise, six thousing; Duke of Edinburgh, twenty-five thousing; Princess Alice, six thousing; Crown Princess of Germany, eight thousing; Princess of Wales, ten thousing; Prince of Wales, one hundred an' nine thousing! The Queen," and here the speaker drew in a deep breath, and the audience held mug and pipe suspended to hear, "the Queen, she gets four—hundred—an'—sixty—*thousing*—pound a year!"

The words were slowly drawn out, and delivered with the utmost force. It was his oratorical climax, and he left the platform. There was a deep and ominous silence. Tom Perkins and Jack Peters began a new game of checkers, conscious of that something about them which makes the air heavy as with thunder slowly gathering toward a tempest.

"Sots, knaves, fools! bah!" Tom Perkins said, under his breath, to his companion. But the American did not reply, except with a warning look. "Who has made them such?" he was asking of himself. The audience was composed of men, not one of whom but would have fought for England in battle with undying pluck. The visitor glanced over the crowd. Through the tobacco-smoke the heads of the men loomed sullen and threatening; they were chained in, but they were mastiffs, manacled by their own ignorance and sensual indulgence, wreaking their vengeance often upon wife and child in horrible brutalities.

"But whose business has it been to educate them?" the American demanded of himself. "There is no better material on earth. It is of such stuff that America has been largely made. Whose duty is it to mold it into manhood? Can a man lift himself into the air by a grip upon his own waistband? Can a man regenerate himself by his own hand? My father made himself what he is," he added; "my mother made herself what she is; but they had the help toward it of the American church, school, press, ballot. Thank God that the poorest in England, the most depraved in America too, are being alike swept toward

> ' The one far-off divine event
> To which the whole creation moves.' "

"By George! this thing ain't goin' to last always," a shock-headed man took his pipe, at length, from his lips to remark, in a voice heard by all, through the silence.

"Take the platform, Harry!" There was new enthusiasm; and, in answer to the demand, the man laid down mug and pipe and mounted the low stage.

"I hain't got no speech to make to-night," he said, "but I'm cur'us to find what you men are thinkin' about. Now I want to know what every man in this room believes is to mend our troubles. Speak up. This is what is called a free country. As you all know, I'm a Cheap Jack, an' I'll mark you off as you speak. This country is goin', goin', goin'! Who names a cure for it?" He repeated it, as if in his cart and auctioneering off his wares. The bids came slowly, now from this corner of the room, and then from that.

"Abolition of House of Lords? Very good. Disestablishment of the Church? Certainly. Educating the masses? Perhaps so. Australia? Thank you. Yes. Peabody lodging-houses? Hah! Trades-unions? Humph! Coöperative stores? Nonsense! Down with the police? Of course.

Abolish army and navy? Yes. Any other gentleman a bid to make for this rotten, old, tumble-down, tyrannical Government of ours? Division of the land? Yes; but how? Down with the Queen? *Much* obliged to you, sir, and yes; if you'll be the man to bell the cat. Revolution? I'm agreeable."

At this juncture the American thought best to lay a strong grasp upon the arm of the one with whom he was playing checkers. It was but too evident that Tom Perkins was becoming very angry, and his friend was glad when, in a pause which followed, the Cheap Jack said, striking an attitude:

"Listen, it is the Poet Laureate speaks, which his name is Tennyson, Al-fe-red Tennyson:

> 'Slowly comes a hungry people,
> As a lion, creepin' nigher,
> Glares at one that nods and winks
> Behind a slowly dyin' fire.'"

To the astonishment of Tom Perkins, his companion, in a loud, clear voice, completed the lines:

> "'Yet I doubt not through the ages
> One increasing purpose runs,
> And the thoughts of men are widened
> With the process of the suns.'"

There was something in the fresh, cheery, decided tones which caused every man to look up with sharp suspicion.

"And who the divvel are you?" the Cheap Jack demanded at last.

"Who am I?" And Jack Peters arose and put on his hat. "I am an engineer, and I am an American."

———

CHAPTER XXVII.

YANKEE ADVICE.

WHEN Jack Peters announced himself as an American, it was as if a gust of wind, fresh and bracing, had suddenly blown upon the befuddled customers of the "Hammer and down wi' 'em." There were some moments of silence, during which the fumes of beer and of tobacco seemed to lift, for the instant at least, from the audience. The Cheap Jack was the first to speak.

"From America, are you? Well, what do *you* bid as *your* dose for our troubles?"

The one spoken to had not intended to say anything when he came in. Like his companion, his sole object had been to study the disaffected and dangerous classes of England and other countries as thoroughly as possible, and he shook his head and kept his seat. But there were cries of "Yankee!" "Yankee!" until he arose.

"My friends," he began, but now the cry was "Platform!" "Platform!" and he stepped upon it, and stood there for a moment in his coarse clothing. His face was bright, open, clear; his eye cool and intelligent; from his first word there was, as in his father's shops in Russia, an instant distinction between him and them of master and men.

"I have no wish to intrude upon you," he said. "It is your country, not mine. But I *can* give you one cure for your disease. You say times are hard, your Government oppressive; very well, go to Canada, Australia, or—I will give you one big pill for your ills—go to America."

The Cheap Jack had resumed his table, his mug, and his pipe by this time, and the American had the platform to himself.

"Look at it, men," he continued, "you can get land over the water for next to nothing an acre. We Yankees are beginning to feed all Europe. Help us to do it. You will be well paid for it. Listen; I happen to have with me the prices paid for work in Europe, say in Belgium, as compared with those paid in New York," and he read rapidly as follows :

OCCUPATIONS.	Belgium.	New York.
Bricklayers........................	$6 00	$12 to $15
Masons...........................	6 00	12 to 18
Carpenters.......................	5 40	9 to 12
Gasfitters........................	5 40	10 to 14
Painters..........................	4 20	10 to 16
Plasterers	5 40	10 to 15
Plumbers.........................	6 00	12 to 18
Blacksmiths......................	4 40	10 to 14
Bakers...........................	4 40	5 to 8
Cabinetmakers....................	4 80	9 to 13
Saddlemakers	4 80	12 to 15
Tinsmiths........................	4 80	10 to 14
Laborers	3 00	6 to 7

" That is plain enough," he went on ; " now look at what food costs comparatively :

PROVISIONS.	Belgium.	New York.
Bread, per pound.................	4 to 5 cents.	4½ cents.
Beef, "	16 to 20 "	8 to 16 "
Veal, "	16 to 20 "	8 to 24 "
Mutton, "	16 to 20 "	9 to 16 "
Pork, "	16 to 20 "	8 to 16 "
Lard, "	20 "	10 to 12 "
Butter, "	20 to 50 "	25 to 32 "
Cheese, "	20 to 25 "	12 to 15 "
Coffee, "	30 to 40 "	20 to 30 "
Sugar, "	15 to 20 "	8 to 10 "

" But it don't say anything about beer," the Cheap Jack said when he was through, and there was a laugh.

" Out west of New York," the speaker continued, " everything is even cheaper ; now—"

" You are talking too rapidly," his friend said to him in a low voice ; " go slower."

"That's a fact," Jack Peters added, as he saw the slow, dull faces of the crowd before him. Evidently they wanted to know what to do. America had long been to most of them a vast Canaan of milk and honey, but a wilderness of water lay between, and where was their Moses?

"All very good, Mr. Yankee," Cheap Jack called out, being the sharpest of them, from his seat, "but how are we goin' to get us there? Where's your balloon? Is it a-waitin' at the door?"

There was a laugh at this, in which the American joined.

"Before I answer that," he said, good-humoredly, "let me tell you another thing. In my country the Government, from constable up to President, is made by the people, from the people, *for* the people. Now, it is in working-people we are most interested, because our nation is made up of that sort chiefly. On that account our Government made our consuls everywhere find out and report upon the condition of workmen all over the world as compared with those in America. Then the reports were digested into four facts. I have them here on a bit of paper, which I want our friend, Old Statistics, to stick up over his bench and to get by heart. Shall I read them?"

There were cries of "Out wi' it!" "Let's hear!" "Read away," and Jack Peters read aloud, slowly and distinctly, as follows:

"All reports from over the world prove these startling things:

"1. That wages in the United States are double those of Belgium, Denmark, France, and England; three times those of Germany, Italy, and Spain, and four times those of the Netherlands.

"2. That the prices of the necessaries of life are lower in the United States than in Europe, and that the laborer in the United States, were he satisfied with the scanty and miserable fare upon which the European laborer must live, can purchase like food for less money than it can be purchased in Europe.

"3. That the French working-people, with far less wages, are happier than the working-people of Great Britain, who receive the highest wages in Europe, on account of the steadiness and economical habits of the former, and the strikes, drinking habits, and consequent recklessness of the latter.

"4. That more misery results from strikes, drinking, socialism, and communism in England and in Germany than from all other causes combined, hard times included."

The company put the information into their pipes and smoked it in a slow and pondering fashion.

"But you haven't told us how to get there," the Cheap Jack cried out at last. "Telegraph *me* over to begin with. I'm willin'."

"I will tell you how to get there," Jack Peters said, good-naturedly, "but it is not by a balloon any more than by a telegraph. There are plenty of ships to put you over for a matter of five pounds. But don't stop in New York when you get there; another five pounds will whirl you a thousand or two miles west. It won't hurt you to have another five pounds in your pouch then to begin on."

"Fifteen pound!" The Cheap Jack but expressed the feeling of the others. "Where's the fifteen pound to come from? Got it in your pocket? Give us a hold of it."

"What can you do here?" Jack Peters demanded in return. "The French may go into revolutions; Englishmen don't straighten things in a rush; they move slowly. As for the French—"

But here there was an interruption.

"Sare," cried a voice from a back seat, "you sall not insult my countree. Behold me! I am of the glorious Commune—"

"Sit down!" the American thundered; "I will be done in a moment, and you can say all you want to."

"Down, Frenchy, down!" arose from all sides. "Go on, Yankee, go on!" And the Gaul was silenced for the moment, but all present were becoming excited. Perhaps the American, being a young man, was more so than he knew.

"I honor France and the French," he said, "but there are two sets of scoundrels there who have done their best to destroy it. They are to the French people what to the Seine is its mud at the bottom and its froth at the top. Louis Napoleon and his *chauvins* were the bloody foam of a time. But the mud, the mire—" Here the Frenchman bounced to his feet; the American looked at him coolly, and added: "The mud, which, alas! is always there, is the Communist and Red Republican."

Before the words were out of his lips the impulsive Frenchman had stationed himself half way down toward the speaker, and was talking vehemently.

"It is not so!" he exclaimed. "*Voilà!* behold me! I am of de Commune! France moves de universe, and we? It is we who *mettre en mouvement*, move France. Who took de Bastile? Who cut off de head of Capet, him you call Louis XVI? Who drove, *enfoncer*, de nobles from France? Who *mettre à l'envers*, upset you call him, de Pope? Who scared away de priests, whish! like a flock of *polisson*, no, crow?—*merle*, what you call him? blackbirds? Who fought wid all de world under Kleber, Hoche? Who made Charles Dix, Charles X you call him, *s'enfuir, s'élancer, se precipiter*, cut, what you call it? his leetle stick? Who ran Louis Philippe out of Paris wid his blue *parapluie*, what you call it? umbrella under his knee, no, his elbow, his arm? Who voted *dechéance* against Louis Napoleon? It is de Red Republicans do de work. So here in your Angleterre. You talk of your beef; bah! of your leetle pound; your *gages, salaire*, wages; your meeserable leetle *poche*, pocket; bah! Behold me! *Lever les yeux à moi! voila!*"

The communist was to the burly Englishmen around him as a terrier is among bull-dogs. His face and head were a whirlwind of hair, which apparently had never known the despotism of a comb; his hairy bosom appeared through the

6

red flannel of the shirt he wore ; his ferret-like eyes flashed
with the fires of absinthe ; his long, lean arms gesticulated in
such a manner that the beer-drinkers about him had to dodge
and duck their heads continually to avoid being struck.

"No, sare !" he vociferated, turning upon the American,
who stood looking at him as a sane man does upon a lunatic,
"no, sare, it is not a question of beef and meeserable what
you call ? pork. It is blood, *sang*, we need in dis, dis *bête
comme une oie*, dis stupid England ; blood, bloo-d-d-d ! It
is sword, fire, barricade ! *aux armes!* What we shall have
is r-r-r-evolution !" and the word rolled from his lips like
the rattle of a kettledrum. To his astonishment, there followed upon it a roar of laughter. He was no more to those
present than a monkey. For a moment he looked around in
astonishment. Then, " *Cochon!* English hogs !" he shouted, and walked out with gestures of profound disgust, which
awakened another peal of laughter.

"No," the American said, with a smile, as the noise ceased,
"we English and Americans don't right our wrongs in *that*
way. But now," he added, as the audience settled itself
again to its tobacco and drink, "I will say one last thing, and
sit down."

By this time the low-ceiled, dingy room was densely
crowded, many others having heard what was going on and
pressed their way in. The air was so dense with smoke
from the pipes, so foul with the odors of the unwashed customers and their, in many cases, steaming tumblers of rum
and gin, that even Jack Peters could not endure it.

"Let me say one word more," he went on. "You can't
raise the twenty pounds or so to take you over the water?
Our friend with the wonderful memory has told us what the
Church and the aristocracy cost. Friends, you are under
the cruel dominion of a master who costs you every year far
more than Queen, bishops, and nobles. Listen ; do you know
what your liquors cost you? One hundred and forty—not
thousands—*millions* of pounds a year ! That is seven hundred millions of our dollars ! How much your tobacco costs

in addition I don't happen to know. Now, if every man would but save up his outlay—"

But the hearers, as he proceeded, were in no mood for that. "We don't want no teetotal talk here," cried at last a shrill voice from the rear. It was the portly barmaid, who was at the door looking in, and there was a murmur of assent. The American glanced around upon the sodden faces, and stepped sadly off from the platform. His friend arose, and the two men went toward the door, from which the barmaid had disappeared.

Unluckily, the burly Cheap Jack had taken too much liquor. Moreover, the last speaker had broken in upon his eloquence.

"I say, stop there !" he called after the departing men. They paid no heed and pressed on, for the atmosphere was suffocating. But the Cheap Jack was a bully and a pugilist, and had resolved upon reëstablishing his importance in the "Hammer an' down wi' 'em."

"Hold on !" He had followed them, and now laid his hand roughly upon the shoulder of Tom Perkins. For an ordinary workman that person seemed to be singularly sensitive. On the instant he had turned around, had struck the Cheap Jack between the eyes with his utmost force, and the brawny orator of the ale-house was lying flat upon his back among his astonished friends. In the same moment the American had put his arm around his companion, and, laying down a half sovereign upon the bar in payment of their bill as he passed out, had drawn him into the street.

"We can not fight all the hammers in the 'Down wi' 'em' at once," he remonstrated. "If you are to go with me into the depths of communism in Germany, France, Russia, you must be more prudent, my lord—Tom, I mean. Besides, yours is a poor way to put down communism.

"And yet," he said to himself the next moment, "a swift knock-down is the only way England has discovered to remedy the discontent of its dangerous classes thus far." And he murmured under his breath :

"'Knowledge comes, but wisdom lingers,
　　And I linger on the shore;
　And the individual withers,
　　And the world is more and more.'"

CHAPTER XXVIII.

DIVINE PATIENCE.

HENRY HARRIS, like his father, was often called away by business, as Lord Conyngham was by pleasure, and the absence of these from Paris had passed unnoticed. One morning after his return the American was loitering with his sister through the Exposition. As if by a common but unconscious attraction, they found themselves standing at last beside the bust which had so arrested their attention. No one else seemed to be specially interested in it, but the brother said :

"It grows upon me. You know I am not enthusiastic about people in general; it is only for a person now and then that I form an attachment, not often. I like a person either very much or not at all. It is so of music; there are certain airs of which I never grow weary : all other music is to me as the rattle of wheels along the street or the roar of the winds. Now, I like this sad and patient face. There is a certain something of home and heart in it of which one no more wearies than he does of the air or of the light."

"So it is with me," his sister said ; "but I think we like it the more because of its contrast to the noisy, shifting, brilliant scene around. It rests one. This peaceful head is patience in marble. Listen, and I will give you the same patience in music," and in a low, clear voice Mary Harris repeated Wordsworth's lines :

"'The little hedgerow birds,
That peck along the road, regard him not.

He travels on, and in his face, his step,
His gait, is one expression; every limb,
His look and bending figure, all bespeak
A man who does not move with pain, but moves
With thought. He is insensibly subdued
To settled quiet; he is one by whom
All effort seems forgotten; one to whom
Long patience hath such mild composure given,
That patience now doth seem a thing of which
He hath no need. He is' by nature led
To peace so perfect, that the young behold
With envy, what the old man hardly feels.' "

"Yes," her brother assented, "it expresses it exactly. Do you know, Mary, it is the accuracy of anything which pleases us; *accuracy*, whether it be in a poem, a painting, a statue, or a machine."

"You mean it must be the expression," his sister consented, "of truth; it is that which strikes and pleases us most in the face, in the tones even, of a friend. But I wonder," she added, glancing around, "where the artist is. I have been here twice when you were away, but could not find her."

Henry Harris made no reply, and they soon after left the grounds. Unreserved as the family generally were in their intercourse with one another, each member had none the less some subjects upon which silence was an instinct. In fact, there are matters upon which one may think and feel, act also, with deepest purpose, and yet refuse to discuss even with one's self. It was so with Henry Harris in regard to the artist of whom his sister had spoken. He had seen her but once. There was no probability of his falling in love with her, since, and to a greater degree than his own family suspected, he was enamored with Lady Blanche. The Englishwoman was to him the flower of her sex. Not even Lord Conyngham could appreciate better than her brother did the loveliness of Mary Harris, but Lady Blanche was different. Her pride of race was to her, in his eyes, like in-

visible wings; it both lifted her and gave to her a flight and
a force above any woman he had hitherto known. "It is
absurd," he felt in his silent soul, "to compare her with such
a thing, and yet she is like, yes, a perfect engine. And gentle and beautiful as she seems, she will crush whatever ven-
tures—presumes—too much upon her gentleness, as an engine
crushes an insect upon the rail."

But it was not an agreeable way of looking at things,
and the young machinist turned to other thoughts. With
all his impetuosity, he was wary. From boyhood he had
rambled about among the whirling wheels and trip-hammers
of his father's shops, among the white-hot masses of iron being lifted and swung this way and that by derricks, among
the showers of flying sparks and spray of molten metal, until
he had grown into unceasing caution as into the habit of his
life. "So long," he reasoned, " as I keep steady watch over
myself I need fear nothing else. But I love her the more
that it is so dangerous a thing to do, and—we will see ! "

With all this he had the interest in Isidore Atchison
which one skilled mechanic has in another. That she was a
woman, that she had made a perfect work of art instead of a
machine, interested him that much the more. He had gone
repeatedly to the spot where he had first seen her, but in
vain. At last, applying in the proper quarters, and obtaining her address, one afternoon he slowly climbed the many
flights of stairs which led to her apartments. The instant
he learned the part of Paris in which she lived, he had
guessed as to her poverty ; the sight of the house, the interior, worse than the exterior, confirmed his fears.

"She is very poor; I must therefore be specially respectful," he said, as he knocked at last at the door. A voice
from within called him to enter, and he took in the whole
situation at a glance as he did so. Pillowed into a sitting
position upon the bed was the old man whose bust he had
admired. The dim light fell upon the silvered head from
above, bringing out the delicate lines, the downward bend
of the neck, the indescribable aspect of peace—it was the

old man who idealized the marble, and not the marble the
man. Upon a cushion on his knees before him in his bed
lay a block of wood, but the flowers upon it seemed to be so
arrested by some winter that they could not unfold as yet.
The hand which held the tool was thin and feeble, but it
persisted, as did the steady patience of the eyes.

Upon the other side of the small apartment the daughter
stood at work upon something at a stand. With the entrance of their visitor the girl had thrown a wet cloth over
it, and now turned to meet him. For the instant she looked
like a beautiful boy instead, for a paper cap was perched upon
her head, and an apron of brown linen covered her from neck
to feet. But her eyes were there, her features so like, and
yet unlike, those of her father. As to that, had she been
wholly invisible, there was that modulation in her voice
which is to speech what carving is to a statue.

"Pardon my intrusion," Henry Harris said, his hat in his
hand, and as if speaking to Lady Blanche in her diamonds,
"but I feared lest I should be anticipated by some purchaser.
I greatly admire and wish to buy, if you will be so kind, the
marble which you exhibit," and he mentioned its location
and number. His manner was as cold as it was respectful,
even when he added other words in praise of the object.
"With your permission, sir," he added, with an inclination
of his head to the father, "will you allow me?" and he became intent upon the unfinished carving while the daughter
slipped silently into her little room. Nor did he seem to
have observed that she had changed her dress, and relieved
herself of the covering which had protected her abundant
hair, when she returned.

It is one function of perfect breeding to place people at
ease with whomsoever they are thrown. Moreover, persons
of the same grade recognize a friend as well as an equal in
each other, although their meeting is but for the moment.
In a little while Henry Harris had taken a seat, but throughout it was he to whom favor was extended ; obligation was
upon his side, not theirs. He made one mistake. "Will

you permit me ?" he asked at last, rising and taking a step toward the covered stand.

"Pardon me, no." The young lady had interposed herself in the same instant with a smile, but, somehow, her No was as decided as any he had ever heard, and he also smiled and resumed his seat. Nor did it take many words to complete his business.

"I regret," he said, "but I will be unable to purchase the marble unless I can have it for—" And he mentioned a sum which brought a flush of rapture into the face of the girl.

"And now she is like Carlo Dolci's Bacchante," the father said, forgetful of all else.

The daughter colored and then laughed. "It is so much more than I had expected," she began.

"It is less than its actual value," the purchaser said, gravely. "Of course, it will remain at present where it is. You will allow me to make sure of my bargain by paying for it," and he handed the crisp bills to the girl, "and to thank you," he added, with feeling, "since it is a present I am making my mother."

A few moments after, he had given his card, had bowed, and departed. As his footsteps died upon the stairway, the girl had fallen upon her knees beside the bed, her face in her father's lap as he sat, the bank-notes lying upon the floor beside her. If she was an artist, she was also a woman, and was weeping as if her heart would break. Her father laid his left hand upon her head, his eyes were closed, his lips trembled. But he remained an artist; for when, after a while, his daughter lifted her face, her eyes sparkling through her tears, her disordered hair about her face, he held his head a little upon one side, examined her critically, and murmured :

"Fra Angelico's Magdalen, only better."

But his Magdalen was on her feet and laughing. "And now," she said, "now ? What is it ?" rapidly arranging her hair. "Wine ? Jelly ? Yes, and white bread for you, father, and roast beef, grapes, medicine, vegetables. Oh, yes, and

that photograph of the Murillo picture you have wanted so !
O father," she said, "I am *so* glad ! "

" Niobe ? " the old man demanded of himself, as she gave
way again to tears. "Yes, and Aurora ? " as she laughed
once more, with rosy face. "Yes, the Aurora of Guido."

" That is because morning has dawned. But I must go,"
she added, basket in hand, and she kissed him and went out,
only to open the door again. " You are sure you are not
afraid to be left alone with *her ?* " nodding her head toward
the covered stand. "Ah, old lady," she laughed, shaking
her finger at the same object, "I'm done with *you!* "

Her father was thinking only of his daughter, she seemed
so happy ; his eyes were fastened upon her radiant face.

" Euphrosyne," he said ; but she shut the door and ran
down-stairs.

CHAPTER XXIX.

AMERICAN GIRLS.

ONE afternoon a number of the young lady friends of
Mary Harris were assembled in the rooms of that family at
their hotel. Virginia Jossellyn and Ellen Ellsworth were
among them, and, having been riding out and shopping together, they were all laughing now and chatting with each
other at a great rate. In a word, they were in that flutter
of high health and overflowing spirits which brings back
their own youth again to the old, even to see and to hear.
They were "training," as Miss Ellsworth calls it, "in a gale,"
as Miss Jossellyn said ; and their merry malice seemed to be
turned upon Mary Harris.

" She tries to make us think that she does not care," cried
the New England belle. "See how placid and peaceful she
pretends to be. Ahem ! How does your ladyship feel this
afternoon ? " And the lively girl courtesied before her with
mock reverence. She herself was as slight as a willow-wand,

as frail almost and as fair as a wreath of mist. But it was
a wreath of mist over Niagara, for, with sparkling eyes and
cheeks of the hue of the inner lips of a conch-shell, the lovely
girl was in unceasing motion from morning until night,
laughing, talking, singing, riding, walking; it was almost as
if she did not know what it was to be weary or to sleep.
The Americans in Paris had seen many like her at home, but
the sober Spaniards, the stolid Germans, even the mercurial
French, watched her with wonder. They could not understand how one so slight could possess such vitality, such
will.

"Ellen dear," Mary Harris said, "you were wild enough
in old Massachusetts, and the air of Paris has made you more
so. Do you know what Hop Fun, the mandarin, said of you
last week?"

"No; what was it?" the other demanded. "Was it a
compliment? Does he want to make me a mandariness?
But, no," and she put out one of her feet; "no; not even to
oblige him could I consent to have my feet squeezed into a
nutshell. What was it, Mary?"

"When he saw you, dear, you chanced to be—as you
always are—laughing and talking with some friends. In
this case it was under an American flag, which was flutter-
ing its silken folds of blue and gold, of white and red, in a
strong breeze. Henry was near the mandarin, and the old
Chinaman caught his eye, pointed first to the flag, and then
to you, and said, 'Kong-fu-tse say, Too muchee shine is
worse than dark.'"

"He is right, Ellen," Miss Jossellyn said; "I wonder you
do not get tired. See how quiet I am."

"Oh, I am a blonde; you are a brunette," laughed the
New England beauty, looking admiringly at the rounded and
olive loveliness of her friend. For Virginia Jossellyn was
plump as a partridge, but beautifully formed, with eyes large
and dark, lips full and scarlet, and a certain languid grace
in her manner, in strong contrast to the swallow-like rapidity
with which her friend moved and spoke. Her very tones

were slow and sweet, and, unless greatly excited, she seemed to yield herself without exertion to the mere current of things. "And yet," Henry Harris had said to his sister one day, "the dark, sluggish, almost indolent beauty of your friend is like that of a sleeping tempest. Only let there be cause enough, and you would find that even Miss Ellen would be but as a frightened bird before the tropical passion of our Southern belle."

But Mary Harris had kept this, as she did many things, to herself. Perhaps her long residence in Europe had given breadth and balance to her character, in addition even to that which she had inherited from her father, whom she so much resembled. Like her mother also, and her brother, an unaffected common sense was the basis of her disposition. In father and brother it was granite ; in her it was as crystal. She merely smiled, therefore, as Ellen turned from Virginia and renewed hostilities.

"Your ladyship ! O Mary, think of having a footman to call out before you, 'Lady Conyngham !' Ah, but does it not sound lovely ? Wealth is nothing to it. A title clothes you more richly than velvet or Valenciennes. I would rather wear it than the finest diamonds. Would you not, Virginia ?"

"I prefer being not even a Duchess of Plymouth—what an insignificant creature *he* is !—but a grand duchess, my child," the brunette said. "Lord Conyngham is a handsome gentleman ; not that he is," she added, "more of a nobleman in his appearance than your brother, Mary. But how will you manage with Lady Blanche, my dear ? She should not rule *me*, I can assure you."

"Oh, please be quiet, girls ! How can you talk so much nonsense ?" the victim said, with a laugh and a blush, "and when you know that there is not a word of truth in—" But at this moment the servant handed her a card, and she said to him, "Tell Lord Conyngham that I will be down in a few moments," while from her friends around her arose a mocking chorus of "Oh, my !" "I thought so !" "There is no truth in it ; certainly not !"

"You will have to excuse me, girls," Mary Harris said, as they seized her tauntingly upon the one side and the other. "He told me at the opera, last night, that he would call to-day. It is because he is about being absent from Paris, I believe. I dare say it is merely to say good-by." But her remarks were received with utter incredulity, and she had to break from her friends with a laugh, shaking her head at them threateningly, as she escaped to her own room.

Apart from the mere circumstance and drapery of his rank and social usages, Lord Conyngham was as simple and thoroughly good and true as any young man who toiled at the moment in his shirt-sleeves in the fields of Vermont or Wisconsin, or in any factory or counting-room in London or Edinburgh. It had been a great advantage to him that his mother had been an excellent woman. And yet, as has been said, Earl Dorrington almost regretted that his daughter Blanche had not been his son and heir instead. It was not because Blanche was so much his superior intellectually as that she had more of the pride of race. Not that Lord Conyngham had not exhibited a greater degree of hauteur than his sister. In him it had been excessive, had amounted to insolence even ; but this was because it had been largely an affectation, a mere mannerism. As it had been a sort of raiment which he had put on, so was it a something which he could put off also, while pride was with his sister a something in the blood and bone. His association with the Harris household had done him a world of good. It was something like the enjoyment he had found when he laid aside his jewelry and his broadcloth to row on the river, or to play cricket, or as when he had laid aside his tight-fitting and fashionable attire to put on a soft hat and flannel for a cruise in his yacht. There were times for Hyde Park, the Queen's drawing-rooms, the ball, Parliament, the club, the opera, and the like, but he had a natural preference for September and game, for dogs and gun, for nature and for Americans.

"I enjoy being with them," he informed his father in regard to his new friends.

"Assuredly so," remarked the old Earl, "and they are most respectable persons ; exceedingly wealthy, I learn. Miss Harris is a charming young lady, I have observed. I do not object to your associating with them, Alfred, up to a certain point, as I have before remarked—a certain point, my son."

As to Mary Harris, she had felt, and from their first acquaintance, almost as much at ease with him as with her brother. Mere girl as she was, strange to say, a certain almost maternal feeling arose in her in regard to him. He was to her, as she came into the parlor on the occasion now spoken of, simply a noble-looking, high-spirited, honest-hearted young fellow, who loved her very sincerely. In all his acquaintance there was not a lady who was more thoroughly a lady, and yet there was no gentleman of his acquaintance, not even Henry Harris, with whom he felt as perfectly free as he did with her.

" Thank Heaven, I do not have to talk with you about the weather," he told her now. "Nor about either opera or Exposition, unless I want to. One does become tired, too, of the trashy compliments. Must I compliment you? How can I?" he said, as she laughed at the idea, "when you are so immeasurably above all compliment. Miss Mary," he added, seriously, " I can not tell you how very much, *very much—*"

"No compliments, my lord," she laughingly interrupted, and, in answer to her questions, he was led off into speaking at last of himself and of his plans more freely than he had ever done with his sister. No wonder. Mary Harris took really a deeper interest in him than any other had ever done. She had drawn from him long before this the story of his life at Harrow and afterward at Oxford. Now he began, encouraged by her, to speak of his efforts in Parliament.

"My sister is eager for me to take an active part," he said at last, "in the questions of the day, but her time is naturally occupied with other matters. Besides, she looks at affairs only from her point of view as a woman and as a member of the Peerage. It is even worse with my father.

He is blind to impending dangers. I tell him that he is like
Louis XVI when he refused to see the awful times which
were coming upon him ; like Charles X, of France ; like
Louis Philippe ; like poor Louis Napoleon; he *would not*
see."

"I suppose the Earl explains that revolutions happen only
in France," the lady said.

"Assuredly so ! " her companion laughed. "In and out
of France it is, he thinks, only idealists who fret and threat-
en. People may edit papers, publish books, make speeches,
roar and rave and rant as much as they please, but England,
he thinks, is rooted off to itself in the ocean like everlasting
rock. Whatever billows may sweep over all the globe beside, they will merely perish in foam when they dash upon
our shores. It is not the thing to talk to a young lady
about, but," and in his eagerness he arose to say it, " it does
seem to me that we may have trouble some of these days.
I am a Tory, like my father, but that rascal Beaconsfield is a
charlatan. His imperial policy is brilliant, but I don't like
it any more than I do his trashy romances. To me it is all
mere gewgaw, flimsy as the spangles upon the gauze of a
rope-dancer. Think of the questions pressing upon us—Irish
Home Rule, education of the masses who are beginning to
govern us, Communism, war in Afghanistan, probably, and
in Africa ; eternal strife with Russia—"

"And disestablishment," the lady suggested.

"Precisely. I am not much of a religious man—it is not
in my line—but," said the Englishman, "things are getting
into a horrible mess. They have upset the Irish Church.
Next the Scotch establishment must go. As sure as you live,
although it is a dreadful thing to say, the English Church
will be disestablished. I am not a saint, yet it is a frightful
thing to have our Christianity, our religion, you know, come
down with a crash ; it is like the end of the world ! "

There was such alarm in the face of her visitor that Mary
Harris could have smiled. She hastened, instead, to describe
to him how, in America, religion only flourished so much

the more by reason of its separation from the state. He listened with deep interest.

"I thank you," he said, evidently relieved ; "but I hope I may be hanged if I ever looked at it in that light before."

"Your father told me," Mary Harris added, "that you had an ancestor in the Crusades, that another led England in its wars against Spain long ago, that your house has always had some one man of mark in its campaigns with France, Russia, in Africa, Asia—wherever it has fought. One of the barons at Runnymede, too, bore your name. Your father is proud of his line, but he believes in sitting still, in controlling matters as by his mere weight, while you—"

"Intend to take an active part, yes," her companion added for her, catching fire from her eyes, "and I thank you for what you say."

"My brother has been studying up China of late," Mary Harris said when at last her visitor arose, after a long visit, to take leave, "and he says that the Chinese have what is called a classic dialect, a kind of dead language, never used except on occasions of ceremony. You can not tell how glad I am that we," it was said archly, "can sometimes do without it. You can keep *your* classic Chinese, my lord," she laughed as she gave him her hand in parting, "until you are conversing with your queen."

"I am conversing with her now," Lord Conyngham said, as he bowed and withdrew.

It may have been because their flame was fed upon more substantial fuel than is common, but when they separated it was with a glow of satisfaction as deep as it was pure.

CHAPTER XXX.

HOP FUN.

AMONG the machinery on exhibition in the Exposition was an engine with certain improvements, which Henry Harris had, with his father's help, himself manufactured for the occasion. The young inventor often visited it, and was as much delighted with its movement, swift yet smooth, as a poet would have been with the cadence of his first sonnet. One morning, as he paused beside it for a moment, a voice from the bystanders fell upon his ear:

"Too muchee fast!"

Looking around, he saw that it was a Chinaman whom he had often observed before about the buildings. He wore a crystal button upon the top of his conical cap, denoting his high rank as a mandarin. His tunic and trousers were of the costliest silks, and so small was he that he stood in serious need of the soles, thick and white, of his boat-like shoes. But that which brought a smile to the lips of the American was his face, which was peculiar even for a Chinese. It was not that the color thereof was yellow, the nose flat, the cheekbones prominent and wide apart, the eyes small and oblique, the mouth a mere slit in the flesh and without any fullness of lips, the queue reaching almost to the ground down his back, nor that the finger-nails were like quills at the end of each finger, long and white, and curiously curved. The thing which struck Henry Harris most was that the face of the Chinaman was as much without expression as if it had been a pasteboard mask. The young man had met multitudes of the inhabitants of the Flowery Kingdom, especially when sent by his father upon errands to the region of the Amoor River, which separates Russia from China, but he had seen none whose face was altogether as wooden as in this instance.

"The others were more or less compelled to exert themselves," he reasoned with himself upon the spot.. "This man is, they say, very rich. Like a turtle, he can repose within his shell in peace. But why, then, should he have come to Paris?"

"Too muchee fast!" the mandarin repeated, coming nearer to the machine and its inventor.

"Why do you think so?" asked the American.

"Kong-fu-tse say, Straws fly about; iron lies still."

It was said with a certain metallic distinctness of articulation as of an automaton, and with mechanical movement the critic walked slowly away.

A few nights afterward Henry Harris observed the mandarin ascending the steps of the Grand Opera House, and was careful to secure a seat as near him as he could. During the music and splendor, the merriment and passion of the opera, the American watched with interest the face of his neighbor. Had the Chinaman been a caryatid of stone, he could not have sat more still; the notes of the singers, the crash of the orchestra, the outbursts of applause, breaking against him as the sea against rock. He must have been aware none the less of the interest in him of the other, for as young Harris went slowly out after the performance was ended, he heard the automatic words at his elbow:

"Too muchee squall! Kong-fu-tse say, The wind howl, the ass bray, the wise man is hushup."

On inquiry the day after at the Bodega, the American learned, in addition to what he already knew, that the Chinaman was a statesman from Pekin whose name was Hop Fun. Notwithstanding his dwarfish size and stolid appearance, he was known to be one of the shrewdest of men. Certain pirates had rifled some French merchant ships near Peiho, and Hop Fun was employed by Prince Kung to settle with the French Government a question as to the measure of indemnity. It was this, and not the Exposition, which was supposed to have brought him to Paris at that time.

But, like everybody else, Henry Harris met too many remarkable people every day to think again of the Chinaman, until one afternoon, when with his sister he chanced to be standing before a picture in the Art Department of the Exposition.

"Yonder," Mary explained to him, pointing to figures in the background of the painting, "is Egistheus, who has supplanted Agamemnon in the affections of Clytemnestra, his wife. That is the false woman beside him. This girl who is advancing toward us is Electra. She has been treated as a slave during the absence of Agamemnon, her father, and she knows that her wicked mother intends to kill Agamemnon upon his return from the siege of Troy. You can read her horror in her face. See her dilated eyes: she sees in the future the murder of her father, then the coming of her brother Orestes, who is to slay Clytemnestra, then the pursuit of him by the Furies. What a face she has! She sees—"

"Woman see too muchee!" a voice remarked by their side. "Kong-fu-tse say, Man see enough for both; let woman remain blind," and Henry Harris did not need to look around to know that it was Hop Fun who had spoken.

To his surprise, his sister turned toward the mandarin and said: "When Shuh-leang-ho, the father of Kong-fu-tse, died, it was his mother Yan-she who trained him from the time he was three years old."

The face of Hop Fun was as that of a mummy still, but his rat-like eyes glittered.

"Kong-fu-tse mourned for her three full years. But," he replied, "when he taught in the Kingdom of Lu, it was the coming of a junkful of women that drove him away. Too muchee women!" And he shook his grave head and walked off.

"He reminds me," Mary Harris laughed, "of the little wooden Noah in a toy ark. And his name is Hop Fun. I would as soon expect the statue yonder to hop; as to anything resembling fun—"

"I do not know," her brother replied, "but would not be surprised if he has many a laugh, perhaps sheds many a tear, underneath the green silk of his robes and the yellow parchment of his face. I am told that he is quite hospitable. He is said to be kind to the poor, is he not, Ishra Dhass?"

The American addressed this question to the Hindoo, who chanced to be near them, and who had witnessed the brief scene.

"I do not know," Ishra Dhass replied instantly; "but Hop Fun is the mandarin who assisted Yung Wing."

"Young Wing?" echoed the American; "some orphan child, I suppose?"

There was a flash of surprise across the swarthy face of the Brahmin, but it gave place the next instant to his habitual good-humor. "I thought you knew," he said. "I thought every American knew about Yung, not young, Wing. Yet," he interrupted himself, "Wing *was* young when he began. Do you know, Mr. Harris, Hop Fun desires to find your father? I think he already knows that you are George Harris's son. If you are invited to dine with him, would you come?"

"Certainly I would," the other replied.

"And not be afraid of having to partake of stewed kittens, salted earthworms, and the like?" demanded the jolly Hindoo, for that word only can express the cordial, laughing good-fellowship of the Brahmin.

"I will gladly risk it. I overheard an indiscreet Englishman asking Hop Fun at the Bodega in regard to bird-nest soup," Henry Harris replied, "but the mandarin, without moving a muscle, responded, 'At least, Chinaman no eat oyster, insides and all.'"

"There are several of us," the Brahmin continued, "who dine with Hop Fun quite soon. If I can manage it, I will secure you an invitation. You shall hear about Yung Wing there. Oh, as to China," Ishra Dhass added, in his rapid and lively manner, "they invented printing, as you are aware. Well, they practice it on the grandest scale in the world. In this way: Kong-fu-tse—Confucius you call him—died four hundred and seventy-nine years before Christ was born. He left nine books of doctrine, as you know, which constitute

the entire literature of the empire. Every child is compelled
to read part, at least, of these classics, as they are styled.
The whole of China was, within a hundred years after Kong-
fu-tse's death, cast into the mold of his teaching. That generation was like a set of type; each of the seventy-odd generations since is merely an exact copy struck off from that.
China is to-day the same China it was twenty-three hundred
years ago. The only thing that ever changes in all the
empire is the river Hoang-ho, which alters its course so
often that it is named the 'Sorrow of China.' Hop Fun is
the living duplicate of many score ancestral Hop Funs going
before. Except," and the Hindoo paused, "for that, China
has known no change, no, not a particle, except for—"

"For English intervention in the last century," Mary
Harris supplied; "and Kong-fu-tse taught, did he not, exclusively as to the duty of man to man?" she added.

"Exclusively. He warned the Chinese not to interest
themselves in anything beyond that. You are fond of
machinery, Mr. Harris," the Hindoo continued; "*you* ought
to like Hop Fun and his people. Click, clack; it is nothing
but machinery in China. From Thibet to the Yellow Sea,
from the South Sea to the Great Wall, the four hundred and
twenty millions concern themselves about this world exclusively. Taouism, like Buddhism, is stone dead there, and
nothing has taken its place so far. An empire—the largest
on earth—of atheists! Think of that. But," and the face
of the Brahmin, always so full of vivacity, became luminous
as he added, "it will not be so for ever; the sun has always
arisen in the East; it is about to arise again. Ah!" he
added, with almost the abrupt frankness of a spoiled boy,
"as soon as I said *that*, your faces turned cold and solemn.
That is always the way with you Christians of Europe and
America. Your churches are vast vaults, damp, dark, and
ah, how chilly! And that," with a shiver, "is like your
Christianity. Now, when *I* think of Christ, it makes me glad
all over, like going into the sun."

Henry Harris and his sister had come to know, with all

who knew the Hindoo, in what direction his joyous talk was certain to run. But, like everybody else, they did not object to it at all, he was so bright and mirthful.

CHAPTER XXXI.

THE ARTISTS.

It was not long after his visit to the old artist that Henry Harris found himself again in his company. It was, however, under different and more favorable circumstances. Zerah Atchison and his daughter had secured rooms nearer to the Exposition and in more accessible quarters. When the American and his sister arrived by appointment, they were shown upstairs to the outer door of an apartment which was given wholly to artistic purposes. Mr. Atchison had covered the walls with some of his best attempts in oil- and water-painting, as well as wood-carving, and was so seated upon a chair made for the purpose that his paralyzed right arm was comfortably supported, while he wrought with his left at a picture upon which he was engaged. He had always seemed so patient that, although his surroundings were changed, he was the same.

This could not be said of his daughter, who was at work, in paper cap and coarse apron, at a mass of clay upon a stand near by. It was evident that she was perplexed as she toiled. Standing first to the right of it and then to the left, she would examine her work, her head upon one side, now drawing back, then going nearer. But it always ended as it had done during months of labor before ; she would make a dart at the offending clay and scoop out here, fill in there, rounding out one curve, obliterating another.

"Stand aside, Isidore," her father said at last, and she did so, her hands dropped, and her air that of a prisoner who already knows the verdict. Holding his brush arrested in his hand, her father examined her work with a critical air. After a while his daughter looked up to see that, without a word, he was painting again, his face as nobly patient as before. It had often occurred, but the poor girl dropped more than one tear upon the clay as, under pretense of work, she bowed beside it again, her face so that her father could not see.

"Do not be discouraged, Isidore," he observed, quietly; "although you do not get it from me, you have genius, and—"

But there was at this moment a knock at the door. The girl, throwing a wet cloth over her work, darted through an opening into her own room, and Henry Harris came in with his sister. Hardly had he introduced her to the old artist, when Lord Conyngham also arrived, accompanied by Lady Blanche and an insignificant-looking gentleman. When he was introduced to the old painter as the Duke of Plymouth, the artist gave him a rapid glance. He was about forty years of age, had thin hair, a feeble whisker, and somehow his whole manner partook of the hue of his eyes and complexion, which were of an undecided, almost watery, hue. During the whole visit he hardly opened his lips, and then only to echo what was said by those who came with him, in a genteel but almost inarticulate murmur. The principal impression produced by him was astonishment that such a man should be a duke, and he was uneasy of eye and of manner, as if he knew what people were thinking of him.

Isidore Atchison soon returned, and for some time all present were engaged in examining the carvings and paintings. Many flattering things were said, but it was in regard to the carving that most interest was awakened.

"I have never seen better in my life," Lady Blanche said; "and I, Mr. Atchison," she added, turning to him with a smile, "am considered something of a judge. Those camellias are perfect, so are those japonicas. Your work is wonderfully good."

The old artist smiled; "I am more, alas! of a critic than

a skilled workman," he said. "When I was young I had passionate desires after excellence. I even hoped, almost believed, that I could attain to it. But I have learned better long ago. With me the critical faculty is too strong for the creative. I have the keenest instinct as to what is and as to what, alas! is not good painting, an instinct so just and keen that I rate my work more harshly, because more accurately, than any other person. My poor pictures will never compete with Titian or Rubens." It was said with a contented smile.

"They are very good," Lord Conyngham said, with a glance around the room; "but as to your carving now, sincerely, it is extraordinary!"

"It certainly is," Lady Blanche confirmed her brother. "It is so good that we are under great obligations to Mr. Harris for telling us of it; and I hope, Mr. Atchison, that you will let me have this panel of grapes, this cluster of roses," pointing each article out as she said it, "and this charming confusion of violets and pansies upon a salver."

The Duke of Plymouth murmured his approval of her choice.

"It is really remarkable"—the old man leaned his white head back in his chair as he said it—"but my life ever since I can remember has been given to painting instead. You would never believe how ardent I once was, how enthusiastic, how almost desperately I hoped and toiled from dawn to dusk at drawing and painting. I would surpass every other American artist, at least, or die in the attempt! All that," he added, with an unclouded face, "is over and gone. It is only since the paralysis of my arm that I have tried to carve. I am a rigid critic, as I said, and my work of that kind *is* good, but it astonished me more than any one else. Yes, the best things, the grandest things descend to us like air and sunshine, apart from ourselves, from—" He only smiled and was silent. What he added to himself was, "from the Father of light, from whom is every good and perfect gift."

"My mother likes you in marble," Mary Harris said to the artist, as she was leaving; "I will tell her how much more she will like you in person." But at that moment Lord Conyngham was entreating Isidore Atchison to allow him to see her work upon the stand. In her flight from the room she had covered it, as has been said, and now stood defending it with laughing face but determined hands.

"No, my lord," she repeated, "no one shall see it, shall ever see it!"

"You had better desist, sir," the father said; "she is shielding you from sorrow."

"O father, how *can* you!" His daughter was so sincere in her exclamation that the others looked at her with surprise, and then laughed, and with many kind words they withdrew.

"And now, father?" Isidore asked, as their steps died upon the stairway.

"Well, my dear," the artist answered, as if in accordance with an agreement going before, "I would have done as you wished without your asking. If you had implored me not to do so, I could no more have helped playing the critic in regard to them than I could refrain from breathing; it is the habit of my life as well as an unconquerable instinct. You can catechise me while I work," and he resumed his brush and palette, the latter being a fixture upon the arm of his chair. "Shall I begin with the Duke of Dundreary, was it not? But I ought not to say that," he corrected himself.

His daughter dismissed his Grace with a laughing gesture.

"Lord Conyngham?" She put the question, leaning upon the stand, which remained hidden beneath its cloth.

"Well, he is above the average of his class," came the reply. "He is of the best material of English manhood, healthful, truthful, brave, despising all meanness. His defects are perfectly natural also, but as external to himself as his coat. But he is in process toward as exclusive a belief in his rank and himself as can be. When he is Earl Dorrington he will—so far as the times allow—be the old Earl over again, unless, indeed, the times clothe themselves in the person of—well, my dear, of Miss Mary Harris."

"Do you think so?" his daughter said, with astonishment of eyes and uplifted hand.

"No, Isidore, I do not *think* so; that is not the word—I *know* so; know so as I know the stamens, petals, subtilest curve and veining of the flower I happen to be carving. The young nobleman loves her because he has an instinctive sense of the fact that she is the one woman of all the sex who can take him as you would take clay, and make him what he should be. Miss Harris is, in a womanly way, the stronger of the two; neither of them look at it in that way, of course, but she loves him because she is blindly conscious that she is necessary to him. They will both be miserable unless they marry each other; miserable whoever else they may wed, because each will know that he or she has done wrong in not obeying their deepest instincts."

"And what do you think of Lady Blanche?" his daughter asked. There was so much of serious meaning in her father's tones, also, that she hesitated long before asking.

"Isidore," the artist replied, as he worked, "let me tell you a little story. Once upon a time, three goddesses strove together for the prize of beauty. They were Minerva, Juno, and—"

"Why, father, I have known the story all my life," his daughter interrupted.

"And Venus," the old artist continued. "Minerva was the beauty of wisdom; Juno, the beauty of power; Venus, the loveliness of love. Do you understand what I would say now?"

"You think—"

"Not think—*know*," the other interrupted her, with a smile.

"That Mary Harris has the charm of wisdom? Yes, you are always right, father. That is the way in which, without defining it to myself, she impressed me at first. Her brow

7

is low and wide, her eyes deep and pure and steady; her manner, her tones, her silence. Yes, she is Minerva; only a more purely womanly Pallas than her of the owl and helmet. Then, Lady Blanche is—" but the speaker hesitated, with a look of trouble upon her face as well as perplexity, "is Venus, father?"

"Of course not—is Juno! and her chariot is drawn by peacocks; it always is, yes." The old artist paused from his painting, and looked up as if he saw the proud English girl as he spoke. "Yes, Lady Blanche," he said, "you are the goddess of power, of pride. You come of high lineage, of the oldest and best of the English, which is by far the noblest nobility in the world. Power! Pride! You have more than your brother, for you are superior to him as you are to the old Earl, your father. You are Juno in your very soul. Even in the Christian heaven I do not see how you can cease to be a beautiful but heathen Juno for ever! Isidore," the artist said, abruptly, "Diana may love Endymion, Venus may love Adonis, but Juno? Juno can never love any other than one of the immortal gods; with *her* it must be Jupiter or no one! Lady Blanche," the artist ended, with a laugh, " your Majesty being a queen, can marry only a king."

But Isidore had turned from her father, and was taking the cloth off from her work. Her hands trembled, her color came and went.

"Do you wish my critical opinion as to young Mr. Harris?" her father demanded, in graver accents.

"No," his daughter said, with great indifference of manner. "I can not say that I do, father," she added, looking with marked despair at her work. "I have been thinking—"

"Perhaps you would like me to say something as to who is Venus, my dear," he added, with malicious accent.

But Isidore was saying, with scornful eyes, to her work, "You horrid old lady! Do you suppose that I am to be your slave for ever? Look at yourself in the glass, now, do!"

The old painter could not refrain from laughing. The
head was a well-executed conception of Sorrow; massive,
stern, sepulchral, exceedingly well done, but it had never
satisfied the father, much less his daughter. Isidore was
holding a hand-mirror before the sad eyes of the clay image.
"Only look at yourself!" the girl said, derisively; "you
flattered yourself that you were going to be a good wife, did
you, for Pluto? Aspired, did you, to be Proserpine? Insolent thing!" And before her father could prevent, the excited girl had boxed the ears of the astonished Sorrow.

"Isidore!"

It was in vain he cried out; the girl seized upon and
twisted off first the nose and then the ears and chin of the
image, dropping them at her feet. Then, with hands rapid
and energetic, she kneaded the face and head into a shape-
less lump, and turned defiantly toward her father.

"Isidore! my child," he exclaimed, and a sudden and
pathetic sadness clouded his usual serenity, as he saw how
her cheeks glowed, her eye sparkled.

"Never mind, father," she said. "I know what I am
about. You remember how hard I have worked at this odious
creature. For all I could do, for all you could suggest, she
only became, not sorrowful, only miserable, basely, degraded-
ly miserable. I could not do it! But I had no other conception before. Now I have another, a better. But it is
not of Sorrow. I see it as clearly before me as if I had finished it. O father, it will be a success, I know—my greatest
success! Wait, and you will see."

Her father looked at her with surprise. He had not supposed she could seem so beautiful. She turned from him
and went to work with eager hands upon the clay; but the
painter said nothing as he plied his brush. Another and a
higher patience sat upon his face, but a tear none the less
trickled down his cheek.

"What was Mr. Harris saying to you?" he asked, after
they had both worked for quite a long time in silence. Although he could not see his daughter's face, the sharp-sighted

old artist saw that her neck had a rosier hue as she replied : "Nothing in particular, sir."

Her father said no more, and the patient endurance burned in a soft, steady flame in his eyes as he continued to work.

CHAPTER XXXII.

THE NEW CHINESE.

ISHRA DHASS GUNGA, the popular Brahmin, found no difficulty in securing for Henry Harris an invitation to dine with Hop Fun, the mandarin, not many days after he had given his promise to that effect. In fact, the Chinese was the first to mention it to the Hindoo. Russia was too near to China, and the services of George Harris in the shops of the Czar had been too great, for the intelligent though dwarfish Chinese statesmen not to have heard of him. There was no telling what need China itself might not have for at least the son, in the engineering of the future.

"Harris he velly muchee man," the mandarin explained to the Brahmin, and then proceeded to acknowledge that heretofore his countrymen would not endure a railway in any part of the Flowery Kingdom. Not only did they abhor the outer barbarians with all their inventions ; the rails must be laid across the dust of generations of their worshiped ancestors, and that every precept in their Book of Rites forbade. Thus far, the regent, Prince Kung himself, was as powerless to grant concessions of the kind as the young emperor would be when he reached the plenitude of his power. But Hop Fun closed both of his little eyes when he told the Hindoo of this, and with a face like a stone wall added, "Kong-fu-tse say, 'Fools reach end before they set out on journey, wise men wait for by-and-by.'"

"The truth is," Ishra Dhass remarked to young Harris, as upon the appointed day they rode together in a carriage sent for them by Hop Fun, "that a vast change impends over China, as over all nations. You have read De Tocqueville, Mr. Harris?"

"Certainly," was the reply, and the American looked at the happy countenance of his swarthy companion, thinking, "Who would have supposed that a Hindoo cared for such things?"

"Then you will remember with what awe," the other continued, "the Frenchman speaks of the day when your republic will stand, in the fullness of its prosperity and power, upon the shores of the Pacific, threatening Japan and China. De Tocqueville prophesied inevitable war and conquest. True, but what a conquest!" added the Hindoo, with animation. "Learned as the author was in the history of all nations, he had no conception that the conquests of America were to be intellectual, moral, spiritual! My friend," the Brahmin said, with pitying eyes, "even you have slight idea of the grandeur of your own America. A nation made up of some fifty nations, present and prospective, yet one, one republic, unparalleled in history! Hail Columbia!"

Although the Oriental laughed, he was in serious earnest. Then his face clouded. "Your nation exists because of your Christianity. At last," he added, "and for that reason, your republic stands with its face toward Asia. The race, starting from its birthplace therein, has made its long, slow, and sorrowful journey around the planet, and is getting back again to the point from which it set out. Has not the race its orbit also as well as the globe? Originating in Asia, the path of history struck through Europe, and so across the Atlantic to the eastern shores of your continent. From Jamestown and Plymouth across the hemisphere to San Diego and San Francisco, the sublime circle is completed. Young, rich, powerful, having ended the long travel of man and of the earth, you have got back at last to Asia once more? Well, Asia, Europe has nothing to tell you which you do not know already in regard to politics, art, science, but—" and the Hindoo looked at his companion with only less pity than he would have bestowed upon a worshiper of the cow or the crocodile in his own land.

"You are always underrating our Christianity," Henry Harris complained. "Frankly, once and for all, what do mean?"

"Mean?" the other said, indignantly. "Fifteen hundred years after Moses, Christ came to the Hebrews, and what did he find? A petrified formalism. Because you are not Catholic you say it is not so of you. My friend," and the other lifted up a warning finger, "suppose the Christ who walked the fields and streets of Syria were to come to even Protestantdom to-day, the living Christ, the truthful Christ, what would he find? Oh! the complicated"—and even the voluble Brahmin hesitated for a word, "yes," he added, "the complicated *catacombs* of mere profession. Do you believe you live, do you *love*, as he says you must?" Once started, the Hindoo launched into such detail of shortcoming among Christians as caused the American to wince. Yet for his life he could not deny a word of it. "I, too, am the weakest of the weak," Ishra Dhass added, "but missionaries will tell you that when the heathen do accept their message, the one person they believe in is the living, loving Christ, as he was to Peter and to John. That is all, and that is enough! I despair of making you understand!"

There was something in the manner, too, of the Brahmin which struck the young man. He had lingered in the Invalides the day before to talk with one or two of the old Imperial Guard, but Ishra Dhass had an enthusiasm for his Emperor beyond anything Henry Harris had been thrilled by among the old *moustaches* of the first Napoleon. *This* Emperor was alive, was landing upon the globe from his Elba, his St. Helena, for eternal conquest, and the Brahmin had the radiant certainty in regard to him of a joyous child.

"But what is it," his companion demanded, "that you intended telling me about Yung Wing?"

"It is soon told," was the reply. "Over forty years ago

a Chinese boy was educated in an American household ; but he did not become a missionary. He had an idea. Returning to China, he studied hard, qualified himself for diplomatic service, obtained access to officials of the empire. When the Tiensin massacre was to be paid for, he was the only Chinaman capable of conferring with the agents of European governments. He was made a mandarin, and talked to Hop Fun, our host of to-day, until he very slowly came to comprehend and accept the life-long idea of Yung Wing. Seven years it took to accomplish that. Just as Hop Fun was getting at the Chinese Government to begin the task of making them understand it, the mother of Hop Fun died, and for three years he had to retire from Pekin and weep. His tears and his appointed years of grief being exhausted, Hop Fun secured at last the consent of the throne, and a certain number of the choicest youths in China were selected by competitive examination, and sent under the care of Yung Wing to America to be educated, nearly two hundred thousand dollars being appropriated for that purpose. Yung Wing is assistant minister from China at Washington. In ten years more there will be, therefore, many score of Chinese like himself in the empire, educated Christians. Even Hop Fun knows," the Hindoo added, "that the end has nearly arrived with his ancient civilization. Very soon it must pass under the scepter of Russia, or England, or— Christ ! "

But there was not an atom of cant in the Hindoo. Henry Harris could as soon have charged hypocrisy upon Damon trusting in Pythias ; upon Clitus, rather, exulting in Alexander the Great.

By this time the carriage had arrived at the hotel in which Hop Fun had established his home. With a great deal of ceremony, the two were conducted to a suite of rooms fitted up in Chinese fashion, with lanterns, screens, lacquered seats, and costly cabinets, embroidered curtains of heavy silk, and cases of curiosities in rock crystal and ivory. There were carvings dispersed about the gorgeous apartments which would have awakened the interest, if not the admiration, of Zerah Atchison; paintings, also, from which he would have recoiled with artistic horror. Between two tall vases of blue porcelain from Pekin stood the handsomest gift Hop Fun had ever received, a coffin of rosewood, with silver mountings, and lined with crimson silk, by which Prince Kung, Regent of China, had expressed his sincere esteem for the statesman in the most grateful way known among the Chinese. Everywhere were displayed the wings and claws, the red ravening mouth and interminable tail, of the Chinese dragon. "The old serpent," Ishra Dhass whispered to his friend, "who has had his coils about China for four thousand years. But his day is nearly over."

In Paris, especially during the Exposition, people took any and every thing as a matter of course, and, after paying his respects to Hop Fun, who was arrayed in silks of brilliant colors, Henry Harris looked about him. Hassan Pasha was conferring, upon one side of the room, with a man of extraordinary appearance.

"It is a nephew," Ishra Dhass explained to him, "of the Afghan bandit of whom you have heard, Dilawur Khan. Did you ever see such a head? It is like the rugged peak of one of the mountains of the Khyber Pass. His enormous nose is another Afghan peculiarity. Napoleon always chose his marshals by the length, you remember, of that feature; it insured clearness and force of intellect, he said, and he was right."

"Who was Dilawur Khan?" Henry Harris demanded.

The Brahmin glanced at him with surprise. "You appear," he said, dryly, "to be ignorant of several of the most important of modern heroes. Excuse me, you are joking; you must know of him. Dilawur Khan had a price fixed upon his head—you will recall it—by the British in India, for his savage robberies. He said he might as well have the cash himself, and so brought it into camp upon his shoulders. As the bravest of men, having enlisted in the service, he rose to the highest grade a native can attain in the British army, and helped to put down the Sepoy rebellion. He would not pocket anything at the storming and looting, i. e., plundering, of Delhi. 'Christ would not like it,' he said ; for," the Brahmin added, " we heathens can not but take him in earnest, if we take him at all. You know the rest ; how the sincere savage, after he believed, turned at least two hundred Moslems from Mohammed. He seized them by their conscience with his powerful clutch, as he used to take travelers by the throat, and, as it were, *made* them believe. The Khan was like a more violent Paul. He was sent at last into Central Asia upon secret service, and is supposed to have been captured and blown from a cannon or martyred in some way. His nephew across the room is Ali Khan, and I see he has already laid his lion's paw upon Hassan Pasha, for, rough and tremendous as Ali Khan seems, like his uncle, he also believes."

"I recognize a Persian gentleman yonder ; I think his name is Meerut," the American said ; " yes, and I see that the rich merchant Aeout, I think it is, of Madagascar, is present. That dark individual beside Hop Fun is an Abyssinian, is he not ? "

"Yes, his name is Cherubin ; a son of the king, I am told ; " and the Brahmin, who knew almost everybody, gave him the names and nationalities of three or four guests besides. But at this moment, and with many ceremonies, the assembly was ushered into the adjoining apartment, in which dinner awaited them.

"Hop Fun loves to gather about him people of all nations," Ishra Dhass explained, as he accompanied his friend. "Although he speaks only to quote Kong-fu-tse, he loves to have his guests express themselves with perfect freedom. All present understand enough English to make themselves agreeable, and at times disagreeable," the Hindoo laughed. "You will not be surprised at whatever you may hear ; you are among heathens, you know. Europeans and Americans constitute but a small part of the population of the globe. The rest of the race are cannibals. You may find yourself part of our repast. Look out ! "

CHAPTER XXXIII.

A CHINESE REPAST.

WHEN Henry Harris was seated at the richly furnished board of the Chinese statesman, he glanced sharply about him. He was glad to find that Ishra Dhass had the seat next to him upon his right, while Hassan Pasha was placed upon his left. Immediately across the table from him, Hop Fun presided—but at the lower, because least honorable, part of the table—while the other guests were ranged up and down upon either side. The table-cloth, was of crimson silk, richly flowered, and each napkin was a marvel of embroidery. From end to end the board was, perhaps, overcrowded with an innumerable quantity of vessels of glass, porcelain, silver, and gold, each containing a very small quantity of food or drink, and not one was left upon the table by the crowd of attendants for more than a few minutes. In fact, it was as if the guests were seated at a diversified and sparkling torrent of food and tableware, so unceasing was the going and coming of the dishes. To the surprise of the American, a *carte*, in French, of the fare was laid beside every plate, so that no one need remain in ignorance of the nature of his food.

But it was upon his host that the attention of Henry Harris was fastened ; as much, at least, as politeness would allow. Although the mandarin could hardly have had a more immovable face had he been carved out of walnut, there seemed to rest upon him now the weight, in addition, of the world. In fact, he was conducting a religious rite. In rapid succession a number of minute dishes were placed and removed from before Hop Fun, who plied his chop-sticks rapidly, but, as the dishes were strictly Chinese, the American preferred not to inspect them too closely, observing only that whales' nerves, fresh tadpoles, and the like, were part thereof, and gave his attention rather to the mandarin himself and his guests. To every one present it was much more

than a mere dinner. The Brahmin broke caste in eating
with the rest, but he had ruined himself with his people by
so doing long before, and seemed to be all the jollier for it.
So with the Mohammedan, Hassan Pasha. Were it not for
the peculiar circumstances of the case, he would much sooner
have seated himself upon his doorstep in Constantinople,
and shared his dinner with the mangiest cur which came
along, than to have eaten with Ishra Dhass, to say nothing of
the others. Hindoo, Persian, Chinese, Afghan, Abyssinian,
American, all felt, however, as if Paris was an eventful pa-
renthesis in their lives. Each was but a grain of corn caught
between the whirling millstones of the time ; they were being ground together, for the moment, as by a force which
revolved the earth and stars. Since they were compelled
to yield to such undreamed-of companionship, they did it
with the reckless desperation of boys who, having got into
some frightful mischief, were determined to rush it through
with defiant energy.

As they ate and drank, the spirits of all arose. There
was a swift circulation of very small cups of brandy distilled
from rice. The cups were small, but the contents were quin-
tessences, and, from a whisper, conversation became loud
and animated. Young Harris had no idea, at the outset,
how closely he was watched, and was glad afterward that
he had confined himself to tea and to a very small glass of
wine.

At last the table was cleared of everything except a
green leaf, laid beside each plate, having in the center a heap
of salt. Every one awaited with curiosity for what was to
come next. Suddenly a servant placed in the center of the
board a magnificent tureen, closely covered. Hop Fun lifted
a forefinger ; the cover was snatched off. The vessel was
almost filled with strong vinegar, in which struggled dozens
of half-grown crabs. Eager to escape the vinegar, the instant the cover was removed they swarmed over the table,
running in every direction for dear life. The American
watched Hop Fun. Without moving a muscle, winking

even, that *diplomate* seized, one after another, upon such crabs as came in reach, dipped them in the salt at his plate, and consigned them in rapid succession, kicking and scrambling, into his mouth, which opened and shut with the remorseless precision of a nutcracker. Several of his friends followed his example, more liquors were served, and the ice seemed to be thoroughly broken. Even the mandarin appeared to have relaxed. He looked at Henry Harris, and opened his mouth :

"America muchee smart," he announced. If, from the orifice in question, one of the martyred crabs had suddenly jumped out, the guest would not have been much more taken aback. But he was equal to the emergency.

"China is much the oldest," he replied instantly, and with a bow.

The little eyes of the mandarin glittered. "India muchee sun," he remarked to the Brahmin.

"Yes," the other replied, with his ready smile, "but too much of our sun goes into the poppy."

"Yes ; too muchee opium," the host acknowledged, and "too muchee English," he added. "Turkish Empire fight," he suggested to Hassan Pasha.

"We are poor ; China is rich," was the reply ; and, as if distributing a higher variety of sugar-plums in addition to the sweetmeats with which the servants were now heaping the table, the mandarin managed to address to every guest a brief compliment in regard to his own country, receiving a more or less pertinent one in return.

This ritual of hospitality ended, the conversation took a freer range. It happened that there was no Frenchman at the dinner, and Hop Fun suggested, by way of variety, a criticism : "Frenchman too muchee cut-a-caper," but it was said with a countenance which had, apparently, never smiled. Perhaps Hassan Pasha had, the Koran to the contrary notwithstanding, taken too much stimulant ; or, he may have been irritated by his animosity to Europeans in general, but he said, with haughty disdain :

"The French are a nation of fools. They are not men. Go to the Chamber of Deputies if you wish to believe in Darwin. No monkeys ever screamed and gesticulated as they do. I confess," he continued, in excellent English, "that it enrages a man of my nation to be at the beck of such people."

As has been said, the Turk was a man of high rank, of considerable wealth, of disappointed ambition. For a brief time he had been Vizier, but, exiled from Constantinople, he had abandoned himself to profligacy and gambling. Although of a fine presence still, his dark eyes had flashes occasionally of a fire which was consuming him within. There was a certain insolence which broke, at times, through the smooth veneer of his politeness; and he was exasperated, also, by his nearness to the Hindoo. Had he uttered his inmost heart, he would have said : "I am the ruined outcast of a nation once the bravest, the proudest on earth. Under the banner of the Prophet we drove out the dogs, the unbelievers, and made a home for ourselves in Europe. But we are going down before the Cross. This accursed Hindoo, for instance, is a specimen. Yesterday he was a heathen; to-day he believes in the Christ of Europe; to-morrow all India will follow at his heels. Renegade ! Accursed *giaour!* In Stamboul we kill such vermin !"

But all that he said aloud was, "I perceive that there are no Europeans present. For once, I think, we may express ourselves frankly. May I ask your Excellency," and he bowed with great respect to their host, "what you think of them ? "

But Hop Fun had not been—and for so long—under the influence of Yung Wing for nothing. Moreover, he was a statesman in Paris upon international affairs. For some minutes his bead-like optics were fastened upon the black and imperious eyes of the Turk. Not a movement was there in hand or face, nor could any one have perceived that he had parted his lips. Yet, in some way, there came, at last, from his direction the word " *Opium!* " and, but separate from it, like another tick of a clock, "Muchee *hell!*" That and no more.

"I thank you," Hassan Pasha replied, "and I agree with your Excellency. Yes; your great nation has had a taste of Europe. When, in 1839, your Government made a desperate effort to prevent the English from poisoning its people with opium, it was brutally attacked. Being Christians, the English devote themselves to the best modes of killing their fellow-creatures, and, in 1842, they succeeded in compelling China to pay twenty-one millions of dollars toward the expenses of the war, and in ceding Hong Kong to them, as also in opening five great ports through which they might pour their poison down the throats of the people at the rate of fifty-two millions of dollars' worth annually, upon which they clear three hundred per cent. In 1857 the French and the English stormed Canton, and forced the Emperor to pay them three millions two hundred and fifty thousand pounds in English money. In 1860 Pekin, your ancient capital, was taken, and given over to plunder. Very grateful your Excellency should be to these—Christians!" It was said by the Turk with bitter sarcasm. "You, also, are greatly indebted to England," he added, in the same tone, to the Persian, Meerut by name, who was seated opposite him.

"Very much so," replied the one addressed—a large man, fat, fine-featured, with olive complexion, and hair, beard, and mustache like silk, jet-black, and, like his eyes and tones, of a soft and luxurious fluidity. He was dressed in embroidered garments, with a red fez upon his head, like that of Hassan Pasha. "Since 1797 we have had a hard time of it," he remarked, with a smile.

"Yes; in that year," said the Turk, "you had to surrender to Russia Derbend and several districts on the Kur. In 1802 you gave up Georgia to the Czar. In 1813 you surrendered all of Persia north of Armenia. In 1826 you had to pay to Russia eighteen million rubles, Erivan, and the rest of Armenia. As in the case of my country, that you exist at all is only because England, France, and Russia can not, for the present, agree how to divide you among them."

The Persian did not seem to share the bitterness of the speaker. He merely smiled, and toyed with the diamonds with which his bosom was enriched, saying : "As Hafiz sings, how much sweeter, O Turk, are kisses than blows, and the flowing of honey than the gushing forth of blood. To you and to the Ottomans will we leave all war, O Prince ! Moreover, I belong," the Persian continued, "to the sect of the Shiahites. You wash before prayer from the wrist to the elbow ; we wash, instead, from the elbow down to the wrist. Furthermore, I am one of the Ali Illahees—the People of the Truth. Most of all do I believe in Hafiz of the sugar lip. For me, pleasure," and the Persian smiled and stroked his mustache.

"Hog !" the Turk exclaimed, under his breath, of this Mohammedan liberal. The truth was, Hassan Pasha had not, since he came to Paris, allowed himself to indulge his mood, but he now drained another glass of sherbet, into which alcohol had found its insidious way, and turned to Cherubin, the Abyssinian. This was a thin and wiry man, of darker hue than Meerut, beside whom he sat. His hair was cropped close to his head, and he wore a mantle of crimson banded with gold. Like the others, he spoke good English and French ; for only such cared, as a rule, to visit the Exposition.

"If England," said Hassan Pasha to him, "had allowed a dispatch from the French Government to lie unopened in its Foreign Office, would France have submitted ?"

"No," shouted the Abyssinian, excited by the liquor and by this mention of the disgraceful neglect of the letter of his king ; "but it was better," he added, "than the insulting reply from France which Theodore, descended from Solomon himself, tore to atoms and trampled underfoot."

"Alas !" added Hassan Pasha, "in 1868 the English stormed Magdala, your capital. Not a man of them was killed, but your king was found among his slaughtered subjects with a bullet through his brain."

"These are hardly topics for a dinner-table," Ishra Dhass ventured, in his joyous tones. "If your Highness would be so kind as to—" But Hassan Pasha was now intoxicated. To the Hindoo he paid no attention. He had been looking furtively at Ali Khan, seated further down the table. As has been said, this Afghan was a man of remarkable appearance. It was not that he was large and exceedingly rugged only. He had a certain bold, yet not unpleasing, aspect, which made him as much unlike as possible to the polished Turk or to the voluptuous Persian. As to Hop Fun, he was a pygmy in comparison. One hand of the mountaineer lay upon the table, as huge and almost as hairy as that of a bear. He had been listening attentively after having eaten enormously, and even Hassan Pasha hesitated to address him. Like all Afghans, he had been a Mohammedan of the sect of the Sunnites, which was abhorred by an orthodox Mussulman like the Pasha. In addition to this, the Turk knew that he was nephew to the famous ex-robber Dilawur Khan; but he ventured to say to him, at last: "It is little thanks you, O Khan, owe English or Russian. But it was a good thing, your war of 1842. Out of an army, under the English, of twenty-six thousand, you allowed only one man to make his escape."

"O Turk," the Afghan replied, "hearken to me!" Even Hop Fun opened his eyes. The voice of the Khan was in keeping with his mountainous frame; it was harsh and loud. "I hate; I, also!" shouted the Afghan, as if calling to the Turk across a pass among his native rocks; "but what I hate is worse than all you have said. Hearken unto me, O son of your father!" And every eye was turned upon him.

At this moment, however, the mandarin arose from the table, and the guests followed him into the parlors, there to hear what Ali Khan had to say.

———

CHAPTER XXXIV.

ALI KHAN.

WHEN, after leaving the table of Hop Fun, the numerous company reached the gorgeous parlors, Henry Harris, seated beside a window on one side, confessed to himself that he had never seen a more picturesque sight. The mandarin had installed himself in a high chair, and sat in it with his little feet resting upon the rounds and concealed from sight by the superb robes which fell about him in silken folds; his hands, with the nails six inches long and twisted about his wrists, rested, crossed upon each other, in his lap. Eked out by silk interwoven with it, his hair descended down his back in a queue which reached the brilliantly colored matting. A hat, with the crystal knob on top which indicated his high rank, was perched upon his head. Thus seated, a fan in his hand but absolutely motionless, he was almost the duplicate of an image carved in ivory which stood in a corner, and which the Brahmin had informed the American was, or rather had been, a god.

"Really, the Chinese believe," the Hindoo had added, "in nothing invisible or spiritual. Taouism and Brahminism, as much as Buddhism, are, as I told you, dead faiths. Confucianism is a mere set of maxims relating wholly to the dealing of men with each other. It is what you would call a Benjamin Franklinism, for there is the strongest likeness between the two sages. There are in China some three hundred millions, also, of fools, who say in their heart, there is no God. An empire of atheists! Think of that!"

"But they worship their ancestors," Henry Harris said. The other replied:

"Merely as a memory, not as persons still existing; and only as the best way of inculcating filial obedience. No, what Hop Fun worships is China. It is a very big and a very old idol, and, like the Vishnu and Siva of my own people, it is so old and hollow and rotten that it is falling to pieces."

Although the eyes of the motionless mandarin were small, they glittered like diamonds, for he greatly enjoyed his company, as he had done his dinner. The Abyssinian had seated himself upon a lacquered chair, with a seat so narrow and a back so stiff that he was prevented from dozing after his meal by the necessity of keeping bolt-upright, if he was to keep his seat at all. The Persian had thrown himself upon a divan and was enjoying a pipe of tobacco mingled with musk, while Hassan Pasha, discarding Europe for the time, sat cross-legged beside him, puffing at a chibouque. Upon an ottoman near by was seated a Japanese prince, fan in hand, who had remained silent but observant; and the American, glancing from one to the other, was struck with the greater breadth of his forehead as contrasted with the Chinaman, and he read in that breadth the exact difference between the two peoples. A swarthy native of Madagascar had made himself comfortable by sitting, draped about in his mantle, flat upon the matting, his back against the wall. Ishra Dhass, smiling and jovial as ever, was here, there, and everywhere. His snowy turban, his white teeth, sparkling as he laughed, his perfect ease of manner, made him seem to be the one most at home there, and his conciliating courtesy to each and all caused him to be really the bond of union and the controlling spirit of the strange and diversified assembly. It was, in fact, under his influence that the mandarin had fallen into the habit of assembling such guests about him.

But the Afghan khan was the center of the group. Like his renowned uncle, he had been in the British army in India, had aided in crushing the Sepoy rebellion, and had acquired a sufficient knowledge of English to use it with a certain rough readiness. "I am glad to have you meet him," Ishra Dhass had said to Henry Harris as they came in from the dinner. "He is absent from his regiment on furlough. It is a matter of pride to him that his voice is such that he can drill his regiment from a distance of a quarter of a mile away. Once he was seized upon, when unarmed, by two Thugs, who rushed suddenly upon him as he slept under a banyan-tree. They say that he took one in each hand and dashed their heads together, breaking their skulls and killing them upon the spot."

"What an uncouth Hercules he is!" the American now said to himself as he looked at the robust, almost rocky savage. But he was yet to learn that the singular strength of the Afghan lay, in its highest form, in something more than mere bone and muscle. It was plain that Ishra Dhass had given him an urgent hint; for, after leaving the dinner-table, he had softened his tones as much as possible, although they still rolled, when he spoke, like thunder through the large and sumptuously furnished apartments.

"There are things I hate worse than anything Hassan Pasha talks about," he now said, refusing to be seated, towering head and shoulders above the rest. "I know the Europeans—English, French, German, Russian," he proceeded, his left hand upon his great tawny beard, only less abundant than that of a lion, "and I know the Asiatics—Sikhs, Hindoos, Chinese, Turks, Persians, Armenians; know them all —know them well. And I don't want to talk; but he," with a gesture toward Hassan Pasha, "has begun it. Very good. Of all people I love the Europeans most, and I hate them most; because they have done the most good and the most harm in the world. Ishra Dhass knows why. Tell them, O Hindoo."

"I will not, O Khan," the Brahmin said, in accents which sounded like those of a woman in comparison with the harsh tones of the other. "Are you afraid to speak, O nephew of Dilawur Khan? Tell them yourself." But the face of Ishra Dhass was very bright as he said it. Plainly, there was a sympathy between the two.

"There are many matters; of which shall I speak first?" and the Khan scratched behind his ear like an enormous school-boy as he reflected. "Hassan Pasha spoke of European weapons," he continued, lifting his head. "True, O Turk. The Europeans can make books, yet they give lakhs of money to making rifles instead. They can build railroads, and lo! they cast great cannon. Millions of rupees are theirs, wisdom and skill beyond all the world, yet do they erect, not schools and churches, but vast ships of iron. They are Christians, yet they crush men in battle; Christians, yet they war upon Christians, British against Russian, and Russian against British. God gives them wisdom, money, power, beyond all other people. The whole world trembles before them. God says to them, Go, save! And they do go, go everywhere, but go—" and the ears of the guests were almost deafened, "go," the Khan said, in thunder, "to kill!" There was satisfaction in the face of Hassan Pasha as he smoked steadily on, his eyes upon the speaker, his lip curled.

"As to the heathen, it is money they seek. *You* love money," the Afghan said, turning with rude frankness upon the mandarin. "And you, O Persian," he added. "You also, O Turk; because it is all you have. You hunger for it, thirst for it, die for it. Shall not the ox desire his grass? But the Franks, they have Christ. Yet it is as if they, too, had no god but gold. I—I *wonder* at them," the Afghan said, with large eyes; "it confuses me. O my fathers, I can not understand it."

"Yes, O Khan," Hassan Pasha suggested, ironically; "but did you never see a Christian drunk?"

The Afghan looked down upon the speaker. "Yea," he said, "and I have also seen a drunken Mohammedan." It was indecorous to laugh, but the eyes of all brightened at this palpable hit at the Moslem, who affected to smoke with a gravity all the sterner.

"Alas! yes," groaned Ali Khan, "to the Europeans are revealed the wonders of heaven as of earth, yet they also drink. They see into the bowels of the earth with all its treasures, and to them God has revealed heaven and himself. Angels might they be, yet are they also swine. You are American," the huge rustic added, turning swiftly upon young Harris; "out of all men your people love money most; do you also get drunk?" The question was like a blow.

"It is not American," Henry Harris hastened to say, "nor Turk; it is not Russian, Syrian, nor English; it is *men* you speak of. Are we not all made of the same clay?"

"True, O Ali," said Ishra Dhass, hastening to the help of his young friend, and, laying one hand on his own bosom, he placed the other upon that of the Khan; "feel it, hear it, know it, is it not the heart, the same heart in all men everywhere?"

But the Afghan was looking gravely, inquiringly, at the American. He hardly heard the Hindoo. "I know little of your country," he said to the American. "They tell me it is big, very big. It also is Christian, and it is different from Europe. In your country do they—do they—" Henry Harris felt his own face growing warm as he saw that the countenance of the Afghan, rugged as a mountain, was actually coloring. "Do they—" the Khan continued, with painful eagerness and with the wistful eyes of a child, "do your people—do your men and women together—do they *waltz?*" The one addressed would have laughed aloud at the reluctance with which the word came out at last, but he dared not do it; the aspect of the inquirer was too serious.

"Our women are pure, pure as snow," Henry Harris said, with energy.

"And your men, are they pure also?" the Afghan asked; but the Brahmin came again to the rescue.

"One thing we all know," the Hindoo said, standing in the center of the group, "whatever may be the sins of Europeans, one thing we *know*—China, India, the Turkish Empire, Afghanistan, Japan, Siam, Burmah, Thibet, everywhere except in Christendom, the government, the religion, is perishing. We are intelligent men. Who of us denies it?"

"And is not Russia to perish before its Nihilists?" Hassan Pasha took his amber pipe from his mouth to ask. "Is not Socialism festering in Germany? How long since France

fell before the Commune? To-morrow this poor republic
tumbles, and then Europe is again overturned. Perish?
The forests perish every year, the world shall perish at last.
Kismet! It is fate. *Mashallah Bismillah,*" and the Oriental
replaced his pipe between his lips with a gesture of contempt.

"True, O Pasha," said the Brahmin, softly, "and yet in
Christendom, not in us, is the enduring life. It falls to rise;
we fall to rot. For they are Christians. Therefore, they of
all men should tremble before him who is coming. It is not
Christ, but opium which they give to China. Listen to me,
O men!" The Hindoo stood before his audience with lifted
hand. "Where do the English get the accursed poison?
The northern states of Rajpootana, whence I come, are
too barren to raise much grain, and heretofore the poor
people have depended upon the southern states, especially
upon Malwa, where the soil is deep, black, rich for food.
Of late Malwa raises the poppy instead, seeing that it pays
better, leaving Ajmere and Mairwarra, north of it, to perish
of famine! They told me, when I stood in Malwa, that the
poppies which crimsoned their fields were red with the blood
also, not of the poisoned Chinese only, nor of the millions
starved to the north of them only—every man, woman, and
child, they told me, among these flowers flaming with the
fires of hell has taken to the use of opium! In your boasted
America," and the speaker pointed to Henry Harris, "opium-
smokers already pay three hundred thousand dollars a year
in customs dues, and the sum is swelling every year. *Your*
Indians ask for the water of life, and you give them whisky
instead. India and China hold out their hands to England,
crying, 'Since God has given to you the bread of life, give it
also to us,' and England gives them—opium! Christ is coming, sword in hand; it is *Christendom* should tremble at
his coming!" and the very lips of the Brahmin whitened
with his fervor. It was as if with lifted eyes he actually
saw the one of whom he spoke.

There was a moment of silence. Then Hop Fun opened
his lips. It was but to utter one word—"Tae-ping."

"Yes," the Hindoo said, eagerly, catching his meaning, "but Tae-ping-wang was a liar. Nearly thirty years ago he called himself Christian, and fought but failed to overturn your emperor. Why did he fail? Because he said that Tien-ma was the wife of God; that he, Hung, was himself, brutal wretch that he was, the son of God. That is the curse of Europe, too, and of America," exclaimed the Hindoo, with intense earnestness. "They pretend that their Christianity is Christ. It is not!" and his voice rang through the room. "Catholic, Greek Church, Protestant, are half heathen in this, that, like idolaters, each makes a Christ of its own, and falls down before that. Pope, preacher, priest, each poor creature, whoever, whatever it is, dreams that he or it is the Tae-ping-wang, the Saviour of men; as if a louse," added the plain-spoken Hindoo, "should crawl across the face of the noonday sun, saying, Behold me! You are right," he said to the Turk; "so far as it is only of man, all systems perish. English gold and Russian force, cannon and iron-clad, American invention and French revolution— these but blast a highway for Him who comes. These are the sappers, the engineers, not the King. Who knows but terrible calamities shall smite Europe, America, as well as China and Turkey? It is not," he added, in gentler accents, "a German Christ we want, nor do we need an American Christ, or British Jesus. The missionaries bring us Christ, but are not themselves the saviours, except in that, so far as the work is only of men, they also fail as the heathen fail. What we need is the Syrian Son of God, the Man of Nazareth himself again, as of old."

But the Brahmin arrested himself as by an effort, and soon after the company dispersed, the last words of Hop Fun lingering in the ears of the American as he rode away: "Kong-fu-tse say, 'Friends no dine at all unless their souls dine too.'"

CHAPTER XXXV.

THE NOBLE DUKE.

ONE evening, Earl Dorrington, confined to his easy-chair by a slight attack of gout, was conversing with his daughter, Lady Blanche. She had been reading the "Times" to him, but the attention of both was given rather to the Duke of Plymouth, who was playing billiards with Henry Harris in an adjoining room, the door of which had been left open. Now, the correct place for such a game would have been elsewhere, but Lady Blanche was fond, strictly in private, of playing with her brother, and the present arrangement was part of what Lord Conyngham described as "the camping out" of the family while in Paris. The article which Lady Blanche was reading to the Earl was leveled at John Bright, and, as she laid the paper down at the end, "Yes," the Earl remarked, "his family extends back through eight centuries."

"Indeed," Lady Blanche exclaimed, "I had supposed he was a nobody of yesterday."

"I am not speaking of the person about whom you have read, nor was I thinking of him," the Earl said, and, by an inclination of his head, he indicated that it was of the Duke he spoke. "It was an ancestor of his," the Earl continued, "who assisted William the Conqueror to his feet when he stumbled and fell, upon his first landing in England. For this, and for helping William off with his boots after the Battle of Hastings, he received an earldom and large grants of land.

"So I have heard," Lady Blanche remarked, absently, and added immediately, "Do you not think that he is a larger man than my brother?"

"Assuredly so," the Earl replied, from sheer force of habit, but corrected himself in the same breath. "Do you really consider him so? The Duke is of a refined, but not of—"

"It was not of the Duke I was speaking," his daughter interrupted, in a tone like that used by the Earl in regard to John Bright. "I was speaking of Mr. Henry Harris."

The billiard-room was near enough for her to see the gentlemen as they played, but too far off for them to hear or to be overheard. From long habit, Lady Blanche could read to her father without giving a thought to what she read, and she had been contrasting their visitors with each other while she repeated the thunder of the "Times" for the Earl. Laying down the paper, and gazing upon the billiard-players, she had said to herself of the Duke : "Yes, he is nervous, thin-skinned, sensitive. He is small enough already ; why will he make himself seem so much smaller by shrinking into himself as he does ? He turns into a mimosa plant the moment he comes near me, wilts and shrivels visibly if I only look him in the eyes. The American seems to expand, instead, when with me, as if I brought summer to him."

"His is a line of royal favorites," Earl Dorrington was saying, in the same subdued tone, while she thus thought. "No less than thirteen of the confiscated Church properties, abbeys, monasteries, priories, and the like, were bestowed by Henry VIII upon an ancestor of his. Another ancestor was greatly enriched by Charles II."

But Lady Blanche looked suddenly and sharply at the Earl, and her color was reflected in that which tinged his fine forehead. No wonder ! It was an ancestress, rather, who, at the price of her honor, had secured the favor for her husband of that dissolute pensioner of Louis of France, and the eyes of Lady Blanche glanced toward the ducal descendant, and then fell to the ground.

"I am not mercenary, as you well know, my dear," the Earl remarked, after quite a pause ; "but I can not endure that your rank should be less than that of your brother ; you should have been my son, Blanche ! " The white-haired old man laid his hand upon her head as he said it. She understood perfectly ; of the two, she was her father's favorite because she was most like him, as Lord Conyngham was

8

most like his deceased mother. So far as a woman can be
so, yet remain a woman, Lady Blanche was an aristocrat in
the intensest sense of the word ; if she had been a man instead, she would have been insufferably so. Her father did
not say it, but she knew what he meant : " You better deserve to be a duchess than he does to be an earl ! " Had the
words been spoken, she could not have understood him more
perfectly.

"No, I am not of a sordid nature," the Earl added, and
it was very true, " but wealth is power. His Grace owns no
less than one hundred and sixteen thousand and, to be accurate, six hundred and sixty-eight acres, in the best parts of
England and Scotland."

" In other words," Lady Blanche added, in a yet lower
tone, and as if calculating, " he is willing to pay for my hand
no less than a rental of two hundred and thirty-three thousand and—let us be accurate—nine hundred and thirty-three
pounds a year, to say nothing of manors, castles, diamonds,
cash in bank, and the like. Oh, yes."

" Neither you nor I care for money as such," the Earl
assented; "but when rank is almost regal, its income must
be in accordance. Assuredly sô. Without a thought upon
our part the Duke of Plymouth throws himself at your feet.
It is the ordinance of Heaven, my dear," the Earl continued,
with venerable, almost sacerdotal air, " that this nobleman
should seek your hand. He belongs to one of the most ancient, as it is one of the wealthiest houses of our nobility.
In England, my child, you are the lady whom he regards as
worthiest of his alliance. It speaks well for his judgment.
Moreover, there is a divine, a quite sacred, fitness in such an
arrangement. Ahem ! assuredly so. I am free to confess "
—the Earl seemed in adding it to know what she was thinking of—" that the Duke has lived what some might call a
wild life. If you please, we will acknowledge that he has
been, shall we say ? dissipated, beyond most of our young
nobles. Consider the temptation to which his rank, his almost fabulous wealth, have exposed him. Of all that he has

grown weary. Blanche," the Earl sank his voice almost to a whisper, "since your mother is not here to say it, the Duke will be as wax in your hands."

"I have not the least doubt of it," the lady spoke in her ordinary tone, with a careless frankness ; "and who is the winner?" she asked, as the billiard-players joined them.

"The Duke," the American hastened to say. "Not only am I but an ordinary hand, but his Grace is one of the best players I have ever known."

It was politely said ; but the game sank in the estimation of the lady as it was said.

"The Duke has had much practice," she remarked, "and you have been occupied with other things."

"Mr. Harris plays very well. To-day he seemed to be thinking of something else." The Duke said it for politeness' sake. The American was as much to him and no more than if he had been a rich young Russian, a successful miner from Australia, anything of the kind, anybody, nobody. In some absurd way, these Americans were received into a society which would not tolerate even the wealthiest brewer or ironmaster, if he were English ; but "Confound them!" the Duke often observed to his friends in private, "I did hope their war would have made an end of them. They are an awful bore. Wherever you go you meet them, and, by Jove, they act, you know, as if they had a right!"

On this occasion, however, the Duke was unusually considerate. He had learned that young Harris was rather a favorite than not in the family of the Earl. It had not entered his head that any man, this American least of all, could be his rival. He forgot his existence as he approached Lady Blanche. The trouble was that, under her eyes, he forgot everything else also. She was known to be extremely intelligent ; he must talk, talk in an energetic way, about something.

"Confound it!" he said to himself now, "don't be an ass! Talk! Yes, but what shall I talk about?" and the perspiration began to moisten his forehead ; his hands sought each other. The Earl, Lady Blanche, Mr. Harris, were conversing freely upon many matters ; it was incumbent upon the Duke to strike boldly in. "We were speaking of America," he suddenly said ; " do you know, I had a queer adventure with a Yankee in Italy last year ? I had stopped, you know, in one of those little towns, you see ; it was at an inn where one of those round and oily landlords wanted me to sit down, you know, at his *table-d'hôte*. But I couldn't stand that, you know, so I ordered a separate table and made my man sit down with the people to their dinner. Wanted to save time, you know. Would you believe it ? A man, a tremendous fellow, looked like a gentleman, got up and made an awful row about it, you know. 'If you can't eat with us,' he said, ' your man shall not !' There was a deuce of a mess. The fat landlord, you know, he bowed and begged and protested, but the other wouldn't give in. What was the man's name ? Harris ? Yes, and it was a George Harris ; large man, rough, stern. Ever met with him ? He was an American, I learned. He was a queer customer ; perhaps you know him ?" And, with the kindest intention, the Duke had turned to his fellow-visitor.

"It was my father," Henry Harris said, dryly.

"Your father ! Oh ! excuse me, I beg your pardon," the Duke hastened to say ; but his confusion was so great, since Lady Blanche's eyes were upon him, that it would never do to smile, and Henry Harris changed the conversation adroitly in other directions.

But it was a severe strain upon even the Earl. Not for an instant had the idea entered his mind that such a mere "person" as this young Mr. Harris, wealthy as his father was, could aspire to the hand of his daughter. Yet, unconsciously to himself, he was wishing that the Duke had something more of the bone and muscle, the manly bearing and ease, of the American. "He looks as if he lived a pure life," the old Earl thought, as he glanced at him, and then looked at the other. "It is so important that my descendants—" But he checked himself, and asked the Duke as to the next Derby.

Henry Harris was conversing with Lady Blanche, who was showing him a carving she had received but the day before from Zerah Atchison. It was a sleeping St. Bernard dog. "He died last year," she was saying, "but Mr. Atchison has reproduced old Chimborazo to the life, merely from my description. Can you wonder that the old dog was such a favorite of mine? Is it not admirable?"

"It seems to be," the gentleman said; and they continued to converse for some time. But it was not while reading dry parliamentary debates alone that the lady could think also of very different matters. She was saying to herself, as she talked: "How strange men are! Here is this duke; as they tell me, he really does love me more than any woman he has known before. It is his devotion to me which makes him so *malaprop* and shy. But this American loves me. He loves me in a way which this—this poodle is not capable of even conceiving. And yet the more he loves, so much the more is he calmly determined never to tell his love. He is strong because he is proud—stronger than I am because he is prouder than I am."

The young American was mistaken in this, that it was impossible for him to hide—from such a woman, at least—what he felt, any more than what he was. "She is the loveliest," he was stammering to himself, under his cool demeanor, "the most beautiful of women; strong as Elizabeth of England; charming as Mary of Scotland; fascinating as Cleopatra; always a *queen;* there never was such a woman before. O Empress!"

At that instant the hands of the two touched in handling the carving. Theirs were strong natures. It was like an electric shock. He lifted his eyes, his whole heart in them, to hers. She met them with the fierce love, as of a lioness. Then her face became pale, her eyes drooped, her hand trembled, and the man remained the master of the woman, because he remained master of himself.

"Your ladyship is right," he said, aloud, and with perfect outward coolness; "the dog is admirably done. He was your dog, too. Poor fellow! big as he was, he was but a dog; and, being *but* a dog, he died."

"Assuredly so," Earl Dorrington was saying of something to the Duke, on the other side of the room, and with a wisdom which was stately enough to be omniscience instead; "what you remark is correct. Assuredly so; assuredly so!"

CHAPTER XXXVI.

THE LOST WIFE.

WHILE the relations between Mary Harris and Lord Conyngham seemed, so far, to be smooth enough, it was very different in the case of her brother and Lady Blanche. Although the affections of the English nobleman were deep and strong, beyond anything he had felt before, neither his love nor his hate could compare in depth or volume with that of either his sister or her lover. Moreover, there were barriers between Lady Blanche and Henry Harris more impregnable than between Lord Conyngham and the fair American. Nothing is becoming more common than for English gentlemen, of rank even, to marry girls from the United States, while, as has been said, nothing is more uncommon than for gentlemen from America to mate themselves with European women. In the case of Henry Harris and Lady Blanche, the ordinary obstacles to such a union were apparently the strongest possible. Both were of a proud and determined nature, and although their natural affection was as strong as was to be expected in persons like them, it was in the case of each as a stream which strove to tear its way through intervening mountains, the peaks of which were rooted in the foundations of the earth, and which towered, covered with the snow of ages, to heaven itself. For the present the yearning of their hearts toward each other was, therefore, as torrents which foam all the more fiercely by reason of the seemingly insurmountable barriers which interposed ; and the affection between Lord Conyngham and Mary Harris was, in comparison, as streams which flow unhindered, except by ferns and pebbles, through level and flowery meadows.

When Henry Harris left the hotel of the Earl, after his game of billiards with the Duke of Plymouth, and his yet more interesting encounter with Lady Blanche, he thought, as he walked rapidly away, of Zerah Atchison. It was strange, but it was the marble patience of the artist rather than even the imperious loveliness of Lady Blanche which struck itself, like a medallion, into his mind at the moment, and almost instinctively he turned his footsteps toward the dwelling of the old man. When he arrived no one was in the studio but Zerah Atchison himself. He was seated at his carving, apparently, but his visitor was struck with alarm when he saw him. The old painter had dropped his tools from his hand ; an old sketch-book lay open in his lap ; a yellow and faded letter was lying upon the flower he had been creating out of the wood. His patient aspect was the same, only he was staring into the air before him as at a vision ; it was as if he had been smitten with paralysis again. The young man laid a loving hand upon his shoulder, spoke to him, but received no reply. In his anxiety he was about hurrying out to send for the daughter, for a physician, when the other seemed to come to himself.

"Stop, sir," he said ; "give me a little time to recover. Pardon me a moment." But he sat silent so long, still looking into space, that his visitor again began to cross the room to call for help.

"No, no !" The artist said it in so importunate a tone that the other desisted and came and stood by his side. "It is wonderful ! It is terrible !" Zerah Atchison murmured at last, and then his eyes turned upon his visitor. The old, critical glance came into them as he looked at his young friend long and steadily. "No, not Antinous, something of the young Hercules," he said aloud, but explained himself immediately with a gentle smile. "I see, sir," he said, " that

you are something more than a dandy, than a man of the
world, than a young millionaire even. You out of all men
happen to be here, and I am glad that Isidore is at the Exposition. Shall I tell you? You are the only person alive
that I would tell, *could* tell, strangers as we are." Then he
glanced over the letter again, which he had dropped from
his hand; after that he gazed into the air as if into the remote past. "Mr. Harris, I do not wish to trouble you, but,"
he asked next, "can you give me a little time this afternoon?
Something has happened to me. It is so strange, so sudden!"

The person to whom he spoke was slow in making acquaintances, not because he did not observe people, but
because he had always observed them too closely. But he
had been drawn to the artist from the instant he had first
seen his face in marble at the Exposition, and he now sat
down in a chair which he placed near him, and listened as a
son might have done to an aged father.

"I will have to go back, far back in my life," the old
man said. "I will have, for a reason you will see in the
end, to cover myself with shame; will have to tell what I
had hoped would remain known only to God. Listen." It
was a long story. Before he had met the mother of Isidore,
years before that, and while quite young, he had gone sketching into the wildest parts of Virginia. Making his home at
the log-cabin of an old farmer, he had given himself up to
his lonely and severe work among the roughest passes of the
Blue Ridge Mountains. But there was, it so chanced, an
orphan girl living with the farmer, as uneducated as a child,
almost untamed as a colt. This daughter of the woods had
formed a sudden and violent passion for him, and the old
artist covered his face with his trembling hands, and was
silent.

"Heaven knows," he said at last, "that I firmly intended
to marry her when a license and person could be obtained to
perform the ceremony. But she was almost as much of a
savage as if it had been in Central Africa instead, and one

day I came back to the cabin to learn that she had run away with a young French surveyor, who was employed in laying out lands for a colony which proposed coming to Virginia, but which never came, owing to a revolution in France. Some months after that, when I had gone back to the State capital, I received this old book," and he took it up, "through the French consul at Richmond. It was a sketch-book I had used when I was at work in the Blue Ridge ; but I could not open it when it came, for I had come to love the girl so far as one could love so wild a thing, and, for remorse too, I could not bear to think of her. Mr. Harris," the old artist added, seriously, "upon my honor, I have allowed this book to be unopened until this hour. I had utterly forgotten it, so long ago was it since it came to me ; but Isidore found it early this morning, I suppose, among my clothes, and laid it upon my stand before she went away. A moment before you came in I chanced, not knowing what it was, to open it for the first time and found this." He took up the faded letter and read it aloud. It was a miserably written note from the girl, informing the painter that she had given birth to a son while she was in Florida in the company of the man with whom she had eloped. "It is your child," she wrote, "but we will take it with us to France, to Paris. He looks like me, they say."

That was all ; except that the old artist was sure the boy, now grown to be a man, was alive, would be found ! "My finding this letter so strangely, and not until I myself came to Paris, proves that to me," he said. "Never before did I understand *why* I came here. I know now my boy is alive. He will be found ! "

Henry Harris looked at the artist with wonder ; there was a new light in his eyes, an aspect of confidence ; his patience had taken the colors of certainty. "Through the years on years since then it all comes back to me," he said— "the old cabin upon the mountain slope, the brawling brook down one side, the rocks and trees and waterfalls I roamed among, the distant summits, the dense forests. I can almost hear the tinkle of the cow-bells, can almost smell the breath of the pines upon the morning air. And that girl Delira; what a singular name, I have not thought of it for so long! I can see her now more like an Indian squaw than a white woman, with tangled black hair, coming up from the spring with a bucket of water poised on her shoulder— "

But at the moment he spoke a messenger handed a note to the artist from his daughter. He read it, his face flushed, he put it, after hesitating a moment, in the hands of his visitor, saying, "I thought so from the first." The note was very short.

"Dear father, you will have opened the book; you will, before this reaches your hand, have read the letter within it," his daughter had written him from the Exposition. "It is many months ago since I first came upon and read the paper, and I did not speak of it because I was trying to understand. I remember you used to tell me of your stay in Virginia. There are scores of your oldest sketches which bear the same date as that of the book in which I found the letter. Dear father, I think I understand. I want you to find my brother." That was all.

The artist and his visitor had a long conversation before they parted, and the next evening Henry Harris visited him again when he knew that Isidore would be at home. The young girl blushed and turned away when she first saw him; but their visitor soon found that father and daughter had arrived at a perfect understanding, and it was not long before Henry Harris was able to say to both, "I think I can help you. At least, your singular faith as to finding your son and brother has infected me also. We do not have even a name to go by. The man doubtless is, as his mother wrote, more like her, whom I have never seen, than like yourself, Mr. Atchison. He may be dead. If he is living and in France, it is more than probable he has been, is, or will be in Paris during the Exposition. It is my custom to see, so far as I can, every person I pass. I know that it is only the merest chance in the world, and yet I will look closely at people.

Who knows what may happen?" As he said it he glanced at Isidore. Her eyes were fastened eagerly upon him. Evidently a new purpose had come into her own life also, and her gaze had fixed itself upon their visitor as upon her only hope of realizing what was to grow with her into a consuming purpose indeed. She hung upon him with an expectation modestly veiled, yet destined to become more and more intense. It was long before Henry Harris could get his own consent to leave his new friends.

"She is very beautiful," he said to himself as he went down the stairs at last; "but she is not at all like my sister, nor like Lady Blanche—not in the least. But isn't it the strangest thing in the world that I, the most practical of engineers, should have become engaged in such a hopeless search? It would seem improbable in a dream or in a fiction; but I have learned that by far the most wonderful things are those which take place in daily real life."

CHAPTER XXXVII.

THE FEMALE PHILOSOPHER.

THERE are in the Rue St. Antoine in Paris many obscure nooks and hiding-places which are known only to the police. In some of these it is possible that even the police have never penetrated, so securely are they concealed in the labyrinth of courts and alleys, cellars beneath cellars, and passages which seem to return upon themselves. In the worst of these lairs many of the vermin of society, the pickpockets and burglars, the counterfeiters and assassins, have, with the reptile-like adroitness of such pests, succeeded in living long lives of crime by night and concealment and drunkenness by day.

In the midst of this district there was a suite of rooms known to those who frequented it as Madame Mosseline's. The apartments are upon the fifth flat of the dilapidated house ; the front room looking down upon the street being, apparently, devoted to millinery, the one back of that being the bedroom of Madame Mosseline, the milliner. Apparently, there was no room beyond ; but a heavy wardrobe in the bed-chamber of Madame revolved upon a pivot, and, by means of an entrance thus made, some twenty men, straying in one at a time, contrived to assemble, at the date of which we are now speaking, in an apartment beyond.

"Now, messieurs," Madame Mosseline said on the occasion spoken of, "on the usual conditions you can say what you will." The persons addressed were evidently artisans. You could have known by the prevailing pallor of their faces that their occupation was sedentary, and that they had but small opportunity to enjoy the sunshine and the open air. From the fact that many wore spectacles and had hands white and delicate, you could have guessed that their labor was that of ivory-turners, grinders of optical glasses, the manufacturers of philosophical instruments, and the like. One or two were engravers. There was one young man, the only fat and florid one among them, M. Portou by name, who was a composer, as he styled it, of anatomy, his occupation being to put together into complete skeletons such bones as he could obtain. Whatever their employment, all seemed to be alike under a certain restraint. It may have been that the room was cleaner than those they generally occupied, for, with its papered walls, polished floor, and deal table of almost snowy whiteness, it was severely neat. Possibly the aspect of Madame was a controlling power. She was a comely woman of forty, dressed in black, with a certain arrangement of lawn about her head and throat which gave her the aspect of a nun, although a more thoroughly wicked woman it would be hard to find.

"Upon the usual conditions, messieurs," she said, for she was seated upon a high chair at the end of the table, a pile of sewing upon the table before her, "you can have as much absinthe or any other drink as you wish ; it is there for pay, on the table ; but I will have no smoking. If any one spits upon the floor he leaves, never to return. Be perfectly free in saying what you will ; but you shall not kill each other, not here."

"But, madame," demanded the anatomist, "how do we know but these friends of yours are *mouchards*, spies of the Government."

"*They!*" and the woman suspended her sewing to cast a pitying eye at the two men seated at the table. "As I told you, monsieur the articulator of bones, they are cousins of mine from Canada. Their association has been with provincials of their own country and with barbarians in the United States. They know nothing, and, being in Paris, they wish to learn. In that all is said. The Government? What cares it for you? You are not *pétroleurs*. It is philosophers you are. Am I not Madame Mosseline? For how many years have you known me? Your fat makes you foolish, M. Portou."

There was a laugh among the leaner kind at the table, and a gaunt-visaged maker of chessmen said, "No, we are not *communards*. They are but the sparks, we are the powder. Yes, they are red ; they fill the eyes of the world when the explosion comes, but they speedily die out and are no more seen. It is we who think, who reason, who write, who talk, who teach the masses ; we it is who do the work."

"It is always so," remarked a beardless man whom they addressed as Achilles Deschards, and whose very black hair and eyes and noble forehead contrasted strongly with a face which showed traces of either disease or debauchery ; "you are right, Pilon. Consider Rome in the hours of its imperial glory. The emperors led their armies, conquered the world, returned in triumph. The city was filled with palaces and wealth. There were caravans along its streets, the amphitheatre was crowded with spectators, the baths with sensualists, the schools with philosophers. All was grand, magnificent, lasting as the universe—that is, as the surface. But look underneath Rome! Consider the catacombs. Hidden in those dark vaults, burrowing beneath the gorgeous show, was the despised Christianity. *Très bien*, it swept the Roman world out of existence!"

"As we will destroy Christianity and the civilization of to-day. You are correct, monsieur our poet. It is we," Madame Mosseline continued, "who toil in the dark because we undermine the foundations of all things. Property, government, religion, marriage, morality, whatever constitutes society, we doom them to the death. Behold them, the provincials!" She pointed her hand, encircled by lace frills, at her cousins and laughed.

The Canadian relatives were plain but intelligent-looking men, coarse as their clothing was, and it was evident that they were surprised as well as interested.

"Take pity upon us, madame," one of them remarked; "we are so new to your ideas. It is that we are here for, to learn."

"Monsieur our poet, instruct them," the woman remarked, contemptuously, as she held up different ribbons, contrasting their shades of color before disposing of them upon the work she had in hand.

The person thus addressed drained a glass of brandy from a decanter before him, and glanced around the board. Evidently all there were persons of the same class; that is, all were poor, some deeply in debt, most of them in feeble health from dissipation or hard work. One or two had fallen asleep as they sat, their heads upon the table. A few were playing dominos; some were listening, with eager eyes. To all the place was a diversion from miserable homes which were also the shops in which they worked. They were there because they had nowhere else to go; because the talk was exciting; because hope of some change in the eternal monotony of poorly paid toil was encouraged there.

"To all of us it is an old story," the poet began, after a contemptuous glance at the strangers. "That you may teach Canada and the United States when you return, listen."

The Canadians gave him a respectful attention, and he began to light a cigarette, was prohibited by the uplifted finger of Madame Mosseline, replaced it in his bosom with a grimace, and continued :

"Know, *Messieurs Provinciales*, that by an eternal process of nature all things grow from within by a decay of that which is outward. The stalks, the leaves, the blossoms, have their day, but perish as the inner principle develops. So of society ; the Roman Empire was at one time but a handful of slaves dwelling in a mud-walled village, but it slowly overmastered the world. As it reached its culmination, the religion of Jesus, working out of sight within it, in due time outgrew it, and lo ! the imperial glories fell from around it like withering blossoms from the ripening fruit. Shall the process end with modern civilization ? Not at all ; why should it ? Men like Voltaire, Rousseau, Marat, were, more than a century ago, the germs of a yet higher civilization. The revolutions of 1789, of 1814, 1830, 1848, the wars of Napoleon, of France with Germany, all events are but the struggles within our existing order, which shall destroy it as all civilizations have been destroyed before. Myself and my comrades, we represent the future. The English, the Germans, the Russians, they too—"

"No !" thundered the maker of chessmen ; "Russia, Germany, England, are savage, stupid ; it is France which leavens the world ; France ! England is flooded with radical papers ; but the English—bah ! they are stupefied with beer like the Germans ; they are slow, oxen, asses. Russia is stirring, but is centuries behind. France is the volcano whose eruptions convulse the planet."

Even before he had ceased to speak there arose a babel of interruptions. Almost every man had something to say concerning the particular oppression under which he groaned. They were loud, eager, almost eloquent, but unanimous only in this, that society as it existed should be utterly destroyed. It was some time before the poet could obtain a hearing.

"We have stormed civilization until it is driven into its last intrenchments," he said at last, refreshing himself with a glass of brandy. "Definitely, it lies trembling within its inmost citadel. A century hence our children will need to be taught as to what is meant by the obsolete phrases, government, religion, property, marriage—"

"Morality, God," the presiding woman completed the list for him. "Why should we rave and roar?" she added, with a smile; "the event marches upon us. As surely as the sea the social republic makes itself to arrive. Let us remain quiet; let us keep ourselves washed, and well dressed, and at peace; with us and without us approaches the end. The *canaille* erect barricades, and bleed, and get sent to Cayenne. It is people like ourselves who inspire the *communards*, but do not soil or fatigue ourselves. We? Are not we the aristocrats of the movement? We destroy the world, but we remain Monsieur and Madame. Recite to us a poem, monsieur our poet."

The request awoke an applauding urgency, to which the poet yielded at last. Drawing from his breast-pocket, he proceeded to rehearse, with abundant gesticulation, such lines in ridicule and denunciation of everything decent people hold dear as caused the eyes of the Canadians to be fastened upon the table. Once or twice they ventured to glance at the woman at the head of the table. It seemed impossible that she could be a woman and endure the atrocity; but she sewed steadily on, with a smile. Almost every man present had his jest, when the lines were ended, at something sacred. It was all that the Canadians could do to keep their seats, the profligacy of sentiment, the blasphemy, was such. Madame Mosseline, maintaining her nun-like aspect, seemed to take malicious pleasure in the evident discomfiture of her cousins, but the *séance* was ended at last.

"I have read of the eruption of mud volcanoes," one of the Canadians remarked to his friend, as they walked rapidly away afterward, "but I never witnessed it before."

"And I am eager for a bath and clean linen," replied the other. "It is worse, I must confess, than I had supposed. When we recover from the nausea of it, I think we will agree, my lord, that it was worth even the heavy sum also which we had to pay the female ogre."

"Having attempted to fathom the depths, I intend to go through with it. I will call at your hotel," his companion added, "as soon as I am recovered a bit, and we will consult as to our next plunge into the mire."

"Next time," his friend replied, "our adventure will be at least more instructive. We can enjoy that consolation anyhow. But out of all in the room there were three persons whom I was more interested in, by far, than in anything which was said," added Henry Harris, for such he was.

"Who were they?" asked Lord Conyngham, for such was the other.

"In Madame Beelzebub, in the fat-featured M. Portou, and, most of all, in the man they styled the poet, Achilles Deschards. I watch people very closely, as I do machinery, and, depend on it, I will tell you remarkable things some day in regard to these three."

CHAPTER XXXVIII.

THE ANATOMIST.

"You seem to notice everybody you pass," Lord Conyngham said to Henry Harris one day, soon after their visit to the house of Madame Mosseline, as they happened to be strolling along a boulevard together.

"Certainly I do, so far as I can," was the answer.

"I never do," his companion replied. "People are current with me as pennies are—I never recognize one from another, unless I know them very well; and I do not know anybody, when I can help it, unless I like him." But the nobleman was vaguely conscious as he said it that it was a narrow folly and weakness upon his part which he must outgrow.

"I know of nothing quite so interesting to me," the American replied, "as men and women, and in each person I find a new and peculiar interest. Did you observe, for instance, the obscene Frenchman who read that abominable poem at Madame Mosseline's?"

"Only to see that he was a dissipated rascal, with long, black hair, and dark rings under his rather fine eyes," said the other.

"Would you know M. Portou, the sleepy-looking and fat anatomist whom we saw there, if you should meet him again?"

"Assuredly not," the nobleman replied, in accents like those of his father, the Earl.

Henry Harris said no more, and the conversation changed. Since he had learned that the lost son of Zerah Atchison might be in Paris, young Harris had glanced with additional sharpness at the people he met. It was as if a problem had been propounded to him in machinery; here was a something to be solved if possible. "I may not hit upon it," he thought, "but then again I may. Mr. Atchison is an invalid, the daughter is closely confined, they have not a friend, apparently, in the world; if I can find the man, I will." And he had his reason for asking Lord Conyngham in regard to the men whom they had seen at Madame Mosseline's. For now, almost as soon as he had parted from his companion, he turned suddenly upon his heel, and, looking full in the face of a man who had been following him, he said, in French, "Well, M. Portou, what is it?"

The gentleman spoken to had on blue spectacles, carried a baggy umbrella under his arm, was like a thousand other of the *bourgeoisie*, a linen draper, possibly a confectioner or tobacconist, a good father of a family in all probability. He looked at the American with surprise. "Did you address yourself to me, monsieur?" he asked. "Is there not some mistake? Whom have I the honor to speak to?"

"M. Portou, I believe," the American said, firmly. He did not inform the other that he knew how, every day since

they had met at Madame Mosseline's, this fatherly-looking
man had followed him about; he merely looked at him
steadily and without speaking. There must have been
something in the unflinching gaze of the American which
acted upon the other as the sun does upon a fog. Certain it
is that the innocently mystified air of the florid Frenchman
changed.

"Is it possible?" he exclaimed. "And this is monsieur
the Canadian. I am delighted to see you. Allow me the
honor of your hand." He shook hands with him cordially,
and they talked in an amicable manner as they walked on.

"I observed at the time that, although present and taking some part in the *séance,* you are not yourself a socialist," Henry Harris said at length. M. Portou colored,
seemed to be for a moment embarrassed. "No, monsieur,"
he said at last, as with sudden frankness, "like yourself, I
am no Red Republican, either philosophic or practical."

"And you *are* an anatomist?" asked the other.

"Certainly, certainly," the man answered, eagerly; "we
are but a square from my little shop. If monsieur will have
the goodness to accompany me, beyond a slight odor, the
place is not an unpleasant one. Will you go?"

Henry Harris had his reasons, and conversing indifferently
upon many matters, the two arrived at last at a basement
room upon a side street. In the windows were displayed
a small collection of stuffed birds, a crocodile, a monkey,
and a wild-cat, also stuffed. When, unlocking the door,
the owner had entered with his companion, a medley of
objects appeared arranged upon shelves—a pair of elephant
tusks, the head of a hippopotamus, a human skeleton, a
Tasmanian devil in the act of fighting with a kangaroo,
both admirably preserved, a number of living parrots and
canary birds, while boxes of bones filled the corners and
gave forth a smell as of the sepulchre.

The visitor examined the collection with unusual interest, asking many and minute questions, all of which were
answered readily and with some pride. Now that the pro-

prietor had laid aside hat, umbrella, overcoat, and spectacles, he was the same florid-complexioned, closely shaven, dull-visaged, slumberous-mannered man he had seemed to be at the house of Madame Mosseline. While the two were conversing together upon natural history, young Harris was saying to himself, " I have a shrewd suspicion that you are no more an anatomist than you are a socialist, but this will do for the present."

"Frankly, M. Portou," he said aloud at last, and after further conversation, " I have no concealments. Like yourself, I am curious in reference to the Commune. I am an American engineer ; my name is at your service," and he handed the other his card. " Whatever you may be kind enough to tell me is, of course, confidential. You are thoroughly informed ; what are the chances of the Republic ? " The speaker might have saved himself the trouble to say all this ; the anatomist was perfectly informed in regard to him already, but he entered now with great cordiality into further conversation. One thing led to another, but this was the opinion of the anatomist upon the whole : The American Republic was a glorious success because of the peculiarity of its size and isolated situation. Doubtless it had before it a yet more glorious future, " although, candidly, I have my fears," M. Portou said. But it was folly to reason from America when France was concerned. The traditions, customs, opinions, surroundings, of the French were wholly different. A permanent republic in France was out of the question. It was purely a matter of a few years at longest. The exiled communists would be brought back. Every day the press would become bolder. Socialism was infecting the republicans with its leprosy. Any day France would have to choose between the red anarchy on one side or the beneficent return of authority. It might be Henry V. Possibly the Empire might be reëstablished.

" But the Republic? No, never. In America ? Yes. In France ? Never," cried M. Portou.

" With us," Henry Harris said, after much more conversation, "the public school is the hope of freedom," and he spoke fully upon that theme. The anatomist listened with great politeness.

"I acknowledge it all," he said in the end, and with enthusiasm. "It is wonderful; for America it is admirable! But it will not do, pardon me, monsieur, for France," and he described with great particularity the Government schools of France, from the primary upward, gymnasiums, colleges, universities. According to him the instructors were ignorant, and taught without ardor and purely for pay. In many of the schools shocking immorality prevailed. There was not one in which the most disorganizing doctrines were not allowed.

"I am but an anatomist," M. Portou said, finally, with modest self-depreciation, "and I consider it in a purely pecuniary point of view. Say that, on the contrary, the Brethren of Christian Doctrine are superstitious, behind the age; at least, they teach cheaply. Having no family to support, these good men can do the work for less than a third of what others would demand," and he entered into quite a detail of the number and excellence of the clerical schools throughout France. It was a question which was soon to strike France to its center, and the listener was deeply interested.

The American arose at last to go. He had been greatly interested, and promised to call again. Before leaving he turned the conversation for a moment upon Madame Mosseline, studying carelessly but attentively the face of the other as he did so. "Yes," M. Portou assented, "she is a remarkable woman. Did ever so unprincipled a female preserve such a neatness, such an almost Puritan order, in the externals of her place? Only in the externals, alas! It was too horrible!" The American looked closely at the dull visage before him; the eyes had fallen; there was a curious twitching about the corners of M. Portou's mouth; there was something in him, in a word, which the visitor failed to understand. He deferred it to the future, and spoke of the depraved poet who had seemed to be the idol of the club.

As he mentioned him, the man himself came into the shop. The American looked at him sharply, but cautiously. He was of an exceedingly fragile build, with a noble head and wonderful eyes, but evidently given over to dissolute courses. He was well dressed, had inky stains upon his fingers, and seemed to be perfectly master of himself. But Henry Harris made his adieus and left. After going a square, he called a carriage, gave the driver a direction, and got in.

"I will drop in upon the artists," he thought ; "but I will say nothing whatever as yet. It must be impossible. In any case, I will get a good look at the old artist, at his daughter especially. Who can tell what may come of it ? And you say that people are not worth looking at," he said, with reference to Lord Conyngham ; "your lordship will come to know that, really, people in this world are the only things in it worth studying."

CHAPTER XXXIX.

THE OLD ARTIST.

WHEN Henry Harris left the ill-smelling shop of M. Portou, the anatomist, he thought of many things as he rolled rapidly along in the vehicle which bore him to the house of Zerah Atchison. He was one of those natural leaders to whom a hunting party among the Rocky Mountains, or a company out on a blackberrying expedition among the stone fences of Vermont, would have yielded itself as spontaneously as did the workmen of his father's shop when anything old among the machinery had broken or anything new had to be devised to meet an emergency. Notwithstanding his knowledge of society and pride of blood, Lord Conyngham had submitted himself to the guidance of his American friend as he had not done to that of his stately father or his proud sister. Now, Zerah Atchison and his charming daughter also were passing into the care of Henry Harris. He had no more an intention to lay his grasp upon them than they had to intrude upon his kindness ; but so it was : the wood did not surrender itself more willingly to the adroit carving of the father, or the clay to the molding of the daughter, than did father and daughter to the hands of their new friend.

At the first sound of his footstep upon their threshold Isidore Atchison threw the cloth she kept ready for the purpose over the clay she was at work upon, and turned to a smaller and lower stand on which was what seemed to be a sleeping Cupid. It was a mere sketch as yet, altogether in the rough so far ; but she busied herself upon it with hurried hands as Henry Harris came into the room. The visitor cast one glance at her, and then, after the usual salutations, he turned to the old artist.

"I see that you are surprised at me," the latter remarked, painting steadily on upon what seemed to be a portrait ; "but I can not give up as yet the dreams of my life. Of course, I know that I can not reach anything approaching perfection as a painter. I know, too, that my highest success is in wood-carving. No one will buy my pictures, while, thanks to your mother, your sister, and yourself, I dispose of all I can carve. But I can not help it."

"Your pictures are far from bad," his visitor hastened to assure him. "Besides, you remember that Thackeray despised his pen in comparison to his brush. No one knows anything about his pictures, while we all recognize his genius in his books. Does our life ever flow as we would have it ?"

"Never ; but it is because it is ordered by a wisdom greater than our own. There is this excuse for me," the artist added, "that, of late, our hearts have turned toward our lost boy, our Valentine, for that is the name I have given him. I am trying to put on canvas what I remember of his mother, of Delira."

"And you," Mr. Harris said to Isidore, as he inspected her work, "are endeavoring to reproduce your brother as you imagine he might have been when a child."

"Yes; but I am only trying," she said; "and my work
is too vague, as it is purely a fancy sketch, of course. Yet,
is it not strange? both my father and myself, and without
saying a word to each other, have been, since you were here,
possessed by the same thought. We do not know that he is
in France. It is very uncertain whether he is living. Even
if he is alive, who can tell what kind of a man he may be?"

Her head drooped lower over her work, and her visitor
asked of himself: "I wonder if she does not moisten her
clay with her tears?" But he said nothing, continuing
quiet, almost cold, in his manner.

"How singularly like his wise mother!" the girl, on the
other hand, was saying to herself. Meanwhile the gentleman
considered the clay growing into life under her small, quick
hand with great care, glancing from it to the canvas upon
which her father had not ceased to toil.

"I paint purely from my memory of the mother, of Delira. I never knew her other name. You see," the old man
said, "that I am making her almost a red Indian. Since I
have thought of her at all, her face has come to me with astonishing distinctness, as they say a language learned when
young does to the old and to the dying, although unused for
scores of years. I could hardly see her more distinctly were
she actually before me."

"But may not she herself be living?" his visitor asked,
after glancing at the daughter.

"Yes, she is living," the artist said, gravely; "I am as
sure of that as I am that her son also is alive."

But the visitor had ceased to study the work of the artist; he was studying the father and daughter instead. "She
has reproduced her father in marble," he thought; "reproduced him perfectly, because he is one whom the memory
holds as perfectly and as unchangingly as does the marble.
You can no more forget his aspect of sublime patience than
you can forget the womanly devotion which transfigures
her." The girl must have felt how fixedly his eyes were
fastened upon her, for the color slowly came to her cheek

and brow. The gazer could not but have observed it, but he gave no sign. In fact, under pretext of examining her work more thoroughly, he placed himself opposite her upon the other side of it, and seemed to the old artist to be studying her instead.

"You see that she is of the purely Greek type," her father said, quietly, at last. "Now, your sister," he continued, as his visitor looked hastily up, "is wide between the brows instead; her forehead is low and broad, calm and sweet and strong. That is the German type. Canova recreated the Venus into that, but it is not the Aphrodite of Phidias; it is Minerva laying off her helmet to put on the cestus. I was telling Isidore of it, how Lady Blanche—" the eyes of the gentleman addressed grew bright at the name; the girl saw it as she worked. "Yes," added the artist, in a slow, critical tone, "she, Lady Blanche, *is* Juno; an English Juno, you know. Let me see: Apelles painted his Venus from the seven loveliest virgins of Greece. Now, into the composition of Lady Blanche has gone, Boadicea as a basis; a little, not much, of the mother of Alfred the Great, a good deal of Queen Bess, something of Mary of Scots. Did you ever think, Mr. Harris," he demanded suddenly, "how much of the blood of the cruel Norman, William the Conqueror, is in her? Yes, and of the dark, fierce Danes, too, of the old pirate days?"

"O father!" Isidore exclaimed, and added, "You must excuse him, sir, it is the force of habit. If Queen Victoria were to come in, it would be only with the criticising eyes of an artist that he would regard her Majesty. Dear father, I am used to it; but people do not like," she begged, with a beseeching look, "to be considered in that way. Lady Blanche is not a marble."

"Do you think not?" the old man meditated, with suspended brush. "Joan of Arc—Charlotte Corday—the Maid of Saragossa—Madame Roland—they are all of the Juno type. Look at this engraving of Maria Theresa," drawing it from a portfolio at his side and laying it on his knee. "Do

9

you see the bend of the neck, the curve of the lip answering to that of the brow, the nose, the ears even? That is the Empress Blanche also. Look here a moment." The enthusiast reversed the engraving and made with a crayon a few swift curves upon the back of it, which was blank. "Who is that like?" and he held it up.

"It is very much like the English lady of whom you have spoken, very much indeed," said Henry Harris, and his tones were more indifferent than his eyes; and he added, "Whenever you intend a queen, you always fall into those regal curves, do you?"

"Always, unless it be the Queen of Love one attempts, or Pallas. There are seven distinct rays, Mr. Harris, in the spectrum of the sun. There are as many in the types of woman. So of man. Lady Blanche—I speak purely as an artist," the old man went on, disregarding the appealing glances of his daughter, "is as brave as her brother. Braver —that is, she would dare and do where even her own brother would hesitate. When need was, Juno defied even Jupiter. Lady Blanche, if victory required, would storm a bastion. What is the name of that poor duke who was with her here the other day? Plymouth? Yes, that is it, the Duke of Plymouth. Sir," said the artist, "if the emergency demanded it of Lady Blanche, she, although of all women she must despise him most, yes, sir, she would marry even that man!" He was looking, as he said it, full in the eyes of his visitor, so unabashed was he in his artless art. Once the gentleman to whom he spoke had seen a locomotive dash, silently and suddenly, upon him from around a curve. Then he sprang aside in time; now he had to stand still and take the unbroken onset of the placid but terrible speaker. The young girl dared not look up from her work. She winced instinctively, so well did she know the force of the blow. Her hands were halted for the moment from the clay before her, were reached out to the wounded man—not in reality, only in sympathy inexpressible.

"Do you think so?" It was all that Henry Harris said,

bleeding inwardly, but allowing no emotion to show itself. His manner became colder than he was aware. After a few words in regard to the picture upon which the artist was engaged, and others in reference to the Exposition and art in general, he took his leave.

"O father, how could you!" It was all Isidore Atchison could say, and then she began to cry silently. But her father was looking at her work with astonishment. It had altered its whole appearance. "Why, my child," he said at last, "that could not be your brother; it is not even a boy. You have made it a likeness of Mr. Harris instead!"

The poor girl did not know it; she flushed, swept rapid hands over the face of the image, but, instead of continuing to cry, she broke into a laugh. It was merry, but not glad. Not being Minerva, the poor girl did not observe until that moment what she had been about. She flushed as Venus might have done; but Juno herself could not have swept her hands more ruthlessly over the features of the clay. Then she ceased to laugh and began to cry.

"I was unconsciously making studies for my 'Purpose,'" she said, in a beseeching way, as she lifted a corner of the cloth covering the other stand and glanced at a head beneath which strongly resembled their visitor; "but I will not work any more to-day," she added, and went into her own room.

CHAPTER XL.

DANGEROUS WAYS.

"My son," George Harris said one day to Henry when they were alone together, "it is time you were married. Choose your own wife, and I will take you as an equal partner with me in my business, which must before very long pass entirely into your hands with half of my property. But, remember what I say to you now, as I say it in my will: so long as your mother lives, everything is as thoroughly hers as it has been since we were married. You know my conviction is that it takes a man and a woman to make a complete person ; 'male and female made He them,' Scripture says. Your mother and myself have always consulted each other at every step, have had no secrets from each other since we were engaged to be married. Poor enough we were then, and our absolute unity has been the chief cause of my success, of our unbroken happiness, of the development of her character and mine, of all that your sister and yourself are and ever will be. Marry whoever you please, marry whenever you please ; but you had better never marry unless it be upon a basis like that."

It was on this account, and because he had rarely concealed anything from his mother, that Henry Harris, when riding one day in a carriage with only his mother, spoke frankly and fully to her concerning—not himself, but—Lord Conyngham and Mary ! "He and I have been associated closely together for some time now," he said, "and he has told me, as he has told her, his whole heart. He is thoroughly in love with Mary, is determined to marry her if she will consent. Apart from his rank, I could not desire a better husband for her. Apart from the mannerisms of his position and training, he is a simple-hearted, manly fellow."

All this was nothing new to the mother, of course. It was Mary's habit to make a confidant rather of her father than her mother, but father and mother had already conferred with each other in regard to the matter.

" We would decidedly rather she should marry an American," Mrs. Harris remarked in the end. " If it must be an Englishman, we would prefer that he should be anything almost that was honorable rather than a nobleman. With your father and myself, as it must be with you, that is a serious objection. Mary is as worthy as any Englishwoman can be of the highest rank, but she—"

" Is not born to the peerage," her son interrupted his mother. " You know how she has teased me by quoting Tennyson's 'Lady Clara Vere de Vere' to me. Well, I read to her yesterday the Laureate's 'Lord of Burleigh.' You remember that in it a village maiden marries one whom she supposes to be a poor landscape painter, and who, to her horror, turns out to be a lord. Yes, I put a solemn warning into it as I read the frightful result. It was after the marriage, remember:

> " 'So she strove against her weakness,
>   Though at times her spirit sank,
> Shaped her heart with woman's meekness
>   To all duties of her rank;
> And a gentle consort made he,
>   And her noble mind was such,
> That she grew a noble lady,
>   And the people loved her much.
> But a trouble weighed upon her,
>   And perplexed her night and morn,
> With the burden of an honor
>   Unto which she was not born.'

Then follows the sad story of how she pined away and died. I read it," Henry continued, "in a way to draw tears almost from the eyes of Hassan Pasha even, but she knew it all by heart before, and I fear it did not have the least effect."

"I understand," Mrs. Harris said. She smiled, but it was very gravely. "Mary is dazzled by his rank, especially by what it will be when the old Earl is dead."

"Do you think so?" Her son appeared to be astonished and almost shocked.

"There is no better girl than Mary, nor a more sensible one," the mother said, calmly; "but she is only a woman, and, like every other woman alive, she can not help coveting a coronet. To be a peeress, and of such an ancient and illustrious house, is the most splendid position, that of a queen excepted, in the world. In addition to, and as part of this, Mary knows that she would live in the highest and most brilliant society on earth, would have castles and palaces in possession, would be a leader of fashion in all the capitals of

Europe, would be flattered, envied. It is not in mortal strength that she should resist."

"I suppose you are right," her son said, with an air of disappointment; "but what Lord Conyngham says is that it is his career in politics which will, he hopes, interest her in him. Since he knew her he has become as ambitious, he tells me, as Lucifer. He intends to take an energetic part in Parliament, and it is astonishing what a change has been wrought in him of late. He used to be little more than a fop and an epicure; not so now. He is investigating communism with me, but that is merely a part of his efforts. Lady Blanche tells me that she can hardly get him away from his books. He is studying up India, Ireland, the Turkish Empire; every land in the world in which England is specially interested. I believe, too, he knows more than I do of agriculture, land tenure, free trade, finance, and all such subjects. He tells me that he has had the most valuable suggestions from Mary, that she has inspired him with the purpose of his life. I do not doubt it. They talk for hours together upon the impending changes in England and Europe. That is all very well, but, bless me, they are in love with each other! Of course, it is all very praiseworthy, but love is at the bottom of it all."

"For one who knows of love merely by observing your sister and her lover, you are very wise," his mother remarked, demurely, while her son colored a little. "Yes," Mrs. Harris continued, "Mary is naturally dazzled, unconscious as she is of it, by Lord Conyngham's rank. She is sincerely interested in his ambitions, and she is capable of becoming to him all" —the mother added, with all a mother's partiality—"that Lady Palmerston, Lady Russell, Madame Roland, were to their husbands; that is, she will be a very efficient help toward his political success. Most of all, Mary is, as you say, in love with the man who is so heartily in love with her. Nothing more natural. Nor do I doubt that they would make a happy couple if they were left to themselves. It is the influence that will be brought to bear upon him that I justly dread. The Earl will never consent, nor, I think," and the face of Mrs. Harris grew very grave, "will Lady Blanche really and heartily approve. There will be hosts of persons in England who will oppose the match with their utmost influence; persons, too, who are not without a certain right to speak. If the question were brought, like the marriage of a son of Victoria, into Parliament—" Mrs. Harris said, with a smile.

"Whatever the House of Commons would do, the House of Lords," her son added, with a laugh, for her, "would vote it down unanimously, no doubt of that! The Earl occupies so high a place in the peerage. Do you think," he asked, "that the Queen would approve of the marriage?"

"Frankly, I do not. Victoria," Mrs. Harris said, "is an excellent and sensible woman, but, with almost the entire nobility of England, she, and it is natural, is becoming, may I say it? jealous of America and of intrusive Americans. Our kindly feeling toward Russia, our prosperity, the unsettled nature of many things in England, the excessive and increasing influence of America there as elsewhere, alarms them. No," Mrs. Harris added, with a laugh, "I do not think her Majesty would recommend the match to Parliament in a speech from the throne. It would be a severe test for Mary," the mother continued, more seriously. "She would have, as Lady Conyngham, to face and conquer an almost unanimous hostility!" But her son smiled to himself, observing how his mother lifted her head more proudly, how her eyes sparkled as she said it.

"My daughter could do it," the mother added, quietly, but with a tinge of new color in her cheeks; "she could do it, but it might wreck her happiness. Henry," she continued, still more calmly, a few moments after, "let us wait. When we are called upon to act we will know what to do. However Mary may set her heart upon anything, so far, at least, she has always yielded to the judgment of her father and myself."

But neither the son nor the mother felt satisfied; no such

test as this had been applied to the young girl hitherto, nor anything comparable to it. Both felt that it was the gravest question which had ever as yet come up in their experience.

"My son," Mrs. Harris said, after a while, "the globe is turning under us all the time very swiftly. Ever since we were born it has been flying also with still more terrific speed into the immeasurable and unknown depths of space. Did it ever occur to you to try and stop the planet, or to change either its speed or its direction ?"

"As Earl Dorrington says so often, assuredly not," the other replied, knowing what was to come.

"When we have done all that we can do in anything, our wisdom," his mother added, "is to cease trying. I dare say that Heaven is as wise as it is irresistible in all its doings, in the least as the greatest. But," and she turned her loving eyes upon her son, seated fronting her in the carriage, "your father and myself are as anxious about you as we are about your sister."

"About me !" he exclaimed ; but he knew what she meant as he said it, and a long and serious conversation ensued. Having entered upon the subject, he found himself almost swept away by it. "I have always been frank with you," he said in the end, and with fervor. "Lady Blanche is superior to any woman I know. I admire and love her as much as it is possible for a man to love and admire any woman. Do you know, I think she—well—she is not wholly without interest in me. The Duke of Plymouth is desperately in love with her too. Poor fellow, I can sympathize with him. Every influence will be in his favor and against me. We love each other more ardently than—I mean," Henry Harris corrected himself in confusion, "that I love her more than Lord Conyngham *can* love Mary ; his nature and mine are different. But I am not going to urge her to what she may regret. And," he added, with a sudden gravity, "I am not a child, nor do I intend to go into either raptures or into desperations, like one of these convulsive Frenchmen. I intend to remain, whatever befalls, master of myself, I hope. As to Mary and her lover, the way seems to be plainer. Mine is a more difficult case than theirs—far more ! I would have spoken to you about it, but there is nothing you can tell me that I do not already know. You spoke about the swift, irresistible course of the globe. I feel as if she or I were speeding on to some terrible crash in the end. But what can I do ? Lady Blanche is out of the usual race of women. She is like—like a lioness, and that is why I love her. She is the one woman in all the world to live, if need be to die, for. But please do not let us talk about it ; I would rather not ! " It was said in the most loving and respectful tones, but Margaret Harris had never known her son to be as decided in his manner. She looked at him with grave concern, but the conversation was turned upon other subjects.

CHAPTER XLI.

ACHILLES DESCHARDS.

HENRY HARRIS had his own reasons for dropping in now and then upon M. Portou, the anatomist, and it was through him that he became well acquainted at last with Achilles Deschards, the profligate poet whom he had first met at the rooms of Madame Mosseline. "That man," the American explained to Lord Conyngham one afternoon at the Bodega, and pointing out the young Frenchman to him on the other side of the gorgeous room, "that man is worth studying. You saw him once before, but observe more closely his fine forehead, his splendid eyes under his profusion of black hair, his hard and dissolute air. He, sir, is a specimen of the literary bandit of the day. He wields a swift and exceedingly sharp pen precisely as the bravo of Italy used to wield sword and dagger, to kill whomsoever he is paid to slay. Enlist him by cash enough, and he will defend you and your party and attack your foes with equal and astonishing power. You

may be a Legitimist, an Orleanist, a Napoleonist, an adherent
of M. Gambetta ; it is all one to him. Take him into your
pay, and until some other party pays him still more to betray
you, he will do you faithful service through the press. He
has a vivid imagination, writes perfect French, is thoroughly
read up on every topic, is absolutely without principles of
any sort whatever ; is a Bohemian in the worst sense of the
word—Gypsy, *sbirri*, literary thug."

"Such men are the curse of France, I would think," Lord
Conyngham replied ; "I have heard of them, but, until we
met him at Madame Mosseline's, I had not seen a specimen
of the species. Let us have a talk with him ;" and in a little while the nobleman would have seriously compromised
himself by entering into conversation with Deschards, but
his friend promptly prevented him and told him why.

"That is an advantage I have over you, my lord," he
said, with a laugh ; "as an engineer, especially as an American, I can be seen with any man, of every sort of character
or no character, anywhere and everywhere in the wide world,
and no one would regard it as anything but natural ; but
unless disguised as Tom Perkins you can not."

With a gesture of impatient assent the nobleman turned
away, and in ten minutes afterward Henry Harris was conversing with Achilles Deschards on the other side of the
Bodega, and as naturally as if they had been the sworn
friends of a lifetime.

"When I saw you at that accursed Madame Mosseline's,"
the Frenchman was saying to him, "I knew you were Americans, but not Canadians. You can tell a Canadian by his
halfness, so to speak ; he is neither English nor American,
and having no independent nationality he has no strong per-
sonality of his own. As a citizen of the Great Republic you,
au contraire, have in yourself the assurance, *pardonnez-moi*,
of your aggressive flag."

"I thank you," the other began, but the Frenchman placed
himself in front of the American, laid his fragile hand upon
his arm, looked keenly at him with his hawk-like eyes, and

dashed on so rapidly that one less familiar with French than Henry Harris would have found it impossible to keep up with him.

"You Yankees," the Bohemian said, "carry your prairies in your aspect ; your Mississippi flows in your veins also. It is not only that you are hurled as upon your Niagara against Europe ; the boundless future of your land breaks over and sweeps away all limits to your personal plans also. The Romans marched everywhere to chain the world down beneath their sway ; the Rome of to-day is America, but, monsieur, the Americans go abroad to unchain the peoples instead. You, sir, are the universal and energetic solvent of the age."

Henry Harris was not at all flattered. He was too well aware that with Deschards such phrases were but the wares of his trade ; that in the twinkling of an eye this literary corsair could and would slay everything American as with the scimetar of his tongue or pen, provided money was to be made thereby.

"Why do you speak so savagely of Madame Mosseline ?" was all that Henry Harris replied. "I supposed the night I saw you there that you were—"

"A *pétroleur*, a Red ? I was as much so as my namesake Achilles was a woman when disguised as such in the court of Lycomedes. No, monsieur, I was there," the other continued with a bow, "only as you were there. You do not love the Social Republic ? Very good ; but I detest it more than you possibly can. *J'avais mes raisons ;* M. Harrees, in me you behold," and the speaker suddenly assumed a solemn air, "a Catholic. Recall, I beg of you, the massacre of the Archbishop of Paris, and ask of yourself what I think of the Commune."

The American glanced at the other with astonishment. It was as when an acrobat turns a somersault so swiftly as to take away one's breath. Could it be that the hollow cheeks, the dark rings under the eyes, the premature age of one who seemed otherwise young ; could it be that what had seemed to be the ravages of dissipation were the results, instead, of

ascetic fastings and macerations in some lonely cell? The
aspect of the Frenchman had become as in an instant that of
a doctor of the Sorbonne, that of an inquisitor even. But,
then, this very man had read the atrocious lines at the socialist club of Madame Mosseline, had read them with too much
zest not to have originated them in his own brilliant but foul
imagination.

"I see that you are perplexed. It is," the versatile
Frenchman said, with almost pity, "because you have not
wholly laid aside the Canadian. I also, monsieur, I also was
constrained to disguise myself when among those sheep of
darkness. *Que voulez vous?* Could I retain my fleece, white
as the snow? No; you saw our friend M. Portou, the
anatomist, there. He, you have learned, was not a Red, nor
was the friend who came with you, nor were you. Distrust
appearances, monsieur. I a Communist! It will suffice to
the Almighty hereafter to turn them into a hell wherein is no
fire. Incendiaries! Each bears enough of fire within himself to kindle the flames of Gehenna. Yet why do I say so?
Alas! poor fools, I pity them instead."

For once the American was fairly puzzled. He knew the
tribe to which his companion belonged. Louis Veuillot, the
savage ultramontane editor of "L'Univers," was, he knew,
but a variation upon Paul Cassagnac, the yet more brutal
Napoleonist writer; and this sharp-featured Frenchman was
as able and audacious as these without being hampered by
any conviction whatever. He knew that this Achilles Deschards was a type of a class of editors—writers for the press,
at least—no longer confined to Europe. A similar species,
he had been told, had sprung up, of late, in America also.
On his visits to Nevada and California he had seen desperadoes who were dreaded for their deadly skill with rifle, revolver, and bowie-knife, and he knew that desperadoes of the
press were beginning to outstrip these—in America, too—by
their more pitiless and terrible skill with the pen. For this
reason he was the more anxious to study Deschards, as belonging to the original type. But he was sorely perplexed

also. The changes in this Proteus were somewhat too swift. The other seemed to read his thoughts.

" You will find," he said, " that we Parisians are not shallow because we are sparkling. M. Portou, for instance—you mistook him ; you mistook me."

" M. Deschards," the American replied, gravely, even coldly, " I may have a profounder knowledge of our friend the anatomist than you are aware. As to yourself, sir, unless I greatly mistake, you are—" Henry Harris paused a moment ; he had a very important task in hand toward the other, and he had long ago learned to proceed with caution. When it was a question of steam and iron there were certain invariable laws, but not so when a man was concerned ; at least, although the laws of the human heart are unchangeable, his knowledge of them was too slight to allow him to act rashly ; therefore he arrested himself for the present, and said instead, " You are, M. Deschards, unless I err, one of the ablest and most effective of writers ; " and, with a slight bow, he rejoined Lord Conyngham.

CHAPTER XLII.

HERR ZOODLEPLAUNTCH.

THERE must have been something in connection with the game of billiards at Earl Dorrington's, already recorded, which smote Henry Harris also even harder than the ivory balls had been smitten, for, in a few days thereafter, he had disappeared from Paris, accompanied by Lord Conyngham, between whom and himself there was every day a firmer friendship. So much were they together that a companionship had sprung up between their servants likewise.

" Yes, I likes mine master," Toffski, the moujik, said to Judkins, the valet of the young nobleman, as they talked together in the cars which were conveying all four on this occasion into Germany. "For one thing I *not* like him."

"Hif his lordship would henjoy himself has hother gentlemen do," Judkins replied, "hi would not complain ; 'e might drink, gamble, go hon larks hof every sort hand hi would not care. But I hasks myself, why should a nobleman go has 'e does hamong the ragtag and bobtail, the degraded lower horders ? Hit his 'orrible ! But what his the matter with your governor ? "

"In my country, in Russia, master beats a moujik with big stick ; every master every man. No stick for me. My little father not beat me once," the other complained, shaking his head sorrowfully, "not even throw boot at me. Where we going now ? "

Lord Conyngham chanced to be asking the same question at the same moment of his friend. "I have read up the German socialists a little," he said, "in the ' Social Demokrat,' and my German is better than my French ; but I'll be hanged if I can understand what they are up to."

"Nor I. We will try Planitz, in Saxony, and see," his companion replied. "I know Herr Puttrich, who is a leader among them. He will gain us admittance into one of their societies. For years I have tried to make out what they are after. It is like trying to fix upon some definite and invariable shape for the froth of a mug of lager or the smoke of a meerschaum. This time I will learn the thing to the bottom, if possible. We go to Saxony because political offenders are allowed pen, ink, and paper in the jails of Saxony and in few other German prisons. Communists speak, therefore, more boldly in Planitz, because, if imprisoned, they can proclaim from behind their bars what martyrs and heroes they are."

It was in pursuance of this purpose that, a few nights after, the friends, dressed as is common to German students, found themselves in the hall used by the socialists of Planitz. A long table ran from end to end of the apartment, plentifully supplied with glasses of lager and other kinds of drink, the waiters hurrying in and out with pretzels, tobacco, and yet more lager in response to the thirsty clamor of the heavy glasses knocked upon the table. Lord Conyngham had furnished himself with, perhaps, the largest meerschaum in the room, but neither he nor his friend could keep up with the others in their glasses. For a time their attention was diverted from the talk going on among the heavily bearded, purple-visaged, square-shouldered Germans among whom they were.

"One thing is plain," Henry Harris said, in English and in a whisper, to his companion at his side, "these men know with perfect certainty that a change is impending in Germany. They are in dead earnest, are sincere patriots most of them, tremendous students. There are more steady thinking, solid learning, deliberate purpose in this room than in all French communism put together. That young fellow is Geib, of whom you have heard. The dogged-looking German opposite is Mosh, the reddest republican of them all. Yonder is Liebknecht. The man with the blue necktie is Bebel. They are comparatively moderate. Karl Marx, at the end of the board, is the leading socialist, as you have read. It will try our patience to the utmost. Now for it."

At this moment Herr Puttrich begged to be heard. He kept his seat, nor did his pipe interfere with his remarks.

"What I must urge upon you," he said in German, "is that the strategic point of our campaign lies undoubtedly in the matter of the Knappschaftskassen," and he entered at length into a history of the Insurance Association of Miners thus referred to, and of the wrongs toward it of the Government. To the visitors the matter seemed tangled and tedious beyond measure, but every German there smoked and listened, drank and listened, with profound attention to the end.

When he was through, they harkened with equal fixedness to Bebel, who proceeded to demonstrate the fact that the energies of ambition were taking a wholly new direction. Once men had gone by millions into the Crusades. Again, when aroused by the discoveries of Columbus, they had rushed into the finding of new worlds across the seas. Under Cortez and Pizarro the search for gold had been the mania, repeating itself in the case of the tulip insanity of Holland, the South Sea Bubble of France. In the days of Napoleon, as of Charlemagne and Tamerlane, conquest had been the rage of the hour. Under and after Luther religion had been the absorbing topic of thought and of action. "To-day it is industry," argued the speaker. "Aided by machinery, the quickened energies of Europe are given to the accumulation thus of vast wealth. Now, whatever the passion of the hour heretofore, it has resulted in the subjection of the many to the despotism of the few. Henceforth our capitalists will be our kings, our Neros. It is against them we must fight. And how? The state must be supreme. It must own and work every railway, telegraph, factory, workshop, as well as all schools and colleges. Abolishing indirect taxes and standing armies, it must grasp and wield as its only soldiers the children of the public schools, the laborers, the money, the—"

But Bebel was broken in upon by Mosh, the Red Socialist. His meerschaum did not prevent his earnest protest against this as, at least, the finality. He could smoke between sentences, and the puffs came from his lips like those from a cannon in battle as he proceeded to show that even the state is but a transition to the individual. "The many principalities of Germany had united at last in the Empire. What was that but a preparation for a confederated republic, such as those of Switzerland and America? The American Republic, it, too, must perish. Upon its ruins would stand the Individual. Every man shall yet be absolutely free, free to speak, think, feel, act; in himself and over himself sole czar and sovereign. That was the grand result, every man his own empire, monarchy, republic, state. Why not accept and aim at the ultimate result of the ages at once?" Much discussion followed thereupon.

Since America had been mentioned, Herr Puttrich stated at length that a friend of his, an American, was present, with the name of whose father, the railway king, they were all familiar. Perhaps he would speak. Henry Harris had not bargained for this ; he doubted if his German was sufficient to the task, but he accepted the work and arose. With great modesty he spoke of his inexperience, then of the vast emigration of Germans to America, and of the benefit they were to the country. He heartily agreed with Herr Mosh as to the fact that, at last, the individual was the supreme result of all government, as of all civilization. History existed for and culminated in the individual man or woman.

"And I hope that every one agrees with me in this also," he added, speaking slowly and using his best German. "The absolute freedom of the individual is the distinctive doctrine of American freedom, its essence, quintessence. By individual freedom I mean individual self-government. It is that which has made us all we are, which is enabling us to mold, may I say it? the race into our image. What is this personal freedom, this self-government, so new to the world, so powerful, so prosperous? Here is no theory ; it is matter of simple fact. It is that no man can be absolutely free in and of and by himself, free apart from government of every kind, empire or republic, to and of himself until—until the individual enthrones in his bosom, as supreme master of his every thought, that Power which alone is the sole, rightful, supreme authority."

"And what is that?" was asked by many about the table as he paused.

"It is," said the American, deliberately, "the God who made him, the Son of God who died to save him. That is American freedom!"

The words were listened to with deepest attention ; they were spoken calmly, clearly, and with the force of certainty. The last sentence struck the intellect of all present, because the instinct of the conscience accepted it. More still, because it was weighted, as well as illumined, with the almost supernatural grandeur, success, and acknowledged future of that America represented by the speaker, which is every day, and more and more, as every man present acknowledged, the haven, and hope, and revolutionizing force of the world.

A vast deal of argument followed, every man eager to establish his own view. The conflict of theories culminated at last in one dissenter, Herr Zoodleplauntch. He was unlike the solid, thoughtful Germans about him in that he was tall and cadaverous. Although he was not fat—far from it—it was not because he did not irrigate his leanness as with a Nile, deep and unceasing, of lager. His hair, long and thin, hung down his shoulders, but his gaunt face was almost beardless, his small, keen eyes glittering with restless excitement.

"No, no, no !" he now exclaimed, in repudiation of what the American had said, and with violence springing to his feet and brandishing his long arms, "that was the baby talk of the ages past. Martin Luther said that. But we? We are centuries beyond such childish nonsense. America? America was born but yesterday, and we intend to change America. We are grown to be men." The speaker drew himself up. "Look," and he waved his hand, "at Berlin. It has a million of inhabitants, with but one hundred and ten clergymen, Catholic and Protestant. Enter their churches on Sunday. Behold a desert ! There is not an average of a hundred worshipers to each, and these at the morning service only. Kaiser Wilhelm still believes, because he is old, very old. We have advanced since 1872. Since then—"

"Has not crime," the American interrupted, "increased more than fifty per cent. since then ? "

"It is," exclaimed the socialist, "because we are in a state of transition. We hasten toward perfection. The ancients sang mournfully of a golden age in the past. It was a myth. Man began with a microscopic infusoria. During the lapse of myriads of æons he developed upward through the ascidian into at last the ape. Through innumerable years he evolved from the ape into the savage of the age of stone. Then came periods of further tutelage under government of kings or republics. His infancy has required to be nurtured in the cradle of the family institution, of religion. But," and Herr Zoodleplauntch lifted the eyes and eager hands as of a prophet toward the future, "man approaches at last his glorious destiny. Already is he treading under his feet governments of all kinds whatever. Throwing off the swaddling-clothes of the family, of religion in whatsoever form," and he threw out his hands on either side as if casting away filth, "he stands erect at last. What need has he of God? Strong, wise, knowing all things, sufficient in himself, under no law but of his own pleasure, man comes at last to be supreme. The God of theology? Feuerbach well says it is but the shadow projected upon the infinite by man himself. With Comte I worship only humanity; unlike Comte, it is the individual I adore, not the aggregate. Look upon me," and the philosopher loomed through the dense fog of tobacco-smoke like the specter of the Brocken, with disheveled locks, gaunt and ghastly, his arms folded upon his breast. "I am the divinity: I worship and adore thee, O Zoodleplauntch, as," and he closed his eyes and bowed his head, "the only God. As God," he added, lifting up a wrathful face, "I henceforth doom to swift destruction not Christianity alone, but all religion. The citadel of superstition is the Christian Sabbath. You insult me with speaking of your Sabbath, your babyish Sabbath," and the speaker paused through intensity of unspeakable scorn.

Now there chanced to sit beside the deity in question a grave and sedate burgomaster, whose pipe was a wonder of art, as it was of size, an heirloom and a treasure. During all the oratory he had smoked steadily on, as if that were the only occupation, as it pretty much was, of his existence. With slow, almost rhythmic, puff he listened still as Herr Zoodleplauntch added, "The Sabbath? Listen. When our great Hermann destroyed the legions of Rome at Wenfeldt, Octavius Cæsar dashed his head against the wall, exclaiming, 'Give me back my legions, Varus!' To-day we wage a greater war with Rome, with Geneva, with America. Soon, very soon, will these lament, and lament in vain, 'Give us

back our Sunday, O Teutons.' For swiftly are we demol-
ishing, in America also, the accursed Sunday. *Delenda est!*"

As he said it he brought down his long right arm with
such energy as to smite the pipe from the lips of his neighbor, dashing it in a wreck of fragments and ashes upon the
table. Even the sedate Germans laughed, but the discussion
was resumed, and it was weary hours before the two visitors
emerged from the fog of tobacco-smoke, a headache each
being apparently all they had gained.

———

CHAPTER XLIII.

THE PIRATE OF THE PEN.

"It is a queer world! It is the queerest of all conceiv-
able worlds!"

The remark seemed to break of itself from the lips of
Henry Harris. Lord Conyngham and himself had got back
to Paris the day before from their trip into Germany. George
Harris was absent on business, but his wife and Mary were
seated in the parlor at their hotel, and the nobleman had
just finished his account of their experiences among the
clouds of Teutonic speculation and tobacco-smoke in the
Bier Halle of the socialistic club. "So far, all I have
learned," Lord Conyngham added, "whether from Old Statistics in London, from Madame Mosseline here in Paris,
from Herr Zoodleplauntch in Germany, may be summed up
in three things: First, the foundations of society are not, as
yet, settled as upon a rock. Far from it. Underneath all
Europe, as well as Asia, is only quicksand. The second
thing I am equally sure of, and that is, that none of the remedies suggested would do more than substitute for what now
exists the most abysmal chaos, out of which, could it be tried,
society would be glad to struggle again for salvation, through
fire and blood, under the leadership, perhaps, of the worst

despot that ever reigned. Last, the people everywhere are desperately discontented, and will never rest until we attain to something better than we now possess."

" There ought to be a fourth conclusion, my lord," Mary Harris suggested, "and that is, that the sooner all Europe follows France, and scrambles out of the quicksand upon the adamant of American republicanism, the better for it."

" You always wave the stars and stripes, my dear," her mother said ; " but, do you know, I have my fears for America, too. We survived the agonies of our civil war, but I almost dread the—yes, the *terrible* prosperity upon which our republic is entering. If we boast ourselves too much, some sudden, unlooked-for disaster may hurl us again into the dust. But what makes you think it is such a queer world, Henry ? "

" I was not thinking of Herr Zoodleplauntch," her son replied. He had been walking to and fro in the room ; now he stopped and said : " Lord Conyngham has told you about the people we met at Madame Mosseline's house. Let me carry on the story by telling you of things which I have found out since we were there. It has taken time, and money, and expert detectives, but I think I have reached the truth at last—almost, at least. First, to be systematic, like your lordship, there is M. Portou, the anatomist." Thereupon the speaker described at length the appearance of the portly, sleepy-faced man, the disguises he wore, the furnishing of his menagerie-like shop. "Now," Henry continued, " that man may or may not be really and truly an articulator of bones, a stuffer of birds, taxidermist, whatever he calls himself ; in any case, his feathers and furs and skins are but the costume of the hour. As I supposed, he is a Jesuit. Fat, sluggish, stupidly socialistic as he seemed, he goes everywhere in the interest of his order, merely to keep him and them informed. To be frank, I can not but honor the fervency of his faith, the utter devotedness of the man, even while I abhor his duplicity. Dull as he looks, he knows that he is liable to be stabbed as a spy by those who hate a Jesuit more than they do an agent of the police. But there is one thing which I have not found out yet. It is not to hear the insane and profligate notions of the Commune that he haunts the house of Madame Mosseline. My lord," and the speaker addressed himself to his friend, "as sure as you live, there is some reason beyond that; some sufficient reason in connection with that woman; some reason why he, a priest—a pure man, I have no doubt—goes to her house. What it is I am resolved to know if I can. I have reasons."

"We know, at least, who that rascal Deschards is," the other replied. "Do you know, he is an entirely new character to me. I study him as I would a newly patented revolver, a recently discovered reptile. We have two or three inferior specimens of the species in London, but I never actually saw one before." Whereupon the speaker gave the ladies a description of the literary bandit, of his appearance, his ways of life. Mrs. Harris and her daughter were greatly interested.

"I think," the latter said, "that he, or men like him, must write the begging letters my father receives. There are so many of them, and some of them are written with wonderful skill."

"Yes," her brother said, "it is only a scribe like Deschards who can write in turns like an old soldier, a shipwrecked sailor, a bankrupt wine-merchant, a starving scholar, a high-spirited youth on the edge of suicide, an aged philanthropist who has beggared himself by giving, a decayed clergyman. I have had to read the letters. But I think it is when the writer lays aside his sex and becomes a perishing female, through all varieties of maid and matron, daughter, widow, sister, struggling to support a consumptive brother, or something of the kind, that the writer is most of a genius. At times he becomes a mere boy of six, a little girl of eight, in his attempts to get a remittance. Of course, the man we speak of is superior to the need of writing such letters. Yet, in manifold ways, I dare say Achilles Deschards keeps his versatile pen going. He is never at a loss, and yet, to do him justice, all lesser efforts are subordinate to his chief occupation—that of political writer."

"He wrote for a socialist sheet," Lord Conyngham said, "and I obtained—you know I want to learn everything— some copies and read his articles with great interest. It was excellent practice in learning French in its purity ; yes, and in its power, also. They were surprisingly good, those leaders. For analysis of the wrongs of the workmen and the causes and remedies thereof, for argument, pathos, invective, wit even, they would not have disgraced Pascal ; they reminded me of the '*Lettres Provinciales*' at every step. He is a talented rascal."

"And I read a number of his articles in a clerical journal given me by our other friend, the Jesuit, " Henry Harris remarked. "Except that they were more aggressive, the ' *Pensées* ' of Pascal were not so much superior to them. It was pathetic as well as powerful, the way in which the writer spoke of the evils of Protestantism and their inevitable outcome in socialistic atheism ; of the stability, glory, conservative power, future triumph, of ultramontanism. You would have thought it was a devout ascetic who wrote, a St. Francis de Sales, a Borromeo. And yet—" The speaker made a despairing gesture with both hands, and began again to pace the floor.

"And yet your pirate of the pen wrote them," his sister added for him.

"Yes, but," her brother stopped to say, "he wrote the radicalism which Lord Conyngham justly wondered over, at the very time he was engaged in his clerical labors. In the morning, let us say, he gives his really wonderful power to tearing socialism to shreds and glorifying the Church. Until late at night of the same day he is engaged with Protean power in depicting, with equal vigor and unutterable loathing, the superstition and villainy of pope and priest. We have all witnessed the rapid transformations of Harlequin ; but the intellectual adroitness of Deschards surpasses that.

You can run a locomotive due north, can reverse its wheels
and back it almost as fast due south; but here is a man who
can run himself, both heart and mind, north and south at
the same moment. Really," the speaker added, "we Americans are 'smart'; but I had no idea of an American as sharp
and thrifty as that. As a Yankee, I am almost proud of
Achilles Deschards."

"Proud of him!" The exclamation broke at the same
moment from his sister and their visitor. "As an American,
proud of *him!*"

"Yes; proud of him, because," Henry Harris said, with
an enjoyment of their surprise, "this distinctively French
individual has not a drop of French blood in his veins. He
is as much of an American as I am."

"What do you mean, Henry? We shall think that *you*
are masquerading next," his mother said.

"No, madam," her son replied with sudden energy;
"the whole world seems to me, at times, to be such a universal *Mabille,* such a vast masked ball; men and women
seem to me, sometimes, to whirl around in such a—yes, universal waltz of dominos and fancy dresses, that I have to
hold fast to the truth myself if I am to remain sane. Every
day I try harder, on that account, to be rigidly, vigorously,
painfully honest, accurate, true in word and deed, in thought
and feeling. Would you like to hear a true story?"

"Not until after lunch," Mrs. Harris interposed. "Come,
my lord; come, Mary." And they went together into the
dining-room.

"Now, listen," Henry continued, as they lingered about
the table. "I rarely touch wine; so you will be confirmed
as to my veracity while I talk. Once upon a time, years
ago, a landscape painter," he smiled at the slight start given
by his sister at the words—"I do not mean Tennyson's Lord
of Burleigh—was sketching among the roughest regions
of Virginia." Beginning thus, he told the story which Zerah Atchison had told him. It required delicate handling,
but he put into a few words the history of Delira, the wild

daughter of the woods, of her love for the painter, of the elopement with the French surveyor, of the birth of the child of the artist, of the flight of mother and babe with the surveyor to Paris, of the desire of the artist and his daughter Isidore to find the relative of whom they had so suddenly learned.

"It may be natural," Henry Harris continued, "for them to desire to find this son and brother—half brother, I should say. They have no other of their blood living. But it has perplexed me why I should have become so deeply interested. It is because it was a something hard to do, I dare say; because they had not a soul to do it for them. Anyhow, I promised to help them in their hopeless search for the missing man."

"Perhaps," Lord Conyngham remarked, "Miss Isidore was not without her influence upon you. She is a charming lady; I do not wonder that she is an artist. There is a clinging, plastic power in her eyes as in her gifted hands; and the perfection of her art lies in her modesty, too."

"I thank you for saying so." Mrs. Harris and her daughter made the same remark in a breath, and when Mary laughed at it and apologized for interrupting her mother, the matron continued, with feeling, "Yes; we thank you. Both Mary and myself have been greatly pleased with Isidore. Nor is it alone because of her genius and devotion to her father. There is a purity of soul which suffuses her. Did you ever see an instance, my lord, in which the very soul seemed to—there is no word but that—appeared to *suffuse* a person? It is like the blush in the cheeks of a girl; like the color, rather, in the face of a child. It is what, in music, is styled expression, effusion. The great masters can pour their very soul through the chords, because—I despair," Mrs. Harris laughed, "to express it; their inmost nature is so deep, strong, ardent, that it trembles to overflow upon lip, eye, hand."

"And the piano, the canvas, the clay, whatever it is they are at 'work upon," her son said for her, "can not but be

10

filled with and reveal the life which is received. That is genius!" His eyes brightened; he had forgotten his story. "Ah, yes," he proceeded, when reminded of it, "there is little more to say. Mr. Atchison painted the mother of the man from memory. When I saw the picture, and then Deschards, it came to my mind that it was barely possible he might be the one they were in search of. I employed detectives to investigate his antecedents. It is too long a tale to tell, but, as the result, I feel almost certain that he is the man."

"And you have told Mr. Atchison?" Mary Harris exclaimed. "Why, Henry, it is like a romance."

"No; I have not told him," her brother answered. "There are points I intend to clear up before I do that. And to find that the person they seek is *such* a scoundrel! No; I am *not* ready to tell them of it yet, if I ever do. We must wait."

But company was announced at this instant, and the circle was, for the time, broken up.

CHAPTER XLIV.

IMPERIAL LOVE.

At every important step of his life hitherto, Henry Harris had consulted his mother if not his father, but in reference to Lady Blanche he could now ask no advice of either. Like his father, he was slow in coming to his conclusions, but, once reached, they were as much a portion of his nature as its grain and fiber is of the oak. And this was because, like his mother, he could neither speak nor act until he was thoroughly satisfied in his own mind. Thus satisfied, his conclusions were to him, and to others also, like sunshine or storm, among the irreversible operations of nature. In other words, his decisions in any given case were but a sure anticipation of the sound judgment in the matter of every other person. As to Lady Blanche, his heart had more to say than in any subject which had ever come before him for final award, and he, like a just judge, had allowed this client to say all it had to say and to the last syllable, but he had also listened to all that his cooler sense had to suggest. This was an unusual course in one so young and so ardent, but this lover was of the stuff also of which kings are made.

He felt himself ready at last to call upon her for her decision, and he had been careful to select a time when he would find her at home and alone. When the footman announced to her who it was awaited her in the private parlor, she was outwardly calm, but inwardly it was as when she had first known that her mother was dead. For a long time she had tried to prepare for the visit, yet it was as if two women were striving in her. But the strife grew only the more desperate as she lingered at her toilet, and she suddenly turned and went to her visitor. Events must decide. Now, if it is by an instinct that lovers hide themselves from all others on such occasions as this, it is by an instinct no less sacred that even the nearest friends shrink from intruding upon them. Yet a few words may be said as to their interview. The American was walking up and down the room when she came in. After the usual salutations she sat down, but he excused himself from doing so and remained standing.

Surely it is at such a moment that a man and a woman appear at their best. Henry was not an Adonis; Lady Blanche met every day hosts of gentlemen who were handsomer, more elaborate in all the details of manner and toilet, than he ; and it was the almost rugged independence of his sturdy form, his open and manly face, his eyes, sincere and steady, which drew her to him. There was in this gentleman beyond any she had known the aspect of self-reliance, of strength to endure as well as to do. She was strong, and she loved him because he was yet stronger. And he was saying to himself as he stood before her : "Surely it was in such a mold as this that the Roman patricians of old were cast. That noble yet lovely head; those eyes, as imperial in the humility of their drooping lids as when lifted to mine; the gracious curve of that lip, of that fair neck; that hand which lies relaxed upon her lap, conscious and yet unconscious of the scepter it holds; yes, this woman is by birth a queen. As such she will be sufficient for this emergency."

"Lady Blanche," he began, "you know already what I came to say, but please listen to me." No man could have begun more coolly. Once begun, his ideas became clearer as he went on. Somehow her presence steadied him, made him even more perfectly certain of the one thing to do. He told her of his exceeding estimation of her, of his ardent affection. He had feared that he would lose the mastery of himself, new as it would be to him to do so. He became more assured as he proceeded, in low and rapid tones, to say all that he had to say. She had glanced up at first with a certain startled look, then her eyes, her head, fell again as he went on. It was very sweet to her to hear what he was saying; but all the time it was as if she had also another self which stood by and listened coldly, angrily even, as a rival might have done. For she was at the moment two women indeed, each how unlike the other! One of these was as simple-hearted as any dairy-maid among the daisies in England. Rosy of cheek and of lip, pure, and good, and true, she was listening to her lover with gladness of heart, as any Peggy would listen, milk-pail in hand, to her Robin beside a hawthorn hedge, their feet wet with the dewy grass of morning. Robin loved her with all his heart, and she loved Robin as sincerely. That was all, and why should they not marry? It was as natural to love and to marry as it was for the larks to sing or for their lips to meet. Of course she would say yes! There was nothing in all the wide world which could or should prevent that! Robin is mine and I am his, and—

The Englishwoman lifted her eyes to her lover as she had done when they had met once before. He stooped, he took her yielding hands in his, he was about to kiss her. She drew back, she arose, she was no longer a dairy-maid ; she was another woman entirely.

"You forget yourself, sir," she said, and the lover found himself confronted instead by the proud daughter of Earl Dorrington. In the same instant he also had grown colder, calmer. He looked her steadily in the eyes.

"You are right," he said. "I had forgotten that you were anything but an Englishwoman ; that you were very beautiful, very charming, and only a woman, nothing more." Even as he said it his heart softened ; she was nothing more again ; was trembling, was weeping.

"You know—" she began.

"Yes," he replied ; "I know everything, and I know it perfectly. I know that not your father only, but that every friend you have, would be shocked beyond expression if you should marry me. It would not matter if I were to become the wealthiest man alive. If I were to hold the highest office in my own land, it would be the same. Even if I could, as inventor, author, orator, reach the loftiest station, it would be the same. It is strange, Lady Blanche," he said, sadly ; "you are, like the beautiful maiden in the German story, the wonder of the world for your loveliness ; you are, like her, locked up in the heart of a transparent globe of crystal ; you live, you breathe, you—yes, you *love*, yet you are frozen in within a sphere of ice, which is also adamant."

"Is it my fault?" But the dairy-maid held herself aloof from her lover as she asked it ; her lashes were wet with tears ; a great perplexity fell upon him ; he dared not come nearer to her. Dairy-maid as she was, she was not standing beside him among the newly mown hay ; her foot was instead upon the steps of a throne ; he had but to attempt to touch her, and at a breath she would be a queen instead, seated high up and out of his reach. He loved her, but there was something which struck at his very manhood in all this. He was a machinist as well as a lover, and it was as if he were engaged upon a task which he knew he could by no possibility accomplish.

"No, the fault is not in you," he said, very sadly. "Why did I come here? Let us be frank with each other, Lady Blanche. Even if you were willing, could I consent to sacrifice you to my love? I am not a fool, for I know what would follow. You might honor me with your love, you might consent to marry me, to elope with me if necessary; but do I not *know* what would follow? It is not that you could not stand up under the storm of reproach which would fall upon you; worse: how could you endure to lose all rank, and be simply my wife and nothing more? The utter change in your entire life; how could you survive it? Would you not come to hate me, instead? Though I loved you a thousand times more, *because* I love and admire you so, I could not take advantage of your weakness, could not plunge you into certain wretchedness."

The proud beauty had become and remained merely a woman again; she was regarding him with reproach; her eyes swam in tears.

"No, Lady Blanche"—he grew firmer as he went on— "if I am to remain a gentleman, I must be steady to what I know of myself, as well as of you. Prince Albert could marry your Queen, but I could never marry a woman who was to be in anything my superior. You would always be my superior," he hastened to explain, "in everything in which a woman is superior to a man, a wife to a husband; but beyond that— No! I admire you, I love you more than any woman alive, but I can not, I will not—"

He did not finish the sentence. At the instant the lady saw in imagination, through her tears, another standing beside him. As the lover lifted his head, as his cheek flushed, his eyes grew bright, the Duke of Plymouth stood before her in comparison with him. He was not a worse man, the Duke, than the *habitués* of London clubs and the theatres of Vienna and Paris generally are, but then he was no better. The lady even at such a moment, and because it was such a moment, could not help seeing the undersized, weak-eyed Duke, his complexion as colorless as was his hair, his eyes, his words, his ways. Just then he appeared to her to be the meanest creature crawling. If his estates measured whole counties, why could he not somehow draw a larger manhood into himself from them? His oaks, his deer, his tenants, throve upon them; he himself was only shriveled thereby in contrast. Why could he not bring something of his vast income into his veins, into his bones? His blood had come down to him through the well-defined channels of eight centuries; why, alas! did it not have a more definite hue, did it not flow in stronger currents?

In a flash the Englishwoman saw and ceased to see the Duke; only the American stood before her. The Duke was but a vaporous individual at best; he had vanished before her clear eyes; only the American engineer stood there in his simple manhood. The tremendous revolution which is heaving beneath the deepest foundations of her country stirred in the depths of her own heart, stirred blindly, vaguely. She was better read, had more capacity, more vigor of heart and intellect, than the majority of her sex and rank. In virtue of that she was beginning to see things as all, even of her own class, will see them in the broader day of a century hence. But at that instant the inevitable future stood before her in the person of the one man she had ever loved. Her heart had lent its flame to the light of her intellect. As she looked, the queen in her came deliberately down the steps of her throne, and lost herself in the simple woman. She was no more than a milkmaid.

"Mr. Harris," she said, "I have thought of all you have said; have thought of nothing else; have thought of it all long and deeply." She interlaced her fingers before her; as she stood with relaxed arms, her head drooped, her bosom heaved before a power too great for her, a soft color suffused her cheek, a gentle light came into her eyes. "Mr. Harris," she said, with a smile that was as sweet as that of the humblest girl, "are you sure? Do you really love me?"

The lover made a step toward her. In the same instant her face changed; she lifted a warning hand; Earl Dorrington entered the room. The lover knew that the Earl could not but be aware of what was passing between him and Lady Blanche. He was glad of it, was about to ask an interview with him, when, withdrawn to one side, the Englishwoman lifted her hand again and shook her head in such passionate entreaty that he forbore to do so, and soon afterward took his leave. On reaching his hotel the lover sat down and wrote to the lady, entreating her to suffer him to speak to her father forthwith. In his letter he endeavored to put his entire heart, but it was several days before he received a reply. When it did arrive he tore it open with eagerness, but was not surprised to find, without date, address, or signature, only a few words :

"Had you spoken, it would have killed him ; he is so old. I can not permit you to do so. Do not call upon or seek in any way to speak to me. It can not be. No one can know that better than yourself."

Whenever Henry Harris saw Lady Blanche after this, at the Exposition, upon the streets, in company, she so evidently avoided an interview that his pride was aroused. For the present, at least, he would make no further attempt.

CHAPTER XLV.

IN PURSUIT.

It had been arranged between Isidore Atchison, Mary Harris, and her brother, that all three were to go upon a ride into the suburbs of Paris quite early one Tuesday morning. The last-named had special reasons for this, which he had told his sister, and, in consequence of their plan, the gentleman called at the studio of the artists immediately after breakfast. The father was not yet up, nor would he arise until after the return of his daughter, but her he found equipped for the drive and eager to go. She had never seemed so fresh and charming. It may have been the perfect taste displayed in her dress, as well as an exuberance of health and high spirits following upon comparative relief after long and severe poverty. The companionship of such friends as Mary Harris and her mother, after long isolation from almost every one, had much to do with it, as also the knowledge that the talents of her father and herself were appreciated—all this went to account for the new gladness and beauty of the girl; but there was more still.

"Just now I had such a flattering letter," she said with glee, while the gentleman stood, hat in hand, waiting for her to draw on her gloves, and, in the fullness of her heart, she waved the letter over her head. "Out of the generosity of his heart, the writer," she laughed, "insists upon it that I shall tell no one, not even my father; but how can I help it?"

It may have been, also, because she had grown up almost out of the world and in the realms of nature and pure art, that Isidore Atchison seemed so unconventional. She was so excited she could not be calm. The dimples came and went in her childlike face; her hazel eyes were full of joyous expectations; her body swayed to the music of her joy as that of a little girl would have done over a Christmas gift, or when full of eagerness to start upon a picnic.

"How glad I am," she said from her heart, "that people think I am a genius! I am not, you know; but if they think so, you see, and if they pay me so, then my dear old father need not carve any more. Nobody will buy his pictures; but then he has long ago given up any hope of that. Ever since he can remember, he has dreamed of being a great painter—has been toiling hard to be one. He has hoped he would certainly succeed *this* time, oh! a hundred times over and over again. But, do all he can, the picture will *not* be what he wants it to be—is determined it shall be. He has a perfect ideal in his mind, you know, Mr. Harris. I do not believe that Titian or Rubens had as perfect a conception of what they intended to produce as he.   He is a great painter," she said, stoutly ; " only—only—"

" The obstinate brush refuses to yield as it should to his hand," the other suggested.

" Yes ; but the genius lies in the conception," she insisted, half in earnest.   " That is why my dear old father—the best father alive—has, through all these long years, grown so patient.   It is because of years of hope, defeat, but undying hope still."

" I understand," Henry Harris said, entering heartily into the reasoning as he did into the mood of the other.   " His ideal hovers in the air before him so vividly that he feels as if next time he will certainly grasp and place it upon the canvas."

" Yes ; and now he can give himself up entirely to trying," the girl said.   " The gentleman who writes to me says that he has desired long and intensely to possess a Venus such as he is sure I can supply him.   I must not tell a soul, but he has already placed, he says, oh ! such a large sum to my account in the Bank of England, for the purpose.   I ought not to have told you," she added, " but you are the first person I have seen, for father is not awake yet, and I am *so* glad."

" Miss Isidore," the other remarked, with a sudden gravity, " please let me read the letter."

The delighted girl, with a sudden trouble in her face, handed the paper, which was still in her hand, to him.   Excusing himself, he walked to the window, read the letter with his face from her.   Then he turned to her, his countenance grown so grave that the gladness died out of her own, too, she knew not why, as he said :-

" Miss Isidore, may I beg that you will say nothing of this letter to your father even—to any one—at present ?   I entreat you to do as I say."   It was said with an authority which was not to be resisted, not even disputed.

And then he turned away again so as not to see the quenching of the light in her eyes, the astonishment, then the crimson shame, which flooded her face.

"My sister waits for us at the door," he said, in a lighter tone, the next moment. "Take your own time to come down. We will have a delightful ride. I will not forget that this is your secret."

He had slipped the letter into his breast-pocket, and went out.

"Mary," he said to his sister, as he stood beside the carriage in which she sat waiting, "Miss Atchison has had bad news which she does not want alluded to. I know you will do all you can to make her forget it."

But it was some time before the poor girl came down. It was plain that she had been weeping; her gladness was gone. As he assisted her into the carriage, and then took a seat beside the driver, Henry Harris pressed his hand upon the letter in his bosom, and said things under his breath, and to himself exclusively, which would have astonished the ladies beyond measure. His sister received their companion with such a loving kiss as caused the tears to flow silently down the cheeks of Isidore as they rode rapidly away. But Mary did not seem to observe them, and conversed with her in a gentle and consoling way.

"My brother tells me that you are not quite well this morning, dear," Mary said, at last. "You have worked too hard. What a beautiful day it is! The ride will do us all good," and she began to point out this object and that as they went. The sun shone brilliantly, the air was clear and bracing. Gradually the spirits of the young girl rallied; her joyousness was sobered for the time, but she grew more and more cheerful as the hours slipped away. It was due to Mr. Harris, she thought, to at least seem to forget.

"I want you to notice the people as well as the places, you ladies," he said, after they had gone some miles, turning to look down upon them. "Ruskin tells us somewhere that one day, in traveling, he took care to study closely the faces of about a thousand people he met. Except in the case of a school-girl, every face, he says, was either very bad or very sad." The speaker had said a word to the coachman just

before, and the carriage was going along quite slowly as he
spoke. "Now," he added, in a light tone, "I wish you both
to observe every face that you see upon the right-hand side.
These men and women have to go to that corner to take a
vehicle for their places of business in Paris. Please," and
he consulted his watch and laid his hand upon that of the
coachman until the horses had come down to a walk, "please
look at their faces very closely. I want to know what you
think of them."

"We will, Henry," his sister said; "there are children on
their way to school, old men, young men, lean women, stout
women, people in uniform, newsboys, market-men—" She
saw her brother lift his handkerchief to his lips as she spoke.
It was a concerted signal. "O Isidore !" she added, "look
at that man coming along, the one with the sallow complexion and the fine eyes. What do you think of his face—the
man with the old woman ? "

"It is a very intellectual face," the artist said, "but he
must have been very ill ; see how thin and haggard he is."

"Is it a good face ? Would you think him to be a good
man, an honorable man ? " her companion asked, hurriedly.

The other was surprised at the eagerness of the question.
She looked steadily at the man indicated, who recognized
Henry Harris at this moment, and a salutation passed be-
tween them.

"N—n—no, I would not regard him as a good man,"
Isidore said, slowly; "he would make an excellent model
for Mephistopheles. He is a French Lucifer," she added,
with energy. "But no," she corrected herself on the instant, and said, with childlike eagerness, "he can not be so
very bad. See how patiently he is supporting his old mother
along."

"How do you know it is his mother ?" Henry Harris
asked, almost as eagerly, but in a low tone. He was taken
by surprise.

"Of course it is. Do you not see how much they are
alike ? And," the warm-hearted girl exclaimed, "see how

she leans upon his arm, how she looks up into his face, how lovingly he adapts his steps to hers, how he bends down to speak gently to her and yet loud enough for her to hear. Oh, I am so glad! His face *is* like Belial, but that may be his character, *must* be his character to others, not to her. He is the worst man in the world, but the best son."

At the word Henry Harris spoke to the coachman, the horses sprang forward, and the conversation took another turn. They had a long and very pleasant ride. The gentleman had left his seat beside the driver and seated himself in the carriage when they turned, at last, to go back, and Isidore suddenly asked him in a pause of their talk : "Mr. Harris, you recognized that good son who is such a bad man ; what is his name ? "

"He is a writer for the press," the gentleman replied, "and his name is Achilles Deschards. Did you notice the woman who you said was his mother ? "

"Yes ; she looks like an old Indian woman. What sharp, black eyes she had! And he is exceedingly like her. But," the girl added, "he is evidently a remarkable man. Tell us about him, Mr. Harris."

The one addressed paused a moment, exchanged glances with his sister, and then told of the talent and singular duplicity of the celebrated writer.

"And he writes as brilliantly for one party as for another," she mused when he had finished. "He can write hymns for the religious papers, and the lowest vaudevilles for the theatres ; can compose sermons for the priests in Lent, and songs which are sung at the *cafés chantants.* Is it not strange ? "

"Oh, yes, and he prepares *feuilletons* for the comic papers, obituaries for dead children, attacks on Germany, anything, everything for pay. He is a universal genius," the gentleman added, "an admirable yet particularly detestable Crichton. He writes anything for money."

"Yes, that is very wicked, but," and the girl lifted her soft and pleading eyes to his face, "he gives the money to his mother. And she is old and poor, and perhaps knows nothing about it. And they love each other so! Not that I excuse him," she added, hastily.

This last was something wholly new to Henry Harris. He was not aware before of the existence of the woman who, he had every reason to believe, had loved and then run away from Zerah Atchison. "And that rascal is, in all probability," he said to himself, "at least a half brother of this unsuspecting girl." He was more perplexed what to do than ever.

But his mind was very clear in regard to another matter. Nothing more was said, and soon after he deposited Isidore Atchison at her own door. Very early next morning he went to the hotel at which Hassan Pasha lodged. That gentleman was not up, but, when a person of the bearing of the American pleaded that he had special business with him, he was allowed to enter the magnificent parlors joining the room in which the Pasha slept, to wait for him there. As soon as he had gone into them he locked the doors behind him, then opened and entered the bedroom. The Turk was still in bed, his servants absent preparing his breakfast, and, awakening at the sound, he sat up with astonishment upon his face.

"Did you write that?" It was all the sturdy visitor said as he handed to the half-awakened man the paper he had taken from Isidore. No name had been signed to it. The girl evidently thought it had come from some wealthy patron of art, American or English, but her visitor had long known the character of the ex-vizier, had recognized his writing. The Oriental was surrounded by the costliest objects. The furniture, the pictures, the silken drapery of his bed, were in keeping with the Sybarite reputation of the man himself, who now gazed with the eyes of a leopard at his strange visitor.

"What business is it of yours?" he almost howled, endeavoring to get out of bed, his black eyes glancing at a pair of pearl-handled revolvers lying upon a table almost in reach.

But the other laid a heavy hand upon his shoulder, and held him down, with eyes more dangerous still.

"The lady is my countrywoman," he said, almost in a whisper. "For that reason, also, I am so quiet about it. If you ever trouble her again, ever breathe even of this visit, you know the penalty, you scoundrel!" Saying which, he grasped the silken beard of the Turk with one hand, threw the fragments of the letter into his face, and slapped his cheek soundly with the other. Then he picked up and tossed the pistols into a bath-tub near by, which was full of water for a morning bath, and went as softly out as he had entered, leaving the wretch paralyzed with wrath and astonishment behind him. The early visitor knew perfectly well what he was about. Had the ruffian been French, American, English, he would have pursued a different course. But a Turk was, he knew, like a red Indian. Such an insult breaks the spirit of the bravest of his species. Whether as an individual or an empire, the only argument understood in that realm is the application of force. By it they came into Europe, by it the Turk must be driven out. At least, what he did was the only course the American could think of, and it was one of the things in which he did not consult any one before acting.

CHAPTER XLVI.

PERPLEXITY.

ONE day Lord Conyngham called by appointment at the Hôtel Bristol. It was early in the morning of a beautiful day, and he and his friend Henry Harris set out on horseback for a ride into the country. The American was mounted upon a favorite chestnut mare, the Englishman rode a black horse of as good blood as the other, and the two gentlemen found it difficult to hold in their spirited steeds as they made a way for themselves through the crowded streets. At last

they reached the suburbs. "Now!" exclaimed the Englishman, who had seemed to be in overflowing spirits, and, giving rein to their horses, they rode almost as if for a race
over the rolling country and between the handsome houses.
More than one of the police called after them in vain; the air
was so exhilarating, the animals so eager, that it was "like,"
Henry Harris said, "shooting the rapids of the St. Law-
rence—impossible to stop!" They were many miles from
Paris when Lord Conyngham at last drew rein—

"Because," he said, "I want to talk to you, and I intend
to do it frankly and fully."

The American had known for some time all that his
companion desired to say, but he had left him to himself.
During their acquaintance a great change had taken place
in the Englishman. He was a sterling fellow at heart, but
his rank and associations had nearly spoiled him at one time.
Affected, foppish, conceited, insolent, arrogant, he had supposed that the world was made exclusively for him and for
his kind. A few years more would have changed all this,
which so far was but a mere outer manner, into the very
nature of the man. But his long sojourn at the Exposition
had benefited him; he had been reading much of late; the
spirit of the times was changing, and he felt it; his association with young Harris had done him a world of good,
as his influence, too, had benefited, although in other ways,
his American friend. Above all, he had come more and
more into the gentle but plastic hands of Mary Harris. In
awakening his heart she had also aroused what might almost
be called his conscience. It was not merely his affection, it
was his judgment which was engaged.

"What I want to say is this," he began boldly, as the
result of long resolve,. then hesitated, stammered. "It is
like putting my horse at a five-barred gate," he said; but
then, as he would have lifted his horse, with spurs in its
flanks, to the leap, he compelled himself to add, "Mr. Harris,
your father is in Russia, and I must say what I have to say
to you instead. Sir, I love your sister; I think she is not

wholly without interest in me. May I beg that you will consult your father and mother at the earliest moment? I want to marry her, if the alliance is agreeable to you, and as soon as you will allow."

"My lord," the other said, gravely, "I thank you in the name of my family for the honor you do us. You have been frank with me; I will be equally so with you. I have learned to like you thoroughly. You will allow me to say, I know no man whom I would be so glad to have as my brother-in-law. There is but one objection."

His companion looked at him for an instant with amazement; then, with a return of his old hauteur, "May I ask what it is?" he demanded.

"It is your rank," was the cool reply. Lord Conyngham gazed at the other in wonder. "My rank!" he said to himself; "why, ever since I was a boy I have had daughters and their matchmaking mammas after me on that account. Yes, and I have had fathers and brothers urging me to come to dinner in hopes I would take a fancy to one of the girls of the family. A lord! Great heavens! it is because I am a lord that I have been pursued from London to Baden-Baden, from Vienna to St. Petersburg, from Rome to Paris, up the Alps, up and down the Rhine and the Nile. Wherever I go there are swarms of girls who, I beg their pardon, would give their souls to the devil if they could get me, and all because I am a lord. What the mischief—"

"My lord," his companion was saying, "if you were a merchant, a farmer, a machinist, anything but a lord, we would greatly prefer it. Not that I am a radical," he continued, with a smile, "but that we seriously object to be included among the number of those who may have sought—"

It was as if the American had heard what he had said to himself, and the Englishman bit his lips.

"Moreover," the other went on, "we are perfectly aware that such a marriage would awaken the utmost opposition in your own family. We are fully as proud as yourself—"

But the blood of the nobleman was up. "Mr. Harris,"

he said, with more energy than the other had observed
in him before, "suppose we deal frankly, indeed, with each
other. Between us there is no need of diplomacy. The
whole thing is this : I love your sister. She won't say that
she does not love me. With her consent I intend to marry
her. We have had, I will confess to you, the deuce of a time
over it at home. It is not that my father does not highly
respect—" he began.

"I understand, understand perfectly," the American said,
with some impatience.

"Very good. But I am of age. Moreover, my father
has never had any of the trouble with me which other gov-
ernors have had. I have not drank, gambled, ran into debt,
eloped with anybody's wife—all that sort of thing. Fact is,
I have been steadier than *he* was when he was young. This
is the first thing he has objected to in me. But I told him,
she told him—"

"She? Excuse me, who do you refer to?"

"My sister, Lady Blanche, of course. From the first she
liked your mother and sister. She teased me awfully. That
of course. But as soon as she saw that I was in earnest, do
you know?" and Lord Conyngham turned in his saddle to
say it, "Lady Blanche has been on my side heart and soul !
It is the most extraordinary thing ! She is as proud as
Lucifer—if a man can speak in that way of his sister—
and I never was more astonished. I can't understand it
yet ! "

The face of the American had grown cold and stern, but
the other was too much occupied with his own matters to
observe it.

"You see," the Englishman continued, " the Earl is old,
is terribly determined. He can not understand the times.
He is sadly shaken in health. We are afraid any great
shock will kill him. There is not a grander Englishman
alive, sir ! " the son said with enthusiasm, " but he is very
determined in his way. We are not rich, sir. You may
know that we own estates enough, but our tenants have failed

in their crops year after year. The Earl has had trouble of late, I may say, severe trouble." The tones of the son had softened as he said it.

"Your father is to me," his companion said, "the noblest of his class, as I happen to know, so far as tenant troubles are concerned. They are, as we are all aware, universal in England. If the next crop fails you will have had five years of failure. Providence itself is fighting against you by the side of American competition. Pardon my saying so, but you are on the eve of a profound revolution in England. Primogeniture, entail, feudalisms of all kinds, all are bound sooner or later to go, my lord! Again excuse me for saying it, but it is so!"

"I am afraid you are right, but," added the nobleman, "you may depend upon us to fight to the last. *Noblesse oblige!* Nothing but Providence, as you call it, can conquer us, and it will be one of the longest and toughest jobs Providence ever undertook! But it was not of that I wished to speak. The Earl is older than you think; he is almost infirm. Although Blanche is younger than myself, he has always regarded her as if she were the older. By Jove! I wish she were his son instead, and his oldest son! Anyway, Blanche has more influence on him than I have. She has done her best for me. Women understand when to speak, and how. We have conquered! The Earl knows that, provided your sister consent, I shall marry her in any case. He will not oppose it. But, for I must be frank, he yields his consent because he has come to know that, if I do not marry Miss Harris, I will in all likelihood go to the devil, whereas if I do marry her I will devote myself to my social and political duties. Mr. Harris," Lord Conyngham said, gravely, "my father holds your family in the highest esteem. For your sister he has the sincerest appreciation. She will be welcomed into our family as she deserves to be. You can rest sure of that."

The American bowed his head in silence. He was aware that more was coming.

"There is another thing I am obliged to say," Lord Conyngham proceeded—"obliged, because it is, to be perfectly plain with you, an additional reason why my father has yielded. It is this." But the speaker hesitated to go on. He glanced uneasily at his friend, spurred his horse on, then reined him in, looked about as if for relief from some quarter, seemed to be sadly put out.

"My lord," the American remarked at last, "I think I know what you are about to say. Please say it. I am not an old man, but I have some knowledge of the world. If I indulge at any time in day-dreams, I know how to endure whatever is inevitable. You were about to speak of the Duke of Plymouth." It was said calmly, for the speaker had, for some time now, accustomed himself to the matter in hand. For many months the gossips had been full of it; intimations of the kind had long been afloat in the papers.

"Yes," the Englishman now said, "Blanche is to marry the Duke of Plymouth!" He did not look at his friend as he said it, and, although the other knew it before, it was as though he had been stabbed to the heart.

"If I could have my way," the nobleman continued, "it is not the Duke who would have married her. I will venture to add that I do not think Blanche would have broken her heart if the Duke had broken his neck the last time he rode a steeple-chase. Oh! he is a good-enough man. The fact is," it was added with an effort, "we are, as I said, by no means as rich as we should be. My father lived freely when in his minority, as his father did before him. After his minority, too, heavy debts were incurred. No, by Jove! we are *not* rich, far from it! Your solicitors will know all about that when we arrange, if I am so happy as to gain the consent of your family, our marriage settlements. As to the Duke, he is clever enough—confound such a state of things!" It was irrelevant, but it was said with the sincerest energy.

"It will be confounded soon enough," the American added to himself, and he remembered a Hindoo proverb which Ishra Dhass had quoted to him one day : "Where there is the least injustice, sooner or later, it shrivels the very sky itself as though it were the cast-off skin of a snake." But the glory had gone out of the day to Henry Harris. He was glad on account of his sister, of his friend, since they loved each other ; but what remained for him?

"My lord," he said at last, "your father, the Earl, must take the initiative in regard to your matter. Until that time I can say no more. As to myself, I must get away from Paris. I leave for Russia very soon. Everything is arranged, and I intend to get to the bottom, if I can, of the Nihilism which threatens the empire."

"And I will go with you," his companion said. "I told Mary—I beg your pardon—your sister, I mean. She opposed it, but afterward consented. We will, if you can obtain the consent of your family, be married soon after my return." But even the joyous lover was sobered by the stern calmness of his friend, and the remainder of their ride was given to a discussion of matters connected with their proposed invasion of the realms of the Czar. But never before had the American endured such agony as that which had now fallen upon him. It was an agony which found relief at last only in silence and solitude.

CHAPTER XLVII.

THE YOUNG ARTIST.

IT so chanced that at the very hour Henry Harris and Lord Conyngham were taking together their memorable ride, Mrs. Margaret Harris and her daughter were on a visit to the studio of Zerah Atchison. It was very rarely that mother or daughter took so decided a liking to any one, but their hearts had been drawn to the artist and his daughter from the first.

"It is impossible not to venerate such a man," Mrs. Harris said to Mary as they rode in their carriage thither

that day. "I have met in Rome and elsewhere those who
are enthusiasts in art, but, alas! their conceit of themselves
is almost always in the degree of their genius, often in advance of it. Now, Mr. Atchison has the artistic faculty to
the highest degree, but accompanied by the sincerest humility. Already refined by his art, his patient trust has
purified even his refinement. He and his daughter have
also been so separated from the world that they are like
children together, simple and good. Their devotion to each
other is one of the most interesting of things. Amid the
uproar and glitter of Paris, the fierce competition of fashion
and business, to be in their room is like getting back to a
quiet rural home in America. That is why I go there so
often. I love to hear them talk. It is pleasant to watch
them at work, too, only I observe that, whenever I am there,
Isidore keeps what I would judge to be her chief occupation
under cover of a cloth, while she trifles apparently with a
Cupid in clay. It is better," Mrs. Harris added, with a
smile, "that she should be at work on Cupid than that the
mischievous imp should be at work on her."

"She never thought of such a thing; she is too much
shut out from all society!" Mary defended her friend
warmly. "I am more interested in her than in almost any
girl I know! Our friends, Virginia Jossellyn and Ellen
Ellsworth, for instance, have nothing on earth to do but to
see and be seen, while her head, her hands, her heart, are full
of art and her father. Now, I think that a girl without some
enthusiasm for music, for sculpture, for painting, for *something*, is a poor creature. And did you ever know, mamma,
so unconventional a girl? She is like, Henry says, what one
reads concerning the virgins of Greece in the days of Apelles,
she is so supple, flexible. When he said that, I read to him
what Wordsworth says of his Lucy."

"Since you have had such a pupil in Lord Conyngham,"
the mother suggested, with a demure smile, "your enthusiasm seems to be for teaching. But what does Wordsworth
say?"

"O mamma!" her daughter said, reproachfully, and not without a blush; "but listen. The words got themselves by heart without any effort of mine:

> "'Through years she grew in sun and shower;
> And Nature said: A lovelier flower
>   On earth was never sown.
> This child I to myself will take;
> She shall be mine, and I will make
>   A woman of my own.
>
> "'Myself will to my darling be
> Both law and impulse; and with me
>   The girl in rock and plain,
> In earth and heaven, in glade and bower,
> Shall feel an overseeing power
>   To kindle or restrain.'

Please let me quote a little more," Mary said, "it describes Isidore so well:

> "'The floating clouds their state shall lend
> To her; for her the willow bend;
>   Nor shall she fail to see,
> E'en in the motions of the storm,
> Grace that shall mold the maiden's form
>   By silent sympathy.
>
> "'The stars of midnight shall be dear
> To her; and she shall lean her ear
>   In many a secret place,
> Where rivulets dance their wayward round,
> And beauty born of murmuring sound
>   Shall pass into her face.'

Now," Mary continued, "Isidore has lived apart from the world with nature until hers has become the beauty of nature itself. In addition, she has conformed herself unconsciously to her father's ideal of art, has grown like living clay under his critical eye and molding hands. Don't you think so?"

"I am not as poetical as you, my dear," the mother said, "although I agree with you as to her lovely simplicity. You know how almost furious Henry becomes at the foolish girls who paste little curls about their brows, and bedizen and belittle themselves, as he calls it. He admires Miss Atchison exceedingly in comparison, and then we are naturally interested in what your brother has told us of her half brother and his singular mother. I never knew Henry to be more interested in a man than he is in Achilles Deschards. He never wearies of reading to us his brilliant papers, and wondering how it is that the intellect can work so vigorously apart from all sincere conviction. He studies him as he would a bit of novel machinery."

"But he can not bring himself," Mrs. Harris added, " to tell Mr. Atchison that he is his son. He fears it would result in more pain to him than pleasure."

"Is he sure that he *is* his son ? " Mary asked. " How can it be possible ? "

"Out of pure curiosity I have encouraged him to investigate it," Mrs. Harris said. " He has had experts at work. The mother of Deschards has had no reason to conceal anything, and, in some way, the detectives have traced mother and son from their first coming to Paris, so many years ago. The French surveyor who ran away with her married her, gave the boy his own name, had him thoroughly educated, but died at last, leaving his widow wholly dependent upon her son, for there were no other children. From a very early age the son has had to struggle desperately to make his way. Henry says that it is this which perplexes him so ; the devotion of the lad and then the man to his mother is the very thing which has driven him to prostitute his remarkable talent as a writer ; it is to make money for her—for himself, too, and his pleasures that he is, Henry says, as indifferent to the nature of the literary work he does as if he were a steel pen or a leaden type. His gratification is in the money he makes, in the rapid exercise of his talent ; except his mother, he cares for nothing, whether it be virtue or vice,

God or Satan. From long habit, too, he is simply an intellect utterly devoid of conscience. His affection for his mother is the one thing which prevents him, Henry says, from being intellectually an unmingled devil. Yes, this increases, of course, our interest in Mr. Atchison, his father, and in Isidore, his sister, who are so eager to know about him and yet so unconscious of the facts. But here we are."

Zerah Atchison was at work, when they had ascended the stairway and stood at the door, upon his portrait of Delira, the girl who had fled from him in his youth. His daughter also was at work, and not upon the Cupid, but upon a bust near by, which so absorbed her that she no more heard the knock at the door than did her father. But the ladies, standing outside, thought they heard an invitation to enter, and, opening the door, they paused for a moment unobserved. The light so fell into the room that the faces of both artists were away from them as the visitors came silently in, but this enabled those visitors to see the work they were at more distinctly, and mother and daughter made the same exclamation :

"It is Henry ! "

At the word the girl seized upon a wet cloth lying near by and was about to throw it over the clay, but "You are too late, my dear," Mrs. Harris said, stepping forward and grasping her hand, while Isidore seemed covered with confusion.

"I am sure you have no cause to hide it," Mary exclaimed, with eagerness.

"O mamma, is it not good? It is Henry to the life ! I am so glad ! "

"Yes, it is a success," Mr. Atchison said, with a glad face, "but it is not a portrait of your son. She had worked for weeks upon her ideal of Sorrow. All that she accomplished was a head representing Wretchedness instead—Misery, I ought to say."

"And it was the most miserable Misery you ever beheld," the girl pleaded, holding the cloth still in her hand.

11

"She had to abandon it," her father went on, "and so she began to work upon her ideal of Purpose instead. If it is like your son, madam, it is his fault, not hers. But," and the artist laid aside the father and assumed the critic, " I could not but approve the work when I saw that she had the genuine inspiration. It is excellent, madam; it is most admirable. But it is not your son, it is her ideal of Purpose, as I said, manly Purpose, noble Purpose, but that is it, Purpose ! See how the lips are slightly parted, observe the lift of the brow, the elastic vigor of the neck, the repose, yet stern intention—" But the mother did not listen to the old critic; her eyes were overflowing with happy tears as she gazed upon the clay. It was not that it was an admirable likeness of her son alone, it was that she recognized as never before the character of her boy. It was a revelation to her, and to the sister, of all that they had secretly hoped for in regard to the son and beloved brother. Here was the authentic declaration of it as from the hand of Truth. Yes, he was full of purpose, noble purpose !

"Why, mother ! " Mary remonstrated, but she was weeping herself—it was so sudden, so unexpected.

"I thank you, my child." Mrs. Harris took Isidore by either shoulder as she spoke, and kissed her again and again. Out of sympathy Isidore also wept, as Mary too kissed her with many thanks.

"It is so with me," Mr. Atchison hastened to say ; "whenever I see a genuine work of art it moves me to tears. The first time I saw the Immaculate Conception of Murillo I wept like a baby. I congratulate you, Isidore ; you have succeeded, my dear ! And I congratulate you also, ladies, that you have the artistic faculty of recognizing genius when you see it. Besides," added the delighted old man, " she has not finished it. Moreover, it will look still better when it is cut in the marble. The solidity of the marble will lend additional strength to the idea of Purpose which Isidore intended. For it is not your son, I assure you, it is not ! " he added, with energy and some trace of mortification ; "it is purely ideal, as Isidore will tell you." With his head on one side, the old man was looking closely and with almost a rueful face at his daughter's work.

Isidore, too, seemed to be sadly disturbed. With her eyes cast down, she shrank as if her efforts were being severely condemned instead. Evidently she was so much distressed even that Mrs. Harris whispered to her daughter, in compassion, "Let us say no more now. We took her unawares. It was a kind of shock. Artists never like any one to see their work until it is finished." As it was said, the young girl had hastily covered the clay over again, but the delighted mother could not refrain from saying to her in a low tone : "You must pardon us for breaking in upon you so, my dear, but remember that the bust is mine. If you will allow me, I have bought it."

There was no consent to this on the part of the girl. She thanked the other modestly, but her eyes were still cast down, or lifted with a troubled look. The visitors had known the girl in many of her varying moods, but when she remained so silent Mrs. Harris took pity on her.

"My dear child," she said, "we called on a little errand to-day. My husband has written to Henry from Russia in regard to a matter which he thinks may interest you. But he must call and tell you about it himself." Then mother and daughter both examined the Cupid slumbering upon its wooden stand near by, with many kind commendations. After that they looked closely at the picture upon which the father was at work.

"It is his latest work, but if that is like Delira," Mary said, as they rode home at last, "there is not a trace of her in the old woman we saw. Yet there is a strong likeness between it and Deschards. And yet he had better have died when a baby. Is it not a strange, strange world, mamma?"

Mrs. Harris did not answer her daughter, did not seem even to hear her ; she was buried in thought. For some days after it was the same. Mary had never known her mother to be so silent, so reserved. She did not know what to make of it.

CHAPTER XLVIII.

THE LAY BROTHER.

ONE day Henry Harris chanced in passing near the shop of M. Portou, the anatomist, to meet his friend Ishra Dhass, the Brahmin, and a sudden fancy seized upon him. "I wish," he remarked to the Hindoo, after conversation upon other topics, "that you would go with me on a visit to him," and he described the Jesuit shopkeeper to Ishra Dhass at length.

"Nothing could give me more pleasure," the Hindoo said, his dark eyes lighting up, his habitual good-humor increasing, as it very easily did to cordial gladness. To tell the truth, the American shrank a little from the Jesuit, as he did from going among the dry bones and stuffed animals of his assortment.

"It is," he explained to his friend as they walked, "like going into a cemetery; especially when I get into close quarters with this anatomist, who is also a Jesuit, I gasp for breath as if I had left the sunshine, the free air, the ordinary common sense of living men behind, and had gone down into the deepest vaults of the dead. It may be because of my practical training, but I feel worse than when I was crawling through the catacombs of Rome, for in M. Portou it is as if I met with one of the dead there, and with a dead man who somehow is alive, and who is determined that I should abandon everything I consider to constitute life, and to force me, if he can, to be a living corpse also."

"I understand," the Brahmin said, with an eager gesture; "only, if one of the dead in the catacombs could talk with you, he would want you to be what I am instead, a Christian of the age in which he lived, a simple follower of the Nazarene, as Christians were in the first and second centuries. You and your good mother and sister, all of you English and American Christians, of whatever denomination, are nearer to the Jesuit than you think."

It was said with that joyous certainty of manner which caused people to accept what the Brahmin said in spite of themselves ; there was a subtle yet substantial and undeniable truthfulness in it, as of sunshine and morning dew. But the two men were by this time at the shop of the articulator of bones. M. Portou was delighted to see his visitors, and, after due salutations, he showed them with alacrity the various treasures of his somewhat ill-smelling establishment. After a good deal of general conversation, the owner led them into an inner room, and entreated them to partake of certain bottles of rare old wine, which he happened to have. As he produced them from a little cellar, brushed off the dust and cobwebs, and arranged the glasses, the anatomist was saying to himself : "Ah, what glory to God and to us if they were brought by me into the light ! This ignorant Hindoo has vast influence in his own land and in Europe also ; what a trophy he would be ! And this clear-headed American millionaire too ! Apart from his money even, he would be, ah, heavens ! what an accession to our influence in America ! His sister, his mother, his father, would follow him into the Church. It would be the making of *me* with the order. Forgive me, O God, my miserable selfishness, and—" But heaven alone knew the intensity of his supplication, even in the act of bustling about with his wine, for help to convert his guests.

"Now, M. Portou," the young American said at last, "you remember how frank I was in telling you that I knew to what order you belong. I have told Ishra Dhass of it, have told him of your courage and energy in penetrating even into the secrets of socialism at Madame Mosseline's. The man must be sincere who hopes," Henry added, turning to the Hindoo, "to benefit such a vile wretch as that unprincipled woman." To his astonishment their host exclaimed, vehemently :

"I beg you will not speak so of her ! " It was said with a sudden warmth of which the speaker seemed to be ashamed the next instant, for he added, as if putting Madame Mosse-

line out of the discussion : "Of myself I am willing to
speak. I am of the order, as you say, of the Jesuits ; for
sufficient reasons I disguised myself ; strategy is always
allowable in war, and we—alas ! upon us all the world is at
war."

"Please let me explain," the American said. "I am the
son of very practical people ; my whole life has been given
to practical questions ; now, what I hate most in anything is
inaccuracy, uncertainty. I like to work, to work hard, but
I must see distinctly what I am at. No man likes more
than I do to go ahead as rapidly as I can, but I must be
sure I am right before I take a step. My time with you
to-day, my time in Paris, is limited, but I am consumed
with a craving to get at the bottom facts, to *know* as perfectly as possible in regard to everything I can. Now, it is
not of mysteries of doctrine that I wish to speak ; of course
there are mysteries in that as in everything. What I want
to know is as to practical facts. You are the first Jesuit I
have been thrown with, at least, when there was such opportunity of frank conversation. I shall esteem it a singular
favor if you will answer clearly, definitely, certain questions
I would like to ask."

Their host was, as has been said, a man generally of a
sluggish, not to say stupid, aspect. It was a natural disguise nature had given him, for under it was anything but a
stupid intellect. He sat now with his hands crossed upon
his breast. Although engaged in almost unceasing prayer
while he talked, he concentrated himself upon the matter at
hand. Too much was at stake not to do so. "I will gladly
do what I can," he said, with courteous humility, "to inform
you and your friend. Please proceed," for he had an intuition of what was coming.

"I deal with iron, with steel, in my business," Henry
Harris said. "In our shops we have to measure and weigh
things with painful precision. The variation of an ounce
in the making of a valve may result in the explosion of a
boiler ; the divergence of a hair's breadth in the construc-

tion of a lever, of a shaft, of a wheel, may wreck a railway train, and massacre scores of souls. Pardon me if I repeat that I do not consider myself to know any matter at all unless I know it accurately and finally."

The Jesuit smiled at the almost peremptory manner of his visitor, but the eyes of the Hindoo glittered with a certain satisfaction.

"Well, monsieur the engineer, will you have the kindness to ask your questions?" It was said by the Jesuit with great good-humor, but, behind his almost pulpy face, he stood upon his guard, like a gladiator behind his shield.

"I have read," Henry Harris remarked, "the Syllabus very closely, have studied what Gladstone, Cardinal Manning, Monsignore Capel, and others, have to say upon the subject, but somehow the matter has been swathed in cloud, wordy assertion, vaporous denial. What I want to get at," the American continued, with almost indignation, "is the simple fact. In the Syllabus and elsewhere, I find certain distinct declarations by the highest authority in the Roman Church, but when I try to learn from Catholics the positive, final meaning, it eludes me, it evaporates, M. Portou," and the young man became slow and cool as he went on. "I am glad I have to do with a brave man. Please tell me this: your Church claims to be the only true Church on earth, does it not?"

"Certainly," the other replied; "when Christ gave the keys to Peter—"

"Pardon me, but all I wanted to get at was the mechanical fact, not the reasons," interrupted the other. "Your Church claims then the sole and exclusive right to marry as well as to bury?"

The other assented. "I will explain—" he began, but the visitor did not give him time.

"As the only Church on earth it has," he asked, "a right to suppress every other where it can by force; is that so?"

"It has; of course we prefer moral suasion, but—"

"Thank you, only this further question: not the State,

only your Church, has a right to control the education of the young?"

"Of course, it alone has the right," their host said, rising to his feet. "There are those, alas! in my communion who would hesitate, prevaricate, endeavor to explain away even that which is most sacred. They charge with duplicity the order I unworthily represent. Gentlemen," the anatomist added, "I am but a lay brother, as we call it, of the order, and yet do I not know that we alone believe in and assert the authority of the Church as it has been held in all ages, as it is held to-day by every real believer? I believe in the Church as I do because I believe in God. The children of Voltaire may scoff, but the day comes when the false and shallow civilization of the times will have perished, when the Church will reign supreme throughout the entire world!"

"As it did in the days of Hildebrand over Europe? As it attempted to do in the days of Philip II of Spain? M. Portou, I thank you," the American continued, rising to his feet, "and I honor you for your sincerity. Also, I thank you for your information. Now I know. If I believed as you do, I would belong to your order. I like a man to be out and out in whatever he undertakes. Good day."

But the anatomist was not willing to part with his visitors so abruptly. He talked long and with impassioned eloquence, entreating them to read certain books which he gave them, beseeching them to pray for divine help, assuring them of his own prayers on their behalf. The man evidently believed, and with intense sincerity, in all he said, and the two men listened respectfully.

"Ah, my friend," the Hindoo said, as they walked away together at last, "mistaken as that man is, can you say that you Protestants are as terribly in earnest?"

"Why, you classed us together before we went into the house," Henry Harris retorted.

"In a sense you *are* one with him. Let me," the Brahmin added, "be as concise and clear with you as possible. I gave up my caste, my gods, my kindred, everything; but it was to believe in Jesus, the Christ; not in you as English or American, not in your church governments, not in your books of theology, but in the Bible, and in the Christ alone."

"We believe in him," his friend remonstrated.

"Do you? Ah, perhaps you do, but," the Oriental said, "yours is a Christ who once lived long ago, a Christ who is to come again centuries hence. Yes, and whenever you think of him at all, you believe you will see him when you die. But I? I believe in a Son of God who walks here this moment between you and me. I am Peter, I am James, I am Thomas with Jesus, precisely (you like to be precise, you say) as when he and they were together by the lake on the slopes of Bethany. He is here now. He means all he says. He made the world, and he is King of the world. It is as when heralds run before to tell a city that its emperor is coming; very little the people care for the heralds when the monarch comes riding up the street in person. John, the first herald, said, 'I must decrease, but he must increase,' and it is astonishing how the heralds of all sects are waning every hour as the Christ of Bethlehem comes himself to possess every land, even although he does it only by means of his servants. Oh, as to your forms, symbols, systems, I dare say that they, like those of the Jews, have been of essential use, but the veil is being rent again, I assure you. People are yearning to tear away the mere drapery and to get at the Christ! Religion is too much an affair of men, men, *men*, instead of him. Not that I don't love men, poor fellows like myself, but," said the Hindoo, with tropical fervor, as vigorous as it was full of joy, "bless your soul, I prefer the Son of God! And 'I, if I be lifted up,' he said, 'will draw all men unto *me!*' How clear and plain God made everything to us by being born as a babe there in Syria! Who knows? He may come to men again by way of Syria. I don't know how, when, where, but as sure as you live, when he does come, it will be in and by poor people, who will love him as the Johns and the

Philips did, with a simple, childlike fervor. Depend upon it, there is nothing in Christianity except one thing—Christ. And be sure of this too," the Hindoo said, with radiant face, "the glory of Christ lies in the splendor of his simplicity. You want exactness, do you? You wish to see and grasp the substance of things, do you, as you do your iron and your steel, your valves, levers, wheels? Well, you know all religion when you know the man Jesus."

CHAPTER XLIX.

DILUTED BLOOD.

RIDING on horseback had always been with Henry Harris his favorite exercise. Whatever else he could or could not afford, he always owned the best horses in reach, and he now possessed, in his chestnut mare Bessie, an animal which he loved and rode more than any he had ever had. Whenever she could do so, Mary rode with him, on a smaller horse which her brother had selected for her. Lord Conyngham had ridden with him on several occasions, but "You ride so fast and so far," he had been constrained to tell him, at last, "that I can not stand it. For days after I am too sore to sleep, to sit, or to walk. You must have learned to ride among the Tartars of the Ukraine."

"I enjoy it more than anything else, and so does Bessie," was the reply.

The time had been when, mounted on her brother's black horse Malakoff, Lady Blanche, also, had ridden with the impetuous American. She, too, had enjoyed it immensely. "It is," she had said to him once, as they rode through the country near Paris, "like the flight of an eagle. I love strength, speed, force, whatever lifts me away from people in general, whatever makes me feel as if I were not merely going somewhere, but doing something. I wish I were a man ! "

" I do not. You are too perfect as a woman. But, suppose you were one of my baser sex, what would you do ? " her companion asked.

" Do ? " and she lifted her head as she rode. " Do ? I would break loose from the miserable falsehoods of society ; would trample down its wretched affectations and meannesses ; would assert myself against mere money and rank and fashion. I would no longer be only what other people try to make me ; I would be myself."

She gave her horse a sharp cut as she said it, and, in the leap which Malakoff made, it was as if he had carried her, with a bound, clean over the barriers which had hitherto imprisoned her. Henry had to spur Bessie to keep up with her. "And then what would you do ? " he said, greatly interested in the spoiled child of society.

" Then ? When I had freed myself ? Then," she said, " I would turn around and," here she gave Malakoff another cut, which caused him to spring forward again, " and charge upon and overthrow the tyranny from which I had escaped."

But all that seemed as if it had taken place ages before, when, the day after his visit with Ishra Dhass to the shop of the anatomist, the American, in riding along upon horseback, saw the open carriage of Earl Dorrington approaching him near the Place Vendôme, and in it Lady Blanche seated beside the Duke of Plymouth. Henry Harris had been riding alone, and for hours, that morning. He had been alone, and yet, from vivid memory of their last ride together along the same road, it was as if Lady Blanche had ridden beside and kept him company. Really, it had been but a short time before, and yet there was the same woman sitting in the carriage, very beautifully dressed, her hands lying relaxed in her lap ; indeed, it was hard to suppose that she was the same person, she seemed so pale and languid.

Yes, and it was the Duke of Plymouth. He did not recognize the American. It was not because he was very near-sighted only, nor because the Duke cared little for anybody. To do him justice, he was not as selfish as many a man, and would do a kindness when he could. Lord Conyngham, like his father, the Earl, had thought himself superior to the race in general; had been insolent, haughty, overbearing, in consequence, until, at last, he had come under the influence of Mary and her brother, which had made him a manlier man, by making him to know things to a broader and clearer degree as they actually were. But the Duke was not like Lord Conyngham. He was, in every sense, a smaller, weaker man. Everything that wealth, rank, the best opportunities at Oxford, the highest association, could do, had been done for him. It had been, however, like exhausting the art of a sculptor upon the pith of an elder-stalk instead of upon marble, or even upon wood. He was of a weakly constitution, and he had done what he could to exhaust even that by his dissolute habits.

"What else could we expect?" the American thought, in the first instant of seeing him. "He has had many centuries of ancestors, who had nothing to do but to spend money made by ancestors before them. It is not in human nature that they should not have wasted themselves as well as their money. Poor fellow! his very tendencies to vice are hereditary. No wonder that his scanty hair and beard are like wisps of hay; that his face is dry and colorless; that his eyes are like the ashes of a dead fire; the sap, the blood, the very life of the man, body and soul, mind and heart, has run so far down the ages that it is run out. I dare say his first progenitors were big and burly fellows, men strong of bone, vigorous of muscle, full of blood and of will—powerful ruffians, who laid about them with their broadswords like the lusty Englishmen they were. The torrent of blood in them has dwindled down in this poor gentleman into the feeblest of rills. But Heaven have mercy upon *her!*"

It was all over in a flash; the carriage went rapidly; so did the mare upon which Henry rode. The lady had sunk into an indifference to everything, but—for there *is* a magnetism in such approaches to each other—she lifted her eyes and saw the American as he raised his hat in passing. He seemed flushed with unusual strength from his ride; his eye, in hers, was as strong and steady as was his hand upon the reins of the animal he bestrode. Only an instant; but in that instant she fell, as it were, down a precipice, and from heaven to hell, in falling back from him to the man beside her. She might, perhaps, recover herself after a while by recalling the vast wealth of the Duke, his exalted position, and the like; but—and here was the trouble with him—it was' exactly his rank and wealth which were the burden of his life, which crushed him to the earth. One day, George Harris was speaking of people in general to his son Henry. It was at the Bodega, and, the Duke happening to pass them, the father called the attention of his son to the shy, nervous little man, not dreaming, however, of any reason why his son should be specially interested in him.

"Do you see that small, washed-out man beside the fountain?" he had asked. "Well, that is the Duke of Plymouth. Do you observe how bloodless he is? He has been bled to death by mosquitoes."

"By mosquitoes? Has he been in Florida, in Cuba? Where was it?" the other demanded, with surprise.

"He has lived in mosquitodom ever since he was a tender and tempting baby," was the grave reply. "Let me explain, for I have met him all over Europe. I know him, and almost every insect, too, of his swarm of mosquitoes by heart. That poor Duke has been pursued ever since he was born by enemies worse than the insects I have mentioned. You have read of Orestes chased by the Furies, of the heroes who had to fly for their lives from the hungry harpies, have read about vampires, and all that. Now, this victim has had parasites too small, too numerous, to be classed as other than the mosquitoes of a Louisiana swamp. Ever since he can remember has he been pursued by obsequious

tradesmen, by thievish valets, by men of fashion, who seek
to fasten themselves upon him, in order to share, in some
degree, both his position and his purse.   He has been game,
hunted down by gamblers, by speculators of all sorts, by
landlords, by disreputable women, by artists even, and architects ; but his most persistent pursuers have been matchmaking mothers of high rank and their fair daughters.
There is no thirst on earth, sir, so desperate as that for
money, unless it be a thirst, still more frantic, for social position ; and this poor fellow unites in himself both wealth
and rank of the grandest degree, and to such a degree that
thirst mounts to frenzy of desire where he is concerned.
Now," George Harris added, "if the Duke were anything
of a lion he might turn on his foes and rend, or at least roar
at them.   If he were only a fox he might double upon them,
dart into some hole, cheat them in some way.   Alas ! he is
only a rabbit, and a rabbit who has not the wit even to hide
under a hedge.   There are only two alternatives for that
man : either he must die or he must marry some woman smart
and strong enough to defend him from his insatiable foes.
He is so run down that he has become shy of every shadow ;
he hears the hateful buzz of a new mosquito in every man,
every woman especially, who speaks to him.   It is only the
female mosquito, you are aware, which sings and bites.
With all his envied rank and wealth, that man told me, one
day, after we had had a particularly good dinner managed
to assure me, on the honor of a Duke and in the strength of
the venison and champagne he had taken and I had not—it
was business in connection with an iron-mine of his which
drew us together—that he didn't care a toss-up whether he
lived or died.   'The only reason, by Jove !' he whimpered
to me, 'why I don't lie down and die, and be done with it,
is that the family will become extinct with me.   I am the
last of my race, sir.'   Of course he was braced up by the
liquor, or he would not have had the energy to confess the
fact.   But he is a good fellow, my son," the father went on,
"a really not bad-hearted man at all.   He means well, but

he is unfortunate, you see. He is nothing, at last, but a poor little pygmy, crushed to the earth by the coronets, castles, rent-rolls, money-bags, chests of plate, hangers-on of a race of giants. That is the merciful provision of nature ; the dodo is not the only thing which has become extinct. Hundreds of the old houses of England have run out in that way. The yellow fever dies, they tell me, for lack of material to feed upon ; well, the ducal house, in the case of this man, is dying out for want of material ; " and the sensible old man would have added much more, although to no one in such a strain but his son. Henry Harris was, however, suddenly called off.`

But he thought of it all to-day when he saw who rode with Lady Blanche. In all his knowledge there was no woman so worthy to be queen of the world as she was, and here she was about to marry a man who, in himself considered, was hardly strong enough or sensible enough to hoe cabbages in the meanest kitchen garden on her father's estates. " And the misery of it," he moaned, as he rode on, " is that they *know* it, both of them. She knows the Duke as well as I do, better perhaps. My father himself has not a more accurate knowledge of him than she has. And *he* knows it ! There is no conceit in him. No man knows better than he does that she is marrying his title and his estates, that there is no possible companionship between them any more than between a pug and its mistress, with the affection between a woman and her pet left out. Ah ! but it is the devil's own world ! "

He remembered, as he said it, that he had a message from his father, who had returned from Russia only to hurry back again—he almost lived on the road—which would take him to the house of Zerah Atchison. His bitterness died out as he thought of the pleasure he would impart when he had told his errand to the father and daughter. Reining Bessie in, he turned down another street and rode slowly toward the home of the old painter. And yet, how he suffered as he rode along ! How *could* he see Lady Blanche married to another! And could his own father have known, when he spoke of the Duke, of what was taking place? It was not often George Harris had spoken so freely; he must have had a motive.

CHAPTER L.

CREATIVE JOY.

WITH her refined nature and sensitive disposition, Mary Harris inherited a love for the beautiful in all its forms. She was an excellent judge of pictures, and her experience and criticisms in passing through the art galleries of the Exposition were invaluable. She intuitively selected the choicest gems, and often became so enraptured with the subject delineated on the canvas that she could readily interpret the spirit of the picture and almost read the thoughts of the artist who placed the results of his imagination before them. Passing rapidly over many of the most imposing and highly colored paintings, she frequently lingered to revel in the sentiment and finish of an unobtrusive canvas half hidden in a secluded corner, and more than once interested her companions in her descriptions far more than they would have been capable of being interested under ordinary circumstances. Her early education in biblical and historic lore enabled her readily to unravel and decipher what seemed to others a mass of mysteries. "Rizpah and her Seven Sons," in the French Department, which attracted the attention of everybody, yet often caused a repulsive shudder, was to Mary Harris full of enjoyment, as typifying the intensity of the mother's love, and her hearers forgot the horror of the surroundings while gazing upon the sublime heroism and unspeakable affection depicted upon the countenance of the unhappy woman.

Without being an artist, she had a sincere appreciation for art, far more skill than the average girl of the period, and her fondness for ceramics, for statuary, mosaics, and bronzes led her frequently to the repositories of art, and induced her friends who were not specially addicted to them to acquire a similar taste, and to prefer spending their time with her, instead of in other and hitherto more congenial departments.

One morning she remained in the studio of Zerah Atchison for some time, watching the painter and his daughter at work. Isidore had removed the "Purpose," upon which she had been so busy when Mary had been there before, and which the delighted mother and daughter had claimed to be a likeness of Henry, and was engaged upon her Sleeping Cupid. She seemed to be almost shy of her visitor and was singularly silent throughout her stay, and Mary felt, she knew not why, that it would be best to make no allusion to the absent bust. It was on this account, also, that she devoted herself to the old artist instead, who was still occupied with his endeavor to bring back again, on canvas at least, the Delira of his earlier days. Mary had almost recoiled with surprise when she first turned her eyes upon the painting.

"Oh, how good it is!" she exclaimed. "It is as if the girl were herself coming upon me out of the woods. She looks like an Indian. What eyes! What fawn-like freedom of step! She seems to be actually breathing between her parted lips. Were she alive, it could hardly be more real. Is it not wonderfully good?" she asked, for information, and as if the artist were merely a spectator like herself.

"Yes, it *is* admirably done. It is by far the best work I ever did," the old man made answer with a species of solemn joy. "As I have told you, my critical faculty exceeds my creative power, exceeds it so much that I have not as yet been able to produce one painting which I cared to preserve; not, at least, until I painted this. Sincerely, it is a masterpiece. I am willing to place it on the walls of any exhibition, confident that it will be recognized as such by every one. I thank God that, for the first time in my life, I have reached my ideal. It reminds me of Thorwaldsen."

"Oh no, father! no, no!" his daughter broke in, almost in tears; "please do not say that, please do not!"

"You foolish child!" the old man said, in loving tones. "Thorwaldsen, the great sculptor of Denmark," he explained, turning to their visitor, "was found lying almost insensible at the base of a Christ which he had just finished in colossal marble. 'Up to this hour,' he told his wondering friends, 'I have never been pleased with what I have wrought. To-day I look at my Christ, and am perfectly satisfied with it. By that I see that I have reached my highest summit. It only remains that I should die,' which he did not long afterward."

"Your picture is perfect, but," Mary ventured, "you are too wise a man to indulge in such notions."

"Who is wise?" the old man demanded; "and what are talent, genius? I have known of great masters who have toiled for years, and toiled in vain, to produce what was so vividly before their very eyes almost that nothing less than that could satisfy them. A painter looks at a completed work; alas! it is but the ghost of what he had intended. Over that he paints yet another, and of the same subject. This also is the merest specter of what he had hoped to do; worse, perhaps, than the other. But his ideal burns in the air before him, and he persists. The next time it is a caricature, a something worse still. But his ideal pursues him day and night, as his murdered mother Clytemnestra did Orestes, and he *must* put the haunting form upon canvas. And so he goes patiently to work once more. On one occasion, when I praised a picture, the artist said to me, 'Alas! yes; but it is painted upon the top of many a failure; underneath that picture are buried a dozen pictures, each of which cost me months of toil.'"

"It is so with me," Isidore said, modestly. "I am not a great artist, yet the bust of my father, which you liked, emerged out of weary months of work, out of cart-loads of rejected clay, of ruined marble."

"But it was worth the effort," her friend said, eagerly;

adding: "Is it not always so? I was visiting once at the house of a distinguished author. He had just published a little volume which was having what is called a great run. When I congratulated him, he said, 'Would you like to see the chaos out of which that book arose?' Taking me to a lumber-room adjoining his study, he showed me the whole floor covered deep with blotted manuscript and scattered masses of printed proof. 'Look,' he said, holding up his wee bit of a book, 'it took all *that* to produce *this*.' 'Yes,' I told him, 'but that is the dirt out of which a diamond has come. Even if there were tons of quartz, the gold we have got from it would be worth the litter and labor going before.' 'I don't know,' he said; 'if you but knew how very often I had to revise every sentence, out of what a vexatious whirlwind of mistake, blunder, blockheaded boobyism of mine this little volume has emerged, you would agree with me that it is ·hardly worth the work.' Dickens says the same," Mary continued—"that every page he wrote was the result of long and hard work. The result seems so simple that anybody could write it, and yet he had to write, re-write, revise, correct, correct corrections, and—"

"Only to reach something at last," the old artist said for her, "as simple as a pearl. It is as when one drives an artesian well downward through thousands of feet of rock, clay, sand, that the pure water may gush up. But it is, when it does come, from the center of the globe, from the heart of the world! Heaven knows what sleepless nights, days of toil and defeat, in addition to years of practice at other work before, I have given to this canvas. At last, at last, the Delira of my youth—the living girl, as I knew her among her mountains—steps out, and, with a smile, says, 'Well, here I am at last!'"

"She repays you for all," Mary murmured, as she gazed upon the breathing result—the hands reached out from the canvas as if to greet again her creator; the eyes, lips, cheeks, instinct with life; it was almost as if they could see the robe lift to the throb of the heart, the heave of the lungs.

"Yes, it is all I can do. And," the artist added, "it is in that way that the Great Artist is at work upon each of us. Ah, what years he has to give to a man or a woman; what severe, repeated, terrible trials! Just as a man begins to emerge, thinking, Now I must be all right at last! his Maker dashes him, as it were, into the dust again, saying, No, not yet! And all the suffering has to be endured again. But in the end, when one comes up out of what seemed at the time to be the utter wreck of death and the grave, then even the Master can smile upon his perfected creature and say, Very good! So good as to be worthy of eternal association with the best in the universe, with God himself."

But at this moment Henry Harris entered. Isidore seemed to awake suddenly out of her reserve.

"O Mr. Harris," she exclaimed, impulsively, "we have found her, have found her!" She pointed, as she spoke, to the wild woman stepping out from the canvas. The next instant she remembered herself and turned away, blushing at her enthusiasm, mortified at herself, almost ready to cry like a child.

CHAPTER LI.

THE YEARNINGS OF NATURE.

HENRY HARRIS was as much delighted when he saw Zerah Atchison's painting as his sister. "It must be an excellent likeness of your Delira," he said, after gazing upon it long and carefully; "because it is true to nature. I do not think that any one can improve upon the Supreme Artist, and therefore my idea of a well-painted landscape, for instance, is when its frame is as that of a window, through which you actually look out upon nature itself. So of historical paintings. Who cares for those, as a specimen, which portray Christ and his apostles as if dressed for a festival, in theatrical attitudes, with voluminous robes, great keys, shepherd crooks, crosses, and the like ? My heart is satisfied when I see Jesus exactly as his own disciples saw him ; as near to it, at least, as it is possible for the artist to put on canvas. That is, I suppose, a defect of my practical character. I don't want a particle of fog to rest upon anything in which I am to be interested ; I must see it as under noonday light ! "

But the old painter was looking dreamily upon his picture. "Yes," he said, "that is Delira. As I sit here it all comes back to me, those young days of mine among the wild woods, when I was so highly resolved to be a great painter. How ardent I was, how eager, how confident ! I would study, would work, work, work ! Oh, how *hard* I would work ! Yes, I would paint pictures which would electrify the world. I would build a studio, would fill it with busts, bronzes, portfolios of engravings, suits of armor. Men would come from far away to see me. I would help poor students, would found an academy of arts. Yes, Delira," he said, sadly, "you will bear me witness that it was not you I loved, it was my divine art. I hardly blamed you when you left me. I was almost glad of it ; it was my art I loved. But you are alive again, Delira ; you rise from the dead, bringing me in your hands those old, happy, hopeful days. The hopes of success have vanished, but—"

"Mary, Miss Atchison, Mr. Atchison, listen to me," Henry interrupted him. "When David, the illustrious French artist, had finished a painting of his coronation for the first Napoleon, the Emperor visited it, attended by a brilliant cortege of courtiers. When he had examined it long and thoroughly, he turned to David, lifted his hat from his head, and bowing low, he said : 'M. David, in the name of France and of the world, I salute you !' I am not an emperor," Henry continued, "but I can represent all men who have eyes to see, and, Zerah Atchison, you have achieved a grand success ; you are one of the masters ; in the name of America and of Europe I salute you ! " bowing low.

It was done by the speaker with gravity, and even the French Emperor could not have spoken with more dignity or grace, and as he spoke his sister went up to the old man, took his hand in hers, and kissed him. A new light flashed in the aged eyes of the artist, the head was held more erect, the patience of the face became radiant, and Mary turned to Isidore, placed a hand upon either cheek, and kissed her again and again. But the girl shrank a little when Henry took her little hand in his to congratulate her. Her eyes were dim with tears, her color came and went ; she was silent, embarrassed. Then she glanced at her father, her habitual gladness came back, and, flying across the room, she kissed and fondled him as a mother might have done rather than a daughter.

As she did so, Henry, by some subtile reminder, saw once more Lady Blanche instead seated beside the Duke of Plymouth. "She, too, is beautiful," he said to himself of the proud Englishwoman, "but she is, at best, merely a part of a system of society. Strong, intelligent, lovely, full of all daring impulse as she is, what at last is she but a bit of brilliant stone ground down, shaped accurately, as by sharp tools, to fit into her place in the grand mosaic of English society ? She is but one figure of the procession which has come down from the Norman conquest. Love her ? I might as well try to clasp to my heart one of those colossal caryatides of marble which I saw at Athens. She is, alas ! but a pillar and part of the British edifice. I dare say she will harden into stone as she feels the pressure upon her more and more. Duchess of Plymouth ! Yes, but I could wish your duke were worthier of you ! "

"Is she not lovely ? " Mary was saying to him of Isidore. "Did you ever know such a child, such a beautiful, gifted child ? She is as much a part of nature as a rose or a lark. Why is it that she has such a dewy smile ? Her face is like morning ; even when she cries it reminds one of an April day. I am in love with her ! But don't tell them about that odious Achilles Deschards ; why should you ? "

"It would," Henry whispered to her in return, "be like letting Satan into Paradise to admit him here. But I can not say as yet what I ought to do. I must wait and see."

"I only lack one thing," the aged artist said, as he began again to touch his picture here and there, while Isidore busied herself again with her Cupid, "and that is my boy."

"You do not know," Henry said, "that he is alive. Even if he is living, who can say what sort of a man he may be? Suppose, for instance, that he is a dissolute, unprincipled, abandoned man. He might be a wretch who would consume your earnings, who would reel home to you drunk, who would insult you, terrify your daughter, break your heart. If he is living, I merely say that he *might* be all this, and worse."

"He would still be my son—my own son, and I have never seen his face. Bad as he might be," the artist pleaded, "he would be, even then, but one of the many things belonging to me which have hurt and tried me to the utmost. There are many men of my peculiar kind," the aged painter continued, "to whom severe and unceasing pain of body and of mind is assigned as their natural atmosphere. It is with me, although I am like them only in my exceeding sensitiveness, as it was with Chatterton, Burns, Keats, Coleridge, Shelley, Alfred de Musset—perpetual suffering is their portion and mine. We live in the tropics of flame. Did you ever read, Mr. Harris, the story of poor Haydon, the English painter? He writhed, his life through, as upon burning coals. But I have no intention of killing myself as he did," the artist added, with a smile. "Ah, no; God is preparing me for something—not here—in the other and eternal life. Moreover, have I not Isidore? and you, too, have been so kind, kind!"

"You have Delira too; you have forgotten her," his daughter laughed.

"Yes, I have her, and the youth, the memories, she brings with her. Old people," her father went on, "love the past. To me it is as a dream; my belief is in the future instead.

My golden age is yet to dawn! The best, the very best part of my life," he said, with a happy face, "is yet to come. Every faculty I have has been but a course of education for that. Think of it, if you can," he said, like a boy who was eager for a holiday; "the entire universe will be thrown open to me, every artistic taste will be gratified. Oh, how I have loved beauty! beauty of landscape; and who can conceive of the grandeur, the sublimity, the varying and infinite loveliness when I shall have free access to the entire range of creation? I have enjoyed beauty, too, of person! My young friend," he said, looking at Henry with kindling eyes, "you, imagine that *you* admire a beautiful woman. Admire? you have no idea how deeply, exquisitely, I *enjoy* female beauty!" The tones were such as to thrill the hearers. "Yes, enjoy until the tears come, until I turn away from it, whether it be in marble, on canvas, in flesh, from the Venus, the Madonna, the living loveliness, with excess of pleasure which is almost pain. Now, just think of it," exclaimed the speaker with zest, "I shall exist in the eternal youth and keenest freshness of my faculties, in a universe peopled only by myriads of the beautiful, by angels, saints, glorious intelligences! Yes, I shall enjoy all that exists of beauty; beauty of form, of color, of character, and "—the eager tones subsided in awe—"I shall see the King in his beauty! whom I shall see for myself, and mine eyes shall behold, and not another!"

The face of the old artist was lifted, was luminous. It was as if his hungry eyes were already feasting upon the scenes and persons of which he spoke. "And beauty," he said, slowly, "is but the divine food; that which feeds and is satiated upon beauty is—love."

There followed silence for some time. Mary was watching the artist as, at last, he resumed his brush, but her brother was standing beside Isidore as she worked. She no longer shrank from him, but she did not seem disposed to talk. Her eyes would be lifted to his when he spoke, but they fell again as she answered. He felt, none the less, more at home with her than he had ever felt with Lady Blanche. It was as if he were enjoying a bit of sunshine, a gentle breeze, a June day, a strain of simple music, a mountain spring— anything and everything that was merely a part of nature.

"But I have almost forgotten what I wanted to say," he said, finally. "How would you like to visit Russia?" he asked of Mr. Atchison.

"Russia!" As the artist exclaimed it, his daughter looked up at their visitor, alarmed as well as astonished.

"The matter is this. You must," Henry said, "have heard of Prince Kalitzoff, the statesman and millionaire of St. Petersburg. My father and all our family know him very well. He was interested in our machine-shops, our railroads across the empire. Events made us well acquainted, for he is a noble-hearted man."

"What I liked him chiefly for," Mary added, "was his devotion to the Princess Aura, his only daughter, a lovely child. He seemed to care for nothing, you remember, Henry, but that golden-haired, motherless girl."

"Yes, and the Princess Aura is dead, my father writes me," Henry continued, "and the Prince has set · his heart upon building a monument to her, upon which he intends to place a full-length statue of her in marble. He spoke to my father to secure an artist for him, and my father has written to me. Now, Mr. Atchison," the young man continued, "I am determined to send, honestly, the best sculptor, the very best, I can find in Paris, for the pay will be almost un- limited. If the very best is also an American, of course I would prefer it."

"I wish I knew of some one, so that I could help you ; but I do not go out, as you know," Zerah Atchison said.

"Thank you ; the fact is I want *two* persons. I must," Henry continued, "have the best sculptor in Paris, and with that sculptor must go the best critic I can find, so that, be- tween the two, the work may be perfect. I know of none who fill my purpose so well as yourself and your daughter. My mother agrees with me, so does Mary."

12

The old artist looked up at the speaker with gratified astonishment; his daughter had glanced up, but was working again in silence.

"You will have a home in Prince Kalitzoff's palace, servants to wait upon you, ample compensation, your own time in which to do the work, the kindest of patrons," the visitor urged; "I am sure you will like it."

"A thousand thanks. And I do sincerely believe," Mr. Atchison said, "that, between Isidore and myself, we could satisfy him. What do you say, my child?"

But Isidore lifted only troubled eyes from her work. "I do not like to—to leave Paris," she said, and she thanked their friend heartily, but was silent again. The project did not seem to please her at all.

"Think over it," Henry said as he took his hat to go; "and, by-the-by, I forgot to say that I am going to St. Petersburg soon, to stay some time, and will be glad to escort you. Think of it. I will call again;" and brother and sister took their leave.

A sudden and remarkable change had taken place in Isidore. "O father, let us go! I shall be delighted to go!" she said.

CHAPTER LII.

M. PORTOU, ANATOMIST.

It was only the afternoon of the day after Henry Harris had told Zerah Atchison of the monument for the Princess Kalitzoff, that his sister and himself, happening to pass Notre Dame, turned into it as by a common impulse. It was at an hour when the huge cathedral was least thronged, and there was a refreshment in the dim religious seclusion. The brother and sister strayed here and there with silent steps, recalling to each other the wonderful events which had taken place beneath that lofty roof.

"To think," Mary said, "of the great orators who have made these walls reverberate with their eloquence, the kings and emperors who have been crowned here ! But I shudder when I remember how the mob filled this very place during the Revolution, roaring with their new freedom. Just to think that it was upon that very altar, now blazing with candles, thronged with priests, that they placed a vile woman as their Goddess of Reason ! "

"Yes," her brother said, "and it was here, too, that the Theophilanthropists set up their newly invented religion of flowery ceremonies and sentimental eloquence. They had to have *some* religion, and they had abolished the old faith."

"What vast crowds have jostled each other here ! " Mary added ; "and century after century they have come and gone like ghosts."

"Whenever I see a great cathedral like this, or those at Milan, at Rheims, at Cologne, especially when I stand under the dome of St. Peter's at Rome, do you know, Mary," her brother said, "the vast edifice reminds me of a fossil ? You remember I described to you the megatherium I saw in Siberia. Perhaps while Adam was still living it had been frozen into the center of an iceberg. An extraordinarily warm summer had melted it out of the primeval ice, wolves had stripped it of hide and flesh, and there it lay, a colossal framework of massive bones, white and bare. As I gazed upon the wreck I said to myself, 'These bones were once filled with life ; this enormous creature once breathed and fed, once filled the air with the sound of its voice, and drove all lesser things before it as it crashed its way through antediluvian forests' ; how," Henry continued, pointing to where the groined arches joined far overhead, "these great arches remind me of its ribs ! For this church, too, was once a living thing. It made its voice heard, made its power to be felt, I assure you ! The time has been when the world trembled beneath its tread, when Jew and Huguenot were glad if they could hide themselves, like the meanest of things, from the glance of its eyes, the weight of its pulverizing hoof. But now it is dead, dead!"

"I do not know about that," his sister said, looking at the women who were scattered about over the church, kneeling in deep devotion at the central and side altars. "There is life in the Church of Rome yet."

"Yes, but remember what it was, and then think of what it is! Spain was," her brother said, "master once of the whole world. Except Great Britain and a handful of Hollanders, who struggled almost hopelessly against it, Spain grasped the entire globe as a strong man grasps an apple or a dollar, and to-day Spain is so dwindled away that, as a general thing, its existence is almost forgotten by men. But even Spain, as it was and as it is, fails to be a symbol of the way in which Rome, once the mistress of the world, has shrunken and pined away into less than the specter of its former self."

"I am glad to see that you are so good a Protestant," his sister said.

"Yes, but you have not heard me out," Henry hastened to add. "You know what a mechanical man I am, and. the way I look at it is this: Every man who ever lived has a craving to know and to be at peace with his Maker. Hop Fun quotes Kong-fu-tse to me, and there is a vast deal of sound sense in what that sage had to say. Socrates, Zoroaster, Epictetus, Marcus Antoninus, Boodha, Bramah—not a nation but has had some great teacher, and I believe that, in a certain degree, each of them was helped of Heaven to instruct men. 'Of a truth,' the Apostle Peter said, 'I perceive that God is no respecter of persons, but in every nation he that feareth him and worketh righteousness is accepted with him.' I have sincere pity for a poor Thibetan kneeling down before his Grand Lama, for a Turk going through his devotions in his mosque, almost for a naked African begging for something of the bundle of sticks and feathers which he calls his god. Provided the poor creature knows no better, depend upon it, every prayer is heard by God. So of the

Roman, the Greek, the Protestant Church—there are bad men and hypocrites in them all, and there are sincere souls in them all."

At this moment a man looked at them in passing, then turned and came back. Really, he had been upon their track all the morning, as for days before, and as he would be for days to come. It was M. Portou, the anatomist. The new-comer drew Henry to one side. "I am just going," he said, in a low and reverential tone, "to a spectacle in a place near by. If the lady and yourself would like to see something of our religion, you can go with me ; it is not far away."

The brother consulted with his sister, made her known to the anatomist, and they walked away together. Although they were side by side, the men were really centuries apart. It was as if they lived in different planets. The American could not even perceive how it was possible for a man to be-lieve in the Roman Church, supreme, infallible ; and the other was almost unable to conceive how any man in his senses could fail thus to believe ! That the Pope was the viceroy of the Creator on earth was as plain to him as the midday sun. Having such belief, he was confident, also, that this young American millionaire would, sooner or later, be converted. With all sincerity, he had given days of fasting and prayer to that very object, and he now prayed silently, but fervently, for this as they walked.

"M. Portou, I have been greatly interested in you, as you know," the American said. "I have conversed with my mother and sister in regard to you. To tell you the truth, you are the first Jesuit I have ever talked with. Let me say this : I believe that if any other denomination had attained to the power of your Church, they would have been, you must excuse me, as corrupt and tyrannical." The Jesuit was pacing along with a peculiarly soft and flowing gait ; he merely closed his eyes and bowed his head, as if accus-tomed to blows.

"You see," the American went on, addressing his sister, "Pius IX has published what he styles a Syllabus, in which, with the help of his clergy, he has stated very tersely what Rome holds and teaches. Among other things he says, for instance, that the right to educate children lies exclusively with the Church. In regard to this, as to all his claims, the Pope says that if any man does not believe that the Church has the right to use force, when it can, for the accomplishment of this purpose, he is a heretic. It is so odd to me to talk with a man who really believes that," the American said, looking closely at his companion.

"Oh, no," Mary exclaimed, "he can not believe it all! I was just thinking about that terrible August day when the Huguenots were massacred along these very streets. Seventy thousand perished, it is said. When the news reached Rome, the Pope celebrated the slaughter, you remember, by a procession to the Church of St. Louis, by a 'Te Deum,' the proclamation of a year of jubilee, and had a medal struck representing the horrible carnage. But that was three hundred and six years ago ; now *you* do not believe in anything of that kind, I know," she said, looking steadily at the rosy and even sluggish and good-natured face of the Jesuit beside whom she walked. " *You* wouldn't kill *me*, would you?" she asked, archly.

"The soul is more valuable than the body ; the life more eternal than this transitory stage. Whatever God, by the mouth of his Church, commanded me, that," the Jesuit said in steady accents, "I would do ! You Protestants only pretend to believe, but I do believe," he added.

"I am glad we were not here St. Bartholomew's Day," Mary said to Henry ; "but I am yet more so that he was not," for as she said it she left the Jesuit, by whose side she had been walking, and took her place so as to have her brother between herself and the fanatic Frenchman.

"We, as an order, have been driven out from every nation on earth," their companion said, with a sad smile. "Multitudes even in our own communion abhor us ; and yet, why ? We simply *believe* what they merely profess, and we carry out, when we can, what we do believe."

"You are logical, consistent! Yes, I understand, and, in a certain sense," the American said, "I both understand and honor you for it. But what is this place?"

They had turned in through the stone gateway of an old inclosure, in the midst of which stood a prison-like structure several stories high. "Come in and you will see," their guide said, in an austere voice. Mary shrank back, but her brother laughed, and led her in after the Jesuit. This last said something to a porter in a clerical habit at the doorway, and the three entered and ascended one or two flights of stone steps, went along a dark corridor, and passed in by a narrow door into what appeared to be the gallery of a chapel.

"I can not stay with you," whispered the Jesuit, "but I wanted you to see that with us there is such a thing as belief. You may find it, sir, to be as practical and positive a force as your steam or iron," and with subdued footsteps he stole away.

CHAPTER LIII.

THE ROMANCE OF RELIGION.

WHEN Henry Harris and his sister had returned to their hotel after leaving, in a manner yet to be described, the building into which the Jesuit had introduced them, they found Mrs. Margaret Harris at the tea-table, in company with Ellen Ellsworth and Virginia Jossellyn.

"Mary, my dear, what is the matter?" her mother exclaimed with anxiety, as soon as she saw her, while Ellen added, "What is it, Mary? you look as if you had seen a ghost." But it was not until they were all back again in the parlor that Mary would explain. Even then she shook her head. "Ask Henry; he can tell you," she said. Her brother was standing beside the piano, and while his mother sat near by, looking at him, the young-lady visitors gathered about him, entreating him to relieve their curiosity.

"Well," he said, "if I must tell you, I will assure you, first of all, that what I have to say is perfectly true. You must know that I have become acquainted with a certain Achilles Deschards, of whom I have had to tell my mother and sister something. From him, for he knows everything, I learned what I am to relate. But," he said with affected solemnity, "if I am to tell my story, you must sit down before me. Moreover, Miss Jossellyn will please take her place at the instrument and play a brilliant overture. I will lift my hand at certain points of my story as I stand, and she must strike in with appropriate music." There were wondering eyes and exclamations and quite a deal of conversation before he could obtain obedience; but they quieted down at last, and he made ready. "Now, attention! audience, orchestra!" He raised his hand, and the music began. The Southern brunette was a fine performer; she played with great feeling, as well as force, an improvisation of her own, and the audience could not help applauding as she ceased. The narrator stood before his company, waiting for them to become silent, as noble-looking a gentleman, so at least his mother and sister thought, as one could wish to see. If the American had done a world of good to his friend Lord Conyngham, he had unconsciously received also a benefit from the Englishman in return. His manner was more quiet, his voice better modulated, his whole bearing more composed and refined than before. "I will call what I have to tell you," he said, his eyes resting gravely upon them,

"THE STORY OF ADOLF AND MICHAL.

"Once upon a time, ladies and gentlemen," he began, "there lived in a village of France, called Quimper-Correntin, two families named respectively Portou and Axelles. They were very plain, very poor, but hard-working people. The Portou family lived out in the fields, and wrought hard as tillers of the soil. They had but one child, a son, Adolf, who was employed as a servant by the curé of the village. Adolf was of a dull and sluggish disposition, but the curé took a fancy to him, educated him in the common branches, allowed him the use of his library,. which consisted only of the ' Lives of the Saints ' and kindred books. It so happened that the curé was a great lover of natural history. At every spare moment he would scour the fields around, with Adolf at his heels, in search of birds, moths, butterflies, beetles, snakes, and whatever he thought worth carrying home he would impale with pins, would stuff, or preserve in spirits. In this way Adolf Portou became as fond of such studies as his master, became even more expert, since the curé was short and fat, in catching and preserving whatever he could find to add to his collection. On Sundays the boy would throw the proper vestments over his coarse clothing, and assist the curé at Mass as an altar-boy. And thus, as the years rolled by, Adolf became at once a naturalist and a devout Catholic. He remained a heavy-featured, dull-visaged, slow-spoken person, and would have lived and died such, if it had not been for one thing. Now, what was that?"

"Oh ! I know," the lady at the instrument remarked with a laugh ; and so certain was she that she proceeded to play a very lively air. "For you refer," she said, when she had finished, "to a young village maiden, of course."

"You are right. In the village of Quimper-Correntin lived a girl some years younger than Adolf, an only daughter in the family of the Axelles, named Michal. She was a very pretty girl, with eyes like black beads, teeth like pearls, lips like scarlet ; above all, a tongue which was as swift and restless as her eyes, her hands, her feet. The village girls called her La Hirondelle, she was in such incessant motion, like a swallow."

The audience glanced at Ellen Ellsworth, to whom the description closely applied, but she shook her head at them threateningly, and Henry proceeded. "Michal was apparently a good girl, exceedingly industrious, a remarkably neat housekeeper ; her only fault was that she was given to excessive fun. She laughed at Adolf when she saw him at work in the onion-field. He could not come home past her

house with a netful of butterflies, a dead snake hanging
over his arm, a box of bugs strapped on his back, without
being stopped, examined, and teased unmercifully upon his
game. Not even the presence of the priest could restrain
her. She carried her spirit of mockery to church. Adolf
dared not look toward the congregation during Mass. It
made not a particle of difference that he had on his robes
as an acolyte, that he held a censer in his hand, that he was
kneeling and making the sign of the cross ; if he forgot himself and glanced at the people, he was sure to see Michal.
She was kneeling, it is true, like the rest ; but as soon as
their eyes met she would make a face at him, and he would
have to smother his laughter and his indignation alike in a
pretense of coughing. The older they grew the worse it
became—the worse, for—" And lifting his hand, Henry
whispered to the orchestra, " Pathetic music, if you please."

" For," he continued, as the sad strains sank sobbing
themselves into silence, " for the poor fellow was desperately
in love with Michal. The curé remonstrated with his charge.
' You are falling into the wiles of the devil,' he said to him
every day. ' It is a just vengeance upon her parents for
naming a child after that accursed daughter of King Saul,
who mocked at David when he was worshiping God,' and
the good priest, who was getting old and short of breath,
waxed red in the face as he spoke. ' You had agreed to
become both priest and a naturalist, and here comes this imp
of darkness—' ' Michal is nothing of the kind,' Adolf would
interrupt ; ' she is an angel of light instead, and we love
each other.' ' You thick-headed oaf !' the priest would say,
' do I not know ? That girl has been a child of evil from
her birth. She looked up at me with a smile of derision
when I baptized her as a babe eighteen years ago. She will
not learn her catechism. Her rosary is worn only as an ornament. I do not believe that she tells me anything but lies
in the confessional. She withholds the truth and charges
herself there with a thousand things she has only dreamed
of. When I reason with her, she laughs. When I threaten

her, she laughs. She laughs when I inflict penance or refuse absolution. I have seen her laugh in the very face of the Blessed Virgin while on her knees before her image, even when receiving the Host. She is possessed of the devil! Fly from her, my son, as you would from Satan himself.'

"But," Henry added, "what good did it all do? What good does it ever do? The parents of Adolf died after a while, leaving him their little home and a stockingful of francs hidden under the thatch. Michal had her way; such women always do. Sorely against his will, the curé married them. Then—" But, without waiting for any signal, the orchestra struck up a wedding-march. The audience laughed and clapped their hands, applauding both Michal and Adolf, as well as the music.

But Henry smiled upon them with pity. "You rejoice too soon," he said, when the music ceased. "For, hardly had they been married a year before a certain Guelf Asnières, who was doing business as a tobacco-smuggler in Paris, came back to his native village upon a visit. As everybody well knew, Guelf was a thoroughly unprincipled scamp, a Red of the deepest dye, an atheist, and given to drink and gambling. He was none the less a handsome fellow. His black mustache, bright eyes, rapid tongue, Parisian ways, made poor Adolf seem in comparison a stupid country lout. It is a sad story; but when Adolf came home one cold January day from his hard work in the fields—came home at night with his usual slow step—hungry, wearied out, he found his house deserted. The dog met him at the gate, whining. The fire was gone out on the hearth; his wife had fled with Guelf to Paris! The unprincipled couple had robbed him also of the last franc; had taken even his Sunday clothes, and an old silver watch which had come down to him for generations. All night the poor, stupid, trusting husband lay upon the ground of his desolate home, weeping, groaning, praying. The next day he borrowed some money and started to Paris in search of Michal. Of course, he might as sensibly have tried to find a coin lost in the Atlantic ; at least, the curé told him that when he persisted in going, and told him so over again when he returned without her, or any tidings of her. 'She is of the devil, and always has been,' the old man said ; 'she has gone back to her father, the black Satan, my son. Thank God for your deliverance !'

"And thus," Henry continued, "matters seemed to slide back into their former grooves. Adolf worked hard ; went to church on Sundays and saints' days ; hunted for butterflies and reptiles whenever he could. At the suggestion of the curé he became a lay brother of the Jesuits. Gradually he gave up the study of animal life in his devotion to his order ; became first an enthusiast, then a fanatic. One day he came to the curé with the key of his house. 'I am going to Paris to find Michal,' he said. 'Never again can she be my wife ; I go to save her *soul !*' He was so determined that the curé saw in it a divine call, and gave Adolf his blessing. But," Henry added, "it is too long and too terrible a story to tell young ladies. Enough to say that the deserted husband found Michal at last. Guelf had robbed and forsaken her long before. She had become an exceedingly wicked woman in every sense ; her very soul seemed poisoned. She was a socialist, a Red, an atheist. There was not a more intelligent, determined, desperate woman in her way than she was ; but Adolf gave himself up to following her. She allowed him to do it out of sheer contempt. 'You want to save my soul,' she would say with scorn, 'when I have no soul, and you persist in telling me about *le bon Dieu !* You might as well jabber to me about Odin or Thor. Poor Adolf, you always were a fool ; that is why I ran away from you. Convert me if you can ; I am willing.'

"It was about this time," Henry Harris continued, "that I met Adolf—his full name is Adolf Portou—for the first time. He had opened a shop in Paris as an articulator of bones ; he had learned the business under the curé of Quimper-Correntin ; but his chief object was to seek and save his wicked wife. She called herself Madame Mosseline, and was at the head of a club of Reds—philosophers, they called themselves." And then Henry Harris told his hearers at length about his visit to the club of Madame Mosseline in company with Lord Conyngham, and something of what they saw there.

The ladies were exceedingly interested. "But how did it end?" They were eager to know that.

"I do not know whether it was his mere patient persistence," Henry added, in regard to M. Portou, "or not. The abandoned woman helped her former husband to pass among her associates as one of them—he would not have been allowed otherwise—but she took special pleasure in shocking and distressing him. She would provoke her atheist companions to say their worst, would herself indulge in horrible blasphemy and all immorality as if to defy the patient-hearted man. No," Henry added, "I can not tell you the whole story, it is too sad ; the woman must have been possessed, as the curé said, of the very devil. She was, as I have said, as comely, bright-eyed, neatly dressed, intelligent a woman as you would wish to see. She made her worst associates obey her. Whether, after a long time, it was the determined persistence of her former husband, or her own, conscience, or a severe illness she had, I do not know— But I will let Mary finish the story ; a little solemn music, if you please ; " and he sat down.

" Well," Mary began, standing up beside the performer as the music ceased ; " this afternoon Henry and I happened to be at Notre Dame, and there I saw Adolf Portou. My brother had told me that he was a Jesuit, and I was anxious to hear him talk ; " and she recounted what had passed between them up to the moment the Jesuit had parted with them in the building into which he led them, and which proved to be a convent of the most austere of nuns.

" When we glanced about," Mary continued, " we found that we were in a small gallery looking down upon what seemed to be a little chapel. It was dimly lighted from the altar, and filled with a silent and kneeling congregation of veiled women. A low music was trembling upon the air from a hidden organ. We waited for some time, but suddenly every candle was lighted, the organ pealed into a wedding-march. Imagine my astonishment when what appeared to be a bridal procession came up the aisle to the altar ! At least, there was what seemed to be a bride, superbly dressed in white satin, with a train, and diamonds, flowers, and a white veil covering her from head to foot. She knelt before the priests, and a service of some kind followed, with responses and prayers. There was no bridegroom, however, and all at once some of the black-robed women began to take off her finery from the bride while the choir chanted a dirge. At last the poor thing was left lying prostrate on the floor. Then she was helped up, clad by this time only in black, a white linen cloth about her face. 'Look at her,' Henry whispered to me. I did so, and will remember her corpse-like face for ever. 'Now look at *him*,' Henry said. It was the Jesuit, and I had been doing so all along, for he was dressed in vestments, and had been assisting the priests. His face was cold and stern. The priest said something to the Jesuit, and he advanced, took the hand of the woman in his, kissed her on the forehead, and stepped back as she sank again upon the floor. Then some women covered her with a black pall to the saddest music I ever heard ; the lights were lowered. As we stole quietly down stairs and into the sunshine again, Henry said to me, ' She is a nun, and he will never see her again. And he has at last, at last ! saved, as he believes, her soul. For that is Adolf and Michal.' "

There were tears in the eyes of all present as Mary ceased to speak, and, her hands resting lightly on the keys, the Southern girl played and sang softly a beautiful song, with which all were familiar, the refrain of which was,

" O love, love, victorious love ! "

" Yes," Mrs. Harris said, when the music ended, " fanatic as your Jesuit is, Henry, in the case of his wretched wife his is a fanaticism of affection, also, which it is impossible not to admire."

"His society has," her son replied, "for its motto, *Ad majoram Dei gloriam,* that is, they will do whatever they think is for the greater glory of God ; *perinde ac cadaver,* obedient as a corpse to authority. France has always been confronted by some terrible foe, the Bourbon, the Robespierre, the Napoleon, of the hour. You admire his spirit, and yet, to-day the Republic seems to be victorious ; but if I were a painter I would depict her as Joan of Arc risen from the dead, and on the alert with keen eyes and ready sword against the twin specters which bar her path and seek to strike her down. One of these is the Jesuit, and the other—"

"Is the atheist," Mrs. Harris said for her son, "and God alone knows which is the worst."

CHAPTER LIV.

THE INEVITABLE.

THE morning after young Harris and his sister told their friends the story of Adolf and Michal, he came, as he was riding out toward Versailles, upon his friend Lord Conyngham, also on horseback. The nobleman was returning from his ride, but was not in his usual spirits. He seemed to be fagged out, and was riding with slackened rein and troubled brow ; but his face brightened as he recognized the American, and, after a few words, he turned his horse's head and went with him.

"What a beastly world it is !" he said, after a while. It was a beautiful morning ; both of the young men had apparently all that heart could wish to make them happy, and Henry said, "Do you think so ?" but he could readily imagine what occupied the mind of the other. However Earl Dorrington might outwardly consent to the marriage of his

son and heir to Mary Harris, such an alliance, Henry knew
as well as his companion, was dreadfully against the wishes
of the old Tory. But there were things which no one outside of the family could know, for, as with the poorest, provided they possess good sense, to say nothing of good breeding, household affairs were the last topics upon which the
members thereof would converse with strangers. Now, as
Lord Conyngham had told his friend, Lady Blanche stood
his ally in regard to Mary Harris. She did so, because she
had learned to love the fair American very sincerely, but
chiefly because she was convinced that her brother's success
in life, as well as happiness, was concerned. In all England
there was hardly a young woman but was, unless already
engaged, at his choice. The old Earl had often gone over
the roll, so to speak, of possible wives for his son; had gone
carefully over it with his daughter, who was his only confidential companion now that her mother was dead. One lady
was wealthy, but too homely to be thought of. Another
was beautiful and of excellent birth, but without sufficient
dower. Yet another was beautiful, rich, of high rank, but
too frivolous to be the wife of a man who aspired to hold
an influential position in the affairs of England and of nations, as also in fashionable circles. Not that Lady Blanche
and her father did not know of many an Englishwoman of
high intellect, but some of these were too old, too opinion-
ated.

"Or too ugly; for," Lady Blanche reasoned, "if Alfred
is to take the stand we wish, he must have a wife whom he
can love and be proud of. Now," she said to the Earl, only
the day before Lord Conyngham had come upon his friend
the American as he rode, "I believe that for every Adam
God makes a definite Eve. So far as I can see, Mary Harris
is the only woman who combines all the qualities with none
of the defects. You know what Aspasia was to Pericles?"

"I know," the Earl remarked, "what Lady Palmerston
was to her husband: the secret soul of his political success,
if that is what you mean."

"Yes, sir. Now," said Lady Blanche, bitterly, "no woman could make anything of the Duke of Plymouth, but in *this case* there is some hope. My brother's entire future depends upon his marrying her, so far as I can see. If he does not, he will dawdle away his life in billiard-halls and club-rooms, like so many of his class, disgracing us, most likely, by disreputable connections, to be married at last to some inferior woman. Let him follow his heart and marry *her*, and she will make him a success in spite, if necessary, of himself. I want to see him made a duke, and so does that beautiful, sensible, ambitious American girl. Our family needs new blood," and then the poor girl thought of the Duke to whom she was betrothed, and turned pale.

"Miss Harris has no ancestry," groaned the Earl. "Her father is not even a tradesman ; he was a common mechanic —an engineer. No, I can not consent ! Whatever I may have said, I can not, can not ! Worse, if possible, the young woman is an American. I detest Americans ! " the Earl continued ; " they are *parvenus*, upstarts, mushrooms. The Spaniard, the Russian, the French, or the German, is bad enough, but the American ! Not only is he insolent, aggressive, boastful, ostentatious, without reverence for his superiors, but he speaks English, is a sort of relative of whom we can not be rid, go where we may."

"Is Mr. George Harris insolent ? Is his son an upstart in bearing ? Is Mary Harris boastful, or her mother, and—"

"Assuredly not," her father interrupted her ; for he was truthful and a gentleman to the core. "It is of the Yankee in general that I speak. Why Heaven allowed their republic to stand I can not see. With all the nobility, I counted confidently upon the success of Jefferson Davis. When Louis Napoleon urged England to recognize and help him, we ought to have done so, as I said at the time. No, I grant you that Miss Harris is amiable, estimable ; but, Blanche, you and your brother must wait until I die ! The traditions, the prejudices, the life-long habits, in me of too many generations, are against it. I can not consent. You must wait. The sacrifice is too great ! "

" Is it as great, sir," his daughter demanded, " as mine in consenting to become the Duchess of Plymouth ? " But as she spoke she observed for the first time a peculiar ashen something in the face of the Earl, generally so ruddy ; his lips were white, his eyes dim, his hand trembled, and, with terror for what might befall, she ceased to contend, and kissed him instead. But her face was cold and hard even as she did so.

" You must wait," she said to her brother, bitterly, " if you would not kill him. I do my part as a daughter when the Duke is in question."

It was of this that Lord Conyngham had been thinking as he rode beside his friend ; but all that he said was, " Have you heard from your father yet in regard to my suit ? "

" Yes, my lord," the American replied, " and it is only what I have already had the honor to tell you myself. Apart from your rank, there is no man we would like better for my sister. To us your rank is a much more serious objection than if you were very poor, or without a profession. But, in any case, it is impossible for my father or myself to give any reply to your suit until we are approached upon the subject by your father the Earl." It was said gravely.

Lord Conyngham uttered something very like an oath, gave his horse a cut, then reined him in. " You do not know the Earl ! " he said at last.

" No, but we do know ourselves," the other replied. " We like you sincerely, my lord, and we are profoundly concerned in the happiness of Mary ; but, whatever befalls, we can do nothing which even seems to place us on a lower level than that which your father occupies. When the Earl asks the hand of Mary of her parents he shall have his answer." It was said very quietly. The American had seen too much of English insolence not to assert himself when it was necessary ; moreover, he had been hurt to the soul by the course of Lady Blanche.

"As things go," he had argued with himself, "the Duke is a splendid match, as it is called, for her. Nothing more natural than that she should yield to the temptation, especially when the urgency of her father and of every relative and friend she has is to the same end. And yet the Duke is a worn-out *roué*, and she knows it. Making all allowance for her education, how a true woman—a pure and noble woman—can sacrifice herself to such a Moloch I can not understand. She need not marry me, but to marry *him !* " He had almost forgotten who rode by him as he said to himself in addition, as he had often done before : " I am an engineer, and have lived too much among machinery to permit myself to be crushed by the wheels. At best, Lady Blanche, beautiful as she is, is but a glittering part of the social mill. You are very lovely, my lady, but I do not propose to perish at your feet ! "

Which shows how little we know our own hearts. Mrs. Harris and Mary had spoken of it to each other ; for, of all persons, Henry was the one of whom they thought and conversed most. "Even if there were no other objections," the mother had said to her daughter, "it would never do. Henry and Lady Blanche are too much alike to be happy together. If she is proud, he is as much, if not more so. In an unhappy moment an unguarded word would surely be spoken by her, by him, it matters not which. It would need but one word. Like a spark to a train, it could not be recalled, and there would follow misery unspeakable."

"There would be no fear of that between—between—" But Mary could not complete her thought.

"Between your lover and yourself ? No," her mother said, with a smile. "I have no fear that you would quarrel ; but your father, your brother, and myself are agreed, and you will agree with us, until the Earl asks your hand, we can do nothing."

And Mary, hesitating a little, had said, "Don't you think, mamma, that a new influence is helping Henry to endure his disappointment ? "

The fact is, as he and his English friend rode together in silence, he had ceased to think of Lady Blanche. The time had been when she was almost his only thought, although she had never come into his very practical mind except as in a sort of halo of impossible possession. When he thought of her now, his mind glanced away to Isidore Atchison. From, in fact, the outset of his acquaintance with her he had fallen into the habit of comparing Lady Blanche with the artist. At first, the Englishwoman entered his mind accompanied by the young girl, as a stately lady is attended by a maid of honor, who lingers behind and smiles and blushes in the shadow of her mistress. Then the two presented themselves to his thought side by side, in strong contrast. Lady Blanche was the statelier, the more striking, but the shy yet joyous Isidore was more homelike, easier of access, appealing to him as a younger sister might have done. Lady Blanche was cold in comparison to the childlike cordiality of the other ; was almost artificial in contrast, so purely native and natural was the daughter of the old artist.

It was a silent ride the two friends had of it. "We have got into a dead-lock," the nobleman was the first to observe.

"So it seems," was the cold reply.

"I say, Harris," Lord Conyngham demanded, "I thought that in your country the young people fall in love and marry without all this accursed red tape. Isn't that so ?"

"It used to be so, my lord, but," the other replied, "our young men, at least, are growing more sensible ; even they are ceasing to yield to mere passion. Now a man allows himself to fall in love only when he can see his way clear to an income which will support a family. In this case we are dealing with something vastly more important than income ; we have to do with Earl Dorrington."

"Do you know," Lord Conyngham said, "we did our best to persuade your sister to run away ? I believe it was Blanche who suggested it ; in any case, she went into the idea with all her heart. We made every arrangement ;

Blanche was to go with us, a clergyman was in waiting, everything was so neatly planned, but your sister would not hear of it ! "

" No, I suppose not," the other said, with a laugh. " You did not know her, or you would not have proposed it, my lord. When will you understand us ? " the American said, with an impatient gesture. " Try and understand ! We are plain, practical, matter-of-fact people. We never act except as in broad day. We ask favors of no one ; fear no one ; consider ourselves inferior to none."

" *Noblesse oblige*, hey ? and," the Englishman exclaimed, "there are millions of you in that remarkable America of yours ! Forty million democratic dukes and duchesses of you ! No, it is of no use ; I can not understand you Americans ! "

" They say that the census of 1880 will make us fifty millions, my lord, but," the other added, gravely, " we have no such inferior order of nobility as dukes among us ; every man is a king, every woman is a queen, I assure you. They had a vague idea of this even here when they dubbed poor old Louis Philippe King of the French — not of France. With us, America is more than a nation composed of nations ; it is a sovereignty composed of sovereigns. Now—"

" Mr. Henry Harris," Lord Conyngham broke in, " Amer-. ica, with every State and Territory in it, Canada thrown in, may be *con*—to put it in the mildest way—*founded !* as also may England, all Europe ! What I care for is your sister. Meanwhile, I have only one thing to say : suppose we go to Russia. We have long proposed to do so. I must either do that or take to absinthe and baccarat. Something may turn up while we are gone. What do you say ? "

A long conversation followed upon this.

That night, just before going to bed, Henry suddenly said to his mother, " By the by, you have not given either to Mary or myself the present you promised for finding your favorite works of art."

" That is a fact," echoed his sister ; " what are our presents to be, and *when* are they to be ? "

"My children," Mrs. Harris said, gravely, "I have not forgotten what I promised. You shall each of you have your gift, and," the wise lady added, with a loving smile, " I will guarantee that each of you will be more than satisfied when I give it." There was so much of meaning in the words that the young people looked at her with sudden surprise; but Mr. George Harris, who had lately returned from Russia, laughed outright, a thing he rarely did.

CHAPTER LV.

ART AND HEART.

THE matter of Achilles Deschards had rested upon the mind, and upon the heart, too, of Henry Harris, as a heavy burden. After long and thorough investigation he had come to know that the versatile and venal Bohemian was beyond doubt the son of Zerah Atchison and the Delira of the artist's youth. And yet so far he could not bring himself to reveal to those most concerned the secret in which they, of all, were most interested. After considering the matter with his mother, he determined to bring the affair to a crisis, for, if Mr. Atchison and Isidore were to go with him to Russia, some final decision must be reached.

In accordance with the suggestions of Mrs. Harris, her son contrived to bring Achilles Deschards to the studio one afternoon when she was present. Deeply interested in the man, Henry had associated himself with him so long and so closely that they were as intimate as persons of character so diverse could be, and the American had little difficulty in inducing the other to go with him. Of a disposition as intense as it was restless, the Bohemian was ever on the alert for a new sensation, and he glanced swiftly about him when he came into the room.

"Is there anything in mere relationship?" Mrs. Harris

had been asking herself, "which will compel this father to recognize a son whom he has never seen? Can this son know a father of whom he has not even heard?" For, as she knew, Achilles Deschards had never been told that the man who had stolen his mother from Zerah Atchison was not his father. He was, in fact, utterly ignorant of the early events in the life of his mother. So far as he was aware, she had herself been born in France, and had never been outside of it. It was natural that Mrs. Harris should await the result with almost painful interest.

When the aged artist looked up from the picture of Delira—for he could not tear himself away from perpetually touching and retouching it—he returned in his usual quiet way the salutations of the gentlemen. As had become the habit of his life, he fastened his eyes upon the stranger who accompanied Henry Harris with sharp, penetrating gaze. A lapidary looks in that way at the stones which come under his observation, however cursorily, and can tell in the first glance the diamond from the imitation. So of a banker: when notes or coin pass within the sweep of his eyes, whether he has anything to do with them or not, and from sheer force of dealing with such things, an instinctive estimate is made, Good or counterfeit? If good, what is the amount? Where, in such case, there is any doubt, one touch with the adroit finger, and the man of money says to himself, almost with his eyes shut: "This note is good, is bad; this gold is alloyed; this silver is pure," as the fact may be. Now, to the artist, men and women were as the jewels, the money, with which he had to do. He might have taken the worst wine for the best, the clumsiest paste for the true diamond, the poorest counterfeit for the good money, but it was very different where a man was concerned or a woman; then his unerring decision struck through the mere outer appearance to the very soul, which is at last the real person.

Even in the act of introduction, the old critic was saying to himself of Deschards: "By what accident is it that this friend of mine is associated with such as *you?* He

is thoroughly true, genuine, reliable, while your inmost nature is adulterated, perverted. And yet what noble eyes !
what an intellectual brow ! Surely some cruel circumstance
has seized upon and twisted this soul awry even from infancy ! "

Both Mrs. Harris and her son were watching the artist
closely. "Yes, he is struck with him, interested in him ! "
they were saying to themselves. "Surely blood will tell ; at
least a father must recognize his own child ! "

Alas ! the only interest of the artist was in Deschards
as probably the best Mephistopheles he had as yet encoun-
tered. Mrs. Harris and her son glanced at Isidore. She had
acknowledged the salutations of the gentlemen with her
wonted modest grace, but it was evidently plain that the
stranger was more interested in her than she was in him.
Had she put her rapid ideas into words, they would have
been : " And here is the man I saw with his old mother that
day. Yes, he evidently *is* what Mr. Harris described him to
be, talented but unprincipled. Poor fellow ! Absinthe !
Intellect ! No conscience ! Atheist—and yet," and she
looked at him again, "he loves his old mother ! "

Meanwhile, Henry Harris introduced him also to Mrs.
Harris, and the conversation became general, even animated.
The sincerest thoughts of every one there were not always
uttered, yet much was talked about. Achilles Deschards
moved around the apartment, looking rapidly at the pictures, the carvings, full of compliment, placing himself near
Isidore, engaging her in lively talk, while a feeling of almost
profound disappointment fell upon the mother and son.

But their expectation revived as the stranger stood at
last beside the picture of his own mother. He seemed to be
exceedingly struck by it, declared it to be a masterpiece, and
was extravagant in his praises.

"Do you know, sir," he remarked at length to the artist,
after gazing upon it steadily, "that your portrait is exceedingly like what I can imagine my mother must have been
when young ? And the likeness grows upon me ! "

Mrs. Harris glanced at her son with eager eyes; her heart rose to her lips; she was witnessing one of the subtlest, profoundest workings of nature. Surely the father would recognize the son!

"Look at it in this light, if you please." As Henry Harris said it, he contrived to place Deschards beside the wonderful painting, so that the artist and Isidore, too, could not help contrasting the son with the almost living effigy of his mother. The likeness was so startling that Mrs. Harris could scarcely restrain herself. "They must be blind, must be absolutely stupid, not to see it!" she said almost aloud.

But they did not, and, after more conversation, in which the visitor praised the painting, as well as the carvings, in the warmest terms, he begged permission to call again and took his departure.

"I am free to say," Mrs. Harris remarked to her son when they were together in their hotel that night, "that I have rarely been more mistaken, more disappointed. It seemed impossible that there should be no recognition. What a pity!"

"Yes, it is a pity!" was the reply.

But, strange to say, her son was thinking of Lady Blanche instead. "That I should not have known *her!*" he was complaining to himself. "That she should not have known *me!* and when we knew almost everything concerning each other, were thrown, and for so long, into such close relation to each other! We even supposed that we loved each other! And yet I knew as little about her real self as if she were Queen Elizabeth instead. And she never saw *me* in her life, never will know me as I am!" But, ah! the dull, deep pain of it all! Yet his pain was as nothing to what Lady Blanche endured. She *did* know, did appreciate him. And with her the alternative was—the Duke of Plymouth. While, irresistibly breaking through his sorrow like spring through the chill of winter, as slowly and imperceptibly too, the daughter of the artist was changing his loss into unspeakable gain. But, if he was conscious of it at all, it was

13

only as is the oak which feels, not understanding it, the blind motions within itself of approaching summer.

"I am coming to understand it," the mother said to her son a few days afterward.

"To understand what?" he asked, coloring almost guiltily under her calm eyes. He was thinking of Lady Blanche.

"To understand why there was no recognition between the father and the son. It is because there was no relationship, at last, of soul between them. The son is a thoroughly bad man, and has," Mrs. Harris continued, "for everybody except his mother a bitter indifference, if not contempt. The father and the daughter have no love except for the character, the inmost heart and soul, of any whom they meet. When the whole person is as utterly perverted as in the case of Deschards, I doubt if in the other world even, and through eternity, recognition, much less relationship, will continue. No, Henry, I would not say anything to them of the matter, at least not yet. Wait. Recognition in this case would only bring misery to the father and to Isidore. As to the son, his character is fixed; even they could not change him."

"And it is circumstance which has made him what he is; is it his fault?"

"Yes, circumstance, and the most powerful circumstance of all is the overpowering influence in him," Mrs. Harris replied, "of the peculiar character of Delira, his mother. But that, my son, is one of the terrible mysteries which can be solved only when we come, in a world wherein is no night, to know even as also we are known. The one thing we do know now is that Heaven makes accurate allowance for everything. No one is punished except for his own deliberate wrong-doing against sufficient light."

CHAPTER LVI.

ST. PETERSBURG.

"I AM glad I came with you ! "

It was Lord Conyngham who said it to his American friend. They were standing together upon the highest of the gilded galleries which ornament the lofty spires of the Admiralty edifice in St. Petersburg. The air was bright and bracing, and the young men were full of the ardor and energy which flushes the very soul also of those who are embarked upon a noble but hazardous enterprise. The capital of Russia lay at their feet like a vast picture. "Yes, and so am I," Henry Harris said, more calmly. "I was weary of Paris and of the Exposition. When I have been shut up too long in what is styled the best society, I become like a bad boy imprisoned in a dark closet ; I batter at the door with fist and foot until I am let out, otherwise I break it down. You have been in St. Petersburg before, my lord, but it is a noble sight, is it not ? When Peter the Great stood here in 1703 upon the bank of the Neva, it was almost as when the Creator took chaos in hand at creation. You see those islands which make up the Delta ; well, this region was then one vast malarious marsh. I like a strong man ! Peter said : 'Let St. Petersburg exist ! ' and here it is ! "

"Yes, here it is," his companion added, "a city of one hundred and fifty bridges, three hundred churches, seven hundred thousand people, covering an area of over forty square miles. I have been informing myself, you see. Five hundred streets, think of it ! and not a lane or alley in the city. Yonder runs the Nevskoi Prospekt, one hundred and thirty feet broad, four miles long, the finest street in Christendom, they say."

"I like Russia," the American responded. "See those long lines of houses, like soldiers in gray uniform. They form themselves in those sixty-four hollow squares you see to the north and the south, or deploy like skirmishers over Aptekarskoi, Kammanoi, and the other islands yonder. Russia is young. Like America, it is rough and very strong." What the speaker did not add aloud was, "And Russia and America are the twin masters of the future."

"Do you know," his companion added, "that the Emperor can put forty thousand troops through their evolutions in the Field of Mars yonder? The Winter Palace over there is acknowledged to be the most magnificent on earth; yonder is the University with its five hundred students, and I can see the roof of the Imperial Library, which has over eleven hundred thousand volumes. There *is* something outside of England, I must confess!"

"There are two thousand pictures and more than a hundred thousand books in the Hermitage Palace across the Neva," his friend said, as they turned at last to go. "I have lived in Russia," he added, as they came slowly down, "since I was a boy, and how can an American help liking it? It has a territory of eight million square miles; think of that! More than double the size of all Europe, with nearly one hundred million people. When my father first came to Russia, in the days of Nicholas, it was as when the first railway engineers crossed the Mississippi going west, only in this case a vaster continent was before him. When the great line was to be thrown across the empire, every town within five hundred miles on either side wanted the road to run by it. Of course, to accomplish their ends, they did not fail to bribe the nobleman in charge. My father was present when they presented their zigzag route for the approval of the Emperor, and he told me that he never enjoyed anything more than when he saw the Emperor spread the map upon a table, place an iron ruler with an end at each terminus, and then, with a red pencil, which he took from my father's hand, draw a line, straight as an arrow, from point to point. 'The road will be built along that!' he said, and left the room. And it was. My father preserves the imperial pencil still. When Nicholas died, less than three thousand miles of rail had been laid."

"I see that you are in haste to return to Prince Kalitzoff's," Lord Conyngham said, with a smile, as the two men stood at length in the great square of the Admiralty. "Do not forget that we are to visit the Annitchkoff Palace. I am by no means as deeply interested in St. Petersburg as you are. Good-by; you know my hotel."

There was that in the manner of the Englishman which caused the American to color a little as he bade him good day, and walked in an opposite direction. Two weeks before they had left Paris. But not alone. Zerah Atchison could see no object which justified him in refusing the offer of Prince Kalitzoff and remaining in Paris. It is true, he had heard nothing as yet of his lost son, but he had long ago learned to wait. He had been brought from Virginia to Paris by no planning of his own. Now that the way, without any thought of his, had been opened for his daughter to go to the Russian capital, "I go there," he had said, "because that is the one thing to do. And I am glad you agree with me, Isidore."

"You dear father!" she replied, "you and I are like a pair of pigeons, except that we have no home of our own anywhere in all the world. Here we are, high up in the sky, with the wide, wide earth lying below us, nothing about us but the sunshine, and the winds, and the immeasurable heavens! The least thing can turn us one way or the other. We curve about as easily as birds on the wing. Yes, I am willing to go to China, if you say so. If the man in the moon were to ask me to visit him a while, provided you went with me, I would say 'Yes.' When you die, father dear, all I beg is that you will let me go with you. I am ready for anything."

Her father looked at her with loving eyes. Until within a few weeks he had been as the child and she as the parent. Of late Isidore had become a child once more. The responsibilities of a father were pressing upon him as never before. A singular change had come over his daughter. Not that she was not as thoughtful of him as before; or that she did not seem outwardly as brave and hopeful as ever. In fact, she talked and laughed and sang and worked more eagerly than before; but the old artist had too sensitive an insight not to know that her outer gladness was put cn. Evidently she had entered into a new world, of thought at least, into which he could not accompany her. She had long periods also of absence. "I was at the Louvre, at the Exposition," she would explain when she came back; but she moved among the miles of pictures in the Louvre as if the walls were bare instead. She threaded her way through the crowds of the Exposition, among the brilliant display, as if she were in an uninhabited desert.

"I must be losing my mind," she remonstrated with herself. "Why is it that I lay awake at night, when I am so tired, too? How is it that Paris is little more to me than a dull village? I have no appetite, no interest in anything. Really, I care no more for art than I do for arithmetic, and I used to be so ambitious, too. Worst of all, I must be losing my very soul. I do not seem to love even my dear old father as I used to do; and here I am crying as if I were a baby. What *is* the matter with me?" But all this took place in the privacy of her inmost heart, and she would bathe her face, arrange her hair, array herself in some new article of dress, and kiss her father, talk with him, occupy herself in some task more feverishly than before. As if from the urgency of the case he had come to be a mother to her also, Zerah Atchison exerted himself more than ever to enter into her moods—to entertain her as he best could. He could not, however, but be conscious that Isidore was not really listening to him. Even when he was talking of art to her in his brightest vein, she would say, "Yes, father;" "No, father;" "You are right, sir;" "So I think, too," and would have said the same had he been telling her of the irruptions more than a thousand years ago of the Goths into Italy.

The old artist saw and knew the meaning of all this, even when he seemed to be blind. He could not have had so unerring an insight as to objects of art if he had not been able to see through mere color and curve in the case of his daughter also, and he was glad to get her away from herself, if possible, by taking her from Paris. Yes, he would fly farther than to Russia if he could bear Isidore with him from that which he began to dread, however patient he might be, with terror. "*He* will be with us only while on our journey," the father said to himself ; "after we get to St. Petersburg we will see him no more for ever."

But the artist did not allow for what might take place during the journey. By some blind instinct Lord Conyngham devoted himself almost the whole way to Zerah Atchison. The young nobleman had come to feel an indifference the most profound in relation to all women except one, and Isidore was given over by him, even more than due courtesy allowed, to his companion, Henry Harris. Now, there are no circumstances which draw people so closely together as when traveling with each other, and where in the world are fellow-travelers drawn as closely together as when riding on the cars through the long and desolate reaches of Russia ?

"It reminds me," Henry said to Isidore, seated beside him, " of the deserts of Southern Russia in the days of Catharine II, when hardly a miserable peasant was to be seen, nor even a hovel, for a hundred versts at a stretch. Catharine made Potempkin governor of the entire region, and when she proposed to go through it to the Black Sea and witness for herself the vast improvements of which Potempkin had boasted, he was at his wits' end. In his desperation he caused an immense number of wooden houses to be so made that they could be rapidly erected and taken down. When the Empress got to the edge of the wilderness, she found what seemed to be a flourishing town filled with thriving villagers. The instant she was through it the entire town was taken to pieces, hurried ahead in wagons—at least, so they say—and set up again by the roadside farther on ; and when, in her slow and stately progress, she arrived, it was to find what seemed to be another town, inhabitants and all, as flourishing as that which she had left behind. Potempkin repeated the device over and over again along the highway, until she wondered at the innumerable prosperous towns through which she journeyed. Arrived at last, after a travel of many weeks, upon the shores of the Black Sea, and standing delighted in the same old town, now erected for her inspection for the twentieth time upon its edge, Catharine heaped additional wealth and honors upon the governor who had made the desert the most populous and prosperous portion of her dominions."

Isidore laughed. "See," she said, as the train moved slowly along, "what a weary wilderness it is. Where do the people live? Nothing but forest and plain to be seen," and she was not sorry that she had a protector by her side. This was great Russia! Her father was old and feeble. Except her father and her companions, she was alone in the wide world! It was dangerous for both of them, since by an irresistible fate each was finding in the other his and her highest ideal. Isidore had never loved before. As to her companion, he had come to know that what he had once thought to be love for Lady Blanche had really been an admiration merely, admiration so great that he had mistaken it for affection. When the Englishwoman surrendered herself to such a man as the Duke of Plymouth, she repelled the American from her with a force which startled him, it was so much like unspeakable disgust. And now he was thrown into intimate relations with a woman who was the most charming because the most perfect of contrasts to the lady of rank. Yes; she was as beautiful, more beautiful, than Lady Blanche! The daughter of Earl Dorrington was a creature of society; here was a woman as fresh from nature itself as Venus arising from the foam of the sea. No palace or castle had she; no retinue of friends or of servants. Except her father, she was as much alone in the world as Eve in Paradise, unless he who sat beside her was a third. The truth is, these two persons were not journeying toward St. Petersburg. They never thought of Russia, or Prince Kalitzoff, or of anything in all the world as they went. Each was approaching nearer and nearer to the other. That was all. To each, life had, at last, no other goal but that.

On reaching, and it astonished them how soon they did so, the capital of Russia, they found the carriages of the Prince awaiting them at the station. Prince Kalitzoff himself stood at the door of their car when they alighted. They were warmly greeted by him, and the father and daughter were driven to his palace upon Nevskoi Prospekt.

CHAPTER LVII.

PRINCE KALITZOFF.

WHEN Prince Kalitzoff assisted Isidore Atchison to alight from the railway train at the St. Petersburg station, she was struck by his appearance. He was quite a large man, with a broad face, kind but sad, of a fair complexion, with dark eyes, his abundant hair and beard being of a color she had never before seen. "It is," her father told her afterward, "of that shade of orange which painters call 'lion's-eye,' and it sets out his pleasing features, his whole person, in fact, as a gilded frame does a picture."

"Welcome to Holy Russia!" the Prince said to the artist and his daughter in good English, for he had once been secretary of legation from Russia to England. "I esteem myself honored by the company of artists above all other of the nobility, and," he added, taking the hand of Isidore again in his, "when one of them is a lady also— But, dear me, madame," he added, with an impulsive ardor which made her flush, as Isidore unveiled herself to reply, "you are only a child, a beautiful child!" In half an hour afterward father and daughter were comfortably housed in their own apartments.

The palace of Prince Kalitzoff was one of the largest upon the Nevskoi Prospekt, but the glory of it was the ample grounds with conservatories and flower-gardens in which it was nestled. At some distance from the stately mansion, and separated from it by a little grove of firs, was a two-storied cottage which the Prince had set apart and handsomely furnished for the exclusive use of his guests. It possessed the appointments and conveniences of a comfortable home, and there was a large studio, lighted only by a skylight, which filled Zerah Atchison with delight.

"I built this cottage," the Prince said, when he visited them a day or two after their arrival, "as an Easter gift to my child, the Princess Aura, of whom you must endure to hear me speak, perhaps too much. You will be wholly independent of me, with, of course, your own table and carriage and servants; but I will be happy to have you consider my palace as equally at your disposal. My bronzes and paintings have remained in the palace, covered from sight since the death of my child, and, at your convenience, sir, I hope you will select such as you wish to be conveyed here. As to the monument, I desire you should take your own time, if it be years. I am a lonely man, and I am honored by your company." But it was the evident sincerity of the Prince which gave to his cordial, almost boyish, manner its chief charm, and father and daughter soon found themselves conversing with him as if he had been an old and intimate friend. They found it easy to lead the conversation back to his daughter, and listened with unfeigned interest as he told them, with an exaggeration which was natural in so devoted a parent, many incidents of her short life.

"Why is it," he exclaimed, when he arose to leave at last, "that you Americans are so different from the English? I have, like you, a passion for art, and I know that popes, emperors, and kings have always considered the Michael Angelos, Rubenses, Titians, Canovas, Thorwaldsens, as more than their equals; but why is it that, unconsciously to yourselves, simply because you are Americans, you make yourselves friends also upon first acquaintance?" And thus, with many kind words, there began between the Russian and his

guests an acquaintance which ripened so rapidly, as the
time passed, into friendship that Isidore could not refrain
from saying in the end to her father, as to herself, "And
this is Russia! Russia? I feel more at home almost than
I did in America."

"That, my child, is," her father replied, "because, for
the first time in your life, you are placed in the sphere to
which you naturally belong. It is not often that God does
this until we die. The happiness, the peace, rather, of heav-
en will consist in our being perfectly fitted for it as it will
be for us; in the deepest sense, dear, you and I will find
ourselves perfectly at home there."

Meanwhile Henry Harris and Lord Conyngham made
themselves comfortable at their hotel. Dressed as students,
and guided by Toffski, the moujik, who was born in St. Petersburg, where he had first become the servant of Henry
Harris, the young men penetrated into every part of the
city by night as by day. But there was rarely a day that
the American did not find himself a visitor at the palace
of the Prince or the cottage of the artists. In fact, the
Prince was to be found of an evening only with Zerah Atchison and his daughter. He had long secluded himself
seemingly from an active part in public affairs, nor had he
gone into general society since the death of his daughter.
The mother of Princess Aura never was much of a companion for him, and she had died many years before her daughter. A man of simple and sincere disposition, of warm and
loving heart, accustomed all his life to do as he pleased,
with little to occupy his attention elsewhere, the Prince
came at last to feel as if he was nearest to the daughter he
had loved so well when in the cottage he had erected for
her, and with the friends who were engaged in bringing her
back to him again, so far as it could be done by the power
of genius. For artistic purposes, also, they were continually asking about the Princess Aura, for the father and
daughter were as eager to hear about her as the Prince was
to speak.

And thus it happened that Henry Harris found himself one evening with them in the cozy parlor of the cottage. The invariable *samovar* of boiling tea was still upon the table, which was heaped with photographs of the dead Princess, for it had been her father's weakness to have her taken in all varieties of costume and attitude. In the studio adjoining there were portraits of her also from her earliest infancy, and medallions. Isidore had, in fact, entered with enthusiasm upon her work.

"I have come," she now said, "to feel as if I knew her all my life. If I had lived with her, I do not see how I could have a clearer conception of her than I have at this moment. When I know and see, almost touch and hear, an ideal, as I am coming to do in regard to her, it is more vividly before me than if it were actually present. Sleeping and waking, I can not be rid of it, even if I would."

"I thank you," said the Prince, whose large, slow eyes had been dwelling upon the young girl as she spoke with deep attention, "but you must not allow even my sainted child thus to haunt you. You look pale; you speak of disturbed repose. I learn from your perhaps over-anxious servants that you eat as little as a canary-bird. We must not allow it," he added to the old artist. "Miss Isidore is injuring her health. As her doctor, also, I prohibit any work for a week or two. You must ride; must go to the opera more; must ramble about the city. I can not," he said, with his eyes again upon her, "I will not, suffer you to sacrifice yourself!"

As it was said, a sudden something smote Henry Harris almost like a blow. He observed, or imagined he did, a tenderness upon the part of the Prince. When he glanced at Isidore, her face paled and then flushed. He did not know what to make of it. "You must remember," the Prince continued, still looking at his lovely young guest, "that you are not in your America now, nor even in republican France. This is Russia; you are under a despotism. If you do not obey orders, you may find yourself in Siberia."

In however playful a manner it might be said, the young man almost resented it, and hastened to change the subject to the political condition of the empire. The Prince had known George Harris, as well as his son, too long not to speak unreservedly in reply.

"It is explained in a few words," he summed up at last. "Your Shakespeare says that there are tides in the affairs of men. He is right. The Atlantic does not ebb and flow with more regularity than does the intellect. With this exception, that as the Atlantic is but a drop of water compared to the depth and breadth of the human soul, so are the tides of the soul deeper, slower, more certain, more irresistible. The mastery of the world by the Roman Empire was one of these tides, and the decay of that empire was its ebb. There was not a soul in Europe that did not feel the rush of the tide in the days of the Crusades, as well as the subsidence of the reaction which followed. So of the Renaissance. What a grand upheaval, and from the very depths, during that revival of ancient learning, with its refluent waters afterward! The Reformation under Huss, Wickliffe, Luther, was another flood; the ebb is in the Protestant rationalism, especially of Germany, which ensued. So of Russia. Peter the Great was but the crest of such an upheaving. Russia rose upon it only to subside somewhat during the reigns which followed. To-day the intellect of the race has broken over all separating barriers. Humanity is one; and over the whole world the awakening intellect is one, as if it were one vast ocean, covering almost the entire planet. Very well. The tide which rises in America lifts also every soul in England, France, Germany, Italy. Even such stagnant bays as Spain, Portugal, and the Papacy are affected by it. Shall not Russia also yield to the lift of the universal tide? If we are Russians, are we not part also of the race?"

"Your Excellency is right," the young engineer hastened to say. "But that is why, if you will allow me, repression is so dangerous a task. There is vast intellectual force in Russia; but how can it reveal itself? You need not tell me of outlets for it in literature, in art, in science, in commerce. God has so made the human mind that if it is repressed in even one respect it is held in check in all. It must have the absolute freedom of the ocean in every point if it is to rise and flow at its highest power in any. America has political freedom, your Excellency; is absolutely untrammeled; therefore it produces also artists, poets, orators, inventors, discoverers. The unparalleled power of our Western farmers to feed the world, of our miners to supply the silver of the world, its coal and oil and gold, is merely a part of the same force, because freedom, of our newspaper press, of our inventive genius. To reach his highest stature, your Excellency, the Russian, like the American, must be absolutely free and in every possible sense. You likened the intellect of the race to the ocean and its tides, and, no more in Russia than elsewhere, can you suppress the ocean—your Excellency, you can not do it!"

"Do you think so?" The Prince asked the question with the gravity of a statesman. Apparently he had suddenly grown older as well as colder. It was as if his face, so genial before, had become a mask of stone. His tones were severe as well as serious. "Being an American, it is natural you should speak as you do," he said, sententiously. "But we are of another race. Our traditions, our religion, are different;" and for some time the Prince continued to converse as became the conservative philosopher he had the reputation of being. A chill, almost a gloom, had fallen upon all present. Isidore gave an almost perceptible shiver, as if touched by the bitter blasts of Siberia. Henry Harris was sorry he had alluded to the matter, and soon after withdrew.

But it was not of political matters he thought as he mounted his *tarantass* and was driven to his hotel. "I had not imagined," he said to himself, "that she could seem so lovely! And what did Prince Kalitzoff mean by his lingering glances at her? He is still young and of a passionate temperament. A Russian is either utter master or utter slave. Under a mere varnish of politeness Kalitzoff is, at best, a semi-civilized savage, a Tartar, and I must be on my guard. Suppose he should dare?"

CHAPTER LVIII.

THE DEPTHS.

ONE evening the young American summoned his man Toffski into a room in which Lord Conyngham and himself were busy preparing themselves for a midnight expedition into the deepest depths of St. Petersburg. The moujik was, as has been said, an undersized and very thickset man. His full and florid face looked, in its environment of hay-colored hair and whiskers, like, Isidore had told his master, "the harvest moon in a halo of fog." Perhaps it was be-cause he was nearly as broad as he was long, but as he now stood waiting he was almost as solid, as stolid, and as still as a block of wood. The young men paid no attention to him for some time, aware that Toffski could stand without mo-tion in the same four-square repose for hours, could sleep as he stood all night, could die, if need be, without movement or the least noise. A being more absolutely the property of his master it was impossible to imagine.

" Toffski Ivanovitch," the American said at last, in Rus-sian, " listen. I want this gentleman to know. Tell no lies. What are the occupations of the Russians in general?"

"Henry Georgeovitch," was the slow but steady reply, "the Russians beat or are beaten. They tell lies, drink vodka, and gamble at *stukolka*."

"Ask him what, then, are their vices," Lord Conyngham said, when this had been translated to him, for, although the man knew a little English, his master and himself always conversed in Russian.

" Henry Georgeovitch," the moujik answered, when the

question had been asked, " the Russians beat each other, tell lies, drink vodka, gamble.　They are *raskolinks*, rascals."

"This *Aglitcha*, Englishman," his master asked next, " demands what are the amusements of the Russians.　Answer, Toffski Ivanovitch."

"Henry Georgeovitch," came the reply, "the Russians go sometimes to church or play the accordeon, but that is not always.　They amuse themselves by gambling, drinking vodka, telling lies, and beating whoever they can with a big stick," and, standing solidly upon his short legs, the moujik seemed quite willing to be questioned, or himself beaten, until the others should be exhausted.

"Who in the devil's name is Bakunin ? " demanded Lord Conyngham, suddenly.

"He is the devil himself ! " the Russian answered, crossing his forehead and each shoulder.

"Oh, as to Michael Bakunin," his master explained for him, " he was a rich native of St. Petersburg, born in 1814, who, bitterly disappointed in his ambition, devoted himself to philosophy and insurrections.　Have you seen none of his innumerable pamphlets ?　He says that right is merely an invention of might, that conscience is the creature of education, that God is only the personification of tyranny.　Here is one of his proclamations—the better to inform myself, I obtained it to-day ; " and, taking it from an inner pocket, the American translated the closing threat : " I, Michael Bakunin, summon you to the destruction of emperor and empire.　Tear out of your souls all belief in the existence of God.　Property, marriage, morality, science, justice, civilization—I doom to eternal death.　No law, no religion, *nihil !*" and a good deal more to the same effect.　" Yet Bakunin," Henry Harris added, putting the paper up, " devil as he is, has disciples all over Russia by the thousands, in all ranks.　Let us go and see what we can for ourselves."

Saying a few words to his man, the three set out.　The two gentlemen were wrapped up in cloaks to hide their coarse student apparel until they got into a *tarantass*, in which, with Toffski upon the seat by the driver, they were driven eastward and toward the worst part of the city. At a certain point they alighted from their vehicle, leaving the driver to wait for them, which he did by falling sound asleep on the seat before they were gone a hundred yards into the darkness.

"We are well armed, and Toffski knows where to go," the American said as they strode on through the dimly lighted streets. It was very late. Now and then a dog barked, or a watchman went by, looking at them closely.

"I see a light glimmering in every house ; why is that ?" the Englishman asked as they walked with Toffski leading the way.

"In every home in Russia," his companion replied, "a lamp burns always before the sacred images. Do you know, my lord, I can not believe that Heaven despises those poor, smoking lights ? Wherever and whenever a living creature tries to pray, and the best he knows how, I believe it is as acceptable to God as if it was the most powerful prayer ever put up in Westminster Abbey by your Archbishop of Canterbury himself. God looks at the intention only, and he knows that very often people are no more responsible for their situation than they are for the color of their eyes or the malaria in which they are condemned to live."

At this moment Toffski halted before the red curtain of a small and poorly lighted house, and said something in Russian to his master.

"This is one of the lowest of the Nihilist *cafés,*" the latter explained to his friend. "We are Russian students, you know. They are the worst socialists in Russia, so that nobody will be surprised to see us. Our flaxen wigs make us sufficiently Russian, but you, especially, must keep silent, whatever befalls." Saying which, the three entered the house. It was not as much unlike the London pothouse as one would have expected. There was the same bar, presided over by a very fat and ugly woman, a large inner room with black walls, an immense stove in the center, a number of tables, about which coarse and heavy-featured men, and men also of more cultivated appearance, sat drinking *kislitchi* or vodka, playing at games, smoking. And yet, and from the outset, Lord Conyngham felt as if almost every one present was disguised as well as himself and his companion. There was no platform, as in "The Hammer an' down wi' 'em," nor was there any general conversation.

Every one looked sharply at them as they took their seats at a table in a corner and ordered drink and pipes. The American conversed with his moujik in angry Russian, as if in continuance of a quarrel, emphasizing what he had to say with a blow on Toffski's ear at last, which was quite in keeping. As he had said, students from the universities were frequent visitors, and very soon their presence seemed to be forgotten. The attention of the nobleman was drawn, he knew not why, to a number of beardless youths off to themselves at a table. Several of them wore spectacles ; the hair of all was cut short ; some smoked cigarettes or cigars. They conversed with each other in whispers, but as a rule they listened instead, continually glancing at each other ; occasionally laughing, as if to themselves also. There was something odd in the manner in which they were grouped.

"They are girls, women, even ladies !" the American cautiously whispered to his friend, "and they are entirely virtuous and respectable, too. They have sons, brothers, husbands, among these men. As in America during our civil war, the women of Russia are, if possible, more deeply interested in the impending revolution than the men. The worst feature of Nihilism is that its female adherents seek to unsex themselves ; they are the most frantic of its disciples —drinking, smoking, wearing their hair short, in sheer bravado. Listen." For two men were engaged by this time in a noisy discussion at a table near the center of the room.

"The Nihilists are scoundrels !" the Englishman was astonished to hear one of them exclaim at last. "Our Emperor has many thousand rubles a day, but does he not deserve it for being the father of his people ? Suppose our army does number nearly two millions, and suppose they are drawn from the shops and the fields, have we not to fight, to fight England, which is becoming a republic? Look at France; it is free, as they call it; it is a republic, and as such is growing richer every day. It must be crushed!" The one who spoke was a powerful-looking man, with broad shoulders and a fierce air as of authority.

"But surely the people of Holy Russia should be free also," remonstrated his opponent, a pale, weak-eyed man, in spectacles, and with a timid manner. "Look at our taxes. Consider our sons torn from us by conscription. Our press— has it any freedom? The Emperor has emancipated twenty million serfs. That was in 1861. Surely it is time to give freedom to the remaining sixty millions of his subjects. Bulgaria is obtaining a constitution. Surely we are—"

"Silence!" roared the other. "You must be a socialist yourself! I dare say if your house were searched we would find copies of the Nihilist papers, the '*Zamlja i Wolja*' or the '*Nabab.*' And to think that even women, respectable la- dies, are taking part in the accursed movement. There are " —and Lord Conyngham observed the intense interest shown at the table of the disguised women as this was said—"there are Vjera Sassulitch, Sophia Löschern von Herzfeld, even a daughter of an imperial councilor, Nathalie von Armfeldt. Mary Kovalerski is one of the nobility, yet she has given money, circulates socialist papers, such as 'The Pole Star' and 'The Clock.' The father of Katharina Sarandovitch is a high official, and it was proved that she was active in the same detestable business."

"But it was also proved," ventured the other man, "that Vjera Sassulitch only knew Netchaieff as the brother of her friend; had no part nor sympathy in his socialistic ideas, and she was eleven years in prison merely upon vague suspicion. As to the assault on the rascal police-chief Trepoff, was it not because she had been driven, after she was released, to desperation by what she knew had been done to Bogoljuboff, an innocent prisoner, whom she had never even seen? The

men who try to assassinate our Emperor, Karakasoff, Ber-
zowski, Solouveff, are madmen. But tell me," persisted the
pale-faced man, "what drove them mad?"

"They are devils!" shouted his burly antagonist. "To-
day sixty thousand political exiles toil, I am glad to say, in
the mines of Siberia. Twelve hours a day do they have to
work, with no such thing as Sunday the year round. Easter and the Emperor's birthday are the only days they rest.
Scoundrels! They will broil in hell for ever! And to think
that there are nobles among them, princesses, too ; judges,
who betrayed the Czar by being too lenient to their prisoners ; learned men, educated men, priests, school-teachers,
scientists, men who ought to know better than to try and
overturn our holy empire. They would try to drag us down
to the level of France, England ; down even to the level of
America, where everybody does what he pleases. Wretches!
It is radical writing, like that of Berzen ; it is treasonable
poetry, like that of Pushkin, which puts the torch to Russia,
as Rostoptchin did to Moscow in 1812 ; it is such rascals
who seek to destroy us." And for some time the conversation continued, the pale man attempting to defend, the black-
bearded giant assaulting the revolutionists with almost eloquent denunciation, in which the labors of the radicals
throughout Russia, of democrats throughout the world, in
fact, were detailed in fierce displeasure. All around them
sat the people, drinking, smoking, listening—above all, listening! It was like bedlam to the English nobleman, who
could see, but could understand nothing. Standing upon
his feet in one corner, the moujik had fallen apparently sound
asleep.

In continuation of his denunciation, the burly defender
of the Government told at last with indignation of an inroad
made, a few days before, by the police at Kief, upon a Nihilist club, their object being the arrest especially of Catarina Simolovitch, the daughter of a university professor,
who had made herself peculiarly obnoxious. As the police
burst in at the front door, Catarina and her husband rose

from the garden behind the house in a balloon held in readiness. The pale man ventured to laugh at this, and in an instant the other, knocking down the table between them, displaying as he did so his badge as an officer of police, took him by the throat. It was a frightful spectacle. The pale man was comparatively small and weak, and the officer, who was a giant, in the extremity of a wrath which it was hard to comprehend, seizing the other about the throat with both hands, lifted him from the floor, strangling, writhing like a worm, struggling, his eyes protruding, his tongue hanging out of his mouth, his face blackened by his agony. Both of the visitors hurled themselves forward to prevent, but Toffski had clasped his arms about his master, and was holding him as he would have held a baby, while the Englishman, exclaiming and making furious efforts to get through the crowd, which had arisen and interposed, could only see at last that the poor wretch hung motionless and dead in the remorseless grasp of his powerful executioner.

"Even the women did not shriek or lift a finger to help!" he said, as they drove home at length through the early dawn. "They are Nihilists, and yet allow a policeman to kill their own defender! Cowards!"

"It is because you did not understand my explanation all along," his friend said. "The defender of the Nihilists was really a Government spy, collecting evidence to send us all to Siberia. I informed myself before I went. The policeman is the celebrated Borozoffski, who is also a Nihilist leader. He edits, they say, the Nihilist paper, 'Land and Liberty,' but his seeming denunciation of the revolution was merely one way of disseminating socialistic news. Except that unfortunate spy, every one there understood. There are over three million Nihilists in Russia. Priests, bishops, students, professors, commanders in the navy, generals even in the army, vast numbers in the police, are active members of the propaganda. I like Alexander, I love Russia, but a revolution is impending which will grind it to chaos, out of which God alone knows what kind of a new Russia is to arise!"

"The most hopeless thing in Russia," he added, a moment after, "is that women are so prominent among the revolutionists—women who are making themselves worse than men. No, there is one thing worse, if possible, than that. It is that the Greek Church—and it is about the only Christianity Russia has—is utterly powerless either to purify the empire or to prevent the revolution."

CHAPTER LIX.

INTO PERIL.

ONE evening, when Henry Harris and Lord Conyngham were spending the evening in the cottage of Zerah Atchison, Prince Kalitzoff being in the room, Henry Harris said to Isidore, "Let me tell you a little story." The young girl had been hard at work all day, and was seated by her father, his paralyzed hand lying in her lap. She raised her eyes almost timidly to his face, and said, "I would like to hear it," whereupon the other began :

"Once upon a time, there was a handsome but bearded ogre, who was extremely fond of young people. Not that he broiled and ate them, but that he loved to give balls at his palace, and to see them dancing, eating ice-cream, and enjoying themselves. One day he was told that he had neglected a girl, who, although the daughter of a poor carpenter, was the prettiest girl in all that region. And so the bearded ogre, who was very rich as well as kind-hearted, gave a ball expressly in her behalf, and when the time came sent his carriage for her. He was in waiting at the door of his palace when the carriage drove up, and helped her off with her wrappings. As soon as he saw her face he exclaimed, 'Why, you dear child, how very pretty you are !' and, in a few months after that, he married her, and they made one of the happiest couples in the world."

"And who was the ogre?" Isidore demanded.

"His name," the narrator replied, "was Count Bodisco. He was minister from Russia to the United States at Washington City, and ever since his marriage to that poor but good and beautiful American girl there has been a sort of love match also between Russia and America." To this Prince Kalitzoff assented, even cordially, confirming the story from his own knowledge. It was plain that he approved of what the ogre had done.

"That is what perplexes me, Prince—you must allow me to say it," Lord Conyngham broke in; "but I never could understand why the Americans always side with you Russians against us English, who are of their own blood. It is absurd!"

"Not," the American interposed, "if you remember that Russia has always been our stanch friend. When the nobility of England—pardon me, my lord—were exulting, during our civil war, in our speedy destruction as a nation, Russia never wavered. It was the hour of our supreme struggle for existence, and centuries hence we will remember that the Pope took sides with the Confederacy against us, the only power that did so; that Charles Dickens, whom we had almost worshiped, was, in his letters, rejoicing in our apparent destruction, heaping contemptuous epithets upon us; that Louis Napoleon, perjured scoundrel that he was, did his utmost to induce England to join him against us. You, my lord, were too young then to have an opinion of your own. You, Mr. Atchison, although in the ranks against us, were always an artist and never a partisan. When England attacks Russia, and especially in defense of the Turks, she must excuse us if we will not weep if she is defeated."

"My father, by the by, writes me to-day," Lord Conyngham said, "that our friend Hassan Pasha is dead. He suddenly disappeared from Paris, you will remember. He returned, it seems, to Constantinople, raised an insurrection against the Sultan, failed, and was found next day dead in a bath-tub in his own palace. Whether he had been killed, or had opened his veins with his own hand and bled to death, no one will ever know." As this was said, Henry Harris was aware that Isidore Atchison had turned very pale ; even he did not know, nor her own father, all the attempts which had been made upon her honor by the Turk. In some way she had learned that the letter over which she had at first re-joiced, but which she had given up to Henry Harris, was but one of these attempts. Her eyes were fixed upon the noble-man as he now said :

"There was a singular story afloat in Paris in connection with his sudden leaving. The landlord of his hotel explained that early one morning a gentleman went into the rooms of Hassan Pasha and gave him a severe beating before he was out of bed. It seems that the rascal had written to some lady. It served him right ! I wish I knew who the gentle-man was. The Turkish villain did well to fly to Constanti-nople."

Henry Harris, as this was said, felt rather than saw that the eyes of Isidore were fastened upon him, her face was in a sudden glow, her lips were parted, and he hastened to change the subject.

"We were speaking of Russia," he remarked. "Your emperor has a terrible time of it," turning to Prince Kalitz-zoff. "He has been very kind to my father and myself, and I am Russian enough to like him heartily."

The same singular change took place, as he said it, in the Prince which the American had before observed. Generally he was the most cordial and off-handed of hosts in his man-ner ; now he became cold and cautious in his bearing, and said, slowly :

"His Majesty has had a severe training. From his earli-est boyhood he was an officer in the army. He had to arise before day, to drill and be drilled for many hours at a time, to live upon hard fare, exposing himself to all weather, even the most bitter cold. There is not a moujik in his em-pire who has had to work as hard as he, not a Tartar of the Ukraine who has lived as much in the open air and on horseback. It was against the most violent opposition that he emancipated, in 1861, over twenty million serfs. People are greatly mistaken when they imagine that he inaugurates war against Turkey, threatens England in Afghanistan, occupies Khiva, annexes fragments of Persia, of China. Holy Russia is immeasurably the largest empire history tells of. It is like an immense ship of war," the Prince added, " of which Alexander II is merely the pilot. If he had only to hold the helm while an unceasing tempest raged, that would task the energies of a Hercules ! that is the least of his work. The empire is made up of many peoples and religions, and there is mutiny on board always. Mutiny among the nobles, insurrection among the peasants, disaffection among the warring religions, and all the time there is the dry rot, as among the very timbers of the ship, of such corruption as no nation has ever before conceived. It is not merely that officials habitually steal, from the lowest to the highest ; in this last war against the Turk, admirals, commanders-in-chief, as much as quartermasters, even grand dukes, bribe and are bribed."

"The Emperor knows all this," the American assented, " and is, your Excellency knows, almost as helpless to prevent it as I am. You speak of the empire as a ship. Yes, and I have been long enough in Russia to know that it is seized upon by unexpected currents, whirled about by cyclones beyond any foresight of the Emperor. Nicholas and his minister Nesselrode could not prevent the disaster of the Crimean War, any more than Alexander and Gortchakoff can help this war with Turkey. But Alexander is a strong, stern, sorrowful man, who fails where God only can be czar. I sincerely honor and respect him. But, your Excellency, I would rather be what I am—an engineer."

"We have all simply to do our duty and to be patient," Zerah Atchison added, with a happy face, as the visitors arose to .go. Isidore seemed to cling more closely to the old artist as they bowed and left the room. She had glanced at Prince Kalitzoff, then at the American. Her face was troubled.

14

"Yes, I fear she is overtasking herself," the Prince said, as he accompanied the gentlemen to the door. "The young lady has shown me her first draughts for the monument. They are beyond my expectations. Even her father approves of them," he added, with a smile. "Miss Isidore is more than a genius, however. She is the most charming of women. Ah! Mr. Harris, yours is a great country. I admire your little story exceedingly. Happy Bodisco!" And he shook his guest warmly by the hand, contenting himself with bowing, almost coldly, to the Englishman.

"What possessed me to tell that story in his hearing?" the American exclaimed to himself, angrily. "Am I becoming a fool?"

But Lord Conyngham was thinking of something else.

"We are bound to have it out with them some day," he said, haughtily, as the two walked away. "We can whip them on the water, but if we go at it in India there'll be the deuce of a mess. You see," he explained, "there's no telling which side those Sikhs, Afghans, Hindoos, and the like, will take. Rascals! I'm afraid the beggars don't like us any too much! We visit the Annitchkoff Palace to-morrow; don't forget. Until the Earl writes that he is ready to let me marry as I please, I stay, you observe, where I am."

But his companion was not listening to him. He was thinking how old and feeble Zerah Atchison appeared to have become; how timid and shrinking his daughter seemed; "and it does appear to me," he thought, "that the Prince might be more fatherly than he is in his regards for her. He is immensely rich; is lonely in his great palace; has such an ardent and despotic nature, who can tell what he— From my very soul I am *sorry* she is here!"

The next day the American and his English friend had, while inspecting the pictures in the Annitchkoff Palace, an unexpected adventure. In consequence of a special permit, they were standing together, no one but a servant with them, before a painting of the coronation of Alexander II, when the door opened and a gentleman entered. At a glance Lord

Conyngham saw that it was the monarch depicted upon the glowing canvas, and both visitors turned and stood with uncovered heads as the stately sovereign passed rapidly by. But his sharp, military eye recognized the engineer, whom he had often seen before.

"Mr. Harris," he said in English, "I am pleased to see you. You were in Paris. What are you doing in Russia?"

Lord Conyngham was as brave, as manly an Englishman as any, but royalty had a glamour for him which it did not have for his friend. "Confound it! how cool he is!" he thought, for the American was standing as erect as the Czar, only less tall than the colossal Alexander, and was looking the other composedly in the face.

"Does your Majesty insist upon knowing?" he asked, with deference, but composedly.

"I do," was the reply, with some surprise in the face of the Emperor, which seemed set into a certain bronze, as of unspeakable sadness.

"If you will permit me," and the American passed from English to Russian, "I am trying to understand Nihilism, even to the very bottom. Does your Majesty object?"

"You are an American," was the reply, in the same language; "but you do so at your peril!"

The next moment the Emperor passed out at the other door.

"I warn you again not to go with me," was all the explanation Henry Harris gave his companion. "But to-morrow I go to Kiev. I want to get through with this thing."

CHAPTER LX.

WOMAN'S WIT.

WHEN the American and his friend returned to their hotel after their interview with the Emperor, they found letters awaiting them.

"I do not altogether like your experiment in regard to Nihilism," Mr. George Harris, who was again in Paris, wrote to his son, "and yet I can not say but that I admire your energy in the matter. Your mother and myself agree that your life must be in many respects unlike mine. I have been obliged to concentrate myself upon my business, and in doing that I have been constrained to remain, as to many matters, merely a spectator. There are things in Europe, as in America also, which are foolish, silly, even pitiful, in their abject folly. The dullest machinist would be an idiot to tolerate in a locomotive any defect which could be as easily remedied as are many mistakes in the working of our civilization. Like you, I have chafed at the horrible forms of wrong which have come down from barbarous times, but I had other affairs in hand. Thank Heaven, we have trained you to do grander work than I could ever do, and that in a grander time than the days in which your mother and myself have lived. We will leave your sister and yourself more money than perhaps you have supposed would come to you. Money is a tremendous force, my son. It is more powerful and dangerous than dynamite or nitro-glycerine. If you do not expend it toward honest effort for the good of your kind, it will recoil and in some way blow you to atoms. That is all I have to say. Be prudent. Learn all you can of Russian explosives. Amazing events are to take place in that empire."

"I am glad," Mrs. Margaret Harris wrote to her son, "that Mary and her lover seem to be so utterly in love with each other. It is doing her a world of good, because she is possessed with the purpose of being more than merely a loving wife. Your father was laughing at her last night. 'From whom do you get your ambition?' he asked her. 'I am an American girl,' she said, 'and I intend that Alfred shall become a leader in Parliament. He has promised me to become some day prime minister! You need not laugh,' she added. 'Look at Lord Beaconsfield! All that lifts him to his position is his life-long and unconquerable purpose. Alfred is superior to him any day, and even if he were not, I will be with him as his undying purpose.' I never saw her look so beautiful as when she said that!

"'It is a singular thing about America,' your father told me when she left us. 'It is coming to be what the Roman Empire once was. That is, Rome conquered the world and drew into itself, as into the vortex and center of the earth, all races of men, only to cause them to rot together until the whole world was poisoned by the deadly corruption.' In the same way all races of men are being sucked in, as if in spite of themselves, under American influence, but it is to purify, I hope, and save them; yet I do not want Mary to become 'strong-minded,' and I told her that she could be a genuine American woman only so far as she was intensely and entirely a *woman*, and in no sense a man. Take care of yourself, my son," and Mrs. Harris added a hundred cautions.

The son said nothing about his letters, but his friend was not so reticent. "By Jove!" he had exclaimed again and again as he read a letter which he had received by the same mail from Mary, "there is a page or two which is none of your business," he remarked to his companion when he had read the letter over once or twice, "but listen to this, will you?" and he read:

"Yes, Alfred, I am only a girl, but I am in good earnest. You are a nobleman in more senses of the word than one!" "Glad to hear it," her lover interjected. "And there is a glorious future before me if I am ever to marry you. Because you are to accomplish so much! For there is so much to be done in the world! Yesterday my father said to me of a mob of Parisian school-boys which happened to pass us:

'Those and the rest of the French boys have a vast work to do ; they have to hold and develop the French Republic against a thousand foes, inside and out ! The work of the world is only beginning, my dear. Why, Mary,' he said, in his calm, methodic way, 'if I were a professor in college I could write out on a blackboard, for the use of young men, the life-work before them.' 'Write it out for me,' I begged, and, sure enough, he scratched it down on the paper I inclose."

Lord Conyngham passed the document to his friend. It was written out, the American saw at a glance, somewhat as his father did his first draughts of work in his machine shops, and was in this shape :

"THE WORK OF THE WORLD.

"*Africa.*—Discover; build railroads ; send missionaries of all sects ; found and build up Christian nations.

"*Asia.*—Obliterate Turkish empire; ease to the ground the impending downfall of Persia, China, Afghanistan, Thibet ; replace Palestine in possession of Jews; Christianize the whole.

"*Italy.*—Maintain unity of Italian kingdom till fit for republic ; ease down Papacy.

"*Russia.*—Transform empire into constitutional monarchy ; then monarchy into the Russian republic ; repress anarchy during transition.

"*Germany.*—Hasten transformation of empire into republic of United States of Germany ; revolutionize excessive use of beer, tobacco, and metaphysical speculation.

"*France.*—Educate children ; separate Church from State ; maintain republic ; see that Napoleonism, legitimacy, ultramontanism, have sure, but, if possible, peaceful decay.

"*England.*—Disestablish Scotch Church ; disestablish English Church ; abolish primogeniture ; smooth the way for the inevitable coming of the republic of Great Britain."

"By Jove !" Lord Conyngham exclaimed, and his friend read on :

"*America.*—Establish civil service reform ; bring South into lines of emigration and commerce ; guard against partisan politics ; prepare to meet and survive unparalleled trials, perhaps, and catastrophes; maintain public schools against all foes; develop power of press; compel world to conform to American example by sheer force of superiority.

"*Everywhere.*—Perfect electric light and force; heat as well as light every city from a common center within same; cook and wash also at same; if possible, navigate air; cut Isthmus of Panama; discover and invent as needs of men demand; abolish war and intemperance; reconcile labor and capital.

" With energy, the above work should be done by the year 2000."

"It is odd," Henry Harris said, as he laid down the paper, "but the year 2000 will be the seventh or Sabbatical age of the world. It will be a remarkable coincidence if the six thousand years of work *is* done by then."

"But you must hear what Mary says," her lover added, and he read from her letter: "Don't think me a fanatic. Who can tell what is to be done! Whatever it is, you will do *your* share, Alfred, if only to please me! As to England, I love and admire it almost as much as you do, because you were born there, and because it is every day more and more one with America. Yes, it is older, slower, wiser than we. No greater poet ever lived, Alfred, than your Laureate, our other Alfred, whom I love almost as much as I do you, but not *quite,* and he sings of it :

" 'Land of just and old renown,
    Where freedom broadens slowly down
        From precedent to precedent,
    Where faction seldom gathers head,
        But by degrees to fullness wrought,
        The strength of some diffusive thought
    Hath time and space to work and spread.' "

"I won't read any more," the Englishman added, as he folded the letter carefully up, and placed it in his breast-pocket. "There is more, but that also is nobody's business but ours. The only thing I want to say is, that your sister is the noblest as well as the most beautiful woman I know!

But if we are to start for Kiev in the morning, it is high time we were going to bed. Good night."

The truth is, the lover wanted to be off by himself, in order to read his letter over again.

CHAPTER LXI.

THE CROWING OF THE RED COCK.

From his boyhood Henry Harris spent much of his spare time in his father's railway shops in Russia. Now, a striking peculiarity of the Russian is his excessive fondness for children, and from his earliest remembrance Henry found small difficulty in becoming acquainted with the workmen of all grades employed in constructing and repairing locomotives. Among these was a brawny, red-headed Russian, who was stone-deaf to any question, remark, or command unless it was addressed to him accompanied by his full name, which was Constantinovitch Miralovinski Stephanoff. His face had been sadly damaged by an explosion, his flannel and sheepskin attire were generally odorous with lubricating oil, and he seemed to wear his name as if it were royal and voluminous raiment which made up for all deficiencies. Now, Henry Harris had long known that this man was deep in the secrets of the Nihilists, and, addressing him by his full name through the mail before leaving Paris, he learned in reply that he was now engineer upon a line running from St. Petersburg toward Odessa. It was from him in person, and after arriving in St. Petersburg, that Henry Harris obtained the information which led to his visit to the Nihilist *café* in St. Petersburg the night the spy was strangled. From him also he learned that there was to be " a Crowing of the Red Cock," as the man styled it, at Kiev, in Little Russia, at a certain date near at hand.

"Yes," the American said to him ; "but, Constantinovitch Miralovinski Stephanoff, what do you mean by the Red Cock?"

"My little father, *Batushka*, if you and your friend," was the reply, "want to know, you can read. If you want, as you say, to *see*, you must go to Kiev. If you will be engineer, I and your friend will be your firemen." And thus it happened that, suitably dressed, with Toffski on a baggage-car, the friends made the journey upon his locomotive as far as the Russian went. At this point he gave them letters, passwords, and grips, which would insure them access at Kiev to all they would like to see. It is true, the man was under the most awful oaths to do nothing of the kind, but for a friend like Henry Harris he would have done, always provided his name was given him in full, much more. "Henry Georgeovitch Harrisinki," the oily and ill-smelling engineer said in parting, "you may be going to your death," and he kissed him fervently. "Constantinovitch Miralovinski Stephanoff, we will risk it," was the reply. Thus it was, within a few weeks after leaving St. Petersburg, the American and his English friend found themselves in Kiev, in Little Russia. They were now dressed as moujiks, and, except that they were taller, seemed duplicates of Toffski.

"I can understand how he has come to be such a block of wood," Lord Conyngham said to his companions one night, as all three strode together through the mire of the unpaved, half-lighted streets. "In such an atmosphere of brandy, blows, gambling, lying, bribing, ignorance, a man must become a brute if he is to escape being a madman. We are centuries behind England and America in this antediluvian region. I feel as if it would take me a lifetime to get back to Paris. How dark it is!"

"Yes, and windy. That," said the American, pointing to a building which loomed through the darkness, "is the beet-root sugar-factory; on the left is the place we visited yesterday, where they make delft-ware. This building which we are now passing is one of the innumerable distilleries. Even Toffski has told you that vodka and usury are the twin

curses of Little Russia. Add to that gambling, conscription
for the unceasing wars—"

" And superstition," the nobleman added, as they passed
a church towering through the night.

" What you call superstition is the only relief to absolute
and utter brutality. Better," his companion added, "*that*
worship of God than none at all! But it will be like going
to heaven to get back to our friends again."

" I know at least one angel there who will welcome me,"
the Englishman thought, but said nothing, for by this time
they had turned down a narrow lane, gone through a stable,
and entered a sort of open court littered with straw, deep in
manure, and having horses, cows, oxen, tethered to the low
stone walls by which it was surrounded. There must have
been nearly a hundred men therein, dressed like themselves,
and all were grouped about a large and Tartar-visaged man,
with small eyes and flat nose, who was saying something to
them in Little Russian. All at once there was a hush, and a
small man in a corner insisted upon being heard. He spoke
in shrill tones and eagerly. After him another spoke, and
then another, all very earnestly.

" What is it all about ? " Lord Conyngham demanded.
He was wedged in with his friend and Toffski between an ox
and an ass.

" They speak in different dialects, and I do not understand it perfectly," was the reply ; " but one says that he
wants all property to be divided ; another is violent against
that, and wishes a monarchy like England ; the last man
seems to be enraged against religion and marriage." A tall,
thin man, his sinewy face illumined by the light of the lanterns which many carried, was making a speech with much
gesticulation at this moment, but Henry Harris could not
understand it, and asked Toffski what he was saying. The
moujik had a face of horror.

" He says," and the man began crossing himself, " that
he wants the blessed saints to be destroyed, the churches to
be blown up with powder, the Virgin, the Patriarch, the Em-

peror, and God to be assassinated. He says he can do it himself. *Batushka*," added the moujik, " let us go away from here ; this is hell ! "

"No two Nihilists in Russia agree as to what they want," the American explained to his friend. "Listen," for he forgot that the other could not understand. "Brethren of light," the burly leader was exhorting, "all *that* will follow in due time. The one thing in which we are now agreed is to destroy the Empire. Chaos first, then cosmos ! " and he recited in a loud, deep voice the creed of Nihilism, which was as follows :

"ARTICLE 1. The Nihilist is a condemned man. He can have no interests, business, feelings, property, or even a name. He must absorb all in one sole and exclusive interest, in one single idea and passion—revolution.

"ART. 2. He must break every bond with the civil order, laws, customs, and moral rules of civilization, and be toward the world a pitiless enemy, living only to destroy.

"ART. 8. He must renounce all doctrines and science, save that of destruction.

"ART. 4. He must neither have pity nor mercy for any one; nor must he expect mercy or pity. He must learn to endure severity, and be severe toward all.

"ART. 5. All tender feelings of family, love, friendship, gratitude, and honor must often be stifled in his breast by the passion for revolution—for this must be his only repose, consolation, recompense, and satisfaction.

.   .   .   .

"ART. 8. He must have no friends, and must regard, as men, only fellow-revolutionists.

.   .   .   .

"ART. 12. If a companion fall into misfortune, it becomes a question whether or not he shall be saved. The revolutionist must not consult his personal feelings, but the revolutionary cause."

At the conclusion a deep "Amen ! " broke from all present. There was the sullen silence after that as of a gathering storm. The air seemed charged with hate and war as a cloud is with electricity.

"I would not be surprised if he is a professor in some college, possibly a nobleman," the American explained, as he translated in a whisper to his companion. "Crouch lower, my lord," he added, suddenly; "I fear we have done a most foolish thing to come here!"

As he spoke, there was a hush as of breathless waiting, then a low murmur of exultation as the sky over the open court began to redden. Next a word, only one, was spoken, and, as if in an instant, the throng had dispersed through every opening, and the three men were left alone.

"Heigh, presto! But what does that mean?" exclaimed the nobleman, aloud, as he came out from among the cattle and stretched himself.

"It means fire, my lord," the American exclaimed. "The signal has been given, and these wretches have dispersed to fire the city in as many places as possible. That is the Crowing of the Red Cock, then! I was a fool not to have known of it. We must get back to our hotel as soon as we can.— Toffski Ivanovitch, lead on." But the moujik had planted himself like a log before them.

"No, my little father," he said, "the streets are full of troops from Odessa. Listen!" and there came the roll of drums and occasional shots in the distance. Then the ringing of what seemed to be, one after another, all the bells of the city; then the galloping of horses, the rattle of wheels, and loud shouts in every direction. Meanwhile the sky had grown almost as bright as day.

"Yes, our best plan is to stay here for the present," the American said. "If we go out we are almost sure to be shot down by the patrol or the troops, or at least arrested. We will wait until it is broad day, and then go boldly home."

"I don't object to a lark," his friend said, as they stood together, "but when I get out of this I will consider that I have graduated in Nihilism. By Jove! I rather like it, only I hope they won't nihilize *me*. Not that I object particularly to death, but I do to Siberia. Hallo!" for as he spoke a man ran in, kneeled in one corner among the straw on the other side of the court, and was in the act of striking a match in it when the moujik hurled himself upon him, extinguishing the flame and the incendiary at the same moment. The two others hastened to his assistance. As they did so a girl stole in from the other end of the inclosure. She could not have been twenty years of age; her dress was kilted about her waist, her feet were bare, her long, black hair had broken loose and was hanging down her shoulders. The others did not observe her until Lord Conyngham, glancing around, saw that she had stuck a flaming mass of burning tow into the hay heaped upon that side, and before he could get to it the whole place was in a blaze. It was a frightful spectacle. Most of the animals were tethered to their troughs. Even the horses, which were loose, tore around and around within the burning inclosure, too panic-stricken to make their escape through the broad and open doorways. The bellowing of the oxen, the furious plunges of the horses were terrible, and the unintending conspirators hastened out, the burning fragments of straw falling upon them as they did so.

But they escaped only to fall into the hands of a military squad outside. In an instant they found themselves grasped on every side by powerful men. Pistols were held to their heads, bayonets gleamed about them, and one man, the corporal apparently, repeated the same phrase over and over again.

"What does he mean by that?" the Englishman asked, as, after struggling in vain to get away, he submitted with the others, and they were being rapidly marched off.

"He says, 'these servants of God are caught in the very act'; it is the legal phrase of indictment," his friend answered.

"I am an Englishman, and, by Jove! they'll be made to know it," said the other.

"Unless they shoot us first. Hark!" for, as his companion said it, above the clamor of the bells, the rush of wheels, the roar of flames, making the scene as bright as day, could be heard the bugle-calls of cavalry, the rattle of drums, and now and then a fusillade of small arms. Strange to say, the spirits of the young men rose as the danger became greater. They thought of those far away who would be terrified when they knew of the danger into which they were entrapped, and yet they thought even of that with a species of exhilaration, and almost enjoyed the peril of the moment. The moujik Toffski had disappeared. At first sight of the soldiers he had rushed back into the blazing building behind them. Better that than arrest. "He ought not to have abandoned me," his master thought; "but, poor fellow, he has perished in the act. He thinks that the fire is better than the ice of Siberia."

There was no time for regrets, however. The building into which the moujik had rushed was a mass of flame, and the Cossacks who guarded them, black and bearded, mere military machines, marched the American and his companion in their center so rapidly along that they gasped in the stifling air for breath. At one time they were rushed yet more rapidly on to escape the walls of some burned-out building, which came down in their very faces with a crash. Now they were thrown to the earth by the shock of an explosion near by. Once or twice they stepped upon the bodies of men lying in pools of blood where they had been shot. The whole city seemed to be on fire. As they rounded a corner through the crush of wagons laden with household furniture, of men and women, children even, forcing their way along, bent down under goods which they had stolen or were trying to save from the wrecks of their homes, they were almost stunned by sudden musketry. As soon as the blinding smoke lifted, they saw a line of men and women lying dead, or struggling in the agonies of death, on the ground in front of a rank of soldiers before a massive edifice. Upon some of these they had to step as they were forced on past the striped sentry-boxes of the prison, for such it was. Door after door was locked upon them, and at last the two men found themselves alone in a species of loathsome cellar with grated windows and dripping walls of stone.

"Well," Lord Conyngham remarked, "Nihilism means the destruction of everything, does it? Then we are beginning to understand it at last. But why didn't they shoot us?"

"Because," the American replied, "they take us to be, as I heard them say to each other, the prime leaders of the whole affair. As it is, they may do so at any moment."

CHAPTER LXII.

THE VOLTAIRE AND THE CHRIST.

UPON the Rue d'Hiver, in the outer suburbs of Paris toward Versailles, there stands an odd little two-storied house with dormer windows. It is separated from the street by a high brick wall, guarded along the slated top by spikes, which incloses also a quarter acre of ground well supplied with trees, flowering plants, summer arbors, and fountains, with statuary. The place appeared, at the time now spoken of, to have nothing whatever in common with the nearest houses on either side, keeping itself to itself under its trees and overhanging roof, like a surly neighbor who folds his arms upon his breast, draws his hat down over his eyes, and has not a syllable to say to anybody. And as the winters seemed but to freeze the household more closely in from the world, so the summers, as they came and went, might cause the windows of the house and the leaves of the trees to open, but could not thaw out the inhabitants, who, for many years now, remained the same. All that Zerat, the bald-headed little cobbler who had his shop near by, could testify, was that there lived in the house an old madame who came out at certain regular intervals to do her marketing, attended by an aged servant-woman with a basket, while a little dog, black and fat, invariably accompanied them to the grated door, but was always locked in and remained whining there until the women toiled slowly back with their purchases. Old Zerat told people who loitered in his shop, waiting for their shoes to be mended, that the old lady was named Madame Deschards, her servant Gretchen, the dog Pinquette.

"Monsieur arrives every afternoon at five," he would add, "evidently from Paris. He is a man far from stout, and looks as if he studied hard and drank deep. *Ciel!* what eyes he has! also, what a forehead! Madame is in waiting at the gate to admit him, as is Pinquette. He kisses her, have I not observed it? invariably. Late in the morning he comes out. Madame, who seems to be his mother, accompanies him for a little walk if the weather be fine. Monsieur knows no one, speaks to no one, but supports her footsteps carefully, and kisses her when they part. He is a good son, although he may also be a *mouchard*, a counterfeiter, a college professor, or a member of the Government—who can say what?"

One gloomy evening Achilles Deschards, for it was none other, sat in what was the largest and best room of the house. Beneath a window on one side was the table at which he always worked. It was littered with MSS., while, under it, and as if trodden contemptuously down, were journals, reviews, daily papers of all sorts—ultramontane, Napoleonist, legitimist, Orleanist, republican, communist, atheist—there was no party in France which had not its representative there—even such comic sheets as "Figaro" and the "Journal pour Rire" were not lacking. A close observer would have been astonished at the almost terrible mixture of the same kind, upon the shelves of a bookcase which filled two sides of the room. The leading writers, past and present, of every faction which agitates the soul and tears the flesh of France, crowded each other upon the boards—Voltaire and Chateaubriand, Pascal and Liguori, Guizot and Thiers, Dupanloup and About, Balzac and Madame Guyon, Lamartine and Alfred de Musset, Buckle and Thomas à Kempis, Darwin and Cardinal Manning. One remained amazed that, with such fierce and warring antagonists brought so closely together, there was no explosion. Facing each other, like the leaders of the opposing hosts, upon iron brackets fastened to opposite sides of the wall, were two busts. One, in bronze, appeared to be that of Voltaire or Satan, it was hard to tell which ; the other, of white marble, was an admirably executed head of Christ.

The owner of these discordant forces had taken from the lowest shelf of his bookcases what seemed to be a large Bible. It leaned against a leg of his table, half opened, but was really no book at all. It was merely a case instead, made to resemble a folio book, and filled with liquors of various kinds in cut-glass bottles. Evidently he had drawn much of his inspiration thence while he wrote during the long hours of the night, yet it was as evident that he had thus arranged matters in order to deceive some one who lived in the house and was closely associated with him. But he had not been drinking of late. Pallid and haggard as was his face, that was evident. He had been writing, and the MS., neatly folded, tied about with tape, and directed upon the back, lay upon the table. The man seemed to be absorbed in thought. Once he arose, walked to and fro, looked at his watch, then out of the front window, lifting the curtain to do so. After that he unlocked what seemed to be a secret drawer, and took out two small boxes. One was full of gold coin, and he counted them carefully over and put the box on the table beside the document. Then he opened the other box with a smile which was ghastlier than tears. It was filled with what seemed to be wafers or lozenges, and he put one to his lips, as if to taste it, but refrained with a laugh, placed it back, and shut the box and let it lie. He glanced again at his watch, walked once more to the window, and looked out. Through the tops of the trees and over the wall, he could catch glimpses of people going this way and that, of vehicles driven up and down. "Rats," he said aloud, "mice, beetles, lice !" and he turned, lit a student-lamp on the mantel, and sat down.

But there was the sound of scratching and whimpering at

the door. "Pinquette," he said, and opened it to let in a little black dog, almost too fat to move, looking more like a leech than a quadruped. It seemed to be very old, too, for it waddled slowly into the room, and, when the man sat down again near his table, it squatted between his feet upon the floor, looked up at him with filmy but inquiring eyes, made an abortive effort to wag its tail, and whined uneasily like a sick child. Then it got up, walked with difficulty into an alcove at the farthest end of the apartment, slipped under the curtain which partitioned it off, and began such an outcry of barking and whining that the man arose and followed it. Looping up the curtain so that the light from the lamp could fill the alcove, he stood over a bedstead upon which lay something covered up. Pinquette, by a desperate effort, had lifted itself up, its forepaws upon the edge of the bedstead, and was actually weeping as it whimpered.

"Yes, Pinquette, she is dead," the man said, and he turned down the sheet, and revealed the face of his old mother. As is often the case, even with the aged, the cold, white countenance of Madame Deschards had taken on again what must have been the aspect, almost the beauty, of her girlhood. Isidore Atchison had been startled at the picture her father had painted from memory of the Delira of his early manhood. Merely as a painting, it was his masterpiece, a work of which the greatest artist might have been proud, because Memory had taken the brush softly from the enfeebled hand of Age, and had produced the girl as she was when the artist had first known her, in her wild home among the mountains of Virginia. Save that color was lacking, here was Delira once more in the white clay of the original master, a clay which was, alas! so soon to be dust. In the picture of Zerah Atchison, the vigorous girl, lawless, uneducated, governed purely by passion, almost stepped, in the eagerness of a deer-like vigor, from the painter's canvas; but in this case she lay sleeping instead, as she used to do in her cabin, ah, how many, many years before! She must have had more in her than merely a passionate devotion to this, her only son ; hers must have been a character also to awaken unusual love in return. There must have been in her an original flavor of her wild country home, a something both peculiar and essential to her, like the sassafras and pine of her native mountains. This old mother was all Deschards had on earth, all he had worked for so long and vigorously. And yet, as he spread the cover again over her face, he merely repeated what he had said as he looked out . of the window at the people passing.

"We are all the same, and she also ! What else are we but beetles, mice, the moths of the moment ?"

As he took his seat again, the dog lying between his feet, in sheer lack of anything else to do, he lifted his eyes to the bust of Voltaire upon its bracket against the wall upon his left. The bracket might have supported a mirror instead, which reflected his own face, so wonderfully like his own was that of the brilliant philosopher of Ferney—the forehead, high but narrow, the face, thin and haggard, the lips, whose very smile was a sneer, the large eyes, through which the eager but eternal unrest looked forth. There was strong likeness, but no love between the two.

"I know by heart, Voltaire, all you have to say," the man murmured at last. "You were very much of a genius, but you had no sincere love even for yourself. Of all men, you despised yourself most heartily, even while you had no other god. And you also, you poor Arouet, you called yourself Voltaire, but that did not make you any the less a rat, a mouse, a fly ; yes, a fly with a sting, not a bee, only a hornet. You buzzed and you stung until all Europe knew your buzz and your sting, and then you too dropped into the dust dead. But *you*," and he turned and looked at the head of the Christ ; "you I can not make out ! I wonder how men got it into their heads that you once lived. You also are dead. The priests say you rose again ; but they are such liars ! I wish I knew you, could come at you, could—" And his eyes rested upon the marble face with a wistful look.

As he sat, the door-bell rang. He was expecting it, and

arose, went out, and returned, ushering in no less a person than M. Portou, the Jesuit anatomist.

"Don't tread on my dog," he exclaimed, with sudden irritation, as the other laid aside his hat and wrappings and took a seat. "Pinquette! Pinquette!" and he stooped down and patted the old dog upon its head. It looked up at him with a loving eye, acknowledged the caress with its tail, but seemed too lazy to do more.

"And so your mother is dead," the visitor remarked, with a singular blending of condolence and austere coldness, as of a man who was visiting him under protest.

"Yes, *Monsieur le Jesuit*," the other said, "with myriads of moths, bats, butterflies, kings, cats, queens, sheep, forest-leaves, and flowers, my mother is gone. We all drop back into the dust, you observe. Old Gretchen was a good soul," he added to his visitor, as he lifted the poodle in his arms. "She loved us, and made *mayonnaise* of chicken better than any servant I know. Her *café au lait* was excellent, and she went, as you are shocked to know, with my mother to the Protestant church." He arose, took the dog, laid it on the foot of the bed in the alcove, and returned and sat down again. His visitor had been speaking meanwhile to him, but he paid no attention.

"Last week I sat beside Gretchen," he now added. "I said to myself, 'Here is a human being I will watch closely, with scientific vigilance, to see if I can detect any difference between hers and the death of, let us say, a rabbit.' My mother was too weak to be with her, but I waited on Gretchen, did what she wished. I read her Bible to her, I heard what she had to say. She was peaceful. I had no idea a Savoyard cook could talk as she did. The poor woman was feeble, but very eloquent. You would have despised her belief, for you are a Jesuit. At least, she was very happy. She truly believed that she was going to heaven. People are not as sincere in the shop, the ballroom, the Chamber of Deputies, as she was then. But I did not listen. You observe, sir, I wanted to see if there is any difference in dying between the human being and the merely animal. My finger was on her pulse as it fluttered, feebler and feebler. Her lips ceased to whisper her prayers. But her eyes, life lingered in them. They were fastened upon me, for she loved me since I was a boy. I bent over and watched the life—no, I mistake, it was the *love* which lingered in them! It slowly died out, as fire does in an ember, and she was dead. What is the difference? None at all. The verdure dying from an aspen-leaf until it is utterly sere and wilted and falls to the earth, the breath ceasing just now from the nostrils of my mother, a snowflake melting, a gnat ceasing to move—it is the same with us, one and all."

The Jesuit crossed himself and engaged, as he sat with closed eyes, in silent prayer. He had discussed matters too often with Deschards ; what good could it do to talk ?

" The only thing I believe in," Deschards began again, " is love ! That is why I wrote to you to come. I don't believe in your Church, my poor Portou. The reverse ! But I saw that you loved the wife who had betrayed and fled from you. Do I not know how you gave up all to follow her, to save her, as you call it ?"

" I love my order," said the Jesuit ; " the Church is more to me than my wife ever was. For it I would gladly die."

"It is *so* odd," Deschards reflected aloud. " This man actually believes in his Church, when, as all history teaches, no organization since history began is so stained with ignorance, brutal oppression, foul corruption. Its inquisitions, St. Bartholomews, Armadas, wars of Alva, this man, he swallows it all ! He believes in infallibility, yet Pope Honorius was condemned for heresy by a council of his own Church, and Pius IX desired to recognize the Southern Confederacy of Jeff Davis. This man believes in his order, yet has it been driven out of every land as the most devilish of all societies ! Yet he so believes in as actually to love these— brutalities. No, my poor Portou, I can not believe in your love for your order, your Church. As to that you are insane. But your love for your wife I do believe in. Therefore I sent for you. The Protestant minister who buried Gretchen comes to-morrow to bury my mother also. He will find, if I should not be here, in this paper on the table, all I wished to say ; in this drawer, the money necessary. But you, and because you loved your wife, I wanted to see—I wanted to ask—"

"You are in danger of damnation ; I would save your soul if I could. If you would but hear me," the Jesuit began, as the other ceased to speak.

"My friend," the other interrupted him, "according to you, Gretchen and my mother are damned already. They alone loved me. Out of all the world, they only have I found to be good and true. Let me be damned with them ; have that kindness, if you will be so good. As to your order, your Church, no, M. Portou ! Do I not already know all you would say ? You would have to take my brain out first, and twist it around. Before then I would have to forget all history. When I can believingly say twice two are ten, you can convince me ; until then, no, my friend, no, no ! "

"And is there anything left you but despair ? " the Jesuit demanded.

"Very true. I have read everything, have defended everything, have attacked everything. No," Deschards said, "I do not deny it. Schopenhauer says it, Hartmann repeats it, existence is misery insufferable. Two thousand years ago, the intelligent Hindoos discussed it to rags. Life is *not* worth living. Man's highest expectation is for *Nirvana*, annihilation. You are right. We are but as bugs, vermin, toads, lizards ; we live, we know nothing, we die. Alexander von Humboldt knew everything, traveled everywhere, and he says : 'Happy is he who was born a Flat Head !' Extinction is man's only hope."

The head of the man sank upon his bosom. But the Jesuit softly began to speak. He told of the necessity of a Creator, Preserver, Ruler, Judge. That it was reasonable this God should give to men a revelation. So far the other hearkened, but when the Jesuit added that of this revelation the Catholic Church is the sole keeper and teacher, he broke out violently :

"No, no! if God can feed me only out of a platter as filthy as that, then must I starve !"

"Why, then, did you send for me ?" the Jesuit demanded, angrily, rising to his feet.

The eyes of his companion were fastened upon the head of the Christ.

"Gretchen told me," he began, "my mother said to me when I was a child and since— My friend," he added, interrupting himself, and with a species of dignity, "I sent for you because I thought you might forget your accursed Church for a little and tell me about *him.*" The gaze of the despairing man lingered upon the face of the marble Christ. "If I had any political belief," he said, "it is in the Republic. Now, in America alone does the Republic really exist, and America is Protestant. Here in France it is not the ultramontanes who love liberty. What care I for Protestant any more than Catholic, except as I see that in Catholicism, men like you thrust yourselves between me and the man of Nazareth more than is permitted among Protestants ? As to the Huguenots, there is this good in them, as I understand it—so it is in England, in America—people take their filthy hands, their thick heads, their hard hearts and foul souls out of the way. People? do any of them know, of themselves, anything more than I do, poor devil that I am ? To the gutter with Catholic and Protestant ! What I wanted was to get to Christ by myself, for myself. I have a terrible deal to tell him, if I thought he was a living person and would hear me."

"The Son of Mary saves only in and by and through his Church," the other interrupted, and proceeded to talk upon that theme. He spoke in a low and gentle voice, but it was no more to the other than the purring of a cat. With his eyes upon the floor, he sat as if listening for a long time, but when the other demanded something of him at last, he looked at him with surprise.

"I had forgotten your existence," he said. "Many thanks, M. Portou, but you are merely a poor ignorant fool like myself. I had hoped you could have led me to—to somebody higher than either of us," and his haggard eyes were lifted despairingly to the marble countenance above him.

Without saying another syllable, the Jesuit crossed himself, went slowly out, descended the stairway, and Deschards heard the door close behind him without moving.

"Alone at last, utterly alone," he said. "No," he added, in a dull way, after a while; "I hear Pinquette."

The dog was whining, from where it lay at the feet of the dead woman. It was cold. The brilliant writer arose, took the animal in his arms as tenderly as he would have done a babe, and sat down with it upon his knees.

"There are only two of us now, Pinquette," he said, and he stroked the black face of the old poodle as it looked up at him and whimpered. "They were women, and this is only a cur," Deschards reflected, as he looked intently in the eyes which were fastened upon his, "and yet here is the same thing we call love. Love! What is love? Who knows? I do not. Love, love, *love!*" His gaze was riveted upon the expression of this, in the filmy organs which looked up at him.

"They are growing dim and dimmer, but it is love, still love, only love. Yes, dimmer and dimmer," he murmured. "They are gone out! No, a flickering spark rekindles; it also is love, only love!" But he sat for some time, the dog in his arms, before he arose. "Gone out for good, but it was to the last—*love!*" Saying this, he laid the dead animal tenderly upon the rug, drew on his coat, took it again in his arms, carried it down stairs and out into a hidden corner of his garden, and buried it.

"And now I am alone," he said, when he had returned. "What does it matter? It is with me also as with the rest. Frogs, bats, lice, lions, dogs, eagles, mites in a cheese,. *infusoria* in a drop of dirty water—we are all alike." He glanced at his watch. It was near daybreak, and it had run down. "And it also!" It was all he said. Then he opened and read over the document upon the table, and placed the box of coin beside it.

"They will be here in a few hours," he said. Then he took out the box containing the wafers.

"Oh, if I could but know you!" he groaned, his dull eyes lingering upon the sculptured face of the marble. "If you were not a myth, but a living person." He turned, he was about to fall upon his knees. As he did so, he caught sight of the scoffing lips of Voltaire. The bronze seemed almost alive, its eyes were lurid, its mouth almost spoke.

"Yes, oh, yes," he said, wearily. Then he crossed the room, the box in his hand, blew out his lamp, went to the bed on which his dead mother lay. Turning the cover gently down, he crept to her side, slipped the wafers into his mouth, laid his head upon her bosom.

"Rats, mice," he whispered; "oxen, moths, the Christ, too, love itself, we are all alike! Death is the end to all."

A moment after profound silence had fallen upon the house. Outside was the roll of early wheels, the sound of feet and of voices, as men and man-like women hastened to their daily toil. A child sang as it went, the hucksters began to cry their fish and fruit, now and then came a laugh as the world rapidly awakened. But the trees clustered, as it were, more closely about the house, the birds chirped upon its roof in cautious ways, the building seemed to draw itself more apart from the houses to the right hand and the left.

"*Mon Dieu!*" the bald-headed cobbler said, as he slouched by to his shop from buying a few sous' worth of onions and mutton. "This house, *ciel!* how it resembles a tomb! But what matters it to thee, Jules Zerat? In twenty minutes thou shalt taste thy soup."

15

CHAPTER LXIII.

THE LAST DAYS OF THE EXPOSITION.

THE French Exposition was drawing to a close; the chestnut foliage on the Champs Élysées was assuming its russet robes under the October frosts; the garden *fêtes* were withdrawn into the great halls of the city; the splendors of the Jardin Mabille were chilled by the searching rains; and there were visible preparations for a long winter campaign. A winter in London is denounced as a season of fog and drizzle and storm, and there are weeks and months of unspeakable gloom; and Paris is, outwardly, as inhospitable as the shrouded British capital: but then it must be remembered that, as Paris is a paradise in spring and summer and autumn, London, most cheerless in its wintry streets, is a perfect saturnalia of inside luxury. The English are accustomed to rains and fogs, and, as they never suffer from our severe American cold, they enjoy the rich comforts of their homes. It is otherwise with the French. They are unprepared for a severe December or January, with their scarcity of fuel, their unsatisfactory stoves, and their out-of-door habits; and so those who can rush to the South of France, to Nice, and Cannes, and Hyères, and Monte Carlo, and Mentone, and the soft and salubrious vicinity of Bay Napoule. Paris, in these two months, is often as repellent as St. Petersburg; not so entombed in snow nor so monumental in ice, but hard upon the poor, thousands of whom have no place in which to shelter, no home in which to hide, and often no occupation for their desperate hands. And now that winter is at their doors, and the fine republican show of the Exposition is being dismantled, they would be objects of pity indeed if the Republic had not provided them cheap amusements within walls, and if they had not acquired the habit of making a little food go very far.

One night Mrs. George Harris, not having heard as yet of the peril to which her son and his companion were exposed in Russia, had a large party at the Hôtel Bristol, including ladies and gentlemen of all nations. The American manufacturer was a royal host. He had not lived in St. Petersburg so many years without acquiring the tastes of high society, and understood the art of entertainment as well as he did the science of practical engineering. He had gone back from Russia after the rebellion broke out, and had thrown his whole soul into the Union side, not as a partisan, but as a patriot. His early years had been lived in Baltimore, and he never was what might be called an abolitionist. He loved the South only less than the Union, and labored long and vainly to dissuade it from rebellion; and when at last his Southern friends insisted upon secession, even as he gave his money and his counsel to the side of the Government, he always cherished the hope that they would finally be induced to return to their allegiance.

The Hôtel Bristol is in the magnificent Place Vendôme, with the tall, gorgeous, carved column, covered with bas-reliefs representing the victories of the first Napoleon, in the center; and on this gala night the superb square blazed with a rare effulgence. It was a glorious evening, and the scene was worthy of the host and of the country. George Harris was a generous patron of the arts, at home and abroad, and had given much time to the American Department in the French Exhibition. His great business operations brought him in contact with official, financial, æsthetic, and fashionable society, and the company that flocked to his wife's levee included the men and women of all these circles. The Hôtel Bristol was also the home of the British heir-apparent, whose long suite of rooms flanked the north side of the Place Vendôme, and whose little court could enjoy the spectacle of the American carnival from their great windows overlooking the square. Beyond the British Plenipotentiary to France, Lord Lyons and his legation, there were no official English among the guests. Mrs. Margaret Harris shared with her husband a great unspoken contempt for the American snobbery that too often sighs for royal recognition.

She held, as he did, that Americans owed nothing but ordinary civility to these dynasties, which had done their work and were outliving their era. The sight of an American lady or gentleman proffering incense to the scions of royalty, either in America or in foreign countries, was simply disgusting ; and as this incense is always laughed at by those who receive it, when they are alone, the practice assumes the aspect of degrading servility. But the republican lady of the great millionaire and manufacturer had no lack of sovereigns at her reception, sovereigns of learning and genius, the princes of the academies, the chiefs of the Cabinet, the leaders of the Assembly, the press, the stage, even the *ancien régime*, and of course the architects of the Republic, including the best culture of the Americans still lingering in Paris to see the close of the Exhibition.

In the lighted space outside thousands of spectators had gathered to see the arriving and departing celebrities. There was no confusion or indecorum. The Marshal-President had sent a detachment of his guard, handsome young Frenchmen, to preserve order, but their presence rather added to the elegance of the pretty pageant than to the order of an occasion made peaceful by the respect of the republican people of Paris. These people knew that they looked upon the hospitality of an American, that the wife of the late President of the United States was the principal lady of the evening, and so they honored the occasion as a tribute to their Republic. The Prince of Wales could not fail, in his frequent visits to the French Exhibition, to ponder upon these lessons. He came almost weekly to the gay capital. The splendors of the Trocadéro, and the richer temple of the Champ de Mars, were enhanced by his own contributions, and his India House, like the costly boudoir which he now and then occupied with Alexandra, his Danish queen, were something more than concession to the spirit of neighborhood ; they meant deference to the improvement of the masses, to the success of the Republic, to *coming democratic empire* in Great Britain, and, perhaps, at the same time, a protest against the too prominent and offensive autocracy of his mother's Prime Minister, who seemed to be never satisfied with his Oriental vision of British supremacy over other nations. And as the Prince stood, with his courtiers, gazing out upon this brilliant scene, in the Place Vendôme, in a certain sense a new panel in the great picture of the French Exhibition, he could not suppress the fear—can we say, terror?—that when the masses work for their rights with the weapons of reason, there is an end to privilege and to royal rule. On the morning of that day the Prince had met Gambetta at a social breakfast, as he had met him before, and that civility had given offense to the Queen and to her Machiavelian Premier. M. Gambetta, who was standing at the side of Mrs. Margaret Harris and Mrs. Grant, with Lady Blanche and Mary Harris, and a radiant bouquet of English and French ladies, in the circle about the American hostess, was no curled darling of power. The Prince of Wales could not make the excuse that he had been entertaining a diplomate, an official, an inventor, an owner of yachts and blooded horses, a republican Sardanapalus, a dilettante reformer, with castles and millions at his command. Gambetta's mission was the destruction of royalism. His purpose was the overthrow of caste. His faith in the people was complete, amounting to blind trust. To him there could be no religion of the state, no class by inheritance, no divine right, no superiority of blood or name, no peers that were not made by the intellect, and no aristocracy but that won by superior excellence and good works. Nor did the Prince of Wales deceive himself by a different belief. He understood and respected democracy precisely as his mother and her minister hated and feared it.

The guests continued to pour into Mrs. Harris's reception. Her husband was a quiet spectator of the brilliant festival, and he pointed out the Prince of Wales, in the opposite window, to Earl Dorrington.

"The Prince, your lordship, is a willing witness to a novelty to-night; but why should I say so? He has been in my country, has met my countrymen in England and here, and certainly knows what he is about. I sometimes think he is prepared for great changes even in his own country, and that his frequent visits to Paris are rather errands for information than voyages of pleasure. His intimacy with M. Gambetta is very manly, and means more than princely courtesy.

"You sincerely think," the Earl asked, in his usually urbane manner, "that political changes are impending? If you speak of permanent change, I am constrained to dissent from you. Revolutions there have been, there will be, but reaction is as sure as revolution. In the madness of a passing frenzy the mob may cut off the head of a Charles I, of a Louis XVI, but the nation invariably comes back again to order and the lawful rule of king and nobles. At the moment, we are here," and the Earl waved a dignified but somewhat disdainful hand toward Paris and France, "beneath a republic. For how long? Do you chance to remember how many republics France has had? The number of them escapes me at this moment. Pardon me, sir, but I prefer the everlasting to the mutable, the divinely ordained dominion of legitimate law to the bubble, however it swells and glitters, of evanescent liberty, as it is misnamed."

His companion looked for a moment at the Earl, steadily, respectfully, silently. He had for him a sad yet profound deference as toward the living symbol of what had been, and for a thousand years, a magnificent and, upon the whole, essential and beneficent supremacy. Mr. Harris venerated the Earl and all he represented as one does the colossal ruins of Karnac or Baalbec. Beneath the calm composure of the old aristocrat there was, as the American well knew, a profound disquiet, an anxious apprehension for what might be coming. The world would stand fast, the Earl believed, during his own day, but what would be the chaos which might befall his country, his children, when he was gone!

"This is neither the time—this is not," Mr. Harris said at last, "the place, in which I should speak upon such topics; yet, if you will allow me—"

"Assuredly so!" said the Earl.

"What I wished to state," the old mechanic continued, "is not theory, but fact. It was not the Republic, my lord, it was the theatrical Empire of France which plunged France into war with Germany and into the most disastrous defeat known to history. It was the Empire which forced it, as the result, to pay four billions of indemnity to Germany. It was the Empire which made the disgraceful debt; it is the Republic which pays that debt. Mr. Gladstone well says that the way in which America, France—republics both—pay off their national indebtedness is something unparalleled in the annals of the race. France is a Republic because America is such. Do you know, my lord, *why* America is becoming so rich?"

"It is a large and fruitful region, sir." It was said with great kindness.

"The reason, my lord," Mr. Harris said, in his steady tones, "is this: in Europe millions of men, men in the prime of their powers, are kept under arms. Their days are wasted in drill or in killing each other in battle. In America—"

"War has its advantages, sir," the Earl interrupted him, warmly. "It suppresses indolence, luxury, the mere shop-keeping baseness of sordid existence. It develops, elevates, teaches manliness, self-sacrifice, obedience, endurance! Terrible as it is, a corrupting peace is worse!"

"Very true," Mr. Harris assented, with energy. "But, consider this, my lord: while no man of the fifty million Americans is forced into the ranks, every soul of them is conscripted instead into a war which never ceases, a battle which demands and develops all the drill, discipline, courage, manhood which is, as you say, essential to a people. Instead of years wasted in waiting, with arms in our hands, for the breaking out of hostilities, ours is a war which knows no truce—it never ceases. But it does not consist in killing any one. During every waking hour we are attacking the immeasurable soil with plow and harrow; we slay the armies of grain with swords which never tire; we use a thousand times as much powder as Europe, but it is in blasting a path

for ourselves through the mountains, in compelling the rocks
to surrender their metals. Our strategy is exerted in a competition which taxes to the utmost every faculty. During the
fiercest campaigns of Wellington, the gallant English never
toiled, endured, dared, as your descendants are doing to-day,
my lord, in America. We discover, invent, experiment. In
educating our children, in controlling our politics between
dangerous extremes, in maintaining a religion which shall be
true to its original, in assimilating our foreign influx, in de-
veloping art as against mere money-making—in too many
modes to specify, we arouse and keep up almost to the fury of
battle the utmost there is in us. All the more, my lord," Mr.
Harris added, "that we are warring in behalf of the entire
race, not to feed it alone, not to supply it only with labor-
saving machinery. Napoleon expended billions of treasure,
myriads of lives—and for what? America has entered upon
its campaign against Europe, Africa, Asia, to revolutionize it
by saving, not slaying. Our fields of Austerlitz, of Waterloo—"

Mr. Harris paused. "I should not have allowed myself
to speak so long. It is because," he said, "everything appears to me, mechanic that I am, so evident, so glorious, because so beneficent in our future. You will excuse an American?"

"Assuredly so, assuredly so!" The Earl was interested
beyond his wont. "And you are confident of impending
changes in Europe?" he asked, gravely.

"I am sure of it. You remember," Mr. Harris replied,
"how your own Beaconsfield says: It is the unexpected that
always takes place. The first step will be the disarmament of
Europe. I know how philosophers like Von Moltke, at Berlin, and Gortchakoff, of St. Petersburg, laugh at such a hope,
and regard it as chaotic intoxication; but these new forces
are organized and organizing, and the fiat has gone forth
that kings must cease killing other men, at least as useful as
themselves, or other men will kill the kings. There are two
tremendous evils unsleepingly engaged in watching each

other, the despot and his assassins. The one may raise an
army, but the other may do more than twenty armies. Depend upon it, the sovereignty, under God, is in the individual,
educated, purified by suffering, prepared for it. I repeat,
the empire of the one ruler is over ; the empire of the million
is here. The future of the race is, my lord," Mr. Harris
added, " in the hands of your great nation and mine. I stood,
one mid-day, upon the center of the suspension bridge below
Niagara, thinking how the torrent was as that of history
itself in its rush, its roar, most of all in the shattering force
with which it plunged at last downward to perish upon the
rocks in the agonies of anarchy and chaos. Then I lifted
my eyes to the magnificent rainbow which spanned the
cataract, and how could I help observing that, if one end
rested upon the American, the other was based upon the
British soil ! Believe me, my lord, in your country and
in mine is the supreme promise, the sure hope of the
world ! "

It is unnecessary to state that the Earl was surprised.
George Harris was cool, passionless, and pale ; and as the two
men looked into each other's eyes, the nobleman seemed to
feel that the earnest language of the American was not a
paroxysm, but an absolute principle—a principle, too, which,
like the axioms of mathematics, carries within itself toward
its execution the omnipotence of the Almighty Ruler. Such
principles are the artillery which sweep the field and invariably conquer.

"I am glad," Earl Dorrington said to Lady Blanche the
next morning, at breakfast, when speaking of his conversation with Mr. George Harris, " I am glad that I shall not live
to see, much less to take an active part in the revolutions of
the future. I am a very old and obstinate King Canute who,
seated on his throne upon the edge of the ocean, sees the
Atlantic tide coming in. The ocean may be advancing upon
us from the American side of the planet, may be coming in
with flood sufficient to roll over us of the Old World, but I
prefer being drowned to changing my seat. And yet I am

glad," he added, musingly, "that Alfred and yourself will live and be actors in the great future."

For some time the Earl pondered as he sat. "If there is to be," he said, after a while, "a new civilization, it will produce, rather, it will be produced, established, maintained, by an order of nobles adapted to it. The word aristocracy means no more than the rule of the best, the strongest. So it ever has been, so it will always be. The old order was by the creation of kings, the new may be by the creation, who can say? of the King of kings, by the gift of character, integrity, sense, vigorous and original manhood. Assuredly so ! There may be a new nobility—who can read the future ? " It was with himself the aged peer was communing, his head fallen upon his breast. There was such dignity in his aspect that Lady Blanche murmured to herself : " The Goths are breaking into Rome, and this grand old father of mine—he endures it as the Roman senators did then, seated each in his curule chair, undaunted, unchanged, unchangeable."

CHAPTER LXIV.

TRANSITION.

ONE morning, some time after Henry Harris and Lord Conyngham had left St. Petersburg for Little Russia, Zerah Atchison and his daughter were in their studio together. Isidore was busy at a table upon her designs for the monument to the Princess Aura. Her father was not at work. He had brought with him to Russia his full-length portrait of the Delira of his youth, and was now feasting his eyes on it as he sat in his easy-chair, his paralyzed right arm supported upon a pillow in his lap. He was evidently older and feebler. Had he been an ailing and only child, his daughter could not have looked at him more often and anxiously as she busied herself with her work. If he had become a child, she had changed from a child to a woman of late, and a very lovely woman, whose lithe form, pliant curves, graceful ways, seemed to move to music. But of late, too, it was a sad music. Evidently it was to interest her father, to hide her own trouble, that she assumed a cheerfulness she did not feel.

"You enjoy your picture," she now said.

"Because it is finished," he replied ; "it is the master-piece of my life ; I will never attempt to paint any more."

It was, as has been said, a wonderful picture. The wild girl of his early years was alive, was breathing, and in gaz-ing upon her the old artist had returned to his youth, and was resting as at the end of a completed circle. The painter had laid aside his brush, but the critic remained.

"We were speaking of drapery," he went on. "Always remember, my child, that the flesh also is but an inner and more closely fitting drapery. What you and I, Isidore, strive to attain is, as you well know, the most perfect expression of the nude. The person is more than what it wears, but never forget that it is the person within the outer person which we would express. It is the soul itself which is really the nude. You pare away the clay, you cut away the marble, to get at that, my child. Yes, you have well illustrated it by what you have said of Prince Kalitzoff, our host. His gracious manners are as much a clothing as are his furs and broad-cloth. Not that he does not have a kind, even a noble, gen-erous, and loving soul, but he has been rich, powerful, pros-perous, all his life. Were he, like Solomon, to write out his experiences of life, he also would say that all is vanity and weariness. He wears the aspect of his earliest manhood still, but who can fail to see how disgusted he is ? Now that his child is dead, what has he to live for ? Politics ? society ? wealth ? all these he has long ago exhausted. Isidore," the old man added, "there is but one thing in the world worth living for, and that is—love."

Almost at the same moment Achilles Deschards was say-ing the same thing in France with dying lips. At last, is it not the verdict of the human heart the world over ?

"Even my art is nothing to me of late," Zerah Atchison continued. "I possess the living image of Delira, but I now feel that she is no longer alive. You know how eagerly I hoped to have seen her son and mine; I desire it no longer. You are all that is left me. Under all his vesture of mere manner I believe the Prince is sincere." It was added meaningly.

"Dear father," Isidore left her drawings and stood over the old man, her hand upon his shoulder; "it is so sudden; who could have imagined such a thing? He is a prince, please remember that; not merely a rich man with estates and servants, not only a Russian—and a few months ago the very word Russia meant nothing to us but Siberia and despotism and awful snow and polar bears—but he is a prince; think of that, a *prince !*"

"The Russians are not cold, like the Germans or the English," her father replied. "Although as fiery as the Italians, more so than the French, there is a solid substance in their passion. If they are barbaric in their ways, sudden at times, and violent as the Tartars from whom they sprang, they are constant. See, for instance, how devoted our Prince is to the memory of his only daughter. Until he knew you, she was his one thought."

"But it is like a wild dream that he should want *me* to be his wife," his daughter pleaded. "When we were in Virginia, who could have imagined that I, your little Isidore, would ever visit this vast, dreadful Russia? Even after we had lived in Paris, if anybody had said to me, 'You little artist, take off your calico apron, tear off your paper cap, wash the clay from your hands, comb your hair, put on your best clothes, here is somebody who wants to make you a Russian princess,' I would have known that whoever said it was crazy, and so would you. Dear father," and the girl placed herself between him and his picture, "please take a good, long look at me, and remember I am *not* a princess; I am only your poor little girl, Isidore. What is more, I do not want to be anything but that." The tears rose, as she spoke, to her eyes.

"I acknowledge that it takes us both by surprise," her father replied; "but the Russians are not like other people any more than are you like other girls, my dear. As I told you, they are Tartars still, sudden, violent, vehement. You remember the Prince told us how his ancestors used to win their brides."

"Yes; the young girl mounted a swift horse," Isidore laughed, "her lover another, and pursued her across the immeasurable steppes of the Ukraine. He had her if he could catch her; but I told the Prince that—"

"He could never catch you? At least, it would be like you to say so," the old artist interrupted. "My dear child," he began a moment after, "let us look our affairs calmly in the face. Here we are in the center of Russia, far away from everybody. Apart from our power as artists—"

"I am not an artist," his daughter broke in, almost vehemently; "there is where the Prince also is mistaken. Say I succeeded in making that head of 'Patience,' what did I do but simply copy your dear head? And I could not have done *that* if I had not loved you so well. This monument to the young Princess—even with your help, I may not succeed in it. No, I am no artist; at best I am an artist only where I love."

"My child," the aged critic made answer, "the ideal head of 'Purpose,' which you made without any help from me, and which Mrs. Harris mistook for the portrait of her son, is far superior to that of the 'Patience.' Any artist will tell you that it is a work of astonishing genius. Was that a result of—"

"Love," he would have added, but that the deep dismay, shame, confusion, upon the face of the young girl arrested him. By a strong effort she turned silently away, and began again to work at her designs.

"My dear," urged her father, "you are an artist of the highest genius. But how will that help you when I am gone? You are here in Russia, far away from every friend of your own sex—a young, beautiful, unprotected girl. Suppose I were to die—"

But Isidore had dropped her crayons, had run to his side, had taken his head in her arms, was kissing his forehead.

"Oh, no, no, no!" she said, "that would be too dreadful. If you were to die I would go too. God would not be so cruel as to leave me here alone—alone. Oh, this horrible Russia! Why did I come here?" And the tears ran piteously down her cheeks.

The more agitated she became, the calmer grew the aspect of her father. His face took the whiteness as it already had the strength of marble as he silently endured, for he had suffered all this in advance. "My dear," he said, as her tears gave place to the quick sobs of a child, "all my life I have known of things only as they came to pass. Nothing has happened as I expected. The great events of life have come to me suddenly, without forewarning, without time for preparation. Hence I have learned, having done all I could do, to wait. When the event befell, there was but one thing to do. That is the benefit of not trying to look into the future; it merely embarrasses and bewilders one, and all the planning and discussion goes at last for nothing. When the hour strikes, however vast, unexpected, the emergency, there remains but one thing to be done. So now, any day I may die. Without thought of such an event on our part, here we are in Russia. Prince Kalitzoff has become deeply attached to you. He is universally known as one of the noblest, sincerest, most generous, of the Russian nobility. But he is a lonely and warm-hearted man, to whom you have come, as he told me, like an angel sent from God. I know it is sudden, very sudden, but he wishes to marry you."

"The Emperor will never consent," began the girl. She seemed bewildered.

"Prince Kalitzoff showed me a letter from Alexander yesterday. I confess it surprised me, but the Emperor has consented. It is with the Prince as it was in the instance of Count Bodisco in Washington. With Russians, all Americans would seem to rank almost as of the nobility. There seems also to be some special reason in this case, I know not what. Therefore—"

"But the Prince is of the Greek Church," sobbed the frightened girl, "while I am—"

"The angels of God are of the most celestial religion of all. At least," her father laughed, "that is the way the Prince met that objection when I urged it. But what I was trying to say, my dear, was that, most unexpectedly, this marriage comes to us as the one thing, the only thing to be done. How could I die, my darling, and leave you alone, my dove, my lamb, in this wide, wild world?" The daughter only clasped her arms more closely about him and wept in silence.

"And what makes your path plainer," her father continued, in a lower voice, "is that you have not already given your heart away. You love no one." But the aspect of the old artist grew stern as he added, "At least, I am sure that no other man has asked you to love and to marry him. You would have told me, had he done so."

He could not help seeing how the cheek of his child glowed as he said it, although her face was almost hidden in his bosom. Yet he did not need that to teach him anything. He knew her heart better than she did herself.

But there came at the moment a knock upon the door. Isidore arose and escaped into her own room through another way, and a servant came in to request permission from Prince Kalitzoff to visit Mr. Atchison. Very soon the Prince came in; he seemed to be holding himself under control, as after a few words of salutation he said:

"I fear I have bad news for you; there has been a Nihilist rising at Kiev, in Little Russia. The city has been burned by the conspirators, but a number of them have been arrested. Chief among them, taking, I am astonished to learn, the most active part in firing the city, are our friends —would you believe it?—Mr. Harris and Lord Conyngham. I knew them to be daring and resolute young men, but I had no idea that they were emissaries of the revolutionary societies. They are lying in jail at Kiev, will be rapidly condemned, and sent to Siberia. I fear there is nothing we can do!"

CHAPTER LXV.

STRUGGLE.

IF a quantity of straws, chips, feathers, trash of any kind, be scattered widely apart upon the surface of a pond, although there is no wind to blow, no billow to heave them together, in a short time they will be found drawn into a mass by we know not what species of magnetism. Certainly it is so of people. Apart even from their own will, those of a like sort are compelled to come together from points however widely separated. Stranger still, there is a certain concurrence of events also. Similar events cluster as by a universal law, which groups into bunches the cherries of a tree, the planets of a system. So it was in St. Petersburg at the critical juncture here spoken of.

When Prince Kalitzoff announced to Zerah Atchison, as related, the arrest of the American engineer and his English companion, each had reasons for an even deeper interest in the disaster than the other could have imagined.

" I have already done all in my power," the Prince said, in the end. "Telegrams have been sent to Earl Dorrington and to the British Government in regard to Lord Conyngham. I have telegraphed to Mr. George Harris in France ; have communicated with the American Embassy. I would have seen the Emperor, but that he is not in the city. The state of things with Turkey, the possibility of the breaking out at any moment of war with England and other powers, the danger from the Nihilists, leave the Emperor no time for the consideration of lesser matters. He is obliged to hurry here and there as affairs demand. Our friends are in serious peril."

"But it is absurd," Mr. Atchison reasoned, "that Mr. Harris, that Lord Conyngham, should be engaged in setting fire to a city !"

"The Chief of Police assures me that they were caught in the very act. There is no telling," the Prince said, "what young men may do in moments of excitement. Why should they have been in Kiev at all ? It is out of the track of tourists, especially at this season of the year—midwinter. It was rash to the last degree. This is worse than a political affair; it is arson; it is felony; it is the most frightful of crimes. How can the Government of England or America protect its subjects when taken, red-handed, in burning a great city ? Have you read, Mr. Atchison, of the Siberian mines ? Except that it is not eternal—for our friends could not long survive—Siberia is worse than hell."

The nobleman shuddered as he said it. There seemed to be a horror resting upon him ; a shadow cast over him by a something behind, and more than the fate of the adventurous young men. He rose and sat down, walked up and down, started at every sound, looked fearfully out, now of one window and then of the other.

"This magnificent Prince is a brave man," the artist said to himself ; "yet he is as sympathetic as he is courageous. It is that which so agitates him."

But the artist was himself to endure more than he had thought. Through all the conversation he had continued to glance anxiously at the door by which Isidore left the studio. As soon as the Prince was gone he hastened thither, pushed open the door, which stood ajar, and was astonished, when he had done so, to find his daughter standing in the center of her room, dressed as for a journey.

"I know all," she interrupted him, with a countenance which was so composed, it was almost glad. "At first I fainted a little—only a little bit, father. But all that is over, you see." And she paused from what seemed to be the hur-

ried packing of a valise to say it. "I did not close the door
when I ran in, and could not help hearing. Siberia! It is
too horrible!"

Her face grew white; her eyes were closed to shut out
the vision; she shuddered. Then she threw on a shawl and
began to tie her hat upon her head.

"What do you mean? Where are you going?" her
father demanded, trembling so greatly in his agitation that,
holding his paralyzed arm in his left hand, he sank into a
chair and looked up at her with a face whose calmness was
white with fear. But his daughter did not seem to have seen
him, even while she talked with him, so absorbed was she in
her preparations. "Where are you going?" the old artist
demanded again.

"Going! Where could I go?" she said. "I am going
to find the Emperor. Prince Kalitzoff said that his Majesty
was pleased with me when I was presented to him last month.
I am going to tell him that he—they, I mean—had no more
to do with the Nihilists than I had. Nihilists, indeed! The
Emperor is not deranged. The idea of *his* setting fire—of
their setting fire, I mean—to anything is too absurd! When
I have explained it to him, Alexander will laugh at the idea
and release them. I hope he will have the good sense even
to apologize to him—to *them*—for the arrest."

And the ardent girl hastened to and fro, opening and shut-
ting drawers, selecting this article for her journey and that.

"My child," exclaimed the father, as the whole truth
broke upon him, "you do not know what you are going to
risk. The Emperor is a sad, stern man. He has been shot
at until he is savage. Besides, he is—"

"I am not afraid of a thousand emperors!" the girl
replied, lightly—gladly.

"But for you, a young and beautiful woman, to go alone,
to risk yourself—"

"God goes with me. You would be the first to say so,
father. Please do not try to stop me."

But even as she said it her eyes fell for the first time

upon the old man. There was that in his face which caused her to hesitate, to halt in her packing. She glanced again at him. There was silent yet unutterable entreaty in his face ; but she saw even more than that, as in a moment she had cast aside her wrappings, thrown off her hat, seated herself on the floor at his feet, her head upon his knee. "You are right, father," she said, simply. "My first duty is to you. I am not going." But not until then did she give way to her weeping ; her high resolves melted like ice into a flood of tears.

An hour or two after she was ready to receive Prince Kalitzoff when he called again. She had become almost stern, so cold and pallid was she with suppressed feeling, as the three conversed in regard to the dreadful tidings. Even in her distress Isidore could not understand why their host should seem to be so deeply concerned. She could learn nothing from him in regard to the Nihilists. Of them and of their plans, their motives, he appeared to be profoundly ignorant. His conversation was concerning the American and his friend. Nor could he cease to speak of Siberia. There was a terrible fascination to him in the theme.

"It is twice as large as Europe," he said, "and is a vast desert of rock and snow, upon whose iron coasts grind icebergs which never melt. Its three immense rivers, the Obe, the Yenisei, the Lena, pour into the Arctic Ocean, gloomy as the river Styx. And yet there are twenty-one volcanoes in Siberia in perpetual eruption—mouths of hell! You remember that it was discovered in the sixteenth century by Vassili Yermak, an atrocious felon, who fled thither on account of his crimes. It ought to be called Scoundrels' Land. More than half the population are those who have been exiled there for political or criminal offenses, or are the children of exiles. Of these, some are at large, under the eye of the police ; some are forced to work in shop and field ; the rest toil without rest in the mines. It is all the same, they are alike in hell ! "

The Prince arose and walked up and down the room in

strong excitement. "I have friends there," he said. "I have read of it. When I was a child I used to dream of Siberia and awaken the household with my shrieks. Dante falls short of its horrors in his 'Inferno.' Your Milton, Mr. Atchison, tells how the damned are hurried from seas of fire and plunged in oceans, more agonizing still, of ice. That is Siberia. Death is heaven in comparison to it!" And he continued to pace up and down.

"But I came for another object," he said, after a little. "In this valise," and he pointed to one which a servant had brought in, "is the amount I shall be owing you when the cenotaph to my child is completed. I have been seized with the whim of putting it in your possession to-night. The amount is large, but I love my child, and have no use for wealth except for her sake, unless—" and he fastened his eyes respectfully but almost eagerly upon Isidore, who was seated beside her father. "Money, my friend, is," he continued, handing the key of the valise to the artist, "only less than God. No thanks! I am a Russian, and my whims are imperious. But that is the least part of my errand. I hope you will pardon my importunity, but, Miss Atchison," and he bowed with deference to the shrinking girl, "I do not intend to press my suit too much upon you. There are reasons for it; but if you could gain your own consent I wish you could promise me your hand. I can not explain, but it must be given, a hope of it at least, very soon if you would have me succeed in rescuing our young friends. No one knows what insurrections may break out, like a Siberian volcano, under our very feet, and I desire to give myself better opportunity of caring for you. I know how sudden, how abrupt, all this is. Young ladies should be wooed for months, if not for years. But in Russia, especially in such times as these—"

"Prince," Mr. Atchison said, "please give Isidore and myself time to think. We are exhausted, all of us, by the events of to-day. To-morrow—"

"Miss Isidore"—Prince Kalitzoff seemed to have hardly

heard the father—"please," he said, "do not misunderstand me. There are reasons. It is not merely as your lover I speak. I would be a brother to you—a friend, if you prefer it. I would be as a father to you!" He had taken her hand, and was looking at her more like a suppliant, magnificent as he was in his bearing and genial aspect, than as a noble. "Think of it. I am true as gold. And now, good night!" And, lifting her hand to his lips, he bowed and left the room.

Father and daughter were almost worn out, but they conversed together long and lovingly before they parted for the night. Isidore had been his nurse for years, and she was glad afterward that she had never tended him as affectionately as on that evening.

"My dear child," he said to her at last, when he was comfortably in bed for the night, "do not misunderstand our host. He would not have placed that money in my hands, and against my protest, too, unless he had good reason. If we wait we will understand. No gentleman is better aware than he that money should not accompany his request for your hand. He has urgent reason. Simply wait, and we will know what to do. Wait; that is all; wait! And now, remember, dear, the child that waits sleeps. Sleep sweetly, Isidore; I am sure I shall."

Several times during the night Isidore stood at her father's door, listening. More than once or twice she crept softly into his room, stooped over, and kissed him while he slept. By reason of her weariness she slept until the sun was high in the heavens next morning. Hastening with many self-reproaches to his bedside, she bent down and kissed her father. The patient face had become marble indeed. She had long expected it. She was hardly surprised. Even in that agonizing instant, it was the sublime patience of his aspect which calmed her. She had long been familiar with it, but now it was patience merged at last into serene and eternal possession.

CHAPTER LXVI.

A RUSSIAN HOME.

"SURELY there never were servants as attached to a mistress as these seem to be to me!" Even in the depths of her grief the young girl, so suddenly orphaned, could not but say it to herself. From the day of her first arrival the women who waited upon her had seemed to live only to do her pleasure. Vadka, her little plump-bodied maid; Ovalinka, the homely old Russian peasant, who brought in the *samovar* and made the queer dishes for her eating; Catarina, who sewed for her, or took the place of a comely lay figure, upon which Isidore tried the effect of draperies for her designs—every servant down to old and ugly Malashoff, her coachman, seemed to be devoted to her. It is the redeeming trait of Russian domestics. Moreover, the young and beautiful American had treated them with such kindness as they had not before known. Even the Princess Aura, if the truth must be told, and of whom they continually spoke as a heavenly saint, even she had boxed, and very often, the ears of every one of them, old Malashoff included. They wondered all the more at the fair girl, their new mistress, who never asked or received their service without a smile of thanks and a gentle word. "And to think," Catarina often said, "that *Matushka*, our little mother, can make blessed images for our worship, and she a woman too, only a child! Surely she is herself very near to God, our Maker!" crossing herself. And now the old father was dead! Even in her darkest hours, during the days which went before the funeral, Isidore was touched by their affection. Little Vadka slept on the floor beside her bed; Catarina and Ovalinka appeared never to leave her during the day, bringing her food, soothing her by their tears, and by words which she understood without knowing their meaning.

Nor could a father, a brother, have been kinder to her than was her host. The Prince brought the American Minister to see her, and he was so much interested that his wife came and insisted that Isidore should make her home at the embassy, at least for the present, when the funeral was over. There were Protestant clergymen in St. Petersburg, and the oldest of these conducted the service, which was attended by many American and English people, by the Prince also and his immediate friends. And then the orphan was indeed alone in the world !

A few days after the funeral Prince Kalitzoff asked permission to call upon her at the house of the American Minister. If he had needed to be more interested than he already was, the sight of the poor girl in her deep mourning would have touched him to the heart. She was pale, silent; but it was not of her father alone that she was thinking. In his cordial way the Prince took her by the hand, led her to a sofa, spoke tenderly of the old artist. The Russian nobleman was a man, as has been said, of imposing appearance, of even haughty bearing, but the tears were in his eyes as he dwelt upon the many happy and instructive hours he had spent in the society of the deceased. And so he came to the chief object of his visit. He would not press her to speak, but she was now her own mistress in every sense. The circumstances were peculiar. Would she not accept him as her husband? His life should be devoted to her. He would take no answer now, would visit her again. After he had gone the American Minister and his wife took occasion to speak of the Prince in the highest terms. In some way the white-headed Protestant pastor, who had buried her father, knew of the intention of Prince Kalitzoff, and he, in calling, spoke of the noble character of the man, of his generosity to the poor. No one stood higher in Russia.

When the Prince called again the mind of the girl was clear. She seemed so strong and glad when she welcomed him that he felt assured of his success. But he was mistaken. Modestly, but firmly, with thanks for his kindness, she assured him that it was impossible. Her father had charged her to wait; she had waited, and now she knew

what to do; knew with absolute assurance. She spoke with
her clear eyes full in his. There was such force of simple
truth and sincerity in her whole manner that he saw the
matter was ended, and turned from her to the window in
silence.

"I never knew how much I lose in you, as I do now," he
said, slowly, as he came back to her after a long silence.
"Perhaps you do not know all I might have been to you.
Even now my deepest regret is that, unconsciously, you
have put it out of my power to help you as to Mr. Harris
and his friend."

While she was wondering what he could mean, he had
turned toward her his face, white, as with an unspeakable
anguish, ghastly to behold. For a long time he pleaded with
her, but it was in vain. She was almost astonished at her
own calm and final resolve; it was fixed as if beyond her
own power to change. The Prince read it at last in the
face which was hardening under its tears into adamant, and,
in utter despair, he took a respectful leave of her, and was
gone. She was to know only too well afterward the whole
meaning of his entreaty. For political reasons, also, the
Emperor had desired that the marriage should take place.
The Prince was, in that case, although he knew nothing of
it, to have been sent as minister to Washington with his
young bride. And why that was a desirable thing Isidore
learned from what took place afterward.

"I have sad news for you, Miss Atchison," the American
Minister said a few days after; "Prince Kalitzoff has been
sent to Siberia."

The shock was almost greater than the death of her father, for that she had expected somewhat, and it took some
days even to believe, and then to understand it. "I might
have been more astonished," the Minister explained in the
end, "if I did not already know how thoroughly Nihilism
has worked its way up and into the highest classes, as it has
down and into the lowest. The Prince is by no means the
only instance in his order. There seems to be no doubt that

he is a leader among the revolutionists ; that he has contrib-
uted immensely toward their funds ; that frequent meetings
of the *raskolinks,* malcontents, have been held by night in
his palace. I do not understand the Russian character," the
Minister continued ; "under their icy surface their blood
boils like the geysers of Iceland, ready to break forth at any
instant. The Prince was a man of generous soul, and he
has long groaned at the dreadful oppression which the Emperor himself can not prevent. He is a man of powerful
intellect, of abundant leisure, of fiery energy, and there is
something in despotism which represses every ambition, until explosion is inevitable. That is the curse of tyranny.
It wars upon the deepest laws of the human soul. To-day,
money by millions, armies of soldiers, myriads of police,
whole swarms of detectives, are sleeplessly employed against
the revolutionists. These we can, to some degree, see and
hear, but these are, in a certain sense, the insufficient measure and evidence of subterranean and unseen forces, yet
more tremendous, against which they are contending. The
Emperor was anxious to save the Prince ; he wanted to send
him to America, and thus out of the way ; but the facts
became known, and at last he could do nothing. We are
very diplomatic, Miss Isidore," the statesman continued,
"very cautious what we say ; but you are prudent, and I will
let you into a state secret. It is this : of all men in Russia,
it is Alexander who most feels and suffers from and is most
helpless under the Empire. Really, he is the sincerest Nihilist of all. Another secret is this : a vast revolution is impending. Whether it is to work slowly, as constitutional
changes do in England, whether it is to burst forth and shat-
ter all things to a chaos in a worse fashion than in France,
who can say ? "

"In other words," Isidore ventured, "all the world *has*
to become like America in the end."

"Yes, swiftly or slowly, through horrible convulsions or
peaceful processes, all nations on earth *have* to work their
way out to the same end. If the miserable politicians at

16

home could but know what America already is! what we
may yet be—" And the astute statesman waxed indignant
as he spoke at length upon the sore subject. But Isidore,
already exhausted by suffering, hardly knew that he was
speaking. She was thinking of her benefactor, of his horror
of Siberia. And then she came back to that which had not
ceased to fill her mind—the fate of Mr. Harris and his friend.

"We have done all we can," her host explained yet once
more, when he saw what so occupied and distressed her;
"all that diplomacy can do for them has been done, will be
done. The Government is by no means sorry as to Lord
Conyngham. You have no idea how bitterly England is
hated just now by the Russians. They are glad to have an
English nobleman in their clutches to mortify the people
in Downing Street, to bring them to their knees. Because,
as you observe, here is in his instance a case of Nihilism of
the worst kind, of arson, which is wholesale murder, not of
Government officials, but of helpless women and children."

"But Mr. Harris is well known, and he is an American,"
exclaimed the eager girl.

"Very true, Miss Isidore; but," her host remarked, "how
can they hold one of the incendiaries and release the other?
They were arrested together."

"He is not—*they*, I mean—are not incendiaries!" the
young girl protested. "The very idea is absurd. That Mr.
Harris should go to Kiev to burn the property of—"

"Of course it is absurd; but how to prove it? How
to single these two out and save them, yet send the others
to Siberia, that is the trouble. I admire your sex amaz-
ingly, Miss Atchison," the diplomate continued, with a smile
at her impulsive ardor, "but it would never do to make one
of your lovely sex an ambassador. You, for instance, would
plunge Russia into war with America and England over
these young gentlemen in less than a week. Provided America was her ally, nothing could please England more. But
we do not care to please England, nor to worry Russia.
America has no warmer friend on earth than Russia, you

observe. *She* did not hunger for our destruction during the civil war."

"At least I would do *something!*" Isidore exclaimed, with her soul in her eyes. "Yes, and I *will* do something!" she added.

"Let me read you a letter I have just received," was the reply. "It is from Mrs. George Harris, in Paris." The Minister paused, strangely impressed by the fire in the tones, the eyes, of the girl. Then he took a letter from his pocket and said : "Mrs. Harris speaks at length of the terrible distress into which the family are thrown ; of the efforts they have made at Washington and elsewhere ; of the wrath, rather than anxiety, of Earl Dorrington ; of the agony of his daughter, and of all that they have done. But she goes on to say that the Earl is confined to his house by the gout. Worse, Mr. George Harris has been so severely hurt while superintending the erection of certain machinery in a beet-sugar refinery near Paris that he can not leave his rooms, nor can he dispense with the attendance of his wife. Ah, here is the part will interest you most," and he read : "'Our daughter Mary insists upon hastening, with friends who go there, to St. Petersburg, to see what can be done. Please see that she meets Miss Atchison, the artist, who is with her father—' Pardon me!" the reader said, conscious of the grief of the orphaned girl, "for not leaving that out ; " and he continued to read from the letter : "'I wish Isidore and Mary to consult with Prince Kalitzoff and yourself. No time is to be lost.' And here follows," the Minister added, "the most earnest entreaty to me to do what I can. As if I needed entreaty! The letter is dated some days ago. I would not be surprised if Miss Mary Harris were to come at any moment."

As he said it, a servant handed him a card. "She is in the reception-room now," the gentleman said, and Isidore arose and eagerly accompanied him to meet her friend.

CHAPTER LXVII.

IN PRISON.

THE attempt of the Nihilists to burn the city of Kiev was not, up to the moment of the arrest of the two friends, as already related, wholly successful. A large part of the place was laid in ashes, but it was not from any lack of purpose upon the part of the revolutionists that the entire town had not perished.

"What in the name of all the devils in hell do they mean?" Lord Conyngham demanded of his companion, when they found themselves alone at last in their prison.

"Do you ask what the authorities mean?" replied the American, who understood the exceeding peril in which they were far better than did the other. "They mean to bring us before a military court and send us to Siberia."

"They had better try it!" the nobleman exclaimed. "As I have already told the old chap who arrested us, I shall write as soon as it is light to the 'Times.' Moreover, my Government will interpose immediately. Oh, I do not object! We are on a lark! It will be something to tell about in the clubs when I am back in London. No, I meant what do the incendiaries hope to gain by burning out the very people they are proposing to help?"

"My lord," his friend said, as he sat in the straw beside the other, "it is best for us to look our situation squarely in the face, and from the outset my deepest regret is that you have insisted upon coming with me on this expedition. You will bear me witness that I did my utmost to dissuade you. Had I known, as I do now, what the Crowing of the Red Cock meant, I would not have come myself. But that you should be involved—"

"Don't mention it, my dear fellow," interrupted the Englishman; "I would not have missed it for the world."

"Yes, but you do not realize how we are placed. We have been arrested in, apparently, the very act of arson. I

do not see how your Government or mine can help us, for
how can we prove our innocence? It was very wrong for me
to come. At least, I ought not to have allowed any one to
accompany me. Poor Toffski! What a horrible death!" The
tears rose to the eyes of the American as he recalled the
many years of dogged fidelity upon the part of his servant.
Toffski had been to him more like a very large and rough
Newfoundland dog than an ordinary servant, but, somehow,
he thought of the faithful moujik the more tenderly on that
account. For some time he did not even hear what the Englishman was saying. Like all of his class and blood, Lord
Conyngham was a perfectly brave man. And now, as if he
were a pugilist going into the prize-ring, he had stripped
himself, as if unconsciously, of the last rag and shred of his
mere mannerism. He was, as it were, naked to the girdle,
and all muscle and quiet readiness for whatever might follow. He even enjoyed it thoroughly.

"But may I be hanged," he was saying, "if I can understand what the socialists can gain by burning towns!" for,
at that moment, the whole prison was illumined through the
bars of their one small window with the glare of what appeared to be a nearer and more terrible conflagration.

"The men who do it," Henry Harris replied, "are desperate rascals who have nothing to lose."

"That's a fact; I remember reading about something
like it at school. Sallust tells of the scoundrels under Cati-
line," said the nobleman, "who went in for a row because,
having nothing to lose, they had at least a chance of plunder when the scrimmage began."

"Another reason," the American said, "is that the Nihilists regard the entire civilization under which they are forced
to live as radically and thoroughly and hopelessly corrupt.
That is the meaning of their name. They propose to make
a clean sweep of everything—emperor, nobility, army, church,
property, marriage, society! In their idea the whole structure is a vast but rotten affair, infested throughout with
malaria and loathsome vermin, and they intend to bring it in

ashes to the earth, so as to begin what they call the social republic from the very foundations."

"Fools! as if," the Englishman said, "there would not be the same human nature in whatever they erected instead."

"That," the American added, "is what Ishra Dhass was always urging, only he believed that the utter destruction of the old in order to the creation of a new civilization is by the power of the coming Christ dealing direct with the heart of every man. He is right! That is American freedom, which these madmen can not understand. But a last reason why some, at least, of the Nihilists turn incendiaries is in order to strike terror into the heart of the Government. Since they can not fight it in the field and with cannon, they burn cities instead. They want to compel the Czar to call a convention which shall make a constitution for Russia."

"And have his head chopped off for his pains, as in the case of Louis XVI. If Alexander has read history, he will see them hanged first. I would!" Lord Conyngham said. "Hush!" he added, in a lower tone, "what is that?"

"It sounds like the gnawing of a rat," his companion suggested.

"By Jove! yes. We are going to be burned out," Lord Conyngham added, gayly. "I don't blame the rats for trying to escape. See how bright the flames are getting! Can't you invent a steam fire-engine, old fellow?"

But the American had just discovered something even more important! He had long known many of the ways of the police, and in the gnawing sound he had detected the scratching of a pen in some hidden recess near by. Nothing could have pleased him more! Spies were listening to and writing down every word they said. The Government would learn what was their real relation to the Nihilists, and he continued to speak himself, encouraging his still more anti-republican friend to speak in the same line. At great length, and with the vehemence of his excitement, Lord Conyngham, while the subdued gnawing continued, broke into yet louder and more heartfelt denunciations of communism, democracy even, in all its forms, the Russian most of all. Had he known that it would be of advantage to him, he would not have said a word, would have denounced the Czar instead; but the American gave him no hint, and even Earl Dorrington would have been satisfied with the views of his son.

Meanwhile, the air grew so hot as to be almost unendurable; the dungeon became as light as day. When at last it seemed to the friends as if they must perish, their door was thrown suddenly open, a body of soldiers marched in, seized upon them, hurried them out, and, leaving their prison to the flames, rushed them along the streets through the blazing city to another and stronger building in the suburbs. There they left them at last, lying exhausted and dripping with perspiration, and begrimed with mire and smoke, upon the floor of an upper room, scantily furnished.

"We would not have been rescued," the American explained to his friend, "if we had not been such distinguished incendiaries. Lesser criminals would have been left to roast," and, utterly worn out, the two stretched themselves upon the bare floor, and fell fast asleep. They needed no covering; the heat of the burning city sufficed. After hours of unconsciousness they were awakened by the entrance of a Cossack, who brought them black bread and water, refused to speak, even in answer to the Russian of Henry Harris, and disappeared. After they had eaten, they tried to look out, but there was nothing to be seen through the small and grated opening, even when, at his request, the Englishman had climbed up for the purpose upon the shoulders of his fellow-prisoner.

The fire seemed, as the day wore by, to be subdued at last, but there was nothing to do but to wait. And thus day after day came and went. In vain did the American endeavor to bribe their jailer to furnish them with pen and paper. The Cossack glanced at the money, the watch held out to him, with keen and covetous eyes, shook his head, and disappeared. That evening the friends were thoroughly searched and relieved of everything except their clothing.

"At least, they have not chained us," the Englishman rejoiced, "and I rather like it, you see," he argued, as the days went slowly by. "I wanted to understand the case of criminals, too, as well as the rest of the lower classes. Well, here I am, a felon myself! There is not a dirtier murderer alive, nor one more thoroughly uncombed. Who could have more vermin upon him than I have? If any rascal in Newgate has fare as hard to swallow, water as foul to drink, smells as awful to endure, a turnkey tougher than our Cossack, walls thicker, or a floor harder to sleep upon, I am sorry for him. My dear friend," he remarked to their jailer, who came in at the moment with their repulsive breakfast, "if you love me, bring me a clean shirt, a bit of soap, a toothbrush, a hot muffin, and a copy of the 'Morning Chronicle.'" The face of the Englishman was so bright as he said it that the Cossack, who did not understand a syllable, grinned, while he shook his shock of red hair and departed.

"Who cares!" the English noble said. "It is true, I would like a chop and a comb, but I know dozens of fellows who have seen rougher times in the Crimea, in India. We have men in the clubs who are everlastingly telling how they were wrecked on cannibal islands, half eaten by lions in Africa, and the like. Anyhow, I feel more nearly of kin to my fellow-creatures, to the poorest, lowest, most unfortunate devil among them, than in all my life. Wait till I get out. I have material to brag about till I die. Why don't they bring us to a trial and be done with it?"

"Their hands are too full just now," the American said.

He was even more patient than his companion, if not as jolly. It was of his mother, of his sister, he thought. Of his father, too; but, strange to say, he thought most of all of the young girl whom he had left with Prince Kalitzoff. "I wish the Prince had not been quite so cordial in his appreciation of her," he said to himself; "and I hope she will hear about our trouble and write to Paris."

"Your sister could not find it in her heart to refuse me now," his companion said. "As to the Earl, he will embrace me and say, 'Marry whom you please, my boy, even if it is a republican.' Blanche will acknowledge that I am somewhat of a hero at last. And then I am sure the 'Times' has already published tremendous leaders about me ; it will help me in Parliament ;" and he whistled "God Save the Queen."

But the days passed by. Then the weeks rolled on. There was a hasty examination before a military board at last. The American told his story frankly—who he and his friend were, how they chanced to be in Kiev that disastrous night. His knowledge of Russian was a great help to him, but he gathered nothing from his grim and formal judges. His request for means of writing was peremptorily refused. Lord Conyngham, who had assumed a haughty bearing, was treated with contemptuous indifference, and the two found themselves again in their prison about as they were before.

"It is becoming somewhat monotonous," the Englishman said at last. "If we could only play billiards, get some cigars, or something of the kind. I wonder how Lady Blanche likes it ! The Earl never did love the Russians, anyhow. Barnum would rejoice in us, for, Mr. Harris, you and I are to-day the most thoroughly advertised fellows in England and America."

To do him justice, ever since they were arrested, and under all his light talk and almost reckless bearing, the Englishman was thinking more soberly and deeply than during all his days before, and every thought revolved about Mary Harris as its center. It would be impossible for him to be again the same man he was before.

"One thing is becoming very clear to me," he remarked one morning, "and that is this : when I see how desperate these Russian malcontents are, I feel satisfied that those must be terrible wrongs which goad them to it. The worst and most ignorant of any nation are left to their vice and ignorance at the peril of the rulers, whose business it is to teach

and elevate as well as to tax and govern them.   If I ever get
out—"

At that instant their jailer came in.

"Two blessed nuns," he said, in Russian, to the American, "and a son of the stick, an accursed moujik, have been
permitted to see you."

As he said it, the three thus designated came in.

"By Jove!" the Englishman said, but not without a
pallid face and a sudden sinking of the heart, as he saw the
black drapery of the veiled nuns; "it is a military execution.
Very good.   I had rather be prepared for death by a nun
than by a Russian priest!"

CHAPTER LXVIII.

RESCUE.

WHEN the two Russian nuns and their attendant moujik
entered the room of the prison in which the American and
his companion were confined, there was an instant of surprise.   The nuns were draped from head to foot in black,
their faces hidden by hoods of crape, a cross of jet suspended by a rosary of black beads completing their mourn-
ful costume, their servant remaining out of sight behind
them.   Henry Harris knew from their costume that these
nuns belonged to an Order devoted to hospitals and prisoners condemned to death, but his sudden dismay at their coming in was as nothing to the amazement which overwhelmed
him when the taller of the visitors lifted her hood and, revealing the face of his sister, cast herself with tears and cries
of joy upon his bosom.

"By Jove!" It was all Lord Conyngham could exclaim before the ardent girl had broken from her brother's
grasp, and had hastened toward him, her face wet with tears,
but radiant with joy.   There was not an instant's hesitation.

It was the first time he had ever dared to do it, but the Englishman had her in his strong arms in a moment, his own face overflowing with joy and love. "Great heavens!" he suddenly cried, breaking away from her, "I'm too awfully dirty to touch you. I hadn't thought of it!"

"No, you are not; I love you all the more for it!" Mary said; and the offense was repeated. Nor did he show any signs of letting her go again, and for a good long while the lovers remained locked in each other's arms, with kisses and murmurs of unspeakable affection.

But the girl tore herself away at last. "I am ashamed of myself," she said. "Alfred, Henry, this is Isidore." Even from the instant of recognizing his sister, her brother had hoped it was the artist. In fact, he had known it was her; but she had shrunk back, and stood veiled and silent beside the moujik. "And her father is dead," Mary whispered in the same breath to her brother. As Henry started toward her, the girl had lifted her hood; her face was an April of tears and smiles, and her lover was on the very point of taking her, as she shrank and blushed, into his arms.

It is a harsh thing, apparently, to say it, but he did nothing of the kind. It was owing, in part, to the unsleeping good judgment which he inherited from his practical father, and especially from his sensible mother. Moreover, he had been trained as an engineer. When driving his locomotive sixty miles an hour, his eye had learned to live, as it were, along the rails in advance. As far as he could see, if a spike had started, a rail had broken, a pebble had fallen on the track, he would have detected it. In that case, before he had time, as it were, to think, he would have acted. His hand would have been prompt, and as if in advance of the intellect, to open the valve which applied the brake, to grasp the lever, and reverse the wheels. But this resulted from a habit which went before everything else—the habit of self-control, instant, and under every emergency. So it was now. He had come to love the girlish artist with his whole heart. She seemed so beautiful in her nun's attire; her sudden orphanage appealed so to his pity ; the daring which had brought her with his sister to his side so awoke his admiration ; he was so thrilled by the instant hope, at least, that it was love for him which had caused her to do it—everything aroused an affection in return which really needed no arousing. But, even in that supreme moment, he grasped and held himself, saying to himself : "Perhaps she has given her heart to Prince Kalitzoff! Even if she has not, I can not commit myself even to her until I have consulted my mother! There may be reasons!" Mary glanced at her brother. Even in the blissful bewilderment of the moment she was astonished at him. Modest and silent as the artist was, she had shown such devotion that Mary was almost angry at her brother for his coldness. All that he did was to take the timid hand of Isidore in his, and to thank her cordially for coming with his sister.

"For coming with me!" Mary exclaimed. "Why, Henry, it is Isidore who made me come with her! It is she who planned everything, did everything. She it is—"

"And how did *you* happen to arise from the dead?" The words were not addressed to her ; her brother was glad to interrupt her, for he had seized upon his moujik Toffski, now noticed for the first time, who stood beside the door as if carved in wood, as if he had been born standing there, would stand there so long as he lived. "But is this Toffski?" he added, looking at him again. "You are sure you are not a ghost?" and, as the most acceptable token to the man of his affection, his master gave him a cuff which would have knocked over any one less squarely planted upon his short, thick legs. The moujik laughed with pleasure.

"But where, where is your beard? and your hair?" Henry asked.

"If he is a ghost, Toffski is the most useful ghost that ever took bodily shape!" his sister hastened to say. "When he saw that you and Alfred were arrested, he dashed back through the burning house into a back street—don't you see how dreadfully he is burned?—and made his escape."

His master laid strong hands upon the man, and dragged him forward. Sure enough, his voluminous beard had been singed away; his hair and eyebrows had gone with the beard. Toffski had never been other than exceedingly like an uncommonly furry bear, and now it was as if he had passed through the hands of a Parisian barber.

"He has become positively handsome," Lord Conyngham exclaimed; but then clapped his hands to his own beard. "Really, ladies," he said, with something of his old fastidiousness of manner, "I am dreadfully unfit to be seen of anybody, much less of you! We are not allowed a looking-glass. If we had a razor we might kill ourselves or cut open the walls of our prison. Soap is contrary to the dogmas of the Greek Church. Please look at us as little as possible," and he shrank back with affected dismay, but somehow he took Mary with him in his arms as he did so.

"You never looked so well in your life," she said, proudly, passing her hands through his tangled hair, smoothing down his tumbled beard, kissing him; "although," she added, holding him off from her for a moment, "your clothing certainly does look—"

"Is it not awful!" her lover assented ruefully, glancing down at his tattered garments, to which the straw of their floor was clinging. "If you ladies will kindly retire and order in a tailor— But you," he said, with enthusiasm, "you look charming! more so than ever! If we are to be shot, you can mourn for us most becomingly. And if we are to be married instead, you shall be dressed as you now are. You could not look so beautiful in anything else." He tried to clasp the nun again to his bosom, but she resisted. All her thought now was for Isidore. The poor girl was standing off to one side by herself, pale, drooping, bewildered, ready almost to fall, her hand grasping the serge sleeve of the moujik.

"You darling!" Mary exclaimed, casting a reproachful glance at her brother, and taking her companion to her bosom. "It is to you we owe everything, everything!" And, with her arm about her friend, she told their story.

The news had broken upon her in Paris of the burning of
Kiev, and of the arrest of the daring investigators of Nihilism. But Earl Dorrington could not escape from his gout,
nor could Lady Blanche from her attendance upon him. "Is
it not strange how things happen?" the excited girl continued; and she told how her father had received his hurt, not a
fatal one, however, in the sugar refinery, and how Mrs. Harris
was kept in Paris to care for him. Application on behalf of
the prisoners had been made to the American and British
governments, to the Ministers in Paris and St. Petersburg.
"But I could not have been held away by chains," Mary
continued. Then she told of her journey to St. Petersburg,
and of the arrest of Prince Kalitzoff, at which Henry
Harris and his friend were astonished beyond measure, and
greatly shocked. "I learned that Isidore was with the
American Minister," Mary hurried on, "and that she had
already done all she could. Oh, but we were so glad
to see each other!" and Mary embraced and kissed her
friend. "Just to think," she went on, "while we were talking and crying together, before we could even begin to plan
what to do next, who should come in but dear old Toffski!
His escape through the burning building was the least of his
adventures. In fact, he had escaped only to go to St. Petersburg and get help for his master; for," Mary added, with a
saucy look at her lover, "Henry is all Toffski cares for. I
doubt, Alfred, if he knows of your existence." It was a long
story of how the moujik had begged, and, at times, fought,
his dogged way back to the capital. "He got there as by
the instinct of a dog," Mary explained, "and, oh! how lovely
his burned face did seem! We made him show us the way
here," she added.

But there was a vast deal to tell of their adventures upon
the very roundabout road by which the girls had come, disguised as nuns.

"We had to go to Moscow in search of the Emperor,"
Mary explained, and told of their perilous wanderings, Toffski at their heels, among the camps of the army, day and

night, through all kinds of weather. "We had a satchel full
of letters from the American and British Ministers, and others, in case of need. It was a sufficient protection to us
everywhere that we were taken for nuns. The Russians
looked upon us, you know, as if we were angels."

"Sensible fellows! they were right!" interjected her
lover.

"But," Mary continued, as she embraced and kissed Isidore in her exultation, "we did not have to use one of our
letters at last; Isidore did it all," and, with a wrathful look
at her brother, the ardent girl took the young artist again to
her heart.

Her brother grasped the little hand of Isidore, and lifted
it respectfully to his lips. Lord Conyngham, his arm about
Mary, did the same, with eager expressions of gratitude, as
well as reiterated apologies for his appearance.

"I am so awfully ashamed," he said, with a desperate
motion of his hand over his hair, "to be seen in such a
plight."

But Mary broke in once more : " We managed to see the
Emperor at last. One morning, he had just mounted his
horse, when, after a weary journeying to and fro, we found
him. I have often seen him, but he looked so sad and stern
that I was afraid to speak. What *do* you think Isidore said
to him the very first thing? " Mary went on with enthusiasm.
" We were led up to him as he sat on his great horse in a
hurry to ride away, and he towered above us like a colossus.
He thought we were Russian nuns. 'What do you want, my
little pigeons?' he said. Isidore knew enough Russian,"
Mary added, "to understand the phrase. Would you believe
it, she answered : 'We are not pigeons, your Majesty, we are
ladies, American ladies!' She said it in English, for he understands it perfectly, and, O you darling!" with an embrace
and a shower of kisses, "you looked like a queen when you
said it. 'American ladies?' Alexander asked, looking down
at her. And what do you think Isidore said then?" Mary
demanded, with large eyes. "She said : 'If your Majesty

will be so good as to get off of your horse, we can talk
to you better. We are *ladies, American* ladies.' You should
have seen how surprised he was. He frowned, then smiled,
then actually dismounted. We were sovereigns, were his
equals; being ladies, as well as Americans, we were his superiors," Mary added, her head in the air, her eyes glittering.
" Oh, yes, he was glad to get off his great horse and listen
to us. I do believe he would have taken off his military hat
if he could; but, you see," Mary added, with a laugh, " it
was fastened on by a silver chain under his chin; he knew
he could not get it off if he tried. But Isidore was very respectful. It was as if she were talking to a venerated father,
and oh, how you talked, you darling ! "

" You did it better than I," the other said; but she was
pale, almost listless; her enthusiasm seemed to have flown
for ever.

" I only came in when you had said all that you could
say," Mary remonstrated. " That was enough, you know,
and the Emperor evidently knew all about it already. Some
report had been made to him. But, oh ! if you could have
seen Isidore ! The Emperor, grave and solemn as he is, was
greatly taken with her, and—"

" With *you*," Isidore said, with a smile.

" With you both, and, by Jove ! an old bear as he is, he
would be blind as well as deaf if he were not," Lord Conyngham broke in, looking at Mary especially with such admiration as brought the glad color to her cheeks.

" It was Isidore, Isidore !" persisted the girl. " Do you
know, when the Emperor alluded to your being incendiaries,
Isidore said, almost angrily, 'The idea of his being an incendiary ! It is absurd.' "

" Of *their* being incendiaries, dear ? " her companion insisted, blushing painfully.

" No, no : 'Of *his* being an incendiary ! Absurd !' That
is what you said, and the Emperor almost laughed aloud.
Then he looked at us as a father might. 'I will give orders
about it,' he said, bowed as a gentleman should, mounted his

horse, and rode away. After that," Mary added, "Toffski showed us the way here. We will tell you some time all about how we traveled in *telegas*, how our *tárantass* broke down once or twice in the horrible roads ; but our nun's dress helped us, and we had money and Toffski, and here we are. And, O Alfred ! O Henry !" she added, with joy, "the commandant has already had his orders from the Emperor. You are free. But you both owe it all to Isidore, Isidore, you darling !" and, with an almost ferocious glance at her brother, the excited girl took her friend again to her bosom. The heart of the engineer struggled within him ; he longed to clasp in his arms the pale and lovely girl. He had almost passed beyond his own control, when the door opened, and the Russian commander entered the room, an enormous document in his hand.

CHAPTER LXIX.

DAWN AGAIN.

It took but a few days after their rescue from the prison at Kiev for Henry Harris to return to St. Petersburg, accompanied by Lord Conyngham, the two fair rescuers, and their faithful moujik. An agreeable surprise awaited them there. Mr. George Harris had recovered sufficiently from his hurt to travel, and, intensely anxious as to their son and daughter, he and his wife had come on to the Russian capital. It is easy to imagine with what gladness the family found themselves together again in the rooms the father had secured at the Imperial Hotel. Almost before eating his first meal, the Englishman had hurried to a celebrated tailor, and, by paying double prices, it did not take long to restore him to his former respectability of appearance.

"You looked better in your rags," was all the congratulation he received from Mary Harris. "If I could but have had you photographed as you and Henry were when we first found you!"

"But why do you still play the nun and wear black?" her lover asked. "Now that the winter of our discontent is past, I had hoped that you would bloom out in bright colors, the first and fairest flower of the blessed summer which is to be ours hereafter and for ever."

"I am sorry that I look so homely," Mary began; but her lover took effectual means to suppress the slander upon the very lips which uttered it, and Mary broke away from him to explain:

"It is of Isidore I am thinking! Her father is dead, you know. She is alone in the world. We did our best to have her make her home with us at our hotel, for the present, at least; but she would not hear of it. The American Minister pressed her to stay with them. But, no, she has gone to board at the house of the old clergyman who buried her father, and who has the best old white-haired wife in the world. And she is so heart-broken! How can I dress in bright colors while she is in black? I am angry with Henry!" she added, with energy, for her brother came in as she was saying it.

Lord Conyngham became very grave. He understood why Mary was angry, but he could not understand why his friend had held himself almost coldly toward Isidore Atchison. It is his lingering devotion, he thought, for Lady Blanche which had come between Henry and Isidore. He could not allude to it, but he said: "I found letters awaiting me on my arrival. The Earl and my sister have not been uneasy about me. My father wrote to the 'Times' and to the Government as soon as he heard of the scrape into which I had fallen, and, having done that, he had not an atom of doubt as to the result. I wish I had the faith he has in our British lion. Lady Blanche," the Englishman added, with troubled face, "is about to marry the Duke of Plymouth. They have gone back to England, and I must be there to attend the wedding. The Duke is a poor stick, but, if

Blanche consents, I have no more to say. Apart from the bridegroom," the brother added, with something of a grimace, "it is a good match. Blanche will have rank to her heart's content. It is what she is suited to. Leaving her husband out of question, I think she will find it very pleasant. A queer world it is, is it not?"

"Give her my congratulations," Mary said, but immediately added: "It is of Isidore I wanted to speak. Do you know, she has gone hard to work already? It is only a day or two since we came, but she is having her room at the old clergyman's fitted up already. When I went there yesterday, she was full of her plans. It seems that the Prince has left large amounts in her father's hands, now in hers, toward the monument for his daughter; and oh! is it not sad, sad?"

"The death of Prince Kalitzoff? Well," her lover said, coolly, "if I were on *my* way to Siberia, I think I too would take the earliest moment to blow out my brains. Hurled as he was from the position of a Prince to the bowels of a lead mine, seven days' toil every week with the pick, eternal slavery and wretchedness, and all as in an hour, who can blame him?"

"Isidore is dreadfully distressed," Mary continued. "The Prince was the noblest of men, the purest of patriots, the soul of kindness. She was weeping as if her heart would break, even while she was hard at work. That is another thing to interest' her in her monument; she intends to add to it now a statue of the Prince in the act of embracing again his dead child. She told me that work, hard work, was the one thing she needed. For my part," Mary added, almost bitterly, "I can not understand you men!"

Her lover opened his eyes, but drew her off to the jewelers to consult with reference to certain diamonds and other gifts he was having prepared for presents to his sister. His own wedding, however, was the subject which most interested them both, and that although Earl Dorrington had so far shown no sign of yielding thereto.

The first thing Henry Harris had said to his mother when

they were alone together after his return to St. Petersburg was in reference to Isidore, and, " I did love Lady Blanche," he remarked, in the end ; " but when I saw her deliberately surrender herself to such a man as the Duke, my whole soul revolted at it and at her. Not that I condemn her. We are too far apart to understand each other, that is all. She is superb in her way, but we were born in different planets."

" In different eras, you mean. My dear boy," his wise mother said, with a smile, " you should have only gratitude toward the Duke. Lady Blanche is as superb a specimen of the Englishwoman as I know ; beautiful, highly cultivated, charitable to the poor, proud, strong-hearted ; but she would have made you miserable. You are too much alike ; that is, you have, both of you, a vigorous will, a determined pur-pose ; it would have been impossible for you not to have clashed ; your training, too, has been so utterly unlike. She will adorn her sphere. That is what she was born into, pre-cisely what she is adapted to. If you were entering into a partnership to lead a party, to manage a business, whatever of money, rank, strong will, daring purpose, each can bring in, would be so much gain. In marriage it is different ; such things are desirable in that also, provided there be a love for each other supreme over all ; love must be the master motive, my son."

" And I do love Isidore with all my soul," he said ; " that I know ! " for he had told her the whole story of his affection for the artist. " And now, mother—"

" There is a change in the world since I was a child," Mrs. Harris mused aloud. " Once girls and boys fell in love with each other on first sight, and married as matter of course. It was St. Valentine's day the year around, and young people mated as readily as did the birds. Now both sexes, almost from their birth, are more cautious. Your fa-ther and I loved each other on first sight, and yet we, too, had to reflect, to wait, to reason long and well, before we married. Your father says the change these days toward caution is because people are more practical than they used to be. Competition is fiercer; the standard of living is raised, but not the salary. Do you know," she laughed, "he thinks that the rage for science and scientific results has its influence? People are making arithmetic the law of their lives. My judgment approves; but, Henry, merely as a woman, I declare"—and the words faltered on the lips of the mother—"I do not know—"

"My dear mother," he soon hastened to say, "I believe in love with all my heart, but I *have* to hold myself in strong control. Besides, I was born practical, as Lady Blanche was born noble. There was my education, too. It takes incessant care to keep from being crushed by machinery; by money, even, when it is your own. People who hold and use power of any sort learn to be careful as well as strong. But who cares for all that?" he broke off abruptly. "The only thing I think of now is Isidore! Mary looks on me as a monster because I have tried to restrain myself. Dear mother, I *am* one, I suppose; but I wanted to consult with you; for if I do not marry her I marry no one. She is the loveliest, most thoroughly sensible, most charming—" and he ran ardently on with fervor long suppressed.

People thought Margaret Harris cold, because she was wise and calm; but she listened to her son with a new light in her eyes, a smile as when she was a girl upon her lips. "Let me speak to your father to-night," was all she said at last, and then she changed the conversation. "To-morrow," she said, "I intend to give you the present I promised so long ago to the one who found in the Exposition the work of art I had preferred. For all these days I have been in search of my gift. There are many rare and precious things to be found in St. Petersburg. I think I have selected it at last."

She drove off in her carriage, and her son hastened to go abroad into the city. Except during the night and when at his meals, he could not endure to remain in the house; it seemed too much like a prison. Even a *tárantass* confined him too closely, and he rode hither and thither on horseback instead. He was glad of the happiness of his sister and her lover, but he knew they would rather be alone, and it was his mood to be by himself. When he wearied of his horse he walked. Up and down the streets he went, through the great squares.

"I am glad, on the whole," he said to himself, "that I have had a taste of life in jail; it enables me to sympathize henceforth and for ever with all who are imprisoned."

But he could not assure himself sufficiently that he was, indeed, a free man until he had ascended to the top of the spires of the Admiralty Building, upon which he had stood with Lord Conyngham, looking down upon St. Petersburg, before their dangerous trip to hear the Crowing of the Red Cock. Once more the great city lay spread out before him like a living map. He was glad that no one was with him; his sense of freedom was more complete on that account. For a long time he stood in absolute silence, feeding upon the vast panorama of palaces and hovels, streets, squares, moving multitudes. The sounds of voices, hurrying feet, rolling wheels, came up to him, blended into one and softened by the distance, like the surge of a sea.

"Oh, how sweet liberty is!" he cried at last. "I had no idea it was so unspeakably precious!" He was like an eagle long caged which had broken loose and was perched again upon its native mountain-top, and which can not at first get enough of the open sunshine, of the free air, of soaring through the infinite blue with powerful wing. The young man drew in deep breaths of the atmosphere; he lifted and let fall his arms. But it was not chiefly of his freedom he was thinking.

"Be ashamed of yourself," he said at last; "are you changed into a spasmodic, gesticulating Frenchman? How can I be master of the sorrows sure to befall me if I do not learn to master my joys also?" And he grew more sober, turned, descended the steps, and went gravely back to his hotel.

He did not confess it to himself, but the truth is, beneath his gladness burned the flames of his gratitude and love to the fair girl who, at her own peril, had hastened to his rescue ; he thought of nothing but her. The next morning he was in all the glow of rapturous anticipations in regard to Isidore when his mother came into his room. She refused to speak about the artist, although eagerly pressed to do so by her son.

"My son," she said, and her face had never seemed so bright, "I want you to go with me from the breakfast table, and I am here so early to make sure of catching you before you go out. It is a glorious day, and I wish to make you the present I have promised you so long."

At the breakfast table, under outward semblance of a calm demeanor, neither had much appetite ; they were feeding instead on things yet to be.

"At last ! And now let us go," Mrs. Harris said, as they laid their napkins aside and rose from the table. She was as eager as a child.

"I am at your service," her son consented, greatly wondering at what she had in view. "When a thunderstorm is coming up," he remarked, with a laugh, "we can feel the electricity in the air before it strikes. Whenever any sorrow has struck me, it is the same way ; for hours beforehand I could feel it in the very atmosphere. It is so this morning ; something serious is impending, so serious that I can not tell whether it is terribly bad or exceedingly good. Let the lightning strike ; I am ready !"

Even as he said it, an official of the telegraph office put in his hand a telegram. Excusing himself to his mother, he tore it open ; his color changed as he read it.

"I can not go with you this morning," he said, after long silence, while he read the dispatch over and over again ; "nor can I explain. This is one of the occasions when a son has to act without his mother. You are the best as well as the wisest of mothers," he added, as he pressed a grave kiss upon her forehead ; "but you must leave me to myself for to-day."

He left the room as he said it, and even then it struck Mrs. Harris that she had never before seen him look so like his father. And even then she was forced to acknowledge to herself, " I know that Mary will grow to be far superior to me, but I did not know before that Henry too, Henry, will be a stronger man than his father ; if possible, a nobler man."

CHAPTER LXX.

TELEGRAM.

To explain the telegram received by Henry Harris, it is necessary that we should hasten to England, whither Earl Dorrington and his daughter had returned from Paris to make the final preparations for the marriage of Lady Blanche with the Duke of Plymouth. To almost every other unmarried woman in England it would have been the most joyful of occasions. According to the universal social estimate, the Duke was the best match in Europe. The papers were full of it. There were pages of statements concerning the antiquity of his family, his estates, his houses in London, his yacht. There were pictures in the pictorial sheets of his magnificent table services, his ancestral jewels. Certain of the more gossipy papers went so far as to give illustrations of the diamonds and other *trousseau* of the bride, and the most fabulous stories were abroad as to the wedding presents which were in preparation for her from the Queen and other members of the royal family. Moreover, the chief residence in London was in course of decoration for the newly married pair, and it was to be on a scale, it was said, of almost wicked extravagance. As the result, there was hardly an unbetrothed girl in England who did not envy Lady Blanche with her whole heart ; nor were pillows lacking which were wet with bitter tears shed by some of the weaker of them while remembering how mean and obscure their own lives were in comparison.

For some weeks now Earl Dorrington had lived as upon the summits of things. With Lady Blanche he had been distressed beyond what he allowed to manifest itself at the peril of his son in Russia. Like her, however, he was all the more proud of his son for entering upon an undertaking so daring. There was this difference between father and daughter : the old Earl had faith so unbounded in the power of his Government, that, as has been said, he had no really serious fears as to the result.

"They dare not injure a hair of Alfred's head," he remarked over and over again to his daughter, while his son's case seemed to be still undecided. " Were he the humblest Englishman, he would have nothing to fear. And when they know who he is, they will be but too glad to release him with infinite apologies. The Czar dare not risk war with us ! I have no fear as to the result. Assuredly not ! "

It was on this account that the Earl read to Lady Blanche the telegram announcing at last the release of his son, with a grave rebuke to her for her fears. " It is merely as I said," he reiterated. " Russia dared not do other than hasten to let him go, and you should have believed what I told you from the outset. I would like to have seen them presume ! Alfred should not have led his young American friend into circumstances so perilous—ahem !—*not* perilous ; so compromising, I should say. Alfred is a man of spirit, more venturesome than I had supposed. I am not sorry that young Mr. Harris, who seems to be a really respectable and deserving gentleman, should have had the guidance of Alfred. For once Mr. Harris will learn that England, at least, is feared by Russia. It is an excellent lesson for him. Really, we must ask him to visit us when we go into the country. Assuredly so ! "

And thus it was that the old Earl ascended, if possible, to loftier heights. Was not Blanche to be Duchess of Plymouth ? There did not exist a better father on earth. Nor

17

did the Earl abhor less than any of the rest of us the abstract vices of which the Duke had long been guilty. Had the man, soon to be the husband of his daughter, been any other than a nobleman, the Earl would have been mortally insulted at his presuming to solicit an alliance with him. If the lover, not being noble, had possessed tenfold the wealth he did, it would have made little difference. Would he sell his only daughter, a pure and high-bred woman, for gold? Perish the thought! But when the worn-out *roué* and gambler was a Duke, the head of one of the oldest families in England—ah, what a difference it made!

When we strike our artesian iron down to the solid facts of the case, we must agree that caste is as strong in England as it has ever been in India. Alas! if we push the artesian inquiry deeper still, we must agree that it would be precisely the same in America, if circumstances were the same. Thank Heaven for our democracy, which originated and exists apart from and in spite of us all! Its charters are only less inspired than are the pages of Scripture itself, and the churches of Christendom are not more evidently upheld, and against the vices and weaknesses of their own membership, by a divine hand than are the republics of the world. We exclaim in wonder at the starry worlds, which are driven along the paths of their inconceivable grandeur and velocities, making music for ever in their orbits about the central sun. Who doubts that these well-ordered worlds were made and are upheld of their Maker? Even so, that man is a fool who does not know that, however men may be overruled as instruments, this constellated republic of ours is the work, grander yet, of God himself. Upon him, and *not* upon us, exclusively depends its continuance.

But it is of Earl Dorrington we are speaking. With the release of his son and heir, and the approaching alliance of his daughter with the Duke, he had reached the highest point in his life. It was as if he had attained to the everlasting ice, also, of Alpine summits. While always a gentleman in his bearing toward even the lowliest, he had now become colder, statelier, more reserved, more intensely the aristocrat than before. Not that he was not gracious enough in his demeanor, unusually so, but it was, more than ever, the gracious condescension of a king. He was unconscious of it, but even his equals laughed among themselves about the increased and almost portentous dignity of the Earl.

"It is all very well for him," even so reticent a man as Lord Derby was heard to say, "and for old noblemen like him; but we younger men should know better. Look at Disraeli; he is the last man living who should play charioteer just now. An adventurer like him, a Jew, fond of flash and dash, is sure to overdo things. If ever there was a day when we should drive the old-fashioned coach of state carefully, it is now, because it is rickety even if it is gilded, and we are going so fast with our imperial policy that I fear a smash. Hang him! who knows but that the very object of Dizzy in taking off the brakes and putting on the lash is that he may demolish things? It would be just like the sensationist he is. I will give him until about the end of Parliament in 1880 to make a finish of his tawdry, un-English imperialism."

As to Lady Blanche, she was not a generation or so younger than her father for nothing. And what Englishwoman had a clearer intellect? Nor was there a warmer heart, in spite of her rank, than hers. Because she regarded Henry Harris as one of the manliest of men, she had first admired, then loved him. When, notwithstanding his passion for her in Paris, he had held himself sternly aloof from her, she admired and loved him so much the more. Such women love none but strong men—men so strong as to be able to stand up and hold their own against the woman herself. That he should have traced Nihilism into its inmost lair, as a hunter follows a dangerous wolf into its deepest den, had intensely interested her in him, and her affection had increased with her interest. When she heard of the capture of her brother and Henry, her anxiety had been, however she concealed it, for the American chiefly, for she rated him highest as well as loved him most. With the release of the two men, had come to her a fever, almost of joy, chiefly on his account. Nor did it diminish her admiration and love when he did not send her a word thereafter. She was proud of his pride.

Who can say what effect the gladness also of her brother, in view of his hoped-for marriage with Mary Harris, had upon his sensitive sister, whose feelings were all the stronger in proportion as she had schooled herself to conceal them under an aspect of pride? The letters Lord Conyngham wrote her, immediately on his return to St. Petersburg from his prison, were as torches to what was already fire. So long as the Earl held out, Lord Conyngham could not marry ; that, of course ; and the Earl was so much the more of an aristocrat of late that there was less hope than ever of his yielding. But, like her brother, Lady Blanche felt sure that some day he must yield, and their hope was something stronger than faith—it was assurance itself ; because that which ought to be always seems to be certain.

Meanwhile, the preparations were proceeding for her marriage with the Duke. From morning till night, Lady Blanche lived in a throng of milliners, upholsterers, jewelers. As rarely as possible was she with her affianced. It was the old story of Beauty and the Beast, except that the beauty became every day more beautiful, and the beast, to her at least, all the beastlier. The loveliness of Lady Blanche was fed, as flowers are by the furnace-fires of hot-houses, by the hidden fever within her heart. She disliked the Duke more and more. Anonymous letters were continually coming to her. Perhaps they were in some cases genuine ; in others they were dictated, doubtless, by envy, jealousy, devilish desire to mar a happiness which, to the miserable and ignorant writer, seemed to be too great for this world. By whomsoever written, they were filled with tales of cheating at cards by the Duke ; of instances of cowardice in moments of sudden peril ; of insults patiently endured ; of seductions concealed by free use of gold. They came to her from the Continent, from various parts of London and England. People even attempted to force their way to her to tell her "things which Lady Blanche *must* be told before she marries the Duke of Plymouth." If she had loved the Duke, these things would have been less to her than nothing; but, as it was—

Poor girl! Her brother was absent, her mother had long been dead, it was out of the question to trouble her father with matters of this kind. She had retinues of friends, but there was not one of them to whom she was not too proud to go for help. She became pale, even while, with a feverish color on her cheeks, she grew lovelier than ever. It was impossible for her to eat, to sleep.

One day she resolved in her desperation to make a confidant of the Duke himself. If he was to be her husband, surely she should be frank with him. When he entered the room, she compelled herself not to see how weak and insignificant he was. She did not know that his Grace had all along been afraid of her, or rather she had been too contemptuous to think of it. To-day there was that in her aspect which positively alarmed him ; he was thoroughly frightened, in fact. Possibly his conscience warned him that she might have been told certain things. He grew embarrassed, persistently refused to see what she would be at, stammered, hesitated, took an earlier leave than he was accustomed to do, and she found it impossible to force herself to speak to him as she intended to do.

Lady Blanche had lost much sleep ; her head was dizzy. On going to her room after he left, she found quite a long letter from her brother, still in St. Petersburg. It was filled with praises, as usual, of Henry Harris, and of his charming sister. He was very happy. For a moment the English peeress lost herself ; she was nothing but an English dairymaid. She could not endure it. She would act; but it should be, as became her, boldly. Rapidly dressing herself as plainly as possible, and throwing a thick veil over her walking hat, she had herself driven to the nearest telegraph station. She was there but a moment, and then returned to her house and room, and lay waiting in an agony of shame, gladness, apprehension, stupor.

And it was thus that Henry Harris came to receive in St. Petersburg the telegram which had separated him for the time from his mother. Nitro-glycerine is merely a transparent oil, and nothing could seem more simple than the line which he repeated over and over again when he was by himself. It was from England, but had neither date nor signature ; it needed neither :

"Are you of the same mind and heart you once were?"

That was all, but it was terrible. At the first glance he understood everything. There had been a time, not so long ago, when he had admired and loved Lady Blanche beyond all women. As he sat locked in his room at this supreme crisis of his life, he could recall every line of her face, every look of her proud eyes, every tone of her voice. From the ashes of his heart the old fires threatened to break forth again with consuming power. He had not whispered a syllable which committed him to the daughter of the artist. And now this proud Englishwoman had laid aside her reserve, had committed herself to his honor. She was ready to risk her father's anger, to break off her brilliant match—all for *him*. He had not imagined she had loved him so. Should he refuse to return *such* love?

And there was Isidore, who had risked what was dearer to her than life to save him. He went over every attribute of her beauty, of her peculiar, childlike charm. It was one of those times which try a man through every fiber. Whatever he did, no human being must know of the telegram which he was afraid to let out of his hand.

And yet he knew from the outset what his answer must be. None the less as carefully as if he had to do with the working designs, instead, of some vast mechanical work, he slowly and deliberately went over the whole matter. When the first tempest of emotion had subsided, he reviewed everything that could possibly be said for and against, in case of Lady Blanche, in case of Isidore. Slowly but clearly he worked out a result which had been from the outset as much the one thing to do as if it had been merely a question as to what twice two might be.

It was very, very long before the head could comprehend and the heart could ratify what the supreme sense had decreed; but at last, when night had fallen, he lit the gas, held the telegram over it until it fluttered and fell to the floor a flake of ashes. Then he drew on his hat and overcoat and went steadily down stairs, out of the house to the telegraph station.

Before Lady Blanche went to her bed that night a telegram was handed her. It was long before she could open it, for upon it depended all her after existence. She did so at last, but the words, as she read them, were merely as one reads what one has already known by heart and perfectly. They could be no other:

"With profoundest respect. Between us alone. But it is too late."

"But I am glad I did it," she said, coldly. "It ends it!" And the dairy-maid had become an English lady of rank again and for the rest of her days.

Strange to say, she undressed herself without a trémor, laid down, slept until morning, and awoke strong and fresh. There could be no more trouble about it now; nor was there.

Let it be recorded here, as it has been upon a thousand bloody fields of battle: in woman, as in man, there is nothing known to the ages which reveals a fiber quite as fine and strong as English pluck!

CHAPTER LXXI.

CULMINATION.

LIKE Lady Blanche, on the reception of the reply to her telegram, Henry Harris felt, when he had sent his message, a sense of instant and exceeding relief; for, like the Englishwoman, he knew that what had been done was the one thing alone which could or should be done. The Duke of Plymouth was surprised and almost bewildered by the manner in which he was received by his betrothed the next time he called upon her. There was in it a gleam of recklessness, of defiance almost, which he could not understand. Henry Harris was calm, knowing that he had arrived at a final and just conclusion, and jubilant too, since he had come to a conclusion also which allowed him to give way to the deep affection for Isidore which had long been kindled in his bosom. It was an unconscious uncertainty still in regard to Lady Blanche which had held him in suspense so long. That was all past. He had attained to certainty at last! His was the gladness a skilled workman enjoys when he has wrought out and verified beyond question a problem which had once seemed to be impossible of solution. "Now I *know*, and I *love*," he said to himself the first thing when he awoke next morning. "When heart *and* head are satisfied, surely the hour of action has struck," and he dressed himself with unusual care.

But his mother seated herself beside him at their hotel table before he was done breakfast. He was always glad to see her, but he would much rather have been left to himself, for he intended to go as soon as he could from the table to call upon the woman he loved. It is true, he had not heard the decision of his parents upon the matter, but he felt sure of that in advance. "You look pale this morning," his mother said, as they arose from the table at last; and at one glance she looked him through and through as she had done since he was a baby.

"I am very well, I thank you," he answered, lifting to her own his eyes so full of the gladness of certainty and expectant love that the tears rose to her own. For she understood perfectly what had happened. Neither then, nor at any time thereafter, was any allusion made by either of them to Lady Blanche, and yet Mrs. Harris knew, almost as well as if she had seen it, that her son had received a telegram from the proud Englishwoman. His mother could have given almost the exact words in which the betrothed of the Duke had telegraphed; she could have written out almost word for word the message he had sent in reply. The numerals of arithmetic produce invariably the same results, however used, whether in addition, subtraction, multiplication, division—to their very decimals are they true to themselves and to each other; and so of human hearts, provided only they act according to the law of eternal right, which is part of their nature; the workings of the heart as of the intellect are as unswervingly the same as mathematics itself. Without a word then or after upon the subject, mother and son knew and rested in each other as in absolute right and certainty, and the peace thereof is as that of heaven.

"No, I can not let you off; you must go with me to-day," Mrs. Harris said to her son. "My present burns, I like it so well, in my hands, and I must give it to you and be done with it. After that you can go where you please."

Henry was in no mood for gifts. He had so long controlled his love that it was flaming in him now with an almost unendurable impatience to declare itself; but he entered her carriage with her, was driven he did not care to observe where with her, but could not conceal his surprise when the vehicle halted, at length, in another part of the city, and before the door of a modest-looking house. Entering this with her son, she begged him to wait for her for a time in the plain little parlor while she withdrew. He strode up and down the room. He looked almost angrily at the pictures upon the walls. What had he to do there when his heart was with Isidore? His mother was trifling with him. It was easier to endure his jail at Kiev! What could she mean? She was gone so long too! He looked at his watch a dozen times. At last he heard his mother call him, standing, as she did so, her face flushed as from weeping, the door of the room across a hall held half opened in her hand.

"Here is my little present," she said, in a whisper, her face all tears and smiles; "looking more beautiful," her son afterward declared, "than I ever saw her."

In amazement he passed into the room, not observing that she had passed out as he did so, and closed the door behind her. Henry Harris, for the first time in his life, lost his presence of mind. On the other side of the room, apparently just risen from her litter of designs upon the table, dressed in black, her face a sweet confusion of blushes and pallor and tears, stood Isidore. But the young engineer was, as has been said, prompt in times of emergency, and in an instant he had the shy and trembling girl in his strong arms, pressed to his heart, was devouring her with kisses.

"I have been starving so long," he explained to her half an hour later. There is no telling, in fact, when he would have been satisfied if his sister had not come running in. Her mother had driven home, had told her all, and, interrupted in her conversation with her own lover, Mary understood everything perfectly. Taking the weeping, radiant girl into her own arms, she was so overbearing as to give her brother a kiss and put him out of the door. There were not two more intelligent and sensible girls alive, and yet, when the sisters, for such they now were, had the room to themselves, the first thing they did was to have a good long cry together.

"Your mother told me," Isidore said at last, laughing through her tears, "that I am to consider myself a gift from her to Henry, the best gift she could find. And she said that you have your gift from her already."

"In Alfred? Yes," Mary replied, "and we must not let them know, lest they should be too conceited; but I am sure we are, both of us, satisfied."

The next day Lord Conyngham left for England, and

there came within two weeks thereafter a description from
him of the marriage of his sister to the Duke of Plymouth.
"She was as beautiful," he said at the end of many pages to
Mary, "as a statue."

But a telegram came even while the letter was being read.
Earl Dorrington had died a few days after the ceremony.
He had been long a victim to heart disease as well as gout;
the excitement had been too much for him. Immediately
after the funeral Lord Conyngham came to St. Petersburg,
but he was Lord Conyngham no more. As Earl Dorrington
he had become a graver, more sedate man.

"Do you know," he said to Mary, almost at their first
interview, "Blanche is eager we should marry? I do not
understand women. She is positively eager for it. The
Duke, poor fellow! is very proud of her, but, unless I am mistaken, he is terribly afraid of her, too. Yes, she sends her
dearest love with this letter," and Mary was surprised at the
ardor with which the Duchess of Plymouth wrote, entreating
her to yield to the addresses of her brother.

But months had to pass, long months, before the marriage
could take place. Not a week before the ceremony the new
Earl, who had been going between England and Russia continually, received in St. Petersburg a letter which he read to
Mary.

"It is impossible for me to understand Blanche," he
groaned. "She had fully determined to bring the Duke
over to our wedding. Now she sends her presents, and says
it will be impossible. I am sure she loves you, is delighted
with our marriage. What can she mean?"

"I think I understand," Mary said, quietly, and added no
more. But she was mistaken.

"No, my dear," her wiser mother explained to her that
night. "You are right in supposing that Blanche can not
endure to contrast her married estate with that of yourself
and the Earl. But she has learned that Henry and Isidore
are to be married at the same time. There are things, my
child, concerning which it is best not even to make a con-

jecture," and she changed the topic. "Henry has not told Isidore in regard to her half brother," she said. "He was glad that he had said nothing of Deschards to his father. Both are dead. It is better as it is, and I am glad that Isidore, dear child! has made such a success of her work in memory of Prince Kalitzoff and his daughter. She was resolved to finish that first, you know. They are singularly adapted to each other, Henry and herself, and so are you and your lover. Both of my sons are to have noble careers," the mother said, smiling, "but they will owe most of their success to women. The question, my child, is not one of poverty or wealth, of plebeian or noble, of England or America—when a man and woman, as in the case of your father and myself, as in the case of yourself and your lover, of Henry and Isidore, are found, after full trial, to be thoroughly essential to each other—it is then that they will possess paradise, for then will they be wedded together, as Adam and Eve were, by their Maker himself."

It is unnecessary to describe the brilliant double wedding, to which Ellen Ellsworth and Virginia Jossellyn came on from Paris to assist as bridesmaids, and at which George Harris and his wife seemed to be in the sober joy of their hearts almost as young as their children. A full account was published at the time in the St. Petersburg "Golos," and so generally copied therefrom into the journals of Europe and America that the reader could not have escaped seeing it at the time. If it is needed, he will recall it by the mention made in the descriptions of the magnificent gifts presented to the couples by the Emperor, who sent an aide-de-camp to represent him at the ceremony.

Invitations were sent to Ishra Dhass and to Hop Fun. The former, however, had left Paris for India, whence he wrote a letter of joyous congratulation, with descriptions of his great and successful work as a missionary among his countrymen. Hop Fun was in the act of returning to China, and he sent his cards of congratulation. Each of these was two feet square, and gorgeously inscribed in letters of purple and green and gold. Henry Harris went to the trouble of having the Chinese characters translated. In addition to the name and titles of the Mandarin, there ran down the side of each card an inscription. Upon that sent to Earl Dorrington it was : " Kong-fu-tse says, He who marries a queen becomes himself a king." " Which," Earl Dorrington assented, with a bow to his courtiers, "is assuredly so ! What a sensible wooden-headed beggar he is ! "

" Mine is better still," Henry Harris exclaimed ; " it reads : ' Kong-fu-tse says, He who has love can do without rice ' ; that is, he who has love has everything ! And it is a fact, is it not, Isidore ? "

" I am a very practical man," George Harris added, and he took his comely wife by the hand and looked with sober happiness upon his four children ; " I am a machinist, and one who has seen a good deal of almost the whole world, and I know something of the value of position, talent, money, and all that ; yet I can assure you that, at last, the only thing in this world worth living for is to labor faithfully in the work given us to do, and—"

" To love," his wife added for him, smiling through her happy tears.

" Yes," her husband assented gravely, " and to love."

MAY 19 1915

THE END.

NEW BOOKS.

MARY MARSTON. A Novel. By GEORGE MACDONALD, author of "Robert Falconer," "Annals of a Quiet Neighborhood," etc., etc. (From advance-sheets.) 1 vol., 12mo, cloth, $1.50.

ANECDOTAL HISTORY OF THE BRITISH PARLIAMENT. From the Earliest Periods to the Present Time, with Notices of Eminent Parliamentary Men and Examples of their Oratory. Compiled by G. H. JENNINGS. 1 vol., crown 8vo, 546 pages, cloth, $2.50.

"As pleasant a companion for the leisure hours of a studious and thoughtful man as anything in book-shape since Selden."—*London Telegraph.*

"It would be sheer affectation to deny the fascination exercised by the 'Anecdotal History of Parliament.'"—*Saturday Review.*

New Volume in International Scientific Series.

THE ATOMIC THEORY. By AD. WURTZ, Member of the French Institute. Translated by E. CLEMINSHAW, M. A., Assistant Master at Sherborne School. Number XXIX of "The International Scientific Series." 12mo, cloth, price, $1.50.

Health Primers. No. 8.

THE HEART AND ITS FUNCTIONS. Previously published: "Exercise and Training"; "Alcohol: its Use and Abuse"; "The House and its Surroundings"; "Premature Death: its Promotion or Prevention"; "Personal Appearance in Health and Disease"; "Baths and Bathing"; "The Skin and its Troubles." Square 16mo, cloth, 40 cents each.

ALL ALONE. A Novelette. By ANDRÉ THEURIET, author of "Gérard's Marriage," "The Two Barbels," etc., etc. Appletons' "New Handy-Volume Series." Paper, 25 cents.

Cheaper Edition.

YOUNG IRELAND. A Fragment of Irish History, 1840–1850. By the Hon. Sir CHARLES GAVAN DUFFY, K. C. M. G. New cheap edition. 1 vol., 12mo, cloth, $1.50.

For sale by all booksellers; or any work sent by mail, post-paid, on receipt of price.

D. APPLETON & CO., Publishers,
1, 3, & 5 BOND STREET, NEW YORK.

NEW BOOKS.

AMERICAN PAINTERS. New and enlarged edition, containing Biograph-
ical Sketches of Sixty-eight American Artists, with One Hundred and Four
Examples of their Work, engraved on Wood in the most perfect manner.
One volume, quarto, cloth, extra gilt, price, $8.00; in full morocco, $15.00.

A new edition of this superb work is now ready, *extending the number of engravings from eighty-three to one hundred and four*, representing sixty-eight of
the leading painters. No similar work, in any country, illustrative of contemporaneous art, surpasses it in the number or excellence of its engravings.

BRITISH PAINTERS. With Eighty Examples of their Work engraved on
Wood. One volume, quarto, cloth, extra gilt, price, $6.00; full morocco,
$12.00.

"British Painters," in size and general character, is a companion-work to
"American Painters." It contains eighty examples of their work, engraved on
wood, representing forty painters, including Turner, Constable, Mulready, Wilkie, Haydon, Etty, Eastlake, Stanfield, Landseer, and Creswick, among earlier
painters, and Faed, Alma-Tadema, Poynter, Walker, Holl, Paton, and Reviere,
among contemporaneous painters.

A PHYSICAL TREATISE ON ELECTRICITY AND MAGNETISM.
By J. E. H. GORDON, B. A., Assistant Secretary of the British Association.
8vo, with about 200 full-page and other Illustrations. Cloth, price, $7.00.

"The want has long been felt of a work on Electricity, which should treat
the subject much more fully than is done in the existing elementary works, and
which should, at the same time, regard it from a physical as distinguished from
a mathematical point of view. In this work the author has attempted to meet
the above want. All the higher and later experimental developments of the science are treated of, but without the use of symbolical mathematics. Every phe-
nomenon is considered, not as a mathematical abstraction, but as something
having a real physical existence. It contains matter which, as far as the author
is aware, has not yet appeared in any text-book."—*Extract from Preface.*

THE ORTHOEPIST. A PRONOUNCING MANUAL, CONTAINING ABOUT THREE
THOUSAND FIVE HUNDRED WORDS, INCLUDING A CONSIDERABLE NUMBER
OF THE NAMES OF FOREIGN AUTHORS, ARTISTS, ETC., THAT ARE OFTEN
MISPRONOUNCED. By ALFRED AYRES. One volume, 18mo. Cloth, price,
$1.00.

This manual will be found invaluable to all persons desirous of making their
pronunciation conform to the best usage and established authority.

**A BRIEF SYNOPSIS OF THE COLLECTION LAWS OF THE
UNITED STATES AND CANADA.** Compiled under the direction
of DOUGLASS and MINTON, Attorneys of the Law and Collection Department of the Mercantile Agency of Dun, Wiman & Co. One volume, 8vo.
Cloth, price, $1.50.

This book will supply a want long felt by the business community, giving in
a nutshell, as it were, the more important features of the laws relating to the
collection of debts throughout the whole country.

For sale by all booksellers; or sent by mail, post-paid, on receipt of price.

D. APPLETON & CO., Publishers, 1, 3, & 5 Bond Street, New York.

ENDYMION.

A NOVEL.

By the Rt. Hon. BENJAMIN DISRAELI, Earl of Beaconsfield, K. G.,

AUTHOR OF "LOTHAIR," ETC., ETC.

In two styles: 12mo, cloth, $1.50; cheap edition, 12mo, cloth, $1.00.

For sale by all booksellers; or sent by mail, post-paid, on receipt of price.

D. APPLETON & CO., Publishers,

1, 3, & 5 BOND STREET, NEW YORK.

UNCLE REMUS:

His Songs and His Sayings.

THE FOLK-LORE OF THE OLD PLANTATION.

By JOEL CHANDLER HARRIS.

"We are just discovering what admirable literary material there is at home, what a great mine there is to explore, and how quaint and peculiar is the material which can be dug up. Mr. Harris's book may be looked on in a double light—either as a pleasant volume recounting the stories told by a typical old colored man to a child, or as a valuable contribution to our somewhat meager folk-lore. . . . To Northern readers the story of Brer (Brother—Brudder) Rabbit may be novel. To those familiar with plantation life, who have listened to these quaint old stories, who have still tender reminiscences of some good old mauma who told these wondrous adventures to them when they were children, Brer Rabbit, the Tar Baby, and Brer Fox, come back again with all the past pleasures of younger days."—*New York Times.*

"The volume is a most readable one, whether it be regarded as a humorous book merely, or as a contribution to the literature of folk-lore."—*New York World.*

"This is a thoroughly amusing book, and is much the best humorous compilation that has been put before the American public for many a day."—*Philadelphia Telegraph.*

"One of the most novel books of the year. . . . If the book in its entirety is not widely read, we shall be greatly disappointed; and, if any one misses the story of the Rabbit and the Fox, he will deny himself much pleasant mental recreation."—*Boston Courier.*

"Uncle Remus's sayings on current happenings are very shrewd and bright, and the plantation and revival songs are choice specimens of their sort."—*Boston Journal.*

Well illustrated from Drawings by F. S. Church, whose humorous animal drawings are so well known, and J. H. Moser, of Georgia.

1 vol., 12mo. Cloth. Price, $1.50.

For sale by all booksellers; or sent by mail, post-paid, on receipt of price.

D. APPLETON & CO., Publishers,

1, 3, & 5 BOND STREET, NEW YORK.

Appletons' New Handy-Volume Series.

BRILLIANT NOVELETTES; ROMANCE, ADVENTURE, TRAVEL, HUMOR; HISTORIC, LITERARY, AND SOCIETY MONOGRAPHS.

1. **Jet: Her Face or her Fortune?** A Story. By Mrs. ANNIE EDWARDES. Paper, 30 cts.

2. **A Struggle.** A Story. By BARNET PHILLIPS. Paper, 25 cts.

3. **Misericordia.** A Story. By ETHEL LYNN LINTON. Paper, 20 cts.

4. **Gordon Baldwin,** and **The Philosopher's Pendulum.** By RUDOLPH LINDAU. Paper, 25 cts.

5. **The Fisherman of Auge.** A Story. By KATHARINE S. MACQUOID. Paper, 20 cts.

6. **The Essays of Elia.** First Series. By CHARLES LAMB. Paper, 30 cts. ; cloth, 60 cts.

7. **The Bird of Passage.** By J. SHERIDAN LE FANU. Paper, 25 cts.

8. **The House of the Two Barbels.** By ANDRÉ THEURIET. Paper, 20 cts.

9. **Lights of the Old English Stage.** Paper, 30 cts.

10. **Impressions of America.** By R. W. DALE. Paper, 30 cts.

11. **The Goldsmith's Wife.** A Story. By Madame CHARLES REYBAUD. Paper, 25 cts.

12. **A Summer Idyl.** A Story. By CHRISTIAN REID. Paper, 30 cts. ; cloth, 60 cts.

13. **The Arab Wife.** A Romance of the Polynesian Seas. Paper, 25 cts.

14. **Mrs. Gainsborough's Diamonds.** A Story. By JULIAN HAWTHORNE. Paper, 20 cts.

15. **Liquidated,** and **The Seer.** By RUDOLPH LINDAU. Paper, 25 cts.

16. **The Great German Composers.** Paper, 30 cts.; cloth, 60 cts

17. **Antoinette.** A Story. By ANDRÉ THEURIET. Paper, 20 cts.

18. **John-a-Dreams.** A Tale. Paper, 30 cts.

19. **Mrs. Jack.** A Story. By FRANCES ELEANOR TROLLOPE. Paper, 20 cts.

20. **English Literature.** By T. ARNOLD. From the "Encyclopædia Britannica." Paper, 25 cts.

21. **Raymonde.** A Tale. By ANDRÉ THEURIET. Paper, 30 cts.

22. **Beaconsfield.** By GEORGE MAKEPEACE TOWLE. Paper, 25 cts.; cloth, 60 cts.

23. **The Multitudinous Seas.** By S. G. W. BENJAMIN. Paper, 25 cts.

24. **The Disturbing Element.** By CHARLOTTE M. YONGE. Paper, 30 cts.

25. **Fairy Tales:** their Origin and Meaning. By JOHN THACKRAY BUNCE. Paper, 25 cts.

26. **Thomas Carlyle:** His Life—his Books—his Theories. By ALFRED H. GUERNSEY. Paper, 30 cts.; cloth, 60 cts.

27. **A Thorough Bohemienne.** A Tale. By Madame CHARLES REYBAUD. Paper, 30 cts.

28. **The Great Italian and French Composers.** By GEORGE T. FERRIS. Paper, 30 cts.; cloth, 60 cts.

29. **Ruskin on Painting.** With a Biographical Sketch. Paper, 30 cts.; cloth, 60 cts.

30. **An Accomplished Gentleman.** By JULIAN STURGIS, author of "John-a-Dreams." Paper, 30 cts.; cloth, 60 cts.

31. **An Attic Philosopher in Paris;** or, a Peep at the World from a Garret. Being the Journal of a Happy Man. From the French of EMILE SOUVESTRE. Paper, 30 cts. ; cloth, 60 cts.

32. **A Rogue's Life:** From his Birth to his Marriage. By WILKIE COLLINS. Paper, 25 cts. ; cloth, 60 cts.

33. **Geier-Wally:** A Tale of the Tyrol. From the German of WILHELMINE VON HILLERN. Paper, 30 cts. ; cloth, 60 cts.

34. **The Last Essays of Elia.** By CHARLES LAMB. Paper, 30 cts. ; cloth, 60 cts.

35. **The Yellow Mask.** By WILKIE COLLINS. Paper, 25 cts. ; cloth, 60 cts.

36. **A-Saddle in the Wild West.** A Glimpse of Travel. By WILLIAM H. RIDEING. Paper, 25 cts. ; cloth, 60 cts.

37. **Money.** A Tale. By JULES TARDIEU. Paper, 25 cents.

38. **Peg Woffington.** By CHARLES READE. Paper, 30 cts. ; cloth, 60 cts.

39. **"My Queen."** Paper, 25 cts.

40. **Uncle Cesar.** By Madame CHARLES REYBAUD. Paper, 25 cts.

41. **The Distracted Young Preacher.** By THOMAS HARDY. Hester. By BEATRICE MAY BUTT. Paper, 25 cts.

42. **Table-Talk.** To which are added Imaginary Conversations of Pope and Swift. By LEIGH HUNT. Paper, 30 cts. ; cloth, 60 cts.

43. **Christie Johnstone.** By CHARLES READE. Paper, 30 cts. ; cloth, 60 cts.

44. **The World's Paradises.** By S. G. W. BENJAMIN. Paper, 30 cts.

45. **The Alpenstock.** Edited by WILLIAM H. RIDEING. Paper, 30 cts.

46. **Comedies for Amateur Acting.** Edited, with a Prefatory Note on Private Theatricals, by J. BRANDER MATTHEWS. Paper, 30 cts.

47. **Vivian the Beauty.** By Mrs. ANNIE EDWARDES. Paper, 30 cts. ; cloth, 60 cents.

48. **Great Singers:** Faustina Bordoni to Henrietta Sontag. Paper, 30 cts.; cloth, 60 cts.

49. **A Stroke of Diplomacy.** From the French of VICTOR CHERBU-LIEZ. Paper, 20 cts.

50. **Lord Macaulay.** His Life—his Writings. By CHARLES H. JONES. Paper, 30 cts.; cloth, 60 cts.

51. **The Return of the Princess.** By JACQUES VINCENT. Paper, 25 cts.

52. **A Short Life of Charles Dickens.** With Selections from his Letters. By CHARLES H. JONES. Paper, 35 cts.; cloth, 60 cts.

53. **Stray Moments with Thackeray:** His Humor, Satire, and Characters. By WILLIAM H. RIDEING. Paper, 30 cts.; cloth, 60 cts.

54. **Dr. Heidenhoff's Process.** By EDWARD BELLAMY. Paper, 25 cts.

55. **Second Thoughts.** By RHODA BROUGHTON. Vol. I. Paper, 25 cts.

56. **Second Thoughts.** By RHODA BROUGHTON. Vol. II. Paper, 25 cts.

57. **Two Russian Idyls:** Marcella, Esfira. Paper, 30 cts.

58. **Strange Stories.** By ERCKMANN-CHATRIAN. Paper, 30 cts.

59. **Little Comedies.** By JULIAN STURGIS. Paper, 30 cts.

60. **French Men of Letters.** By MAURICE MAURIS (Marquis di Calenzano). Paper, 35 cts.

61. **A Short Life of William Ewart Gladstone.** By CHARLES H. JONES. Paper, 35 cts.

62. **The Foresters.** By BERTHOLD AUERBACH. Paper, 50 cts.

63. **Poverina.** An Italian Story. Paper, 30 cts.

64. **Mashallah!** A Flight into Egypt. By CHARLES WARREN STODDARD. Paper, 30 cts.

65. **All Alone.** A Story. By ANDRÉ THEURIET. Paper, 25 cts.

APPLETONS' NEW HANDY-VOLUME SERIES is in handsome 18mo volumes, in large type, of a size convenient for the pocket, or suitable for the library-shelf, bound in paper covers. A selection of the volumes bound also in cloth, 60 cts. each.

Any volume mailed, post-paid, to any address within the United States or Canada, on receipt of the price.

D. APPLETON & CO., Publishers, 1, 3, & 5 Bond Street, New York.

CPSIA information can be obtained
at www.ICGtesting.com
Printed in the USA
BVHW041431210721
612411BV00007B/1460

9 780343 837426